RIKER'S APOCALYPSE: THE PLEA

(Book 4)

SHAWN CHESSER

ISBN:978-1-7371106-5-1

CONTENTS

ACKNOWLEDGEMENTS

For Steve P. You are missed, friend. Maureen, Raven, and Caden … I couldn't have done this without your support. Thanks to our military, LE and first responders for all you do. To the people in the U.K. and elsewhere around the world who have been in touch, thanks for reading! Lieutenant Colonel Michael Offe, thanks for your service as well as your friendship. Larry Eckels, thank you for helping me with some of the military technical stuff. Any missing facts or errors are solely my fault. Beta readers, you rock, and you know who you are. Harry "Dutch" Scholtz (RIP). You are sorely missed. Thanks, George Romero, for introducing me to zombies. To my friends and fellows at S@N and Monday Steps On Steele, thanks as well. Lastly, thanks to Bill W. and Dr. Bob … you helped make this possible. I am going to sign up for another 24.

Special thanks to John O'Brien, Mark Tufo, the late Joe McKinney (RIP), Craig DiLouie, Nicholas Sansbury Smith, Heath Stallcup, Saul Tanpepper, Eric A. Shelman, and David P. Forsyth. I truly appreciate your continued friendship and always invaluable advice. Thanks to Christian Bentulan of Covers by Christian for the great cover. For technical help, in no particular order, thanks to: Paul Whitmer, W.J. Lundy, Ted Nulty, and Stephen Knight. Once again, extra special thanks to Monique Happy for her work editing "The Plea." Mo, as always, you kicked butt and took names in getting this MS polished up! Working with you over the years has been nothing but a pleasure. I truly appreciate having a confidante I can trust. Huge thanks to Adam Paul for being the voice of my two ongoing series! You truly bring my yarns to life. If I have accidentally left anyone out … I am truly sorry.

***

Edited by Monique Happy Editorial Services
www.moniquehappyeditorial.com

Chapter 1

Trinity House

Santa Fe, New Mexico

The plea for help coming through the tiny speaker on the desktop caused Amelia Earhart to sit up straight in her chair. The reedy voice was that of a young boy. It was faint and full of desperation, the underlying static adding a heightened sense of urgency to the overture.

As the newest and youngest inhabitant of the sprawling mansion tucked away high in the foothills above Santa Fe, New Mexico, Lia was still trying to find her place among the myriad cast of characters calling Trinity House home. When she wasn't sitting on her butt in the high-ceilinged great room and reading one of the many books left behind by Trinity's eccentric former owners, she was in the cramped bunker below it, trying to make contact with the outside world. At least that's what she told anyone who asked. In reality, she was hoping to make contact with survivors in Portland, Oregon. She wanted desperately to learn what had become of Portland International Airport—the last known destination of her airline pilot father.

Releasing the HAM radio's HF tuning knob, ever so slowly lest she inadvertently jump frequencies and lose the connection, she snatched the radio handset off the desk blotter and depressed the Talk button. As she removed the cap from a Sharpie with her teeth and hovered the pen over a blank page in her spiral notebook, she said, "I can hear you. My name is Lia. What's yours?"

"Cole Parker," replied the kid. "You need to send help *right now*. The people who have us are really, really bad." His voice was full of fear and heavily accented. Somewhere in the Deep South, Lia thought. Louisiana, perhaps.

Us, she thought, a cold ball forming in her gut. "Who's *us*?" She paused, the channel still open. "Are there other kids with you?" She blurted the last part out, her voice rising an octave or two. *Keep it together, Lia.* Releasing the handset's Talk key, she instinctively glanced at her right wrist. No watch. Only a stark white stripe on a sea of deeply tanned skin where one used to be. The Rolex had been a gift from her father. A man of few words, platitudes especially. The expensive timepiece had been his way of acknowledging her clinching a spot on the United States Olympic biathlon team. The watch had been taken from her, stripped from her wrist at gunpoint by some very bad people. Although Lia's stint as a captive of the desperate trio had been a short one, a horrific experience that led to her pushing a knife into a woman's neck and watching her bleed out, she immediately identified with Cole's situation in more ways than one.

Glancing at the row of dinner-plate-sized clocks high up on the wall to her left, clocks displaying multiple time zones the world over, as well as Zulu time in Greenwich, England, Lia jotted down the kid's name and noted the time and day of the week. The airwaves had been mostly quiet the last couple of days, yet her notebook still contained dozens of entries detailing her contacts with groups and individuals from New York to California and everywhere in-between. So far, though, she had failed to fulfill her main objective, with a couple holed up in Seattle the closest she'd come to learning the fate of Portland International. If Sea-Tac Airport was any indication, she feared the worst for her dad.

A handful of seconds ticked by with no reply from Cole.

"Are there other kids there with you?" she repeated.

Finally, Cole said, "There are six of us—"

Interrupting, Lia said, "Where are the bad people keeping you?"

"In a store with old stuff."

"An antique store?"

"I'm not sure."

"Where are you now?"

"I'm in the store next door. It has something to do with criminals. There are wanted posters on the walls." He paused. "Right now, I'm in a small back room connected to a larger room. The others are in the store next door."

Why don't you run? Instead of posing the question to Cole, a question Lia feared could lead to him actually taking her advice and becoming an easy meal for the dead, she said, "So you snuck away from the bad people?"

Cole quickly told her how he had stood on the toilet tank in the bathroom, pried a vent cover off the wall, and discovered the overhead duct system. Not only did the duct starting above the bathroom connect to the room inside the office he had already described, it crossed over a bar and ended at a liquor store, both of which he could not access because the vent grilles wouldn't budge—not even when he tried kicking them.

On Cole's wrist was one end of a long length of twine. A girl he called Maggie was tending the other end of his *lifeline.* "She's supposed to tug on it the second she sees Kurt or Janice start to wake up," he explained. "We've done this three times so far. This is the first time I've gotten ahold of anyone on this radio. I was beginning to think it didn't have an antenna."

"You two are very brave," Lia said. "I'm twenty-seven. How old are you, Cole?"

"Twelve, going on thirteen."

Must be small for his age, thought Lia. She said, "Maggie and the other kids … how old are they?"

"Maggie is nine. Her twin sisters, Diana and Dena, are five. Charlie's six. The littlest just holds up two fingers. That's all. She won't tell us her name." He paused. "She hasn't talked since Janice found her and brought her back. Anyway, we just call her Missy. Me and Maggie are supposed to be watching the littles when Kurt and Janice sleep. They tell us to take shifts."

"So the radio is in a manager's office?" Lia probed. "And there are wanted posters on the walls. Are you in a post office? Maybe a UPS store? Do you know what city you're in?" After she said it, it dawned on her those places probably wouldn't have a HAM radio.

"I honestly don't know the answer to any of that," Cole conceded. "But you *have* to help us. They aren't good people. They don't respect our boundaries. When Kurt is drunk, he does bad things to the littles. Janice doesn't even try to stop him—" Cole's voice suddenly choked up.

Lia felt the first tickle of bile in the back of her throat. She wanted to reach through the radio and pull Cole over to her side. Swallowing the acid-tinged saliva, she said, "Kurt and Janice … where are they now?"

"Passed out drunk, I think. They also like to put needles into their arms. Whatever it is they're taking, it does the same thing to them as if they'd been drinking all day."

Addicts, thought Lia. *This kid is really in harm's way.* "It's just the two of them?" she asked.

"For now," Cole said. "Others are coming. I don't know much more than that."

That was going to be her next question. So instead, she asked, "Do Kurt and Janice have a car?"

"A Suburban," replied Cole.

"Have you ever driven a car?"

"Just in video games." He paused, thinking. "There was one time I sat on my dad's lap and steered our Jeep. I was really young, though."

"Maybe you can steal the keys from them. Think you can gather the others and make a run for it?"

"I can't. They keep all the doors locked. When Kurt and Janice sleep"—he went quiet for a beat—"Kurt leaves his shotgun aimed at the window to our cage. I think the glass on the door is bulletproof. Kurt has a string tied to the gun's trigger. The other end is tied off on the doorknob. If I open the door, the gun *will* go off." There was an awkward silence. When Cole came back on, in a near whisper, he added, "That's how Sophia died. She didn't believe Kurt cocked the gun. It was awful. The sound was so loud. So were her screams. Blood was everywhere. She was dying." He went quiet. Lia heard muffled sobs. Choking on the words, he added, "Kurt opened the door and put her out for the walkers to eat. The screams ended real quick." Another long pause. "They made me and Maggie mop the blood off the floor."

"I'm so sorry you had to experience that," Lia soothed, her stomach tightening with anger. "But right now, I need you to focus. Look around, tell me what you see. Any business cards with an address? A wall calendar, maybe?"

After a prolonged silence, he said, "There's a calendar. It has naked ladies on it. There's a round thingy on the desk. It's full of cards with writing on them. I don't see any business cards."

"Is there a corkboard on the wall?"

After a brief pause, he said, "There is. It's got pictures of naked ladies pinned to it. And a couple of pictures of mean-looking men. Some receipts and scraps of paper, too."

"How about an alarm permit? Maybe a city business license?"

"Nothing like that I can see," Cole said.

Hoping to draw out something useful in learning the kid's whereabouts, maybe mine a snippet of memory from what had to be a terror-clouded brain, she said, "How did you end up with Kurt and Janice?"

"They helped me and my parents get away from some other bad people." A brief silence, then, "Once we were safely away and my dad pulled our van over so he could thank them, Kurt's son killed him. Shot him in the chest with Kurt's shotgun. I couldn't run. My mom was so scared she couldn't talk. Kurt took me away from her and put me in the back of an SUV. There were eight other kids and two younger women Kurt said were his sisters. Us kids were all cuffed to each other and told to be quiet. If we talked or cried, the switch would come out and one of the sisters would lay into us."

"Where's your mom now?"

"I don't know."

"Did Kurt or Janice talk about where they were going next? Did you see anything on the way to where you are now that stands out? A landmark, maybe?"

"They make us wear hoods when we're on the move. Said it's so we don't get scared by the walkers."

"Did you hear them talking about any landmarks? Did either one of them say anything that stands out?"

"Janice did say something about an awful tower. A bit later, Kurt was mad because there were too many monsters to stop and look at some pirate ships."

Somewhere upstairs, Dozer, the gunmetal-gray pitbull who'd quickly taken to the new additions to Trinity, emitted a guttural growl. A beat later, Rose was at the top of the stairs and going on about seeing zombies on the security monitor.

"Are they inside the perimeter?" Lia called.

"Nope," Rose came back, "but there are already three at the main gate and more coming into the turnaround."

The news didn't surprise Lia. During her short stay here, every time someone left the compound in one of the vehicles, the walking dead would make an appearance eventually. She said, "Can't you go out and take care of them? I'm in the middle of something."

A short silence was broken by Dozer barking upstairs.

"I'm not ready yet," Rose called back.

"If Mister Rossi doesn't return soon," Lia said, "I'll come up and take care of them for you." The words were barely out of her mouth when the bookshelf to her right sucked inward. There was a rush of air as the section of wall, maybe a yard wide and crammed floor to ceiling with books, disappeared into a dimly lit tunnel.

Vern Rossi emerged carrying a Rubbermaid bin and wearing a hat Lia had never seen. While it was a trucker's hat with the mesh back, it wasn't one of the gas station items with the crude messages Shorty was known to wear. *White Sands Missile Range* was stitched in gold on the front. Clusters of gold oak leaves decorated the brim. Vern smiled, showing off straight white teeth. His tanned face wasn't that of a man nearing his seventieth year. It was taut and devoid of worry lines. His hazel eyes sparkled. If he was still mourning the recent loss of his wife, adult son, and the hardware store they had worked so hard to make a fixture in northeast Santa Fe, it didn't show.

Although the concrete-and-rebar-reinforced tunnel connecting the Lazarus bunker to Trinity House was narrow, the ceiling, at best, six feet off the sloping floor, the man didn't need to duck as he emerged from the gloom. Pausing at the tunnel's narrow mouth, he pressed a recessed button on the spine of one of the larger tomes occupying the top shelf. The section of wall made no sound as it sucked closed behind him.

Meeting Vern's gaze, Lia held a finger vertical to her lips and showed him the handset.

"Who is it?" he mouthed.

Silencing him with a raised-brow stare, she said, "Cole? You still there?"

"I am," he came back, "but Maggie just pulled the string. I got to go." Like a person who'd just seen a ghost, his voice choked off at the end.

Face going slack, Lia depressed the Talk button. "Cole?"

Nothing.

Lia hung her head. Speaking softly into the handset, she said, "I'll be here tomorrow, Cole. Same time. I promise." Backing her thumb off the Talk key, she pressed the microphone to her forehead. "His name is Cole," she told Vern. "He's in trouble." She slid the pad around so he could get a better look at it. It was filled with specifics she'd jotted down during the short conversation.

After skimming the page, he sneered, voice full of contempt, "*Pedophiles.* One would think that God would have taken them first." He was still not over losing his adult son. All his life he had expected to precede Shane in death. A month ago, he couldn't have fathomed Santa Fe being overrun by living dead things, let alone Shane getting bit by one of the shambling monsters. But it had happened. Just two short weeks ago. The loss had given him a new purpose: to rid the world of as many of the things as humanly possible before he rejoined his wife and son wherever one ended up after shuffling off this mortal coil.

Rose called down again.

"Coming," Vern replied, heading for the stairs. Looking back at Lia, he asked her to man her two-way radio and give him a play-by-play until he got into position. While he really wanted to give Rose the benefit of the doubt, he'd come to the conclusion the young woman was their weakest link after just a couple of days observing the group that had accepted him with open arms.

Dozer resumed barking.

Lia nodded. Vern didn't need to say the quiet part out loud. She'd noticed Rose's hesitancy. The woman's penchant to ask others to do the dirty work. But worst of all was how the woman would suddenly freeze up without warning. Bottom line: Rose was strung way too tight for the horror-movie-come-to-life they were all living through.

Going for her right calf to scratch an itch, Lia grimaced as her nails instead raked against the smooth plastic of the below-the-knee prosthesis Vern had fashioned for her out of items taken off the shelves of his hardware store. Two weeks removed from the life-saving amputation and Lia was still being ambushed by the sensation that her leg was still whole. Missing Limb Syndrome was what Lee called it. It was a major pain in Lia's ass. One time it would manifest as an infuriating itch she could never scratch. Next, the phantom appendage would be under assault by a squadron of murder hornets. The latter made the old pins-and-needles that came with a limb falling asleep seem like a lover's caress.

Nothing compared to the excruciating pain of the zombie's crushing bite. At the time she was certain the burning that followed the bite was the Romero virus surging into her bloodstream. She could still see in her mind's eye the creature coming away with a bloody, jiggling hunk of her flesh in its mouth. Last thing she remembered was Sarah Rhoad's face looming over her, the blade in the helicopter pilot's hand a blur as it simultaneously saved and changed her life forever.

Lee had assured Lia the sensation that her leg was still there would diminish with time. But that assurance had also come with the warning that she would never really be free of it.

Lia powered on the desktop monitor. It was one of many scattered throughout the home. The screen took a moment to refresh. Once the cathode-ray tube had warmed up, nine panes, each containing an image beamed in from a different camera around the compound's vast perimeter, filled the monitor's curved screen.

The zombies were picked up by the hidden camera trained on the turnaround. The ones already pawing the driveway gate appeared to have been dead since the first days of the outbreaks. The pair of males, both pushing middle age, were dressed in summer attire: above-the-knee shorts and polo-style shirts. On their feet were ratty golf shoes. *A final round gone wrong,* thought Lia. Imagining being pursued by the pair, the steady *clickety-clack* of metal spikes on cement, started a cold chill tracing her spine.

The lone female of the trio had been attractive prior to first death. She had died wearing a sheer yellow nightie and looked totally out of place next to the golf buddies. Her long blonde hair was tangled and home to twigs and leaves. Speaking to miles logged, the soles of her dainty bare feet left behind crimson prints wherever she stepped.

Purple-rimmed bites peppered the left side of the undead woman's neck. The responsible parties had made a meal of most of the cheek and all of the fleshy bits ringing the ear on that side. The earhole was crusted with dried blood and teeming with wriggling white maggots. A wide gash starting just below her right ear traveled across one exposed breast before ending a few inches north of her navel, where a deep puncture wound still wept a viscous yellow fluid. The damage must have been inflicted by a single swipe of a large knife or machete. The edges of the arcing wound were raised and dark with dried blood. A row of yellowed molars peeked out from an inches-long tear that ran horizontal to where the gash began.

In the background, more zombies were streaming into the turnaround. While Lia counted another five on the move, she couldn't tell whether they were all Slogs or if a Bolt or two was present due to the monitor's poor resolution. She supposed the moment Vern showed his face, all would be revealed.

There was movement in the panel displaying the feed from the camera mounted above the multi-car garage. It was a bit grainy, but Lia could still make out a large portion of the brick driveway and twenty yards or so of the backside of the exterior wall, including the pedestrian and automobile gates.

The door on the rear of the garage swung open. Vern emerged wearing a helmet, the attached visor flipped down in front of his face. In one hand was a pink pool noodle, in the other a steel cylinder about half the size of a SCUBA tank. A length of black hose snaked from a brass fitting atop the cylinder. Sprouting from the other end of the hose was a thin metal wand. The wand was nearly the same length as the pool noodle and tipped with a flared metal shroud. Ensconced in the shroud was the lethal component of Vern's modified bolt gun: a foot-long spike fashioned from aerospace-grade titanium.

While Lia didn't know exactly how Vern's *Mule* worked, she was impressed by its lethality. That the bolt was fired by compressed air and remained in the shroud kept the group from constantly having to dip into their dwindling supply of ammunition. So far, the only instance in which the Mule's kick had been ineffective was when Vern had tried to put down an undead prison guard decked out in full riot gear. The spike had barely made a dent in the 3A ballistic helmet strapped to the guard's head, the very helmet Vern was now wearing. The polycarbonate visor attached to the helmet had also proven impervious to the spike.

She watched Vern close the door at his back and trap the noodle under one arm. After cinching down the helmet's chin strap, he made his way to the smaller of the two gates and set the cylinder and noodle down on the herringbone pavers. Plucking an aluminum folding ladder from the ground, he lugged it to the wall and deployed it where the wall met the pedestrian gate.

Scooping up the cylinder and noodle, Vern scaled the ladder with ease. Feet planted on the second rung from the top, upper body hinged over the top of the wall, he waved the pool noodle over where Lia guessed the dead had congregated.

Lia shifted her gaze to the pane on the monitor showing the entire run of the wall's south-facing exterior. She saw the trio, faces and bodies in profile, straining mightily to reach Vern. The other zombies were still transiting the turnaround. After coercing the trio into standing shoulder to shoulder, he drew back and the noodle disappeared. Having switched out the pool noodle for the cylinder, he reappeared a few seconds later brandishing the spike-tipped wand.

Even with the audio on the monitor turned off, Lia still imagined the subtle *pfft-thwak* made by the Mule each time Vern triggered it. Not lost on her was the spritz of blood and flecked bone produced each time the spike punctured a zombie skull. In a matter of seconds, the zombies went from viable threats to the living to an unmoving jumble of arms and legs on the ground at the base of the wall.

Upper body hinged over the top of the wall, Vern was peering down on his handiwork when a Bolt broke from the knot of dead traversing the turnaround. It was a younger specimen, maybe in its early twenties when the Romero virus snuffed its first life. The younger ones were always faster and more dexterous. A small number of the newly turned were capable of near-normal locomotion. A fraction of those could flat-out sprint.

After barely surviving an encounter with a fast-mover in the tunnels underneath a high school stadium in Middletown, Tara's last city of residence before everything changed, she started calling them Bolts. Inspired by Olympic sprinter Usain Bolt, the name had stuck.

Lia snatched up the two-way radio. Before she could get it to her mouth, Rose beat her to the punch, hollering "Bolt!"—a warning that instantly had Vern hinging up and squaring off to meet the threat. Ladder wobbling under his weight, he dragged the wand over the wall and braced for impact.

Eyes glued to the monitor, Lia could only watch it all unfold. While she had seen a Bolt hit smaller fences at full speed, flip head over heels and end up on the opposite side, she doubted that would be the case here. However, she thought glumly, if the Bolt reached the wall and the pile of dead became its launching pad, Vern would be in trouble.

The young male zombie's eyes never left Vern's helmeted head. Barely missing being tripped up by the low curb ringing the turnaround, the Bolt hit the gate with a full head of steam.

Lia watched the gate vibrate and imagined the solid *thud* as the creature was repulsed by the thick wooden item. Then she was again hearing in her head the *pfft-thwak* of the Mule as Vern reached over the wall with the wand, pressed the spike to the back of the struggling Bolt's cranium, and pressed its trigger.

In less than a minute, thanks to Vern's new toy, nothing was moving in the turnaround.

But the work wasn't done. He was going to need help clearing the accumulation of twice-dead corpses.

Chapter 2

"We should be out cutting firewood," groused Benjamin Sistek. "Winter's coming. This"—he gestured at the structure a few feet off of his left shoulder—"is stuff we could be doing *after* the weather turns. For Christ's sake, Trinity is already flush with solar panels. Plus, the colder it is, the slower the biters are. Especially the *Bolts*."

Though Steve-O was next to Benny, his stocking feet planted on the dash and the remote control to his deployed drone clutched in a two-handed grip, the older man said nothing.

Standing watch nearby and well within earshot, Tara Riker also ignored the latest addition to Benny's constant stream of glass-half-full thought.

Benny was at the wheel of his longtime friend's Ford Shelby Baja, awaiting, rather impatiently, word to pull forward and reposition the attached U-Haul trailer to the spot behind the mansion where they would soon be loading the liberated solar panels. With the number of dead in the area steadily increasing, leaving the truck and trailer out front of the mansion and lugging the panels around was no longer safe.

The south-facing array of panels atop the multi-level architectural monstrosity built on a mesa north of Santa Fe had originally consisted of four rows, ten to a row, forty in all. Each individual panel was roughly the size of a large flat-screen television. Initially, all the work that had gone into getting them off the roof and into the trailer had seemed more risk than reward.

Now, after perfecting their system through trial and error and having already removed and trucked two rows of panels to Trinity House, Leland Riker was back atop the gently sloping red-tile roof. He was roped up and down on one knee, the size twelve Salomon laced to his carbon-fiber prosthetic providing a fairly stable platform as he worked.

Though the through-and-through gunshot wound Riker had received during the shootout with Tobias Harlan was still healing, the handful of 800 milligram Advil he'd taken with breakfast was doing a pretty good job of dulling the periodic stabs of pain that accompanied the process. The constant itching was a different story. It was all he could do to not rip what he had affectionately dubbed his *bionic* off of the stump and scratch the puckered pink lump of scar tissue until it bled.

Riker had lost the lower half of his left leg to an IED explosion in Baghdad, Iraq. The artillery shell buried on the side of Route Irish had been detonated remotely, completely destroying the up-armored Land Cruiser he'd been driving. The VIP passenger and two security personnel he'd been transporting had perished in the fire that followed.

Along with other life-threatening injuries, Riker had suffered a closed head wound that put him in a weeklong coma. Emerging from the coma, he was quick to anger and prone to headaches. He left the hospital diagnosed with CTE—also known as Concussion Syndrome. A decade later, the symptoms were still a constant companion.

While initially the below-the-knee amputation had taken a lot of getting used to, dozens of physical therapy sessions at the VA hospital had transformed that first prosthetic from a pain-in-the-ass necessity he'd been loath to strap on over the lump of healing scar tissue to an extension of his body he rarely removed. As a symbolic graduation from those VA-provided crutches to that first professionally fitted prosthetic—a separation that was both mental and physical—he had taken a saw to those clunky sticks and then burned them in a barrel in the alley behind his late mother's home in Middletown, Indiana.

Muttering under his breath, Riker scooted closer to the fifth panel in the new row of ten. Thumbing the wheel on the crescent wrench for what seemed like the hundredth time, he got the jaws to where he wanted them, then went back to attacking the stubborn bolt.

Having lost yet another round of rock-paper-scissors, Riker had gotten stuck with the manual wrench. While the chrome item was adequate for the job, it was incredibly small in his mitt-sized hand. It was also prone to slipping off the bolt which had led to him bashing the first two knuckles on his right hand several times, leaving them bloodied and throbbing mightily. Only consolation to losing and getting stuck with the tool he had was that the maddening itch of the healing gunshot wound was just a couple of slips of the wrench from taking a backseat to the pain radiating from the battered knuckles.

Opposite Riker, the rope around his waist also tied off to the stone chimney at the roof's peak, Jimmy "Shorty" Twigg was busy *wrenching* the bolts on his side. The battery-powered ratchet in his hand produced a constant hum as he moved it quickly from bolt to bolt.

The panel the pair was currently removing was tied off to the chimney, the excess rope coiled and sitting on the roof between Riker and Shorty. Once the panel was free from the supporting frame, it would take both of them working a separate rope to keep the panel from spinning and bashing into the mansion's glass façade as they lowered it to the ground. With a thirty-foot drop from the roof to the yard below, the process required a good deal of coordination and concentration from both men. Easier said than done, considering every dead thing within earshot was acutely aware of their presence.

"We've got company," bellowed Tara. She was a few yards from the pickup, her position putting her equidistant to the mansion and infinity-edge swimming pool that took up a major portion of the backyard. Beyond the pool, the ground fell away gradually to the arroyo separating the mansion from a distant subdivision, the main source of the constant stream of zombies.

Clutched in the petite woman's hand was a semiautomatic Glock 19 pistol. Over the course of the last few weeks, a chunk of time that had seen Tara go from barista slinging hot drinks in a university lobby in Middletown, Indiana, to hardened survivor capable of killing to keep from being killed, she had become quite the marksman. Whether putting down zombies at point-blank range with the compact Glock, dropping them en masse with the suppressed HK MP5 submachinegun currently slung across her back, or sniping them over great distances with her brother Lee's scoped Klepto rifle, she was more than capable of holding her own against the hungry ghouls.

She wore her jet-black hair in tight, skull-hugging braids. The braids were tied off with rubber bands, tipped with white beads, and snaked from beneath her woodland camouflage boonie hat. Usually the same light shade of brown as a latté—her least favorite drink to make before the world went to shit—all the time spent outdoors had turned her skin the same inky black as a shot of espresso.

Edging over the center console to sneak a peek at the remote control's screen, Benny said, "That's a lot of biters climbing out of the arroyo. Once they reach flat ground, think you can lure them away with the drone?"

Steve-O shook his head. "They're not interested. They started to ignore the drone as soon as they caught sight of Lee and Shorty on the roof." He glanced sidelong at Benny. "And now that they are on to Tara, even if Lee and Shorty hide, the monsters are *our* problem."

Fingers tightening on the steering wheel, Benny said, "Then tell Tara to get her butt inside the truck."

Brows arched, his prescription glasses making his blue/green eyes appear unusually large, Steve-O said, "I'm not telling Pretty Lady anything. She's in her thirties. That makes her a grown-ass woman."

"Just humor me, Steve-O. Stick your head out the window and call her in."

Focused intently on the remote, Steve-O bit his lip and tried his best to tune Benny out.

Pulsing the passenger window all the way down, Benny called out to Tara at the top of his voice. Nothing. She was turned away from the pickup, the Glock pistol in a two-handed grip, arms at full extension.

"Lee wants us to conserve ammo," Benny muttered. "Am I the only one who follows orders?"

Steve-O looked away from the screen. "I follow orders, Benny. Just not from you." He adjusted his glasses. "You may be taller than me, but I think I can take you. My center of gravity is lower than yours. I get you off your feet and"—he made a punching motion at the dash—"ground and pound, baby."

"You've been watching those mixed martial arts training videos, haven't you?"

Steve-O smiled wanly and returned his attention to the screen.

"Better bring your drone on in," Benny suggested. "We may be forced to pull up stakes and leave with only half a load."

Steve-O was one step ahead of Benny. He had already punched a button on the remote that had the drone returning to its landing pad on the Shelby's hood. Acting on the new command delivered via radio frequency, the drone was making a beeline for the GPS coordinate Steve-O had designated as home.

While most people born with Down syndrome, also known as trisomy 21, possessed an IQ of around 50, in that department Steve-O had won the extra-chromosome lottery. Shortchanged a bit in the height and dexterity column, where IQ was concerned, the forty-five-year-old authority on all things country and western had scored high up on the chart among those like him.

Hearing his sister's shouted warning, Riker rose up to get a better view of the mansion's vast backyard. After several weeks of inattention, the lawn was a sea of brown. Numerous flower beds spread around the lawn's perimeter were now islands of bone-dry soil sprouting withered stalks and littered with sun-bleached petals.

The swimming pool ran away from the banks of sliding glass doors dominating the mansion's rear elevation. It was half full, the brackish algae-polluted water teeming with bloated corpses.

When Riker and Benny had found the place two days prior, there were only three zombies trapped in the pool. Upon returning earlier this morning, that number had risen by thirteen.

One by one, Riker had lured the new arrivals to the pool's edge and put eleven down with his razor-sharp Randall Model 18. After a little prodding and words of encouragement, Steve-O accepted the big blade from Riker and handled the final two, dispatching them both with well-placed knife strikes to the temple. Slowly but surely, the man was coming to the realization that what he was being asked to do was not going against all he had been taught growing up. It was not an act of violence or an affront to the living, breathing human beings the reanimated dead used to be. It was, in fact, an act born out of compassion. Riker had explained that by killing them, their souls were being released from the decaying husks which—through no fault of their own—they had become trapped within. Riker's gut feeling was that Steve-O was on the verge of fully embracing the necessary act that, pre-Romero, would have earned any one of them a long stint in prison.

Stepping around a skylight to gain a better view of the ground below the eaves, Riker caught the toe of his Salomon on the raised metal flashing. Pitching forward, he instinctively twisted to his right, away from the roof's edge. The streaked glass of the double-paned skylight came at him fast. Instead of putting a hand out to arrest the fall, an action that would only break the glass and leave that hand a bloody, shredded mess, he resisted the urge, opting instead to cover his face with both hands and allow his shoulder to bear the brunt of the impact.

There was a sharp *crack* and the glass spidered and imploded under Riker's weight. With a lightning bolt of pain coursing the length of his right arm, and the sensation of weightlessness gripping him, he wasn't worried about the possibility of Vern mining his shoulder of shards of glass and the dozens of stitches it would take to sew him up. Nor was he concerned about the broken bones in his future if the chimney the rope was tied to crumbled and he ended up on the floor in the chef's kitchen, some twenty-odd feet below the skylight opening. All of that would suck. But it was the home's undead owners that had his full attention.

Every time Shorty and Riker had been up on the roof, the geriatric couple had been their constant companions, standing in the kitchen, their blank, shark-like gazes directed skyward. The only time the withered zombies stopped staring the meat from their bones was when the Shelby's engine firing up drew them to one of the gore-streaked windows overlooking the backyard.

That wasn't going to save Riker now. Benny was in the truck with the big V8 engine stilled. With the two-way radio stuffed deep in Riker's pocket, there was no way to call for a diversion.

Mercifully, the rope arrested Riker's fall a yard and a half shy of the Italian marble island. The rope he'd threaded between his legs and tied off around his waist made a high-pitched *twang* as it went taut. As he reached behind his back to get a hand on the island, the rope suddenly reached full extension and his entire body was jerked back toward the skylight. Arched forcefully due to gravity and inertia working in direct opposition, all of the vertebra in Riker's spine cracked in unison. It sounded a lot like a Vegas dealer ruffling a fresh deck of cards. It *felt* like the Predator was taking a trophy.

While Riker couldn't see Fred and Ethel—nicknames he'd given the undead denizens of the mansion—he certainly could smell them. Although they'd likely been dead for weeks, the gasses put off as their flesh and organs slowly putrefied remained trapped inside the sealed-up home. The stench was palpable. He could almost feel it envelope his suspended body as the change in pressure drew the warmer air toward the blown-out skylight.

The rope was strangling Riker's waist and balls like a pissed-off anaconda as it again accepted his full weight and went taut. Before he could take another swipe for the island to steady himself and maybe relieve some of the biting pressure, pent-up momentum started his body spinning counterclockwise on a flat plane. He was no Tom Cruise in *Mission Impossible*, suspended from wires and on a controlled descent through probing laser beams. There was nothing graceful about this entrance, nothing controlled about the bind—both literally and figuratively—that he now found himself in.

Initially, due to being upside-down, gravity working to pull his head groundward, the room started to spin in front of Riker's eyes, and all he could see was an interior wall. It housed a double door freezer/refrigerator that looked as if it could contain half a cow, an eight-burner Wolf range complete with an industrial-sized stainless-steel vent hood, and a built-in wine cooler, its glass door streaked with dried blood and ghostly handprints.

As the rotation picked up speed, Riker felt his arms being pulled away from his body. The island a white blur beneath him, he caught a fleeting glimpse of the yard through the window above the massive double sink. Tara was out there on the brown grass, backpedaling away from the threat she had just warned the others about. The bell cow zombie was a big specimen. Riker figured it weighed a few pounds north of two-fifty. About twenty more than he was carrying. Only this thing was a foot and a half shorter and half a dozen belt notches wider around the waist. It must have been roaming the desert for some time. Nearly every inch of exposed skin was punctured by what appeared to be cactus needles.

No sooner had Riker set eyes on his sister than the rotation continued, and he found himself eye to eye with Ethel. Teeth bared, a guttural moan rumbling its narrow chest, the beast made a two-handed grab for his face. Too slow. While Riker's head had spun away from the gnashing teeth, the cracked fingernails raked him over the left eye, reopening one of the superficial wounds he'd received during the gun battle with Harlan.

As Riker continued on the high-speed 360-tour of the kitchen, he reeled his right arm in close to his body and groped blindly for the Randall in the scabbard on his hip. He was just dragging the knife free when undead Fred entered the picture. Well within arm's reach, the zombie threaded the gnarled fingers on one hand into Riker's beard. As the other bony hand snatched his shirt sleeve, the ashen face suddenly loomed large in his peripheral. Maw open wide, Fred dipped in for a taste of fresh meat.

But instead of tasting flesh, the equal and opposite components of Newton's Law kicked in. Chattering teeth an inch from clamping down on Riker's nose, the zombie was yanked off its feet. There was no look of surprise, nor was there recognition whatsoever on the zombie's part as centrifugal force caused its slight frame to go horizontal to the floor.

Simultaneous to the zombie's pistoning jaw and twisted countenance retreating from Riker's side vision, he heard fabric tearing and felt a sudden sting as a sizeable patch of his beard was rent from his cheek.

Having lost purchase on Riker, Fred spun a flat 180, then smacked Ethel broadside and took her to the ground with him. They ended up a tangle of arms and legs face down on the floor a short distance from the island.

"Damn it!" Riker bellowed. "That was uncalled for, Fred."

Trapped underneath Ethel, the shock of curly black hair clutched in one hand, tattered strip of fabric in the other, Fred fixed Riker with a dead-eyed stare as if it knew it was being addressed.

Seeing it as a personal affront, Riker felt a sudden flare of heat rush up his neck and spread to his face. He was getting angry and there was nothing he could do to halt the process. It was a byproduct of the CTE. One therapist recommended humor as a remedy. Too late for that now. There was nothing funny about a man his size stuck in the predicament he had gotten himself into.

The sound of nails raking the floor echoed off the kitchen ceiling. Riker craned and saw that Fred had released the hair and fabric and was struggling to rise from under his undead better half.

Contorting his body, Riker was able to get himself turned around. Getting a knee planted on the island top, he sawed through the rope with the Randall. Eyes locked on the opposite end of the island, he climbed off and went into a combat crouch.

Undead Fred was kneeling across the island from Riker, dead hands palm down on the white marble and squeaking loudly as it struggled to rise. Approaching from the thing's blind side, he focused on a spot on its head an inch or so in front of its left ear. Taking a little hop-step forward, he twisted his body counterclockwise and delivered a swift roundhouse kick. The toe of Riker's Salomon caught the thing right where it was supposed to: squarely on the left temple. The follow-through sent Fred's head whipping clockwise and had the wispy strands of gray hair standing on end. When the zombie's head reached the extent of its natural range of motion, there was a pronounced *crack*. On the heels of the distinct sound of vertebrae shearing in two, the zombie's arms went slack and it slammed down hard onto Ethel, neck bent unnaturally, gaunt face aimed at the ceiling.

It was clear to Riker that the force of his kick had paralyzed Fred from the neck down. The only movement happening now was a constant opening and closing of its mouth and the eyes roving their sockets as they tracked his slow and steady approach.

Keeping clear of the snapping teeth, again Riker went to one knee, only this time he planted it on Fred's sternum, trapping both zombies to the floor. Anger subsiding somewhat, he grabbed a handful of hair and pressed the tip of the Randal to the side of Fred's misshapen skull. "I'm sorry it had to come to this," he said. "Just know the watch I see on your wife's wrist is going to someone who'll cherish it every bit as much as I imagine she did."

As if the promise had been understood by Fred, his eyes suddenly went still in their sockets. They remained fixed in that thousand-yard-stare as Riker finished his grisly deed, pushing the knife to the hilt and stilling the chattering jaw. A second quick stab to the base of the other zombie's skull stopped its struggles.

Glancing in the direction of Fred's dead-eyed stare, Riker caught sight of Shorty. He was peering over the skylight's edge. His head looked ridiculously small in the four-by-six opening. He chuckled, then said, "That there is elder abuse, Lee."

"They didn't feel a thing," Riker shot, rising up off the unmoving corpses.

Pained look on his face, Shorty said, "Ouchie. That rope looks like it's *encroaching*." He let out a low whistle. "Looks like *you're* feeling something. Your trouser snake OK?"

Riker said nothing.

Shorty said, "We should have found ourselves a couple of proper climbing harnesses before going *mansioneering*. This could have ended badly for you." He shrugged. "If it's any consolation, I'm damn impressed by your knot-tying skills. Were you a Boy Scout or something?"

"Or something," Riker said as he untied the makeshift harness and tossed the short length of rope aside.

Shorty said, "All kidding aside, your sister is being pursued by a roly-poly biter. There's also a pretty good-sized pack of the fuckers coming up out of the arroyo."

Nodding, Riker said, "She can handle herself with the lone biter. The others might be a problem. Especially if there's a Bolt or two in the mix. How about Benny and Steve-O? What are they doing?"

"What you told them to do. Both are still sitting inside your rig."

"I'm going out back to help Tara," Riker said. "You stay put. When we're done with the biters, I'm coming back up. Won't take us but a half hour or so to unbolt the rest of the row and get them into the trailer."

Shorty shook his head. "Change of plans, boss. Benny called up from the truck to tell me Lia just radioed. She wants us to return to Trinity ASAP. Guess she has something she wants to tell us—"

Interrupting, Riker said, "What's so important it can't wait?"

"You know what they say about women," Shorty said.

"Off the top of my head … no, I don't," Riker said. "Better enlighten me."

Smiling, Shorty said, "You can't live with them, and you can't kill them."

"And you wonder why you haven't been laid since George W's second term."

Shorty flashed a pair of middle fingers down at Riker. "And you're a regular American gigolo. *Magic Mike* in the flesh."

Ignoring the barb, Riker cocked an ear and listened hard.

Nothing.

The mansion had gone as quiet as the tomb it had become, the dust motes scudding the putrid air the only thing moving. Confident he was all alone in the mansion, he hinged over and lifted Ethyl's thin liver-spotted arm off the floor. He removed the watch and let the limp arm fall to the floor. Seeing the word *Rolex* etched on the watch's white gold face brought a smile to his. The way the second hand smoothly swept the dial told him it was the real deal. He'd seen plenty of counterfeits on the street being passed off as legit by corner hustlers. A ticking second hand was the dead giveaway the thing was a *Made In China* knockoff. Removing the watch, he dropped it into a pocket for safekeeping.

Chapter 3

"Get in here, Tara," Benny hollered. "We need to leave … your brother's orders." A moment after hearing the plea for her to board the truck, Tara had lined the lead zombie up in her sights, transitioned her finger from the Glock's slide rail to the trigger, and was drawing up a few pounds of trigger pull. The thing waddling her way had garnered her undivided attention. It was bristling with thousands of cactus needles, the tattered tee shirt pierced through by the inch-long spikes and pinned smartly to its ample belly. Dozens of the needles had become embedded in one of its pale, filmy eyes. Tara recalled a movie starring a monster that strongly resembled this shambling pincushion but couldn't drag the title from her overstimulated brain. Whatever the case, there was no way she was letting this thing get anywhere near her. Killing it with her blade was *definitely* out of the question.

Aiming for the bridge of the zombie's bulbous nose, the only needle-free square inch of skin on its cherubic face, a point of impact where a slight deviation of aim would still likely result in a kill, she let the round fly. With Lee's admonition to save ammo echoing in her head, she instead implemented one of the prime rules laid out in a zombie comedy she had caught at the theater when zombies were just a construct of someone's wild imagination: She gave the trigger a second press.

The *double-tap*. Or *two to the dome*. The rule was right up there with *cardio*. Though she was a better shot with the MP5, especially when facing multiple zombies, she really enjoyed shooting the Glock. Lee had purchased it for her in Florida as the East Coast was slowly falling to the dead. She tried to push herself to use it in situations like this when faced with only one or two slow movers. It taught her patience and perseverance. Which in turn helped to bolster the confidence she needed to keep putting one foot in front of the other.

Before Romero, the only handgun she had held was the little Smith & Wesson revolver her brother had picked up long ago at a pawnshop in the seediest part of downtown Indianapolis. That gun had a very short barrel and was highly inaccurate beyond twenty feet or so. Another downfall: the snub-nose .38 only carried five rounds and had to be reloaded by first extracting the spent shells, then inserting each individual new bullet into the empty cylinder—a time-consuming task she couldn't fathom having to accomplish with a zombie stalking her.

The first 9mm round from the Glock punched a nickel-sized hole through the zombie's septum, sending its head snapping backward and putting the underside of its needle-studded chin in the path of the follow-on shot. While the first entry wound was a mostly bloodless affair, the second was a gory sight to behold. Traveling at nearly 1,200 feet per second, the 115-grain copper-jacketed missile struck with a wet slap and opened up a hole magnitudes larger than the first. Even as the zombie was pitching backward, its body contorting into an upside-down U, the kinetic energy rippling through decaying fat caused the entry wound to blossom like a flower.

There was a sickening crunch as its skull smacked cement. Needles quivered as a ripple transited the twice-dead corpse's fat rolls. As the body settled into its final resting place, face-up, milky lifeless eyes staring at the blue sky, escaping gasses produced a long-drawn-out farting noise.

Nose crinkling, Tara took one last look at the damage caused by part two of the *double-tap*. The gaping chasm was impossible to miss. Even if the report of the second of the closely spaced shots had gotten by Lee, there was zero chance he was going to miss the fresh fist-sized hole in the thing's pale, fleshy neck. Which meant that another of his *ammo conservation* talks was definitely in Tara's future.

She had sidestepped her kill and was putting the swimming pool between her and the remaining half dozen zombies when, simultaneously, the Shelby's engine roared to life and its horn blared. It wasn't a cordial *toot* meant to get her attention. Far from it. Seemed as if Benny was putting his entire weight behind the effort. Which told her the large pack of biters Steve-O had spotted navigating the arroyo had just crested the rim.

So much for luring them into the pool.

As Tara turned toward the mansion, she received two distinct messages from two different sources. The first was from her brother. He was standing *inside* the mansion, his frame nearly filling entirely one of the floor-to-ceiling windows. How he came to be there was a mystery. Last time she had glanced at the mansion, right before she issued her warning, he had been up on the roof and wrenching on one of the solar panels.

Now he was staring at her wide-eyed, a radio pressed to his lips and frantically stabbing a finger toward the pickup. Although she wasn't hearing what he had to say, even from halfway across the estate's vast backyard the message was clear: *Get to the truck.*

The second message to Tara *was* emanating from the two-way radio in her pocket. It was Benny confirming her hunch about the zombies emerging from the arroyo. They were locked on and heading in her direction.

Didn't need to tell her again. Leaping over the face-shot zombie, she slalomed through the upended pool furniture. Sprinting the remaining thirty feet to the idling pickup, she holstered the Glock and fished the radio from the pocket. Half the distance to the pickup, she was on the radio and asking Lee who had taught him the teleportation trick.

"Wasn't a magic act," he explained. He was already on the move through the mansion and sounded out of breath. "More like an act of gravity." He went quiet for a second. Coming from the speaker was the sound of a door lock being thrown. As he emerged from the mansion through a ground-level door somewhere out of sight, he admitted to her what had really happened.

Tara reached the truck about the same time Shorty was coming down off the roof. He had already shucked off the rope and was halfway down the extension ladder, a metallic ringing issuing each time one of his low-top North Face hikers came down on a rung.

Entering the Shelby through the passenger-side, she slammed the door and scooted to the center of the backseat.

Steve-O was already turned around, a broad smile on his face. "Good shooting, Tara. You need to teach me how to double-tap."

His greeting was quickly drowned out by Benny shouting at Shorty. "Grab the drone on your way in and put it in the bed," he ordered, goosing the throttle to get the point across that he wanted to get a move on.

Tara stripped off the MP5 and placed it on the floor by her feet. Hinging up, she met Benny's gaze in the rearview mirror. "Lee's going to be coming around the far corner any second. Don't you think you ought to give up the driver's seat?"

Benny broke eye contact long enough to assess the zombie situation. Seeing that only four of the initial group had walked into the pool and that the other three—as well as another ten or so marching over from the arroyo—were making a steady advance, he said, "I'm not getting out of the truck. Besides, I'm already belted in, and the seat is set up for me." He hooked a thumb at the backseat. "Lee can get in back with you. I'll stop once we've made it to Veterans Memorial and change seats with him then."

Tara grimaced. "He's not going to like it."

Steve-O said, "You suck at backing this thing up with the trailer hooked to it."

"Steve-O has a point," added Tara. "But suit yourself." She laced her fingers behind her head and locked eyes with Benny in the mirror. "You make that bed … enjoy sleeping in it."

Entering through the passenger door behind Benny, quadcopter in hand, Shorty pulled the door shut and fumbled for the seatbelt. As he clicked it home, he got the sense that something was wrong. Looking up, he saw that all eyes were on him. Gaze jumping from face to face, then settling back on Tara—by far the easiest on his eyes—he said, "What's going on? You all got that guilty look. Conspiratorial might be a better word."

Tara said, "Benny's afraid to go out into the wild. He doesn't want to relinquish the wheel." She detailed the driver dilemma and explained Benny's reasoning behind his reluctance to move to the backseat.

Benny changed the subject, saying, "You were *supposed* to put the drone in back."

Seeing Riker emerge from behind the mansion, maybe twenty yards off the Shelby's left front fender, head down and in a full-out sprint, Shorty said, "Sooner or later, Sistek, you're going to have to water your balls and face a big group of eaters. I recommend you do it under your own terms and on your own time. That way you'll know what you're capable of. We'll also find out what you're capable of. And there'll be fewer moving parts. Less room for error. That way, if you do shit the bed, only one who dies is you." Riker had halved the distance to the truck and was pulling the Sig Legion from the holster on his hip. Going on, Shorty added, "But right now is not the time for experimenting. Things are about to get interesting."

Benny's response to that was to point to the quadcopter. "Lee is going to be here in a second. Better make room for him."

"How about I shove this toy up your ass, Sistek." Shorty shook his head. "You'd probably enjoy it too much," he added sarcastically.

Benny extended both middle fingers.

Steve-O had planted both hands on the dash. "Hurry up, Lee! There's a Bolt on your tail," he warned.

Sure enough, the Bolt, a twenty-something male with a ripped physique and a pronounced limp, had just made a sharp cut around the corner. The pursuit wasn't blistering fast. It was more of a lope thanks to the hitch in the thing's giddy-up. But Riker was also moving much slower than normal. His gait was different, too.

After reacquiring its prey, the Bolt was quick to close the gap.

On the run, Riker twisted halfway around, leveled his Sig Sauer pistol at the Bolt, and snapped off four rounds. The first two found their mark, hitting the zombie in the chest, but only staggered it. Due to muzzle rise, the follow-on rounds sailed harmlessly over the charging beast's head.

"Sunroof," Tara barked.

Biting a knuckle, Steve-O said, "Please don't shoot Lee."

Benny triggered the button that started the sunroof sliding open. As he did so, he instructed Steve-O to run his seat as far forward as it would go.

Contorting her body, MP5 in hand, Tara leaned against the seat back and poked her head and upper third of her body past the slow-moving pane of smoked glass. She planted her elbows on the roof's leading edge, widened her stance on the seat, then tucked the little sub gun into her shoulder. After lining up the iron sights, by feel, she rotated the selector from safe to three-round burst.

Making eye contact with Lee, the zombie but a dozen feet off his six, Tara aimed for the particular spot in space she expected them both to pass through. Once Lee had crossed the imaginary plane, she exhaled slowly and pressed the trigger.

Triple-tap was what she was thinking as the soft recoil vibrated her shoulder. Out of the three 9mm rounds she sent downrange, a single slug was all that struck home. It smacked the Bolt upside the head, entering just above the right ear and, inexplicably, exiting through its left eye socket. Trailing a plume of pink mist, the Bolt face planted on the brittle grass behind a good deal of pent-up momentum. The shallow furrow made by its forehead as its bare feet caught up with the decelerating upper body was bloody and littered with clumped brain matter.

Skidding to a halt beside the passenger door, Riker said, "Good shooting, John Wick. Now get back inside the truck." Seeing the seating order, he reluctantly hauled open the rear passenger-side door and folded his frame behind Steve-O's seat.

As Tara plopped back down on the backseat, a finger of gun smoke curling from the suppressor, she caught the drone full-on with her left elbow. There was a sharp *crack* and one of the four propellers was left a broken mess.

"I have more," Steve-O said nonchalantly. "I'm just glad you and Lee are both safe."

"We're not out of the woods yet, buddy." Meeting Benny's gaze, Riker commanded him to drive.

Working the steering wheel and accelerator in unison, Benny got the Shelby and trailer rolling straight backward. They hadn't moved but half a truck length in reverse when everything went to shit. First, there were a series of bangs as a trio of zombies caromed off the truck's bed on the passenger side. Then the trailer bounced over something, probably a zombie skull on account of the wet pop. That started the trailer to jackknife. As the trailer tracked toward the mansion, the load of panels shifted and crashed into the rail opposite of where they'd been propped.

Benny hit the brakes, cursing.

Riker tapped Benny on the shoulder. Meeting his narrowed gaze, he said, "Watch my hands and listen close."

Prior to his stint shuttling VIPs around Iraq in armored Land Cruisers and Suburbans, Riker had logged thousands of miles at the wheel of just about every type of truck in the Big Green Machine's inventory—double and triple trailers notwithstanding. Palm out and fingers curled, pretending *he* was the one driving, Riker spun the imaginary steering wheel clockwise.

Benny mimicked the movement, then flicked his eyes to the rearview.

Riker said, "Give it some gas," then slowly moved his hand in a counterclockwise motion.

Benny followed suit.

Peering over his shoulder, Riker said, "Good … it's coming back around. Now hold the wheel steady and give her some gas."

Head on a swivel, Steve-O had been watching the interaction between teacher and pupil. Just as the engine revved and the pickup started to roll backward and gain momentum, he said in a near whisper, "Don't screw it up, Benny. We're all counting on you."

Riker shot Steve-O a look that could be construed only one way: *time and place.*

The zombies raking the metal on the passenger side fell away as the truck picked up speed.

"OK, Benny," Riker instructed, "now do this and slowly apply the brakes." He spun his hand clockwise.

Again, Benny did as he was told. With the Shelby bleeding speed and the trailer's tires carving a fresh pair of Js in the dry grass, a Bolt slammed full speed into the rear of the trailer. It had come from out of nowhere and caused Steve-O and Shorty to visibly start.

Going heels over head, the Bolt's forward momentum carried it up and over the top edge of the drop-down ramp. It landed flat on its back on the trailer floor, the impact rattling the solar panels and causing them to shift yet again. Having become wedged between the passenger side wall and two-hundred-some-odd pounds of glass and steel, all the thing could do was take futile swipes at the air with its one free arm.

Seeing the old tire tracks in the grass, Benny threw the transmission into Drive, tromped the accelerator, and got the truck pointed toward the gravel access road they had come in on.

"Color me impressed," Shorty said. But instead of the praise being directed at Benny, he was addressing Riker. "That was some stellar backseat driving, Lee. Captain Dyslexia would be lost without you."

"To be fair," Steve-O interjected, "Benny was never a sea captain. He didn't own a barge. And he didn't own a boat ramp." He looked to Benny. "How many times have you put a boat into the water?"

Benny took his hand off the wheel long enough to make a circle with his fingers and flash it at Steve-O. "Zero times," he said. Steering one-handed onto the gravel access road, he turned right and gunned it.

Coming to Benny's defense, Tara said, "Squash the last name game, Shorty. And if you don't have anything good to say, don't say anything at all. Advice my momma gave me."

"Gave *us*," added Riker. "She ran a tight ship. Especially during Dad's drinking years."

Shorty ran a finger across his mouth. "My lips are sealed, M'lady."

Pointing in the direction of the pool and arroyo behind it, Steve-O said, "We got monsters. Step on it, Benny."

Spread out across the backyard was a herd of dead things two dozen strong. They were in various stages of undress and showed advanced signs of decay. The clothing some still wore hung in tatters. Speaking to miles logged traipsing across the desert landscape, cactus needles bristled from any skin that had been left exposed.

After apologizing profusely for nearly getting them stuck, Benny offered to pull over once they got to the interchange. "We can change drivers there. I'll drag that thing out of the trailer while Lee gets the seat and mirrors back to how he likes them."

"No need, bud," Riker said, again peering over his shoulder. "That thing's not going anywhere." He put a hand on Benny's shoulder. Gave it a soft squeeze. "Just drive. I trust you."

Chapter 4

After the short, uneventful drive from the mansion, Benny nosed the Shelby up to the Trinity House gate and ran his window down. The alarm keypad was on a pole, its lighted keys protected by a smoked plastic shield. Reaching out his window, he tapped in the code that started the gate moving.

The gate was slow to open, revealing in little slices the inner courtyard, three-car garage, and front entryway to the sprawling mansion.

Rose was standing in the open front door and waving at Benny. It was clear she was happy to see her man return home unscathed.

Vern, on the other hand, was waiting for them off to the side of the circular parking pad and watching with indifference as Benny pulled forward and struggled to get the Shelby and attached trailer parked in the limited space. Trapped under one arm was the riot helmet. On the ground by his feet was the Mule, its hose wrapped around the steel cylinder.

Seeing the zombie pinned beneath the half-load of solar panels, Vern hitched up his pants and shot a questioning look at Riker through the pickup's open window.

Beating Riker to the punch, Shorty said, "Lee doesn't adhere to Shorty's *rules for riders*."

With a *here we go again* tone to his voice, Vern said, "And exactly what would those rules be, Jim?"

Shorty leaned forward and made eye contact with Vern. Wearing a crooked smile, he said, "*Ass*, *gas*, or *grass*. No one rides for free."

"You're nasty," shot Tara, elbowing him playfully. "Always trying to get over on people."

"It's called survival, sweets. And that's not entirely true." Shorty threw off his seatbelt. "I stuck my neck out for you and yours. As a result, I lost a lot of paying customers *and* a perfectly good ferry."

"Lee gave you gold to take us across," Steve-O said.

"I have to admit, Shorty did give me a break on the price for passage," Riker conceded. "Although"—he looked sidelong at the man in question—"he was heading out to search for his son and daughter anyway."

"It's just a saying I lifted off a trucker hat," Shorty said sheepishly. "Probably not the best thing to be repeating in mixed company. Hopefully, you all don't see it as an indictment on my character."

Tara said, "The jury is still out on that. You can be pretty pervy at times. And you definitely *are* a character."

Shorty said nothing. Grabbing his stubby Shockwave shotgun off the floor, he shoved open his door and climbed down out of the truck.

Killing the engine, Benny exited the truck and went to meet Rose.

Steering the conversation away from the sensitive subject just raised by Tara, Riker said to Vern, "You were wondering about the thing in the trailer?"

Vern nodded. "Pretty hard to miss those flailing arms cresting the side rail. Thing reeks to high heaven, too."

"It's got a lot of competition from the corpses by the gate," Riker said.

"Slog or Bolt?" Vern asked.

"It's a Bolt. Damn thing hit the trailer full tilt as we were leaving the job and got itself stuck back there. It wasn't an imminent threat, so I saw no reason for us to stop in the wild to put it down."

Vern hefted the Mule off the ground. There was a twinkle in his eyes. "Good thinking. Speaking of putting it down"—he smiled wide—"want me to take care of it for you?"

"Go ahead. Put another notch in your belt." While Riker didn't mean what he said literally, it certainly wouldn't hurt. Since coming into the picture, Vern had lost a couple of inches off his waist. Wiry and spry from the get-go, now he was showing some muscle tone. It was mostly in the arms and legs, the once flabby folds of skin drawn tight over pronounced biceps and calves.

Riker attributed the rapid muscle gain to all the walking back and forth between Trinity and the Lazarus bunker. In addition to killing zombies, the man had taken it upon himself to unearth all of Lazarus's secrets.

After pacing off the distance from the hardened basement bunker underneath Trinity to the redoubt's steel blast door, Vern had declared the roundtrip to be just a tick under three-quarters of a mile. Better than making laps inside the Santa Fe Place mall, he had declared at the time. Three or four roundtrips a day, thought Riker, coupled with the physical exertion the man expended cataloging the bunker's vast stores, uncovering its many secrets hidden in hard-sided cases and wooden crates, would transform any man's physique—no matter his age.

Before Benny had reached Rose's side, Riker was elbowing open his door and unfolding his frame from the backseat. Gesturing toward the zombie corpses stacked outside the wall, he said, "You put all of those down by yourself?"—he flicked his gaze in Rose's direction—"or did you have some help?"

Vern nodded. "Lia was busy manning the radio." He paused. "Rose was just *busy*." He had made air quotes and flashed Riker a pained smile. "Just trying to pull my weight." Smile fading, he added, "I still owe you for what you did for my boy. I'm not the squeamish type. But when it came to doing *that* …"

Shaking his head vehemently, Riker said, "I get it. We're way more than square. You saved my life. Lia's, too. Believe me when I say we *all* appreciate everything you bring to the table. In my book, age is a number, *not* an indictment. You're a shining example of that." He paused. When Vern didn't respond to the accolades, Riker asked him what was so important that necessitated them coming back early.

Vern said, "I'll let Lia fill you in on all that." He arched a brow. "But when she's done saying her piece, I want the floor. There's a couple of things I discovered up the hill that I think might be game-changers when we decide to range further out from home base."

"*If* … we decide to range farther out," Tara said. She had exited the truck and, up until now, had been following the conversation, arms crossed and with a look of indifference on her face. Uncrossing her arms, she stepped between the two men. "We need to have a *group* discussion about how much we want to expose ourselves to the outside world."

Vern bowed his head. "Sooner or later, we're going to have to do some reconnoitering," he stressed. He regarded Tara with a pained look. "We need to expand our foraging territory. If we don't get out there and liberate the supplies we're going to need to ride out winter, someone else will."

"How are the winters here?" Riker asked. He'd already picked Lia's brain on the subject and came away not liking her answer. Knowing Vern, a man not prone to sugarcoating things, Riker had a hunch he wasn't going to like what the man had to say any better.

Vern rubbed his hands together. "Numbing cold at times. We'll definitely need to amass more wood to augment Trinity's geothermal heat."

Riker grunted. Minus the firewood comment, it was pretty much what Lia had said.

Rounding the front of the Shelby, Shorty said, "How's the War Wagon coming along?"

Vern removed his ball cap. Ran a hand through his tangle of thinning hair. "She's been sitting for a lot of years. She'll need new tires. Off-road items would be nice. Definitely needed her fluids changed. Job took me about an hour to complete. How the seals and gaskets held up over time is something we'll learn when we fire her up and take her for a spin."

Tara said, "It's obvious the former owner's kin didn't share the same end-times fears as he did." She shook her head. "If I was in their shoes, I would have never put this place up for sale. Not that the zombie apocalypse was on anyone's radar."

"I don't think they knew about Lazarus," Riker stated. "If they did, you would think by now one of them would have made it here. Since nobody has shown up unannounced, I think we're in the clear."

Vern said, "I think you're both going to have a change of heart when I show you what I came across in the big bunker. It contradicts all of your assumptions."

Riker said, "Can you give us a clue?"

"Patience," Vern implored. "It's a lot to digest. Probably best heard sitting down." He called Steve-O over.

Closing the passenger door behind him, Steve-O took up station next to Riker. "What do you want, Mister Rossi?"

"Please call me Vern. Saying my last name takes my mind back to all the family members I've lost. That's a bad neighborhood for me to be spending time in."

Steve-O cast his gaze at the ground. "Sorry," he said somberly.

"It's OK, Steve-O. You meant nothing by it." Picking the Mule off the pavers, Vern went on, saying, "You know what this is, right?"

Steve-O nodded. "It's for putting cows down before slaughter."

"It was initially. I modified it to pack more of a *punch*."

Steve-O smiled. "A *mule* kick of a punch."

"Exactly," Vern said. "Delivers way more of a punch than your Nerf guns." He met the man's gaze. "I want you to have it, Steve-O. I went ahead and put straps on the tank. Might have to do some fine-tuning to get it to fit you how you like it. I also just finished calibrating the air pressure. It's ready to rock." Although he did want to be the one to put down the unwanted undead passenger, instead, he handed the wand to Steve-O, helped him position the straps on his shoulders, then proceeded to go over the finer points of the Mule's operation. Finished, he said, "You got all that?"

Steve-O plopped his Stetson on the ground and took the helmet from Vern. Snugging it down tight, he pushed his glasses up on his nose, then deployed the visor.

Some things requiring fine motor skills still gave Steve-O trouble, especially when he couldn't watch what his hands were doing, so he had Riker help him with the chinstrap.

Riker palmed the helmet with one hand and tugged gently in a couple of different directions. "How's the fit?" he asked.

Steve-O said, "Like a glove," and stomped off toward the trailer.

While the others filed into the mansion, Riker tagged along with Steve-O.

The Bolt was an average-sized adult, mid to late twenties, and wearing only a soiled wife-beater tank and frayed blue jeans. The ragged divots running up and down both forearms, where mouthfuls of flesh had been excised, spoke to how it had become infected with Romero. The shaved head, corded neck muscles, and bulging biceps had Riker thinking of the Mr. Clean character from a certain brand of all-purpose cleaner.

The Bolt was on its stomach and struggling mightily to stand. Every time it pressed its upper body off the trailer floor, the weight of the panels on its back would stymie the effort.

The growling and *clackety-clack* of its teeth snapping rose to a crescendo when Steve-O peered in on it. Biting his lip, he lifted the wand over the trailer's side rail and pressed the business end to the Bolt's exposed temple.

Steve-O looked at Riker for permission.

Delivering a barely perceptible nod, Riker raised a hand in front of his face, just in case. Last thing he wanted was to catch a piece of flying bone and become infected.

Seeing the cue, Steve-O triggered the Mule. The *pfft-thwak* produced as compressed air moved the spike in the wand was not much louder than Riker had remembered. The damage to the Bolt's skull was definitely more noticeable. The spike left a bloodless hole in front of its ear. The crater created by the impact and follow-on blast of air encompassed the majority of that side of its cranium. Whatever tweak Vern had made to the Mule, it was paying dividends.

"What do you think? Can you work with that?"

Tilt to his head, Steve-O said, "You don't trust me with the little gun?"

"I do, Steve-O. But this is better. It doesn't use up precious ammunition. You can clear the dead from fence lines for us. It'll also be ideal for putting down sickos trapped inside of cars. You'll be the tip of the spear, so to speak."

"You're demoting me, Lee Riker. It doesn't feel good"—he tapped his chest—"inside here."

Riker shook his head. "This is *not* a demotion, buddy. Consider it adding a new skillset to your expanding repertoire. We come across more ammo for your Mosquito, we'll resume target practice."

Steve-O said nothing.

Riker pressed a finger to the man's chest. "Feel better in here?"

"I guess."

Riker moved the panels off the twice-dead Bolt. Lightning-bolt-like cracks marred the black glass face of the panel that had been resting atop the zombie. The other four panels had survived the fall and all of the jostling that followed. "OK," he said, grabbing a limp arm, "help me with your kill."

After depositing the Bolt on the pile of corpses outside the wall, the disposal of which Riker was not looking forward to tackling, he closed the gate and shored it up at the base with the pair of steel spikes Vern had fashioned from rebar taken from his store.

Ushering Steve-O ahead of him, Riker said, "Let's go and see what's got Lia all worked up." As he fell in behind, he touched his fingers to the spot on his cheek where the zombie had torn away the patch of beard. It was tender. No blood. A good thing. A little moving around of the surrounding whiskers mostly concealed the irritated skin.

"Maybe Lia got ahold of the Army. Or the *President*," Steve-O speculated. "Maybe we're winning the war against the dead and everything will soon be back to normal." He paused, thinking. Finally, eyes a bit misty, he asked, "If things do get back to normal, can I still stay with you and Tara?"

Riker made no response to the former. Lately, he was trying to avoid assumption and speculation. It took up way too much energy. Energy best spent devising ways of surviving all this madness. So, taking a cue from Vern, a man whose wisdom knew no bounds, Riker had begun employing Occam's razor to everything having to do with life in the zombie apocalypse: *The simplest explanation is usually the best one.*

Shorty had pointed out a perfect example of the principle's application. Riker had fucked over Harlan at the boat ramp. Stole Abigail out from under him and his family. So if he'd simply employed that reasoning when Tara had gone missing, the identity of her captors would have struck him like a bolt of lightning.

In this instance, if Riker were a betting man, he would be all in on Lia having learned the whereabouts of her father.

Responding to Steve-O's heartfelt question, Riker rested one muscled arm on the smaller man's shoulder. Looking him in the eye, he said, "We're brothers now, Steve-O. That makes us family. And *nothing* comes between me and my family."

Chapter 5

Riker and Steve-O entered the great room and found themselves in the middle of several ongoing conversations.

Lia was standing near the fireplace, giving all of her attention to Shorty, who was in the process of recounting Riker's fall through the skylight. "It was like a Cirque du Soleil act gone horribly wrong. Lee's spinning around over the island, his balls in a nylon vice," he said, grimacing. "All of this is going on and the rotters of the house are crowding the island and straining to get a piece of him. Only thing missing from the act was an undead clown or two."

Throwing an exaggerated shiver, Lia said, "I hate clowns. Living or undead, they creep me out."

Seated on the knotty pine sofa, Rose and Benny were engaged in an animated conversation that had something to do with her need for him to stay home more often.

Nearby, both sitting on pub chairs wrapped in fabric with a faux palomino print, Vern and Tara were theorizing on what had become of the United States east of the Mississippi.

Seeing the two men enter the great room, Lia stuck a finger up in the air to indicate she was aware of their presence, then urged Shorty to wrap up his story.

"I cede the floor," quipped Shorty. He backed away from the fireplace and plopped down on a dark walnut Shaker-style chair with thin cushions sporting a green and burgundy Navajo-inspired design.

"Crowd around," Lia prompted. "I'd have you all sit at the table, but it's covered with all of Vern's stuff."

Once everyone was within earshot, she went over some of the contacts she had made with outsiders over the last twenty-four hours.

"I'm amazed anyone's left alive on the Eastern Seaboard," commented Tara. "Cape Hatteras is where, exactly?"

"It's part of the Outer Banks off the North Carolina coast. Perfect place to ride this crap out," Vern opined. "I'd want a pretty big boat if I was planning on making foraging trips to the mainland."

"Or a fast ferry," added Steve-O. He nudged Shorty. "Miss Abigail would be perfect."

"I'm with Vern," Shorty said. He could see himself captain of a thirty-foot Grand Banks. "Flat bottoms aren't great in open water, Steve-O. But I like how you're thinking. Ferry or cruiser, you can be my co-captain any day."

Steve-O fist-pumped the air and turned his attention to Rose, who had raised her hand and was waiting to be recognized. Next to her, Benny seemed perplexed by her schoolroom etiquette.

Riker nodded. "What is it, Rose?"

Clearing her throat, she said, "I'm going on record to say that me and Benny want nothing to do with what Amelia is about to ask of you all."

Benny's eyes widened. Clearly, he didn't see that one coming. Whether he was privy to Lia's coming overture or not, he didn't let on.

Eyes narrowing, Riker said, "Can we at least let her get to the *ask*?"

Rose said nothing. She had removed her glasses and was busy giving them a polish.

Dozer sauntered into the room, looked the humans over, then made his way to the fireplace, where he sprawled out on the thick rug concealing the bunker entrance.

As an uneasy silence descended on the great room, Lia went over all she knew about Cole and the others being held captive with him. Though her voice was far from commanding, the room's high ceiling and sharp angles that made up the central spire acted as a sort of natural amplifier. With all the thought that went into the design of Trinity House, Riker wouldn't doubt it if someone told him the acoustic property was intentional.

Raising his hand, Riker said, "That's not much to go on."

Lia said to Rose and Benny, "You guys didn't have much more to go on when you set out looking for Crystal."

Catfight. Out of the corner of his eye, Riker saw Rose don her glasses and park a narrow-eyed gaze on the speaker. Tara's body stiffened and she scooched to the edge of her chair and crossed her arms.

Riker knew where this was going. Little sister would pick a side. And he knew it wouldn't be Lia's. Hoping to diffuse the situation, he said, "That's like comparing apples to oranges. We knew Crystal. Well, some of us did."

"Rose and Benny, right?" Lia pressed. "Crystal was basically a stranger, too. Considering what she brought here, did she really deserve a search party? Was she worth saving?"

"All people who have a pulse are worth saving," Steve-O posited. "There's some good in all people."

Shooting Riker a skeptical look, Shorty said, "Debatable, Steve-O. Each case needs to be judged on its own merits. Where there are kids involved, I tend to feel that takes priority over a woman who knew what she was getting into with that ex-con, Paul."

"Raul," corrected Rose. "We had no idea she was bringing *him* until it was too late. I'm just saying, if you all go, that's on you. We"—she glared at Benny—"are not leaving this mountain." She turned on her heel and announced that she needed to get back to her job.

When Benny didn't respond, and followed after Rose like a puppy, Riker knew his friend was cowed.

Vern rose from his chair. Hands raised in mock surrender, he said, "We don't even know where the kids are being held." He looked to Lia. "The kid said he overheard the adults mention an awful tower and pirate ships."

She tapped the legal pad. "That's what I wrote down."

Vern paced the floor for a few seconds, thinking. Finally, he stopped beside Dozer and looked up at the ceiling. "Vegas," he said. "The kids are being held somewhere in or around Las Vegas."

Shorty said, "There are pirate ships in Vegas. But an awful tower?"

Riker was following the conversation closely; nevertheless, he was still lost. His only exposure to Vegas was through a screen. He wasn't a gambler and didn't see the draw of all the amusement-park-like amenities.

Still on the edge of her seat, Tara addressed Lia. "You said the boy had an accent that sounded Deep South, right?"

"I'm not totally sure," Lia admitted. "He sounded a little like Adam Sandler in The Waterboy."

Crickets.

"You know … *mama always said* …" It was a fair impression, although the put-on accent was more Bo and Luke Duke than Louisiana Cajun.

Nothing.

Nodding, Vern said, "*Eiffel* is what he said. *Awful* is what you heard. There's a replica of the Eiffel Tower in Las Vegas. I've been with Shane a couple of times. He and his buddy made it an annual event. A sort of pilgrimage. They'd go down and see Aerosmith or ZZ Top. If a good rock and roll act wasn't playing, they'd go catch a comedian they could both agree on." Vern smiled. It was clear he was reminiscing over good times. "Shane showed me some pictures of their escapades. There was this one I remember where his buddy is mounting a camel in front of the Sands Hotel and Casino."

"Did he ride it?" asked Steve-O

Vern chuckled. "Oh … he *rode* it all right."

Steve-O scratched his head. "I don't get it."

Unable to contain himself, Shorty turned toward Riker and sent a couple of frantic hip thrusts in his direction.

"Leave it to Pervy Perverton to start up a game of lude and crude charades." Tara singled out Steve-O. Speaking a little slower than normal, she said, "It was a statue of a camel. Vern's son and his friend were likely drinking and carrying on. His friend probably decided it would be funny if …" She looked a question at Vern.

He said, "Scott was his name. Kid's last name was Campbell, if my memory serves. My boy had to have put him up to it. Shane was usually the one instigating things. At least every time they got into trouble as teens, it was my boy's brilliant idea that brought the hammer down on them."

Tara said to Steve-O, "Scott thought it would be funny if he humped the camel statue."

Steve-O was growing more confused by the second. "Did he ride it or have sex with it?"

Riker had had enough of the banter. "Mount, hump, screw, bang, have sex … they all mean the same thing, Steve-O."

All the back and forth about Shane and Scott had resurrected the headache that had just recently begun to subside.

"*Fuck* falls in there somewhere, too," added Shorty. "I think the Sands is gone now. Wonder what they did with the camel."

"Doesn't matter," Riker said, grinding both thumbs hard against his temples. "We need to focus. There's still those trees across the fire lane. They aren't going to cut themselves into firewood. Got to get around to moving the corpses from the turnaround, too." He looked at Lia. "I'm on your side. That being said, we're going to need more than just the city. Vegas is a very big place."

Lia shifted her weight onto her good leg and planted her hands on her hips. It was clear she was tired of standing. Riker got it: Breaking in a new prosthetic was far from a comfortable experience. Especially one created in a garage from off-the-shelf materials. Wavering slightly, she said, "We know there's a liquor store. It's next to an antique store. Then there's the place with the mugshots and naked lady calendar in the office. A post office is my guess."

Shorty said, "That's probably a bail bond joint. I did a little skip tracing back in the day. Anyone think, given today's climate, a fella … or a gal who likes gals, could get away with putting nudes on the walls of a federal institution?"

Riker said, "Good point."

Having recently embarked on that jaunt down memory lane in which she'd been hefting her brother's .38 revolver, Tara said, "Liquor stores next to bail bond joints usually only happen in seedier parts of town. How many alcoholic thugs you think are going to be drawn to an antique store?"

Riker saw where she was going with this. "It's not an antique store. It's a pawnshop. Hence the bulletproof glass divider the kid mentioned."

Tara unfolded her arms and sat back in her chair. "My thoughts exactly."

Lia said to Riker, "That's plenty to go on. We have to do *something*."

He nodded agreeably. "They don't call it Sin City for nothing. All the gambling—"

"All the losing," Vern corrected. "Which means there's probably a dozen strip malls with the same caliber tenants."

"We could check the phonebook," Steve-O suggested.

"If you can find one," Tara said. "I think we're better off waiting until Cole comes back on the radio."

"There's no guarantee that will happen," Lia pressed. "But I see your point. I'll keep trying to raise him on the radio." She looked over the faces staring back at her. "If I can narrow it down, will you all consider helping him?"

"We'll cross that bridge when we get to it." Riker met Vern's gaze. "Your turn. What have you got for us?"

"We could kill two birds with one stone," interrupted Shorty. "We range out and get some foraging done before winter hits. I've got the portable HAM setup in the Roamer. We take it, and should we come into contact with Cole again, we'd already be out and about and could make our decision then. Base it on any new intel the kid might provide. Only caveat is the lack of range. We'd need to be inside Nevada, or close to the state line, to pick up his transmission."

"Then we can either forge ahead to Cole's location," Riker said, "or we can turn around and bring our spoils home." He liked the idea. There was a house on the lower flank of the mountain where they'd found a motherlode of dog food for Dozer. A number of rain collection barrels were connected to its downspouts. They could take a few of those and siphon fuel along the way. With Shorty's electric pump, filling the barrels would be a lot less time-consuming than the traditional siphoning method. The motor was relatively quiet. It would definitely cut down on the time they'd need to spend outside the vehicles.

Vern had made his way to the walnut dining table. It was large enough to accommodate all of them and then some. He stood on one side of the table and remained tightlipped until everyone had crowded around the side opposite him. Lia and Steve-O sat on wooden chairs on one end of the table. The others remained standing.

On the table was a map of the United States. It took up a good portion of the center of the table. Vern had pinned down all four corners with heavy clay drink coasters. A number of red dots meandered across the states, most of them east of the Continental Divide. Each dot was labeled with the word associated with a unique letter in NATO's phonetic alphabet. Alpha through X-Ray was represented. Strangely, Zulu was not.

The red dots were vastly outnumbered by black dots that were clustered around them like stars in a constellation. There seemed to be no rhyme or reason as to how far away or in which direction they were located from the central red dot. These, too, were more concentrated east of the Colorado Rockies.

Riker said, "What are we looking at, Vern?"

"I found this in the … for lack of a better description for the RV, I'll call it the War Wagon. First, I should lay out what I learned about the former owners of this magnificent home of yours." He pulled a thick stack of passports from a pocket. There must have been a dozen of them. "These were in a secret lockbox I discovered when I was underneath the Wagon."

"Whose are they?" Tara asked.

"The man who built this place had a son and a daughter. The son was an aviator. His F-4 Phantom was downed somewhere over North Vietnam. His body was never recovered. The daughter went on to marry a man just as adventurous as her father and brother." Vern tapped a finger on the passports. "Six of these are his. Only they're all different covers. The others are the daughter. Also different names. She inherited this place when her father died."

Steve-O rubbed his hands together briskly. "Was the man she married James Bond?"

Vern pointed a crooked finger at Steve-O. "Pretty damn close. Not exactly X gets a square, though." He caught everyone staring at him, questioning looks on their faces.

"Hollywood Squares," Shorty explained for Vern. "Before most of our times. I only watched because teenaged me thought Barbara Eden was pretty damn hot. *Milf* hot, to be exact."

Tara stopped thumbing through the top passport long enough to paint Shorty with a disapproving glare. Dropping her gaze back to the tiny photo of a swarthy-looking fellow flashing a toothy grin, she said, "What did the son-in-law … this Harry Dowden dude do for a living?"

"That's a pseudonym," Vern stated. "His name was James Lee Whitman."

"The guy who turned FEMA around after the Hurricane Andrew debacle," Shorty said. "I'm guessing this was his own little sanctuary from the Cold War madness."

"Nope," countered Vern, "Lazarus … or site Zulu if we're using its intended moniker, was here before Whitman. He just put his mark on it. The bunker downstairs was the original owner's baby. The dated tech and old maps are the dead giveaway. Clearly, Whitman put more stock in the Zulu bunker. Though the weapons and vehicles up there all predate the Y2K scare, he *was* keeping the tech current. But all that ceased a couple of years ago."

Tara was back on the hook. "Why? What happened to him?"

"He suffered a massive stroke seven months ago," Vern said. "He hung on for a couple of weeks but ultimately passed away."

"Damn," said Shorty. "Zombie apocalypse hits and the man isn't around to enjoy the fruit of his labor."

"I had assumed the original owner was the seller," Tara said. "The real estate agent danced around the question when I asked. The fact that the downstairs bunker wasn't used as a selling point tells me the seller didn't know it was here."

"The widow sure wasted little time putting the place on the market," Vern noted. "Maybe she wanted to get rid of everything associated with her late husband. Grief has a way of shifting priorities. Maybe she just forgot to mention it to the agent. Or," he added, "she didn't want to. If she had, knowing the local government, she probably would have tons of red tape to wade through to get it to market."

Riker said, "I bet Whitman was keeping her in the dark about both bunkers. At the very least, because of national security and all that, the Zulu facility had to be known only to him."

"If so," Tara said, "the only thing we have to worry about is the government coming back and repossessing their property."

Steve-O said, "I hope we don't get kicked out of here."

"It's our place now," said Riker. "We paid cash for it." While he had a good idea what he was looking at, he still regarded Vern and tapped the red dot due north of Santa Fe. "What do the dots represent, Vern?"

"The one you put your finger on is roughly where we are standing right now."

Riker said, "It's Zulu, I presume."

Vern nodded. "Unofficially. It's off the books. Built sometime after continuity of government protocols were established but before nine-eleven. Everything changed after that. This place was probably realized using money siphoned off of a line item in the defense budget. Those twelve-thousand-dollar hammers and ten-thousand-dollar toilet seats pointed out by whistleblowers didn't really cost that much. Not even close, even if you're figuring in R&D costs. Inflating numbers is the deep state's way of hiding what they are really doing with our tax money."

Steve-O said, "How did you learn so much about the end of the world, Vern?"

"I read a *lot*. I'm on my fifth Kindle. Believe it or not, though I'm … I mean, I *was* the owner of my own business, there's a lot of downtime between selling a neighbor potting soil and trying to keep spray paint out of the hands of the local graffiti crew."

Shorty leaned over the table. "So these are all locations that have something to do with continuity of government. In the east, you'll have Mount Weather, Raven Rock, the White House bunker. Closer to us is NORAD. I watched History Channel a lot. Still, that's all I can name off the top of my head."

"A lot of the sites are military bases, mostly Air Force. Some are meant for families to convene. Some are strictly for command and control."

Shorty tapped the black dot closest to their location. It was equidistant to Santa Fe and Los Alamos. He said, "These black dots are either repeater stations or supply caches, right?"

"The latter," Vern said. "The red dots represent locations where our heads of government are supposed to convene in the event of an impending national disaster. The War Wagon is actually a specially designed roaming command post. Its communication suite is hardened against electromagnetic pulses put off by an airburst nuclear explosion. DARPA built dozens of them for the DoD. The caches are their resupply points."

Lia said, "The cache between here and Los Alamos is near a place I used to mountain bike. That'd be a good place to start."

"Agreed," said Tara. She looked to Vern. "Her bringing up Los Alamos jogged my memory. How far along did you get in repairing the bunker blast door?"

Vern grimaced. "There's no undoing the damage I did with the acetylene torch. Lazarus is no longer sanctuary in the event of a nuclear strike. That being said, with the external garage door and the MacGyver job I did on the internal blast door, we don't have to worry about zombies infiltrating the place."

Brows arched, Riker said, "Humans?"

"They'd have to be really motivated to get past both doors. But it's not outside the realm of possibility," Vern conceded. "Anyone gets inside Lazarus when I'm there, they'll wish they hadn't."

That was good enough for Riker. He was about to ask what the War Wagon needed in the way of repairs to be fully operational when Rose's voice came over the radio in his pocket. Extracting the radio, he pressed the Talk button. "What is it?"

"We have company at the front gate."

All eyes were on Riker. "Living or undead?" he asked.

"Just zombies," she reported. "About ten or so. They're pretty beaten up. Engine noise probably drew them up from the valley."

Jumping up from his chair, helmet trapped under one arm, Steve-O said, "Tell them to set up the ladder by the gate. I'll be right out with the Mule."

"Be careful on the top rung," Vern warned. "Last step is a doozy."

Shooting the older man a stern look, Tara said, "Steve-O is a grown-ass man. You have to let him be. Quit with all the hand-holding."

Chapter 6

The axe head struck the zombie with a meaty *thunk,* angling downward through its clavicle where it became stuck fast. Nearly losing purchase on the smooth hickory handle, Tara firmed her grip and struggled to yank it free. Nothing doing. It wouldn't budge. It wasn't helping matters any that her arms and shoulders were still sore from pulling grave-digging duty the night before. While she rocked the axe back and forth, hoping to break it free from the tangle of tendon and muscle and protruding bones, the male zombie was taking one-handed swipes at her face, the dirty, cracked nails leaving deep furrows after each pass.

"A little help here!" she bellowed in Steve-O's general direction. She had been engrossed in the monotonous task of splitting wood, entrusting security to the man with the Mule. The day before, he'd proven himself proficient with the tool, culling nearly a dozen newly arrived zombies from the turnaround, all without falling off the ladder or letting the grabby creatures knock the wand from his hands.

When Tara and Steve-O arrived in the clearing east of Trinity, her instructions to him had been simple: Keep your head on a swivel and holler if you see, hear, or smell anything.

"I'm sorry, Tara," he called from across the clearing. "I told you I had to pee."

Extending her arm and locking her elbow put her face just out of the zombie's reach. It also created enough separation for her to reach the Glock with her off-hand and work it free from the drop-leg holster.

Acting on her brother's advice, she always kept one round in the chamber and the magazine loaded to capacity. The Glock's safety was on the trigger. A blessing. Because with snippets of her childhood flashing before her eyes, fight or flight instinct starting an avalanche of adrenaline dumping into her system and making her heart race, if she had to chamber a round and recall how to throw off a safety, she probably never would have considered reaching for the gun in the first place.

Contorting her body sideways, right hand still clamped on the very end of the axe handle, she picked up Steve-O in her side vision. He was a few yards away, pants around his feet and struggling mightily to pull them up.

Having confirmed the man was nowhere near to coming into her line of fire, she brought her off-hand up and around, right to left, and thrust the squared-off muzzle between the zombie's snapping teeth.

Hoping the constrained space would help to lessen the pistol's report, one of the main reasons she had Steve-O backing her up with the much quieter Mule, she angled the muzzle upward and pressed the trigger.

With the zombie basically sucking on the Glock, a double-tap was not necessary.

The typical sharp crack of the Glock discharging was reduced to a hollow *pop*. Jaundiced eyes bugged from their sockets. The expanding gasses and follow-on shockwave took the path of least resistance. The blowback was substantial, the rush of superheated air rife with the stink of gun smoke and decaying flesh. Tara flinched as her face was peppered with needle-like fragments of pulverized teeth and a wet slurry that was once the thing's bloated tongue.

As she released the axe handle, an action that sent the stilled zombie on a one-way trip to the forest floor, her jaw locked open and a torrent of bile and the remnants of her MRE breakfast came rushing forth.

Tara was on her knees and still retching when Steve-O reached her side, stammering and apologizing for letting her down.

In truth, she was partly to blame. Swinging the axe for hours on end had a way of dulling one's senses. At one point, she felt like it was lulling her into a trance-like state. She should have stopped sooner and given them both a break. Whether she hadn't heard him due to the noise the axe made as it cleaved the rounds, or she had heard him and the words had gone in one ear and out the other, the point was moot. She supposed she would never know. What she did know, however, was that it was close to noon, and a check-in was in order.

As she dragged the back of her hand across her mouth, her eyes took a tour of the clearing. Seeing that once again they were all alone, she holstered the Glock and bowed her head. And though she saw she was kneeling in a puddle of her own vomit and could feel the mask of human detritus surrendering to gravity's pull, sloughing slowly off her cheeks and chin, she remained rooted in place. Raising her gaze to meet Steve-O's wide-eyed stare, she made a reverse peace sign and pointed to her own eyes. "It was a miscommunication, Steve-O. Next time," she stressed, "when you tell me something, make doubly sure I'm looking you in the eyes." She paused to let it sink in. "Just like this, OK? Once we're engaged and have established eye contact, I will acknowledge that I heard you by saying *OK* or *copy that* or *understood.* Do we have a deal?"

"X gets a square," Steve-O said, the look of concern morphing quickly into a wide toothy grin. "That's *exactly* what happened to me the first time I shot a sicko up close." He adjusted his glasses on his face and stared down at the corpse. "There's a hole in its throat. Did you do that?"

Tara craned to get a closer look. "Nope. The round I fired couldn't have taken a U-turn like that. It went straight up into its brain." She examined its dirty black tee shirt, poking at it with a stick she plucked off the ground. The shirt was home to tiny black insects and shot through with three small holes. The holes formed a small triangle about where she guessed the sternum would be. Pulling the shirt up revealed a pair of deep bite marks just above the navel. Matching the holes in the shirt were three dime-sized bullet entry wounds. They were bloodless and nearly identical to the hole in its throat. "Someone already shot it up. Missed the brain, though. I'm guessing the one to the throat destroyed its voice box. Probably why I didn't hear it as it snuck up on me." She rose and stripped off her shirt. Seeing a noticeable red flush creep up Steve-O's neck and color his cheeks crimson, she used the shirt to quickly wipe the mess from her face.

"I'm s-s-s-sorry, T-t-t-ara," he declared, stuttering and diverting his gaze to the ground. "I d-d-d-didn't mean to look at your b-b-boobs."

"I'm not naked, Steve-O. It's just a bra. Remember Madonna? Seemed like that's all she ever wore."

He nodded, his gaze slowly leveling off at her. Matching her stare, he said, "She was *not* a virgin."

"Neither am I, Steve-O." She laughed and stared at the sky. "Neither am I. Though, nowadays, at times, it seems like it."

"I am," Steve-O conceded. "Marcy said I would not be one forever. She promised I would meet someone special one day. Someone I could give it to." He went quiet for a long couple of seconds. "Marcy was wrong. But I forgive her. She didn't know the sickness was coming."

Tara didn't know what to say to that. It had caught her off guard. Completely flatfooted. Grabbing her coat off the ground, she shrugged it on. Taking hold of both handles of the wood-laden wheelbarrow, she said, "What do you say we take a break? Get this load down to the house and have a bite to eat? While we're there we can check and see if Lia has had any luck contacting the kid."

Steve-O tightened the shoulder straps on the Mule and gestured at the trailhead with its business end. Making a point of looking Tara square in the eye, he said, "Good idea. I will keep my head on a swivel and watch our backs." He didn't break eye contact with her until she came back at him with a firm, "Copy that," and started off for Trinity House, the wheelbarrow bouncing as its single tire rolled over the bed of discarded branches littering the clearing.

Two miles southeast of Trinity House, Riker and Vern were busy loading empty rain barrels into the trailer hitched to the Shelby. The copse of trees rising up between the two-story home and narrow drive connecting the property to the main road cast its shadow over the entire backyard. A large portion of the side yard was darkened by a patchwork of shadows, too. Strangely, although the house was currently unoccupied and appeared to have been vacant since the dead began to walk, the lawn on all sides was green and thriving. Riker's best guess was that the knee-high grass concealed a timer-operated sprinkler system.

Quite a few things in the dying world were operating in much the same manner. A smattering of lights in homes equipped with solar panels downslope from Trinity House still burned around the clock. And though there were no vehicles on the move or people on foot, in small pockets of the city, traffic signals and streetlights on timers still went about their daily business. When viewed at night, all of it gave the false impression that Santa Fe and its suburbs still belonged to the living.

Shorty stood guard near the downhill corner of the house where he could see the entire drive, a hundred or so yards of the main road, and, bisecting the desert floor several miles distant, a wide swath of car-choked US-84.

After working in the shade for the better part of an hour, Riker was longing for the afternoon sun on his exposed skin. It made him feel alive when just about everything around him was not. *Soon it will be winter.* He'd been told to expect sunlight to be plentiful but offer very little in the way of warmth.

Oh, how he wished the Romero virus's spread hadn't reached Miami so quickly. What with the beach and the warm water, not to mention all the fine women in their skimpy bikinis, he could have stayed at Villa Jasmine all winter—zombie apocalypse be damned.

Finished lashing the barrels together, Vern said, "Shorty told me about the Rolex. How'd it go over when you gave it to Lia?"

Riker said nothing.

Incredulous, Vern said, "You didn't give it to her last night?" He shook his head. "George Bernard Shaw was right … youth is *most definitely* wasted on the young."

Riker looked at Shorty, let his gaze linger, then returned his attention to the inquisitionist. "He told you?"

"He didn't behave like he was divulging a state secret. And it didn't seem like an act of sabotage. Seemed as if he was just looking to make small talk with me. I think he's still trying to navigate foreign waters. Find his place in the scheme of things at your place."

Riker exhaled. "I've always been afraid of rejection. I'll probably just leave it lying around. Somewhere she's most likely to stumble upon it. Maybe I'll put it on the table next to that damn radio she's tethered to."

"Then deny you know anything about it? That's a pretty chicken shit move."

I didn't ask you, Riker thought. Out loud, he said, "Do you really think any of those caches are worth the side trip to check out?"

"You familiar with the Law of Economy?"

"Doesn't ring a bell."

"Occam's razor?"

Riker nodded.

"Same thing, basically."

Riker made a face. "So far, I haven't been successful when applying it."

"I think you and Tara stumbled onto something special in Trinity House and the Zulu slash Lazarus bunker. Considering the times we're living in, all that's out here working against us, discounting those black dots would be criminal."

"That windfall came at a great cost." Riker paused. "We lost both parents. I'd give up all of it to have them back."

No stranger to loss, Vern said, "I get it. But think of it this way: The money they left you and Tara is them taking care of you two from the grave. Honor them by making full use of it."

All the *woo woo* Deep Thoughts by Jack Handey stuff was way too much for Riker to process at the moment. That Vern thought the side trips would be worth the time and expended fuel was enough for now. In fact, a simple *yes* would have sufficed.

"Rotters coming in from the road," Shorty called. "We're leaving soon, right?"

Riker flashed a thumbs-up.

Hefting his stubby Shockwave, Shorty called back, "I got 'em. Pick me up on the road."

"Will do," Riker hollered.

Waving that he understood, Shorty turned on his heel and started walking the drive.

He wasn't too worried about the man going it solo. Shorty was a survivor. Riker had seen the man come out of a scrape with nary a scratch more times than he could count. It was as if he had a whole host of Guardian Angels looking over him.

The noise from the shotgun discharging was of no concern to Riker, either. They'd be well on their way before the reports drew them any additional attention. The only other argument, one Riker used often to stem Tara's desire to go to the gun first, was the finite supply of ammunition. But that really wasn't his problem. Shorty had come loaded for bear. Crisscrossed over the man's black Trans Am jacket was a pair of ammunition bandoliers. Both leather items were laden with several different types of shotgun shells. And according to Shorty, there were plenty more of them stashed in the EarthRoamer. He'd scored the vehicle after shooting his way out of a poorly planned ambush. From the way he told the story, the ambushers had been way out of their league. They paid dearly for it, too.

The zombies were crowded into a loose knot, maybe two deep and three across, and just arriving at the T where the drive and road met. If any of them happened to be a Bolt, it would have already burst from the pack and be barreling straight for the approaching meat.

Climbing into the Shelby, Riker snapped his seatbelt home and fired the 6.2-liter V-8. Only when Vern had taken his seat and was situated—belt clicked, door closed and locked, MP5 sub gun stowed safely on the seat beside him—did Riker get the rig moving.

After flicking his gaze to the rearview and verifying that the load was secure in the trailer, Riker asked Vern what he figured they would find stashed away at the GPS coordinates on the map.

"The red dots are facilities. Whether they're manned or not is anyone's guess. The caches are going to be like scratching a lotto ticket. No telling what we'll find. Fuel, water, and food. I'd bet some of them were established in the fifties as part of the government's COOP program. Stands for continuity of operations planning. The program was aimed more at seeing to the survival of government at the state and local level. CoG on the other hand, continuity of government to us laymen, was established to ensure that enough of the politicians survived a germ attack or nuclear first strike to keep on screwing up our country."

Riker steered from the home's RV pad and onto the drive. The shadow from the trees rippled across the windshield, creating a hypnotic effect, and gravel popped under the tires as gravity pulled the pickup downhill.

Up ahead, Shorty had drawn to within a dozen feet of the advancing zombies. Knowing Shorty, he had the shells in the Shockwave staggered, alternating between shot and slug. That he hadn't opened fire yet told Riker the round in the chamber was likely a shot shell. While highly effective at opening a locked door at close range, shot spread too quickly to destroy a zombie brain at anything but.

As Riker slow-rolled the Shelby forward, eyes locked on Shorty, he unholstered his Sig Sauer Legion and placed the semiautomatic pistol on his lap. "So wouldn't any food and batteries and stuff of that nature be worthless by now?"

Vern scooped up the MP5 and chambered a round. Checking that the safety was engaged, he said, "After the nine-eleven attacks, the President declared a state of emergency that put the nation on high alert. That alert status was never rescinded. Although the threat of thermonuclear war was thought to be very unlikely thanks to mutually assured destruction, as proven by those weaponized jetliners, terrorists and rogue nations were still deemed to be a viable threat. Especially an EMP attack or decapitation of government due to a suitcase nuke or dirty bomb."

A rapid-fire series of loud *booms* broke the still. The first report dislodged an unkindness of ravens from the nearby trees, sending them airborne, wings aflutter and squawking bloody murder. The expanding lead shot from the first discharged round enveloped the lead zombie's head, erasing its features and sending it flying backward into the others. The second round, a lead slug, caved in the narrow face of a geriatric creature.

Shorty was a blur as he stalked the rest, crunching rounds into the shotgun and sending lead head high into the dead. Once they were all down, he came back to the face-shot zombie. It was blinded and struggling to stand. Shorty drew a black dagger from the sheath on his hip, grabbed a handful of gore-slicked hair, and thrust the blade deep into one eye socket. The zombie went limp at once.

It was all over in a handful of seconds, the final act of kindness on Shorty's part taking place as the Shelby came rolling out of the shadows. And though all Riker could hear during the entire melee was the cawing of the birds, the low growl of the Shelby's engine, and the hollow-sounding booms rolling across the lawn toward him, in his head he heard Shorty hollering: *Shocky's gotta eat!*

"Damn impressive," Vern gushed.

"Even for a guy my size," Riker noted, "that Shockwave is a wrist breaker."

"Quirks and all," noted Vern, "Shorty's definitely an asset."

Shorty slung the still-smoking shotgun on one shoulder and sheathed the knife. As if he sensed he was being talked about behind his back, he performed a perfect bow and scrape.

Riker pulled up to the T, stopping short of the drift of twice-dead corpses. Throwing the transmission into Park, he said, "I do appreciate the comedy relief he brings to the group."

"There is that," agreed Vern. "Every good circus needs a clown."

Low blow. Riker grimaced. Much like Steve-O and Shorty, Vern Rossi was proving that he also possessed no filter. Voice adopting a more serious tone, Riker said, "So what do you think we're apt to find inside those red dot sites?"

Watching Shorty grab the geriatric corpse by the wrists, Vern said, "Those sites aren't going to be easy to find. And if we do find one, it's not going to be like opening someone's forgotten garden shed. It will take some work to get to the prize. No doubt some of the sites will be behind double or triple layers of security. Means we'll need to bring heavy-duty bolt cutters to defeat locks and snip through fences. No doubt the more remote caches will be behind steel blast doors, so bringing the acetylene torch and spare tanks would be a smart move." He grimaced as brains sluiced from the zombie's broken skull when Shorty deposited it into the roadside ditch.

Riker had been watching, too. He was about to get out and help when a barely perceptible electronic warble emanated from the radio in his pocket. It was Lia, and her message was more detailed than the one she'd delivered over the radio the day before. Finished listening, he depressed the Talk button. "We'll be there in ten."

She said, "Copy that," and signed off. Riker detected in her voice a certain optimism that had been absent since their first meeting aboard the fire engine two weeks prior. That day had begun with her being abducted, peaked with her escaping from her captors, and had culminated in her helping him rescue a number of corrections officers from a prison southwest of Santa Fe.

Vern said, "You *must* be smitten. She says *jump* and you do just that." He went quiet and watched Shorty roll the final zombie corpse into the ditch. Finally, pinching tears from his eyes, he said, "My wife had the same effect on me."

Chapter 7

Trinity House

When Riker pulled the Shelby through the compound's front gate and set the brake, Shorty was first to set foot on the pavers. Before the engine cut off, he had thrown the lock and was pushing through Trinity's front door.

"So what's this definitive *proof* of yours, Lia?" he called to an empty foyer.

"Take a seat and show a little patience, Shorty." Her voice had carried from the direction of the great room.

Riker came through the door a couple of seconds behind Shorty. "Where is she?" he asked.

Gesturing straight ahead, Shorty said, "In the *tribunal* room."

"The *great* room," Vern corrected. "Sitting down and hashing things out like adults does not a tribunal make."

"There you go talking like Master Yoda again."

Vern ignored Shorty's barb. Edging past Riker, he said, "Where are the others?"

"Right here," said Tara. She was coming from the kitchen. In her hands was a large serving platter piled high with steaming homemade tortillas. The tortillas were ringed by crackers of all shapes and sizes. Steve-O was on her heels and carrying a wooden cutting board. Arranged neatly on the board, like soldiers in formation, was an assortment of cheeses, cured meats, and several different types of olives.

"Oooh," carped Shorty, "it's charcuterie Tuesday … *again*."

"Beggars can't be choosers," Tara said. "If you don't want to partake in what we made, you can take your sorry butt back to your Roamer and get yourself an MRE. Surely, you've not yet grown tired of shredded BBQ beef. I hear the tortillas are the *bomb*."

"Hard pass," Shorty said. "Just pokin' the bear."

"With an attitude like that," Tara said, "a bear is the *only* thing you'll be poking."

Placing both hands over his heart— à la Redd Foxx of Sanford and Son fame—Shorty feigned a coronary.

Riker shook his head as he craned to see past Shorty. Reaching over the shorter man, he placed a hand on Tara's shoulder, stopping her in her tracks.

Steve-O was slow to react to Tara's sudden halt. Running into her from behind, he came real close to having everything slide from the cutting board.

Tracing with one finger the longest of a series of scratches marring Tara's cheek, Riker said, "You get into a fight with a feral cat?"

"Nope," interrupted Steve-O. "I fucked up."

"Swear jar," Shorty said with a mischievous grin.

"Language, friend," Vern added.

Riker turned his attention to Steve-O. "What do you mean you *fucked up*?"

"What he means," Tara said, "is it's none of your damn business. A zombie got too close for comfort, that's all. The problem has been rectified. So get out the way so we can move this tailgate party into the stadium."

Raising his hands in mock surrender, Riker took a step back and let the pair make the corner.

As Tara passed him by, Shorty whispered, "At least you didn't get tased again."

The comment landed like a lead balloon. Tara shot him a murderous look and mouthed, "We'll talk later."

The front door opened behind them all and in walked Benny and Rose. The former was rubbing his hands together and inquiring about the lunch menu. The latter was wearing the riot helmet and lugging the Mule.

Seeing Rose with the Mule made Shorty forget the veiled threat. Perking up, he said, "Did you kick some zombie butt?"

Rose shook her head. "I spotted for Ben. Held the ladder still while he put the things down."

"You'll get your nerve up sooner or later," Shorty promised. "It took me a few dry runs before I finally pulled the trigger. And believe you me, shooting one of those beasts in the face with a pistol … no matter the caliber, is a lot messier than going at one with Vern's pneumatic toy."

"It's Steve-O's … *toy*," Rose reminded Shorty. "He just let Benny borrow it."

Shorty looked to Vern. "Can you build one for me?"

"We'll see," Vern said. He gave Shorty a gentle shove in the back. "Let's get in there. I'm so hungry I could eat a horse."

The comment drew a look of horror from Steve-O.

Riker met Steve-O's gaze. "It's just an expression, buddy." Raising his voice, he said, "Everyone move it. I'm jonesin' to hear Lia say her piece."

When Riker emerged into the great room behind the others, it was clear to him that Lia was really taking this thing seriously. She had tacked maps of New Mexico, Arizona, and Nevada to the wooden support beams bracketing the big picture windows overlooking the rear courtyard and the guesthouse that Steve-O, Shorty, and Vern called home.

Given the determined expression on Lia's face, Riker was fairly certain that if she could have scrounged up a projector, they all would be sitting through a lengthy PowerPoint presentation. Instead, she read her handwritten account of the most recent conversation she'd had with Cole Parker, stopping only after she'd made her case that he and the others were, in fact, being held in Las Vegas.

"Good ol' *Lost Wages*," Shorty said. "I'm amazed the kid remembered that little detail from a snippet of a one-sided drunken conversation. If we play our cards right—pun not intended—it should be an easy in and out."

Benny said, "This new person who brought the two new kids … the guy Cole called a *scout*—who was he again?"

"Cole said Janice called him Wayne. He's a white guy much younger than Kurt. Cole said Kurt never referred to him by that name. Just called him *Brother* the entire time he was there."

Vern said, "Brother by *blood*? Or was Kurt using the generic term? Bikers tend to call each other brother. So do men who have gone to war together." He went quiet for a second. "Men who have certain skillsets and aren't afraid to kill. Because if that's the kind of brotherhood they share—should we get into conflict with them … I'm afraid we're going to have a fight on our hands."

Lia said, "My gut tells me it's the former. Cole overheard Wayne say to Kurt that the rest of the family was going to be two or three days late getting there."

Rose put a hand on Benny's thigh. "Great … you've confirmed they're in Las Vegas. Where exactly in Vegas?" she asked. She gestured at the map of Nevada. In one corner was a detailed overview of Las Vegas. "That's a lot of ground to cover. It's not going to be an *easy in and out* like Shorty suggested. Vegas is probably crawling with zombies. Whoever goes on this fool's errand will be running a gauntlet of them as they bounce from strip mall to strip mall trying to locate the right pawnshop."

Lia made a face. "There's more." She moved to the maps and pointed to an area northwest of the Vegas strip. "Cole said that someone clogged the only toilet. So when he and the others had to go, Kurt or Janice made them do their business in the fenced-in area behind the place where they are being held. Based on Cole's recollection of what he saw this morning, I think the pawnshop is somewhere in this vicinity."

"How did you come to that conclusion?" asked Vern.

"Cole remembered seeing two mountain ranges in the desert behind the strip mall. I asked him to describe what he saw between the strip mall and the desert. He insisted there were no tall buildings blocking his view of the mountains. There was also desert behind the building. He thinks he saw a wall in the desert. I'm not sure what to make of that."

Vern said, "What makes you certain the desert he was looking out on is northwest of downtown? Maybe those mountains he's seeing are the ones showing on the left or right side of the map."

Steve-O said, "Las Vegas is in the desert. Tall buildings stand out like sore thumbs in the desert. Wouldn't Cole have seen at least one of them?"

"Same with Indiana," said Tara. "It's so flat a corn field can blot out the horizon. That being said, sounds like Cole has limited visibility from where he's being kept. Lia's drawing her conclusion from all the evidence put together."

Steve-O harumphed, then returned his attention to Lia.

Riker wished he *was* watching a PowerPoint. It would have cut down on all the chatter.

"Good question," Lia said. "I put myself on the map. Pretended I was staring out over the desert. I did this from all points of the compass."

Shorty said, "Kind of like Google Street View."

"Exactly," Lia said. "I did try Street View, but for some reason that option was disabled." She took a sip from a bottled water. "So Cole said the two ranges were roughly the same height and split in the middle." She pointed to the map. "La Madre Range and Sheep Range are divided by a few miles of desert." She moved her finger to the top right corner of the map. "These are Sunrise and Frenchman Mountains. They're the tallest in the valley. One of Vern's red dot facilities is located at the base of Sunrise. Might be something to check out."

Vern said, "So now we have the wall in the desert, a pawnshop, a liquor store, and a bail bond place to work with." He regarded Rose. "That's a lot of information for us to cross-reference. We find a phone book, I'm very confident we'll find the correct strip mall."

Lia said, "I'm pretty damn confident I'll be able to find it using the Shelby's navigation computer."

Wisely, Vern made no comment. It was clear to him Lia had a dog in the fight.

Riker was leaning against one of the rough-hewn wood support columns. Looking out over the faces of the other seven people occupying the great room, he said, "So the question is: Who's going and who's staying?"

Lia was first to raise her hand. "I have a rapport with the kid," she stated, her gaze finding Riker. "I'm definitely going. And there's more I need to tell you."

Riker had hoped she would be one of the ones to stay behind. But knowing her competitive drive, he should have squashed the notion the moment it crossed his mind. No way she was going to let her new *condition* slow her down. Nodding at her, he said, "What kind of *more*?"

"The sat phone rang shortly after I summoned you guys back here." She looked the group over. "It was Wade."

Interest piqued, Riker pushed off the column and stood up straight. "What did he have to say?"

"He and Sarah will arrive here sometime in the next few days. He was pretty vague about it. Only thing set in stone is that they'd be coming in under cover of darkness. Less chance of drawing too much attention to Trinity."

Riker felt the beginnings of a headache. A faint throb behind the eyes. He was pleased Clark was thinking strategically, but he wished the window of arrival provided by the aviator wasn't as wide open as a cable repairman's. "They coming in the Lakota?" he asked.

"That I don't know," Lia conceded. "All he said was that on the night of their arrival they'll need a clear landing pad and some chemlights strung up in the trees on all four corners."

Clapping his hands, Steve-O said, "Maybe Mr. Clark and Miss Country Rhoads can fly us to Vegas."

"That would be the easy way to do it," Riker said. "But the Lakota can carry passengers or supplies—not both. We need to stock up before winter hits. The more I think about it, the more I like the idea of checking out the caches. If we leave just after first light tomorrow, we'll be able to make a couple of stops along the way and still make Vegas before nightfall."

"If we time it right," Lia added, "we may be able to find out where Cole is being held and get into place while Kurt and Janice are boozing it up."

"What are we going to do," asked Shorty, "yell *freeze, police* and barge right in?"

"Something like that," Riker said. "We'll put our heads together when and if we find the pawnshop. No sense war-gaming an assault when we don't know a single variable."

Steve-O threw his hat in the ring. "I'm coming, too. You'll need someone to operate the Mule."

Vern said, "Sure you don't want to stay back and use that thing on any rotters that show up?"

"He's a grown-ass man," Tara reminded Vern. "We don't treat him any differently. He wants to go … he gets to go. It's still a free country."

Vern bowed his head. "Duly noted. I'm the new guy. Definitely wasn't trying to step on anyone's toes."

Rose raised her hand. "I'm staying." Catching a sharp elbow to the ribs from Rose, Benny raised his hand and stated that he was staying with her.

"Good," said Shorty. "The two of you and Dozer should be able to hold the fort down until Wade and Sarah arrive."

"It's settled then," Riker said. "We better get busy. We still have a lot of work to do before we roll out."

Chapter 8

The next day Riker awoke at first light with a pounding headache and a severe crick in his neck. To add insult to injury, the second he opened his eyes he was blinded by a bar of sunlight lancing in through the east-facing windows.

In his old life, waking up on a sofa in this condition would have been a byproduct of a long night of heavy drinking. The nearby table would have been covered with empties and half drank bottles of whatever brand of beer that had been on sale at the nearest convenience store. In all likelihood, mixed in among the dead soldiers would have been an empty fifth bottle of some kind of inexpensive liquor: Claymore scotch, Evan Williams bourbon, or McCormick's vodka. Name brands didn't matter to Riker; he had never been a connoisseur of anything. If he had booze and a place to flop—he was content.

But this was different; he was sober and sofa surfing by choice. He'd insisted Lia take his room inside Trinity House. There had been a brief argument over it. She had won, initially, taking the sofa for a couple of nights, even though her battlefield amputation was fresh and needed constant attention. Riker's relentless harping had finally worn her down. Which was a good thing. If she needed anything in the night, her new room was close to both the room shared by Benny and Rose and the master bedroom Tara had claimed long before anyone had seen Trinity House in person.

Though, as co-owner of Trinity, Riker could have commandeered a room in the guesthouse and sent one of the three bachelors to the sofa, there was simply way too much farting and snoring going on underneath that roof.

Shielding his eyes against the relentless bar of sunlight, Riker remained still and listened hard. *Nothing.* No snoring. No farting. And, thankfully, few and far between were the telltale moans of the dead things that had shown a propensity to accumulate at the gate overnight.

Alone with his thoughts, he cracked his neck and did a quick stretch. Rolling off the couch fully dressed in black fatigue pants, black tee shirt, and wearing the below-the-knee prosthetic, he knocked out his customary twenty-five pushups. The first twenty-two were in remembrance of the veterans who used to commit suicide on a daily before the dead rose. The final three were in honor of his battle buddies who didn't return from their deployment to the most recent war in the desert.

Finished, he sat on the sofa and firmed up the prosthetic's hold on the tip of the residual limb. Next, he slipped on the worn Salomon hikers and cinched the laces tight. After gunning up and strapping on the Randall, he rattled a few ibuprofen from a nondescript bottle and swallowed them dry.

Feeling the Rolex banging around in the bottom of his pocket, he spent a couple of seconds debating whether he should leave it behind or take it with him. Taking it with him won out. He didn't want to be presented with the perfect situation to offer the watch to Lia and *not* have it on his person.

Conscious of the fact that he may have been the first to rise, he padded down the hall, taking every precaution to remain quiet as he made his way to the kitchen.

Before reaching the T near the foyer, he picked up the scent of vanilla. And as he ranged further down the hall toward the kitchen, he detected the unmistakable nose of roasted Arabica beans. While the former had only caused his stomach to growl—a low rumble confirming what he already knew: that his last meal had been scant and was consumed about a dozen hours ago—just the portent of a steaming cup of the latter had put some pep in his step and kicked his taste buds into overdrive.

As Riker entered the darkened kitchen, he saw he wasn't alone. Lia was standing by the sink, her upper body awash in the blue-gray glow coming off the rectangular monitor displaying the incoming feeds of the myriad of security cameras ringing the compound. Clutched in one hand was an oversized coffee mug, a curl of steam rising above it. *Rocketeers Do It With More Thrust* was emblazoned on the side of the mug facing him.

"Get any sleep?" she asked.

Suppressing a smile, he shook his head. "Not enough. You?"

"Same. I'm all jacked up by the thought of doing some good for a change." She gestured with her mug. "Coffee?"

"Thought you'd never ask." A lie. He knew she would be quick with the offer. During the short amount of time he'd known her, he couldn't remember her ever displaying a *me first* attitude.

She dragged a mug from the cupboard and poured until the steaming dark liquid was close to overflowing.

While Riker watched her pouring the coffee, he came to the realization that her need to *do some good for a change* might be her way of saying she was hoping to offset the lives she had taken by doing her part to save Cole and the others. Although the teenagers had shot first, that she had been forced to kill again that day to survive still weighed heavy on her heart.

As Riker accepted the mug, Lia grimaced. "When does the itching stop?"

"When it's done healing. Mine happened so long ago, if I were to give you an estimate, I'd be lying." He gestured with the mug. "My wounds are healing slowly, too. If it's any consolation, the through and through itches like a mofo. Woke me up twice last night."

"How about the phantom limb thing?" She sipped her coffee. "It's freaky when my brain is telling me my leg is still there and it's really not."

"Never goes away," Riker said soberly. "But it does seem to diminish in frequency over time." He tipped his mug and drank greedily.

"You wake up with a headache?"

He nodded. "Every morning. Today's is a combination of caffeine withdrawal and the CTE." To steer the conversation elsewhere, he gestured at the monitor with the mug. "What's going on outside?"

She stepped back from the counter. "Take a look for yourself."

Riker moved closer. Although the sun's first rays were blotted out by the trees in front of the mansion, in one of the panes on the monitor he could see that the ladder had been erected near the pedestrian gate. Two people were out there, too. Thanks to the combined shadow cast by the trees and nearby wall, plus the fact the two survivors were close in size, he couldn't immediately discern Benny from Rose.

One person was spotting the ladder. The second person was up on the ladder. He or she was wearing the Mule and leaning over the top of the wall. It looked a little reckless, being top-heavy and all. The hose attached to the Mule was coiled around the person's right arm, but the wand and hand holding it were both out of sight.

"That's Rose on the ladder," Lia pointed out. "She volunteered for morning rounds right in front of me. She wolfed down a pancake, threw on her boots, and hustled out the door with Benny in tow and Dozer not far behind. I think she'd been steeling herself for it all night. The desire to pull her weight is strong in her."

"She just getting started?"

Lia shook her head. "She already put down a few that had shown up overnight at the rear gate. She was super tentative at first."

They drank their coffee and watched Rose work for a couple of minutes.

Finally, Riker said, "She looks like an old hand at it now."

"Could be that the one who puts them down gets out of burial detail. That's a pretty good incentive."

"Good point." Riker raised the mug to his lips and stared at Lia as he drank down the remainder of his coffee. His other hand was in his pocket and worrying the dainty gold watch.

Noticing all the fidgeting, Lia said, "Playing a game of pocket pool?"

Riker felt a flush creep up his neck. Thankfully, the combination of melanin in his skin, his thickening beard, and the dim lighting helped to conceal his embarrassment. He opened his mouth and was about to present the watch when in walked Steve-O. He was dressed in his usual country and western attire: stiff blue jeans held up by a wide leather belt, the silver buckle Texas-sized and inlaid with turquoise. His long-sleeved denim shirt was festooned with authentic mother-of-pearl buttons. Sitting low on his head was the white Stetson cowboy hat he was rarely seen without. The heels of the prized Stetson Outlaw boots Shorty had picked up for him at a feed store outside of

Thompson's Station, Tennessee clicked against the floor tiles as he approached.

"What's up, guys?" He paused and sniffed the air. "Is it already oh-coffee thirty?"

"It's too early to be oh-beer thirty," countered Lia. "If we were tilting beers before noon, wouldn't that make us alcoholics?"

"Too late for that," Riker divulged. "I reached my lifetime beer quota years ago. Unfortunately, at the time, the consequences weren't enough for me to stop. Apparently, it took the gravity of animated corpses walking the streets to convince me to stay stopped."

This was the first Lia had heard of his problem. She was visibly taken aback.

Steve-O, on the other hand, simply said what was on his mind. "I don't like beer. It tastes like dirty socks smell." He made a face. "And it makes my hands tingle and leaves me with a headache the next day."

"That's called a hangover," Riker said. "Agreed. They're no fun."

On the monitor, Benny and Rose were moving the ladder. Their shadowy forms blipped from one pane to another pane in which the camera showed a handful of zombies standing in the cul-de-sac and blocking the vehicle gate.

Lia said, "How about hard liquor? Ever tried a shot?"

"One New Year's Eve, I had one of each." He pursed his lips and stared Riker and Lia in the face. After a couple of beats, he went on. "I barfed. Threw up all over the toilet seat. Marcy was *not* happy. She told me that when she was in college her sorority sisters called what I did 'praying to the porcelain god.' I didn't get it then. Still don't get it now."

Riker let go of the Rolex and put his hand on the counter. In a way, he was grateful for Steve-O's sudden intrusion. The conversation's change in course led to him remembering that Lia was ten years his junior. Which was still considered college-aged in most circles. An age gap his mom would have judged worthy of informing him he was robbing the cradle. While he didn't classify as a *boomer*, he figured—at thirty-eight— he was likely considered an antiquity in Lia's eyes.

As Shorty and Vern filed into the kitchen, both fully dressed and looking chipper, Lia said to Steve-O, "When you're puking in the toilet, you're usually down on your knees … like you're praying. The toilet is made of a glass-like material called porcelain."

Steve-O nodded. "Makes sense to me now, Lia. Thanks for that."

Patting Steve-O on the shoulder, Lia looped around the island and pulled from the oven a plate heaping to overflowing with golden-brown pancakes. "Everyone take a seat," she ordered. "Good news is I've been keeping these warm for you all. Bad news is we're out of butter."

"Have been for a week," Steve-O grumbled. "Not your fault, Lia. At least we still have plenty of Mrs. Butterworth's syrup." He sat on a stool at the island and stuffed a napkin into his collar.

Tara entered the kitchen, rubbing the sleep from her eyes. She was dressed similarly to her brother, the belt around her waist sagging under the weight of the Glock 19 and trio of fully loaded seventeen-round magazines.

As everyone took their seats around the island, Lia followed with mugs and the coffee urn, placing a mug and pouring as each person got situated.

Looking to Riker, Tara said, "You and the boys sure were up late last night."

Between bites, Riker said, "Me and the *boys* got the rigs gassed up and their fluids checked and topped."

Steve-O said, "I helped clean the guns and got some practice loading magazines."

Shorty couldn't resist. Wearing a lopsided grin, he put down his fork and knife and regarded Tara and Lia. "All that leaves for you *girls* to do is be pretty and choose who you're riding with."

"I'm riding with Shorty," blurted Steve-O. "I call *shotgun*, too."

Lia looked at Riker. "May I?"

He nodded.

Vern said, "Got room in your rig for me, Lee?"

Before Riker could answer, Tara stood and pushed her plate forward. "Oh hell no," she shot, "you all are *not* going to stick me riding with Mister Misogyny and his sidekick Go Along Cassidy."

Riker shrugged. "Early bird gets the—"

Interrupting, Tara said, "Me and Vern need to draw straws. Only fair way to do it."

Nodding, Vern said, "Sure thing. I'm feeling lucky."

Still fuming, Tara strode off in search of something suitable to use to break the stalemate.

Tara returned as Lia was clearing plates. In her hand was a pair of long wooden matches. "Who's doing the honors?"

Smiling, Shorty said, "Give them here."

Tara shook her head. Handing the matches to Lia, she whispered, "Girl power. Hook me up."

Lia said nothing and turned her back to the island. A beat later, she was facing Tara and Vern, arm outthrust, both matches protruding an inch or so from her closed fist.

Vern said, "Ladies first," and stepped aside.

Tara stared long and hard at the level ends of the pair of matches. Finally, she reached out and chose a match. Without looking at the inch and a half long sliver of wood that was about to decide her vehicular destiny, she said to Vern, "Bring it."

He plucked the remaining match from Lia's hand and held it up for all to see.

Clapping Vern on the shoulder, Steve-O said, "Winner, winner, chicken dinner."

Looking down at the smaller man, Lia said, "Sticking with your first choice, Vern?"

Vern handed over his plate. Regarding the others, he said, "I'll let you all know when we get out in the courtyard."

"Understood," Riker said. "We leave in five. Know that I'm good whichever way you go with it. Won't hurt my feelings if you roll with"—he looked at Shorty and Steve-O—"what'd my sister call you all?"

Shorty shook his head. "Downright rude. I'm not even going to repeat it."

Steve-O shrugged. "I don't remember."

As Tara stalked off to her room to get her things, she called over her shoulder in a booming voice, "Mister Misogyny and Go Along Cassidy."

Chapter 9

To say Tara was pissed off about losing out to Vern and being relegated to riding in Shorty's EarthRoamer would be the understatement of the century.

Before boarding the massive Ford F-550 at Trinity and taking her place in the backseat behind Steve-O and Shorty, she had spent a couple of minutes schooling Rose and Benny on how to operate the Iridium Extreme satellite phone Clark had left them. It was an encrypted DoD item and one of a matched pair. The second phone would be going along with Riker in the Shelby. After activating both phones and inputting pertinent contact numbers, Clark had stressed to the group that they were likely being monitored by someone somewhere, and he recommended they be used in case of emergency only.

Finished coming down off the mountain from Trinity House via the twisting two-lane ribbon of blacktop called Paseo Encantado, the two-vehicle convoy—the Shelby rolling point—used Veterans Memorial Highway to circumvent the static dump trucks and long lines of snarled vehicles blocking US-84 into Santa Fe.

Flanked by grass and juniper shrub, the divided four-lane curled north by west through sparsely inhabited range. After the short jaunt that had them backtrack slightly, the bypass took a hard left and plunged due south. The straightaway quickly transitioned into a left-to-right arc as Veterans Memorial continued its descent through a wide arroyo toward its eventual terminus on the outskirts of Santa Fe, almost twelve miles south by west from the highway entrance.

Tara had remained tightlipped the entire time they'd been on the road. However, from the second the convoy rolled through Trinity's front gate to just a moment ago when her brother radioed to warn that they were coming up on the overpass known for its falling zombies, the little man at the wheel with the crooked nose and cocksure attitude had been doing just the opposite.

When Shorty wasn't yammering on about all of his pre- and post-zombie apocalypse exploits, he had been bouncing ideas off Steve-O of places they should visit, covering everything from the S.E.T.I. facility with its vast array of building-sized dish antennas, the site of the purported Roswell UFO crash, to Area 51, which he said was somewhere deep in the Nevada desert. The only place he mentioned that would not be so far out of their way that it was doable, so long as time allowed, was Four Corners Monument, the only point in the United States shared by four states—Arizona, Colorado, New Mexico, and Utah.

Tara was about to ask Shorty if he was going to dominate the conversation all the way to their final destination when Steve-O twisted around in his seat and fixed her with an earnest stare. "If we're going to all be stuck in here together for"—he glanced sidelong at Shorty—"how many hours did you say it would take to get to Vegas?"

"Fourteen hours," Tara shot. "And I'm counting down the seconds to arrival."

"Take off the half-hour since we left home, and we still have more than half of a day to go," Steve-O noted. "You've been quiet the whole time Shorty has been driving. That's not like you, Tara. So I think that if we're all going to be stuck in this truck together, you will need to contribute to the conversation." He pushed his glasses back to their usual perch on his squat nose. "I'm already tired of listening to Shorty's lies."

"Embellishments," Shorty corrected. "Every good storyteller does it. It's like adding icing and colorful sprinkles to a cake donut. Nobody likes *plain* cake donuts. They're *always* the last ones left in the box. So you gotta dress them up."

"I like cake donuts," Steve-O announced. "It's the ones with coconut on top that I cannot stand. *Blech.* Those are nasty."

As the Shelby made the turn onto I-25 south, Shorty braked and did the same. Once he'd made up distance lost during the wide turn, bringing the Roamer's boxy steel bumper to within a truck length of the trailer hitched to the high-performance off-road pickup, he met Tara's gaze in the rearview mirror. "If we make any side trips or have to stop and winch vehicles from the road, fourteen hours is *not* going to happen. Anyone who thinks we'll be anywhere near the Vegas suburbs before dark is living in a fantasy world."

Tara felt the drumbeat of anger finally subside. Keeping her tone civil, she said, "None of it matters anyway. We won't even be in range for Lia to try and connect with the kid until well after their usual check-in time."

"I think your brother and Vern wanted to get there in time to find a place safe enough to loiter overnight," Shorty noted. "Choosing a spot and setting up security is a dangerous undertaking during the day. After dark, lights ablaze, sound traveling far and wide over the desert … forget about it. Every zombie from there to Timbuktu will come a-calling." He had his eyes parked on the road the entire time he'd been talking. Working the brakes and gas, he slowed the Roamer to a crawl and followed close behind the Shelby as it slalomed through the beginning of a long stretch of highway littered with vehicles—a substantial number of them blackened with soot and sitting on the remnants of melted tires.

The pileup had been a horrific affair no different than the dozens Shorty had encountered throughout his travels. During those first days of the zombie apocalypse, the people surging from the cities had not only been fleeing the dead but also the living. The dregs of society had started the ball rolling, stealing with impunity jewelry, electronics, furniture, and sneakers. The pharmacies came next. They were overrun and ransacked, most of the spoils going home with the addicts. Then, with the populace finally slipping the reins of normalcy bias—oft described as a cognitive bias that leads a person to disbelieve or minimize threat warnings even as a catastrophic event is occurring all around them—the looting of grocery stores reached a fever pitch. By that point, the National Guard was cordoning off cities, and the military was engaged in a tactical retreat. Their failure to contain the outbreak to the cities was a shock to the system that saw the Joint Chiefs, heads of all the alphabet agencies, and the President and his entire cabinet scatter to all points of the compass. In the end, the dead were rising faster than a D5 avalanche barreling down Mount Everest.

There was no stopping Romero as it cut through the terrified citizenry like a scythe through summer wheat. No matter how fast and far one ran from the population centers, there was virtually no escaping the undead hordes.

At the rear of the pileup, a long-dead corpse remained at the wheel of a Volvo wagon—one of the few vehicles nearby not consumed by fire. The rear-end collision with a large American SUV had left the Volvo's windshield spidered and its front end a mass of mangled metal a couple of feet shorter than normal. The gas flap yawned open. Which told Shorty that someone had already beaten them to the fuel. Mouth agape in a silent scream, the long-dead geriatric driver's bony hands remained glued to the steering wheel.

"It was Grandpa's lucky day," Shorty said. "Unlike these poor fuckers coming up on Steve-O's side, this one died and stayed dead."

A trio of bullet-riddled corpses slid by outside Steve-O's window. Two men and a woman, all in their twenties, their slack faces aimed skyward. The lack of blood from the entry wounds suggested all three had been zombies when the majority of the damage had been done. Each of them sported a single dime-sized gunshot wound to the forehead—the classic coup de grace to ensure second death.

Navigating the long row of inert vehicles at slow speed burned fifteen minutes. At the head of the mess was an eighteen-wheeler and a crushed minivan. Both were completely immolated, the fire so intense that the blacktop had buckled in places. Several vehicles in the vicinity had also been consumed by fire.

Nearby, occupying the expanse of blacktop between the slow lane and guardrail, sat a tow truck. It was painted in woodland camouflage. On the open door, gold leaf reflecting the sun, were the words *Sergeant's Towing*. Still hitched to the wrecker was a lipstick-red Jeep. The Cherokee had taken a big hit to the left rear quarter panel. The coating of dust and numerous tumbleweeds lodged underneath the rear wheels indicated it had been sitting in the elements for some time.

Just as the Shelby and Roamer emerged from the quarter-mile chute of death and destruction, a jumble of charred corpses that had been left to rot on the inner breakdown lane awaited them. Each one wore the rictus grin of the truly dead. Arms frozen in position and missing fingers reached indiscriminately for the cobalt sky. It looked as if the half dozen unlucky souls had gone out requesting a final hug. More likely, they had all been in their individual vehicles and bracing for impact when the minivan's ruptured fuel tank exploded, ending their mortal tenures on Earth with a bang as opposed to the proverbial whimper. Why someone had extricated them from their vehicles and posed them on the road was anyone's guess. It wasn't the strangest thing the group had encountered since the fall. Certainly something else would come along that would make them all forget about this strange sight.

Shorty was shaking his head when his two-way radio came alive, and Riker's voice spilled from the tiny speaker. "No gas to be had here," Riker said. "Someone beat us to it."

"I noticed," Shorty radioed back. "We should probably be looking in less obvious places. Maybe find a large farm off the beaten path. Something with farm equipment in clear view." He released the Talk key to let Riker respond.

Coming back, Riker said, "A business park outside of Albuquerque with a lot full of eighteen-wheelers might have both fuel types we're looking for. A truck stop could be the ticket, too."

Bringing the radio to his lips, Shorty said, "Copy that. We also need to be looking ahead. Sound travels far out here. Wouldn't want to be on the wrong end of an ambush."

Riker came back, saying, "I'm one step ahead of you. Lia's on high alert. She's glassing the road ahead with the Steiners." There was a short pause, after which he asked, "Is my sister still salty?"

In the Roamer, Tara thrust one hand between Shorty and Steve-O and made the *gimme* motion.

"Here she is," Shorty warned as he relinquished the Motorola.

"I was way past *salty* when we left Trinity," Tara spat into the radio. Voice softening, she apologized to Vern for being indignant after his win. "Everyone has been getting their way but me," she confessed. "I want to *spend* my millions. I was going to go to Europe and Australia and Hawaii. Last thing I thought I'd be doing after Mom died is watching the fruits of all of Dad's hard work become worthless because some assholes trying to make super soldiers got sloppy and released their virus on the world."

Steve-O was turned around, hand to his mouth, the knuckles red from him gnawing on them. "Tara's angry," he said to nobody in particular. "More angry than I've ever seen her."

In the Shelby, Riker made a face. He was trying to think of something to say that would simultaneously comfort Steve-O and placate his sister. Bringing the radio to his lips, he said, "We really don't know what's going on in the bunkers in and around D.C. You all saw those red dots on the map back at Trinity. There's a bunch of them on the East Coast … Mount Weather, Raven Rock, the White House bunker, Greenbrier hotel and many more. Hell, the Cheyenne Mountain Complex in Colorado Springs is sealed to the outside. North American Aerospace Defense Command operates out of there. NORAD is supposed to be able to survive a direct hit from a nuclear warhead. There's got to be some kind of command and control working out of there. And I'd be willing to bet all my inheritance that some of our military is holed up off the beaten path … well away from the big cities. Right now they're probably eating MREs and awaiting orders from the President or Joint Chiefs." He stopped talking long enough to draw a deep breath and glance at the navigation information on the Shelby's SYNC display. It showed they were nearing Albuquerque. Which told him a decision needed to be made soon.

Having collected his thoughts, Riker addressed Tara over the radio. "The government will be back up and running in no time, Sis. Then you can get on your travel app and book us a trip to anywhere in the world you want to go. Hot or cold climate, you'll hear no complaints coming out of me." He grimaced and released the Talk key. He didn't believe a word of his last statement. And from the similar expressions worn by Lia and Vern, they also knew he was spewing complete and utter bullshit.

Hearing the electronic tone that meant the channel was open, Tara thumbed the Talk button on her Motorola. "The government is *not* in control of anything, Lee. Have they ever been? That was a rhetorical question. I'm going to keep this line open and give you the sauce." She paused and took a deep breath. Outside her window, the ubiquitous brown and gray countryside scrolled by at sixty miles per hour. A sign promising the best Mexican food for a hundred miles could be found at

Abuelita's Kitchen in Bernalillo was a colorful blur as they passed it by.

Shorty took a hand off the wheel and pointed to the Motorola. "Pretty sure your bro is still all ears," he said to Tara. "He can't talk unless you open the channel."

Pressing the radio to her shirt, she mouthed, "Big bro needs a few more seconds of timeout to think about trying to bullshit me on an open channel in front of friends and family."

"My mom used to give timeouts," Steve-O divulged. "One time I dressed our dog, Clover, in my old baby clothes. I didn't make her wear the boots or hat, though." He smiled wide. "She was *not* happy."

The mental image Steve-O's story conjured made Tara forget about why she was angry in the first place. Apparently, humor worked both ways, she thought. Her brother resorted to it to diffuse situations that used to get a person his size in trouble. He couldn't help it. The CTE he suffered from was a byproduct of war, therefore his propensity to see red in certain situations was not indicative of his true character. The same couldn't be applied to her, she suddenly realized. She had no excuse for acting like a baby, for being so selfish and self-centered when everyone around her was doing what they were doing for Cole and the other kids.

The desire to lash out at her big brother diminishing by the second, Tara smiled at Steve-O and released the Talk key. "Who was more pissed about the cowboy getup? Your mom or the dog?" she asked the man.

"The dog," Steve-O said, smile fading. "She bit me. Made me bleed. Mom was mad at the dog but gave me the timeout because dogs don't learn anything from timeouts."

The radio clutched tight in Tara's hand crackled to life. "You finished?" Riker asked. "Going to let me get back to driving?"

She said, "You're off the hook," and passed the radio to Shorty.

Thumbing the Talk button, Shorty said, "Maybe we can swap passengers when we stop next."

Riker replied at once. A playful tone to his voice, he said, "Not a chance, sir. I'd rather walk than take on as passengers a rabid wolverine and the human fart machine."

Chapter 10

Between Santa Fe and a spot on the Shelby's navigation screen dominated by a cluster of towns and small cities, I-25 was mostly clear of automotive snarls. The wandering bands of zombies so prevalent in and around Santa Fe were also few and far between.

As the interstate cut through forty-some-odd miles of sparsely populated high desert, it was shadowed to the north by the once heavily traveled historic Route 66. From time to time, the old haunts that had survived the advent of the interstate could be seen in all their faded glory.

The convoy didn't make it to Abuelita's Kitchen, though. They didn't even make it as far as Bernalillo, a town of roughly eight thousand. Instead, Vern instructed Riker to exit I-25 near Algodones, a town with one-tenth the population of Bernalillo. From there, they followed the twisting Rio Grande River for a short time on a little-used road, then got off on US-550, a four-lane that angled diagonally, north by west, across the Shelby's nav screen.

When it was clear the state route was navigable, Vern had Lia plug a destination into the computer that would have them automatically bypass Albuquerque, a city of half a million that would not only be crawling with undead, but likely also teeming with gangs of breathers with bad intentions.

Settling back into the passenger seat, Lia parked her gaze on Riker. "You didn't really believe that crap you were spouting about the government and military, did you?"

Eyes fixed dead ahead, Riker said, "Not all of it."

Incredulous, she said, "Which part is feasible to you? You told me how fast things went to hell in Indiana. National Guard roadblocks going up almost immediately. I got the impression your trip from New York to Florida was sketchy as hell. Were the military units streaming east near the Texas border chilling and eating MREs and awaiting marching orders? No, they weren't. Their fate had already been sealed. They were heading into the grinder those big cities back east had already become." She crossed her arms. "All of that, if it's true, pretty much debunks the bulk of your *unicorns and lollipops* speech."

Vern said, "I think Lee's NORAD theory isn't far off. Poor bastards are probably all crammed in there like sardines and watching the world fall apart on satellite feeds. I couldn't imagine being in their shoes"—he dipped his head and shook it slowly side to side—"trapped in there and wondering what had become of *my* family."

Sometimes knowing is harder, thought Riker. After all, Vern *had* stopped short of begging him to put down his undead adult son, Shane. And it was clear Vern's inability to complete the grisly task himself was a burden he'd carry for the rest of his life. While it didn't compromise the man's ability to function in the new world, the man did struggle with the sadness of outliving everyone he knew. Riker couldn't imagine losing Tara and Steve-O, the latter of whom may as well be kin.

Riker purged the thoughts and looked sidelong at Lia and Vern. "The other day in the Lazarus Bunker I was by myself and started thinking about the movie War Games. So, yeah, you're right, Lia," he admitted. "I did pull that NORAD part out of my ass. It's the leaders in bunkers part that I think I really want to believe. Need to believe. I guess NORAD fits into that equation. Sure feel for those folks if they are watching the world fall to shit knowing full well what's awaiting them when they do finally emerge."

"If they ever emerge," Lia said, "it'll likely be years from now when we're all dead and gone."

"Glass half full, please," Riker chided. "My *unicorns and lollipops* speech was delivered over that open channel mainly for Steve-O's ears."

"He's a resilient old soul," Vern said. "He wouldn't have gotten this far in life if he wasn't. What is it you and Tara are always saying? Something about Steve-O being a grown-up ass?"

Smiling, Riker said, "Grown-ass man. Thanks for the reminder to heed my own advice."

Lia had relaxed somewhat and was busy jamming the eraser end of a pencil into the top of her prosthetic. "The itching is driving me effin crazy."

"Is the skin hot to the touch?" Vern asked.

Lia shook her head. "Just from the friction." She dipped her head and sniffed the air. "Doesn't stink, either."

"You keep jamming a dirty pencil in there and it will," Vern warned. "You're introducing bacteria. It starts bleeding again, that dressing will be a bastard to change."

Lia popped open the center console and tossed the pencil inside. *Out of sight out of mind.* A sentiment that would be meaningless to her when the urge to scratch the itch once again pegged ten on the irritation meter.

When the nav system prompted, Riker slowed and prepared to make the shallow left turn onto Unser Boulevard.

"What's that place?" Lia asked. She was pointing to a cluster of brick and steel structures off the Shelby's right front fender. The green-tinted windows reflecting the mid-morning sun had drawn her attention. As they drew within a quarter mile or so, they saw that the parking lots surrounding the one- and two-story buildings were home to an assortment of dusty vehicles. A lot sandwiched between the buildings was occupied by a handful of eighteen-wheelers and pickup trucks, all wearing desert-tan paint.

Coming to a complete stop at the curb adjacent to the sprawling facility, Riker said, "It's not named on the nav screen. While it looks like a business park, the design and materials all scream government. And with the amount of barbed wire strung around the place, there's got to be something worth protecting inside."

Vern said, "The 111th Sustainment Brigade, if my memory serves. Read an article in the *New Mexican* about some recruitment shindig they were hosting. It's a New Mexico guard unit tasked with providing mission command for combat support and combat service support units."

Riker nodded. "My unit worked with similar guard brigades in Iraq. Before I was driving for VIPs … generals and the like, I was part of a fuel and general resupply detail and was driving rigs much bigger than the Land Cruiser I nearly died in."

Lia said, "The differing states of the two parking lots tells me quite a few Guardsmen showed up when the shit hit the fan. The lack of military vehicles inside the fence makes me think the owners of the civilian vehicles were deployed somewhere and have yet to return."

Vern pulsed down his window. "Probably never coming back here." He asked for the binoculars. After glassing the facility and deeming it free of zombies, at least the parts he could see, he proposed going in to see if the cars in the nearby lot contained any fuel. "When we're done there," he went on, "we can get into the motor pool and see if the big rigs have any diesel in their tanks."

The radio crackled to life. It was Shorty. He said, "I have a feeling you all are thinking what I'm thinking."

Riker snatched up the radio. The beginning of a plan was working its way through his head. Thumbing the Talk button, he said, "You bet. It's a National Guard depot. Vern says it's a logistics unit. I'll bring the bolt cutters. You and Steve-O bring the siphon gear and Mule and meet me and Vern at the gate. When you park your rig, make sure you leave good lines of sight. We'll have Tara watch our backs from inside the cab." He looked to Lia. "And Lia just volunteered to drive Dolly. She can follow behind us while we're on the lot. We'll go car to car and get as much fuel as the barrels will hold."

"Copy that," said Shorty. "When we're done with the outer lot, let's check the big rigs and see if they're holding any diesel."

Riker said, "Great minds," and broke squelch. Looking sidelong at Lia, he busted her glaring at him.

"You can do it," he insisted. "Even with the trailer out back, she's nowhere near as hard to maneuver as Shorty's Roamer." Then, remembering why she had been running from the Bolt when he had first met her, he smiled and said, "Plus, there's no pesky clutch and stick shift to foul you up."

As Lia was flipping Riker the bird, Vern said, "I second that. You've got to test yourself, young lady. Because when the chips are down and we're in trouble, it's good to know you are an asset, not a liability."

"Stick shifts can go to hell," Lia said, punching out of her seatbelt. "Even though this truck is an automatic, working the gas pedal with no tactile feedback is going to be weird."

"Driving a right-hand drive car on the wrong side of the road is weird, too," Riker pointed out. "You get used to it real quick."

Riker parked the Shelby and relinquished the driver's seat. It was all he could do to refrain from telling her how to drive his baby. He'd heard Tara refer to the practice as *mansplaining*. Wouldn't want to be guilty of that, so he just got out, drew his Sig Legion, and closed the door.

After checking all points of the compass for dead things and seeing nothing moving but a lone tumbleweed crossing the flat parcel of land opposite the armory, he opened the door for Vern.

Riker and Vern met up with the other two men at the gate to the outside lot. It was on the western edge of the rectangle of blacktop and towered over them, the coiled razor wire up top adding another foot and a half to the already twelve-foot-tall run of fence.

At the far northwest corner of the perimeter fence, maybe a hundred yards distant and sitting in the shadow of a copse of gnarled trees, was a bullet-pocked pickup. On the dirt behind the pickup, all laid out in a neat row, were a half dozen corpses. From this distance, it was impossible to discern true cause of death. That there weren't birds feeding on the carrion told Riker that the dead bodies were either Romero infected or they were freshly killed and the buzzards and crows and ravens had yet to discover them.

No reason to investigate. At this point, obtaining fuel was the number one priority. And the fuel, if any was to be had, would be in the vehicles parked on the lot inside the fence.

To draw to the fence any zombies that might be skulking the lot, Riker ran the bolt cutter's business end back and forth across the chain-link. He did this for a good thirty seconds. After another long minute ticked into the past and nothing stirred amongst the static vehicles, Steve-O said, "Looks like it's our lucky day. No sickos, no guard dogs, and no soldiers."

"Don't count your chickens yet," warned Vern. He gestured at the main building with his suppressed MP5. "We still don't know what's inside there. Then there's the courtyard we saw from the road. It could be crawling with undead Guardsmen."

"You guys are gonna jinx us," Shorty declared. "Just be quiet and let the master work."

Riker opened the bolt cutters and instructed Shorty to steady the big Schlage padlock for him. The thick chain looped through the two halves of the gate rattled as the shorter man lifted the lock so Riker could get to it with the bulky tool's yawning metal maw.

"Lee," said Vern, his tone all business, "you're going to want to cease and desist at once."

Head down and concentrating on getting a good bite on the lock, Riker said, "If it's zombies, have Steve-O put them down with the Mule."

Steve-O said, "Uh oh … looks like I fucked up again."

Following Vern's not-so-subtle order, Riker lowered the tool and lifted his gaze. What he saw stood the hairs on his arms at attention. Crouched down behind a nearby pickup, most of his body protected by the truck's rugged rear bumper, was a soldier clad in desert-tan camouflage fatigues and wearing a snug-fitting full-face respirator. While finding himself staring down the barrel of a shotgun had had one effect on him, the *schlack-schlack* noise the weapon's slide made as the mute soldier crunched a round into the chamber was entirely different. It spoke volumes. Riker's brain processed it as *don't fucking move.*

Even as Riker froze, adrenaline was dumping into his system. In his brain, the change was visceral and snapped awake his fight or flight impulse. At the same time he was experiencing all of this, maybe a fraction of a second ticking away into the past, he was getting a weird vibe from Shorty. Like the man had been jolted by an unseen electrical impulse, his entire body had gone rigid. No doubt at the same time Riker had been clued in to their situation, Shorty had caught his first look at the soldier aiming the shotgun at them. Only Shorty's reaction had been different. He didn't freeze after tensing. Instead, he stabbed one foot backward and exhaled sharply.

Clearly, Riker thought, the man had already performed a cost-benefit analysis that was going to get them all killed. For if there was one lightly armed Guardsman in full battle rattle, there had to be more where he or she had come from. And, more than likely, the others were armed with high-powered long-range weaponry.

With a cold sweat breaking out all over his body and detecting in his peripheral vision the Shockwave's stubby muzzle already beginning an upward sweep, Riker did three things simultaneously. Shooting his left arm out to his side, he wrapped his mitt-sized hand around the Shockwave, thumb trapping Shorty's trigger finger to the weapon's blued frame. Thrusting the other arm in the air, Riker stood tall and backed away from the fence, bringing Shorty and the shotgun along with him. The steps Riker took were slow and easy and prompted Vern and Steve-O to follow his lead.

Voice muffled by the black gas mask, the soldier said, "Leave now and don't come back." It was a woman. No waver to her voice. She definitely meant business.

"My bad," said Riker, one arm still reaching for the sky. "We were just hoping to find some gas for our rigs." A strong tremor ran up his prosthetic and his entire body was suddenly jarred when he stepped backward off an unseen curb. Gritting his teeth against the new wave of pain radiating from the old wound, he went on, saying, "It was terrible judgment on my part, ma'am. We're leaving right now. Rest assured it will not happen again."

"We're good guys," added Steve-O. "We won't tell anyone you're here. Scout's honor."

"All those miles we logged together as road dogs and you never thought to tell me you were a Boy Scout," Shorty whispered to Steve-O. "What other secrets are you holding back?"

"I saw boobs yesterday."

Vern shushed Steve-O. "Time and place."

Unexpectedly, the soldier rose and peeled off her mask. Snaking from one ear was a flesh-colored earbud. Attached to the bud was a coiled wire that disappeared into her collar. In addition to Old Glory, the soldier's uniform was adorned with a subdued gold oak leaf and nametape that read *Littlewolf.*

Littlewolf was very tan and lean of face. Liquid brown eyes and an aquiline nose were framed by high cheekbones and a strong chin. The shock of dark hair poking from beneath the helmet's brim, combined with the other features, convinced Riker she was Native American.

Stunning instantly came to mind. But it wasn't her beauty that stopped Riker in his tracks, it was that she shared the surname with the warden he had rescued at the Santa Fe Adult Detention Facility a couple of weeks prior.

After looking Riker up and down, the shotgun unwavering, Littlewolf said, "Are you Leland Riker?"

Riker was speechless.

"You're about the right height," said Littlewolf. "And judging by your gait, I'd bet the house that you're wearing a prosthetic."

"Guilty on both counts," Riker finally managed. "Apparently my amputation precedes me. Is Warden Littlewolf your mother?"

Now the major was speechless. Her chinstrap didn't stop her jaw from hinging open and staying that way. After a couple of beats, Riker said, "Can't be that many Littlewolfs in Santa Fe."

Cocking her head, Littlewolf said, "I know you from the *New Mexican's* front-page spread. You were wrapped up in the Clines Corner murders. Got yourself mentioned in one of the last newspapers to make it onto the shelves before everything went completely sideways. I remember it only because your face was right next to the Romero coverage." She paused, thinking. Finally, after a few seconds of strained silence, during which Steve-O shifted foot to foot and Vern and Shorty exchanged questioning looks, Littlewolf said, "The article said you were the one who killed the CC killer. It was self-defense, right? If so, you wouldn't have been released on your own recognizance. Instead, you would've been put in general population. Begs the question: How do you know my mom?"

Riker said, "It's a small world," and explained to Littlewolf how he had defended himself at Trinity. He then went on and told her all that had happened at the adult correctional facility, leaving out only the grisly details about how her mom's men had died at the hands of the undead inmates.

Stunned, Littlewolf said, "She didn't go into all of that. She just told me some civilians helped her and some of her men off the roof. She was mostly mad at herself for losing so many people under her command. The virus turned most of the prison population into zombies before she could do anything about it. Then she lost most of her staff trying to contain the damn zombies." She dropped her gaze to the ground. "Romeo Victor has burned through our ranks, too."

Riker said nothing. He got it. Nothing he could say would bring any of them back.

Lifting her gaze, Littlewolf said, "If it weren't for you and your friends showing up when you did, my mom would have died up on that roof." A tear traced her cheek. "I owe you a debt of gratitude, Mr. Riker."

Showing her his electric pump setup, Shorty said, "You can make it up to Lee by letting us inside so we can do a little siphoning. Motor's whisper quiet. Quick in and out?"

Pinching away the tears, Littlewolf said, "I can't. This gate only opens for authorized personnel."

Vern slung his MP5 on one shoulder. "Nobody has to know," he urged. "Those cars aren't going anywhere."

Littlewolf shook her head. "Not going to happen. I can't break protocol." She flicked her gaze to the road behind the men. "You should be able to refuel at the Double Eagle Airport. As of yesterday, the perimeter was still secure. It's twenty miles south of here. But you gotta stay frosty out there. Keep on the lookout for bandits. They're thick as thieves between Rio Rancho and the airport. Know that they *always* shoot first. The Rust Medical Center is a no-go. The Walmart is sacked. If I were you, I'd make a thunder run from here and not stop until you have eyes on the airport and you've determined it hasn't been compromised." She paused and let the shotgun's barrel drift toward the ground. "I sent a patrol out a few hours ago. A Humvee and a Jimmy pickup. I could only muster six troops. Four men and two women. Lieutenant Murphy is commanding the mission. He's pretty green. But my sergeant and two of the other four are seasoned veterans." Lips pursed, she shook her head. "I'm a bit worried, though. They're an hour past due for a radio check. If you see anyone from the triple one, and their radio is hashed, pass the word that Fort Apache is still secure. Then tell them I said to get their asses back to base."

The warden did a bang-up job raising this one, Riker thought. "I'll do you one better," he promised. "My friend's rig has long-range comms capability. We'll keep our eyes open for your patrol. If we do come across them and they need our help, we'll do what we can. Lend them our radio. Give them fuel—"

Interrupting, Vern added, "I'm a combat medic. I'll render first aid if necessary."

"And I'll put them down if they're already zombies," Steve-O said, turning and showing off the air tank strapped to his back. "Lee says being a zombie is like being in limbo. Like getting stuck between heaven and hell." He tipped his Stetson at Major Littlewolf. "It's the least we can do."

Littlewolf pressed a finger to the earbud. She made a face. "You all better go now. There's a substantial-sized herd of zombies coming in from the east. The things are beginning to gather together. To coalesce. Reports have come in that put some of the herds in the thousands and tens of thousands. Nothing you want to be in the path of."

Didn't need to tell Riker twice. Although he wanted to pick the major's brain, ask her about things on the ground west of Albuquerque, inquire where the warden had set up shop in Santa Fe and, most importantly, to get from the horse's mouth the answer to his questions regarding command and control over the Continental United States, he instead simply snapped her a crisp salute and about-faced.

Riker and Vern were nearly to the Shelby when his radio came alive with a burst of white noise. It was Tara. Her message was brief and to the point. Confirming Riker's initial hunch, she reported that two soldiers on the roof were covering the gate with scoped rifles. A third soldier had just emerged from the main building and was hustling toward the gate. The soldier was toting, in Tara's words, *a big ass machine gun.*

Thankfully, Riker thought, as he reached the Shelby, the act of surrender on his part was acknowledged by the snipers before Shorty's kneejerk reaction had led to all of their heads being reduced to clouds of fine pink mist.

When Riker flung open his door, he couldn't get into the seat fast enough. He didn't even wait for Lia to dismount and return to her seat. Instead, he herded her over the center console and hauled himself behind the wheel.

Lia's transfer to the passenger seat was far from graceful, her prosthetic banging loudly against the steering wheel and dashboard as she scurried over the shifter.

"Pushy much?" she scolded. "You could have let me get out and walk around."

Riker said nothing.

"The little powwow at the gate between you guys and the soldier … what was that all about?"

Slamming his door, Vern said, "Lee is a celebrity, that's what. And his notoriety earned us a pass."

Riker had the engine running and the pickup rolling south on Unser before Shorty and Steve-O had closed their doors.

On the nav screen, the nearly straight yellow line that was Unser Boulevard dove south. After a short distance, it jogged a couple of times west before becoming Paseo Del Norte Boulevard, the arterial that would deliver them to the point of interest Lia had inputted earlier. Flicking his eyes to the rearview, Riker saw the EarthRoamer nearly go up on two wheels as it made the right-angle left turn at speed.

Littlewolf was dead on: The text displayed on the nav computer screen indicated the POI was twenty miles ahead. The accompanying icon showed that, once they reached the POI, they would have to turn right and take a short feeder road to access the facility.

Getting on the radio, Riker opened the channel and told Shorty he was taking the major's advice. "Thunder run to the airport," he said. "We don't stop for anything."

Chapter 11

We don't stop for anything. Famous last words, thought Riker. They'd successfully navigated twelve miles of car-choked surface streets that cut through Albuquerque's western suburbs, passed by the looted Walmart that Littlewolf had mentioned, avoided being swarmed by the throngs of undead milling about the parking lots fronting the Presbyterian Rust Medical Center, and were well on their way to the point of interest inputted by Lia when Riker's words came back to bite him in the ass.

Ahead on Unser, a block or so before it intersected McMahon Boulevard, was a merged mass of twisted and bent sheet metal. Front bumper and grille badly mangled, a full-size Dodge pickup sat atop a pair of silver imports. It appeared that the pickup had rear-ended one of the cars and then proceeded to ride up and over both of them. No other way Riker could see it coming to rest where it had, four feet off the ground, with all four off-road tires hanging down over the blown-out windows and effectively blocking the interiors of both of the imports from prying eyes.

It looked as if the two cars had been stopped, the drivers waiting for the light to go green. The only skid marks were wide and black and belonged to the pickup. The collision had been so violent that Riker couldn't tell where one import began and the other ended. If there had been people inside either one of the little cars, they were definitely closed-casket material. He also had no doubt, seeing as how both vehicles' trunks were compressed like an accordion's bellows, that their fuel tanks had ruptured upon impact. It was a miracle, he marveled, that the whole tangled mess hadn't gone up in a ball of flame.

The Dodge's front doors were open. Riker could see all the way through the cab. Nobody home. A deployed airbag drooped over the steering wheel. A strong and prolonged wind gust caused it to flutter and pop. Caught in the vortex, the metal latches on the dangling shoulder belts banged repeatedly against the inner door frames.

Slowing the Shelby, Riker pulled hard to the curb. Beyond the sidewalk on their right was a square block of scrub-covered dirt sprouting a For Sale sign. Beyond the empty lot was an animal hospital, its windows dark, the handles to the double doors wrapped with a length of chain. To the right of the animal hospital was a squat, windowless building made of cement blocks. A sign fluttering in the wind bore the words *Desert Wind Taekwon-Do Academy*. Beyond the bare block was a Circle K, its fuel island hemmed in tight by empty vehicles that had arrived after the station's tanks had run dry.

Lia shot a furtive glance at the wreck. Although it was twenty feet at most from Riker's open window, she could smell the ripe pong of carrion coming in from outside. "You said we weren't stopping for *anything*," she reminded.

Riker nodded. "That I did. But if we pass this wreck by without stopping, we'd be missing an opportunity to get Shorty some fuel. That Dodge high-centered on those cars runs on diesel. Unless the driver was a complete idiot, I imagine there's still fuel in the tanks."

Lia said, "Tanks? Plural?"

He nodded. "That's a ranch rig. They usually have a reserve tank." He pointed out the rectangular box in the bed. It was affixed to the rear of the cab and was fitted with a hose and nozzle similar to those on the Circle K's pumps. "If we're lucky," he went on, "and that external tank is full, we could be leaving here with sixty to a hundred gallons. Maybe more if the driver had just topped off."

"He's right, Lia. But it's no benefit to us," Vern pointed out. "This rig runs on regular gas." He shifted his gaze to Riker. "Seeing as how Shorty almost got us killed back there, why should we stick our necks out for him now?"

"If Shorty doesn't keep up," Lia said, "there's no radio for me to use to try and contact Cole."

Riker said, "Nail on the head. Plus, my sister is a direct beneficiary of this momentary pit stop."

Vern said, "We still have hundreds of miles ahead of us before we're even close to being in radio range." He looked at

Riker. "I'm certain this is going to be the first of many crackups we're going to encounter. That's both good and bad. There could be fuel for us to siphon from some of them. The bad is that they're going to mostly be in and around Indian country."

Lia said, "I don't get it. What do you mean by *Indian country*?"

Vern looked first to Lia, then craned and locked eyes with Riker. "There's more. I withheld some information from you all."

"What kind of information?" Riker asked, a chill to his tone.

"While I told you we were going this route to avoid Albuquerque's population, which last I checked was around half a million, I wasn't forthright about the tradeoff."

"What tradeoff?" Riker asked.

Gesturing at the beginnings of suburban sprawl outside the windows, Vern said, "Rio Rancho's population is eighty or ninety thousand. Granted, we're avoiding the more populous east side of town, but we're still dancing with the devil if we stay stopped here for much longer."

"So we backtrack," Lia suggested. "If we cut west back near the armory, we should be able to skirt Rio Rancho on backroads."

Vern shook his head. "It's mostly desert. Roads are unimproved. It'd be real slow going with a trailer out back." He pointed to a scraggly ridge of upthrust desert. "And we can't just keep going west because eventually we'd come to that escarpment. It runs north to south. It mirrors Unser all the way to the airport I had you input. The airport sits pretty close to where that ridgeline ends."

They'd been sitting for a couple of minutes, burning fuel as they talked. Thinking it prudent to maintain radio silence this close to the city, Riker stuck his arm out the window and made a swimming motion. While he waited for Shorty to figure out he was supposed to pull up and park beside the Shelby, he took in more of their surroundings.

Beyond the east/west boulevard, windows of the homes in a newer-looking subdivision reflected back at Riker the warm glow of the midmorning sun. Behind the pitched roofs, at the far edge of a vast sea of cactus-studded desert, the escarpment Vern had pointed to shot off to the left.

Distance was hard to gauge in the wide open. Be it five miles or twenty, the ridge stood as a barrier to a vast desert landscape pressed down on by a seemingly never-ending swath of cobalt blue sky.

East of Unser, the windows fronting a smattering of business concerns were black as obsidian. Signs were darkened, too. Here and there, flashes of movement could be seen down side streets. Closer in, zombies slalomed between parked cars and flitted from building to building. For now, though, the majority of the dead were far away and few in number.

The only clear threat was a male zombie clad in a red shirt and naked from the waist down. It had emerged from the Walgreens a block distant and was standing on a carpet of glass from the smashed-out windows. There was a definite tilt to its head. After standing still for a few seconds, the head started to swivel slowly, left to right. It was trying to establish a lock on the idling engines.

At this point, Riker thought, just a few weeks after Romero's introduction to an unwitting population, the few people who had survived the initial wave were either holing up and waiting for the cavalry to arrive or were venturing out only when absolutely necessary. Both actions were the polar opposites of what Lia had convinced him and the others to do. And all for a few kids who, for all Riker knew, could be bait to a trap meant to ensnare anyone attempting a rescue. No sooner had he thought it than he was stuffing the glass-half-empty thinking back where it belonged: on the pile of unrealized fears that'd been growing steadily ever since the dead began to walk.

A few blocks in front of the idling Shelby, where Unser cut across the wide east/west arterial, the traffic signals swaying above the intersection were not operating. Trash, blown by the wind, had accumulated against a trio of vehicles that had tried, rather unsuccessfully, to occupy the same patch of asphalt at the center of the intersection. Stuck fast to one another were a full-size SUV and a rust-streaked early-model Ford sedan. A faded gray minivan had speared into the side of the SUV. On the inside of the minivan's rear window was a bright yellow *Baby On Board* sign. A single zombie sat trapped behind the wheel. Filtered through the gore-streaked auto glass, the lone zombie's constant movement came off as a fluid dance of shadow and light. In Riker's mind's eye, the baby was still *on board.* It was strapped into an out of sight car seat, its stick-thin zombie arms straining futilely to touch the undead driver. Whether it was there or not was irrelevant. The thought alone made the hair on Riker's arms stand at attention.

To the west, in the middle distance, a dog pack appeared in the boulevard's eastbound lanes, their bays and yips reaching Riker's open window a half-beat after he'd spotted them. No sooner had the odd collection of canines coalesced on one spot in the road than a dozen or so zombies hunting them ambled from a connecting arterial. The sudden appearance of the zombies sent the entire dog pack into a frenzy and scurrying away to the south. The growling and barking coming from the pack grew louder and more ferocious as the walking dead things changed course and resumed their unending pursuit.

Finally catching a clue, Shorty slow-rolled the Roamer forward. He parked the taller rig broadside to the Shelby and used his master controls to pulse down Steve-O's window.

Riker turned his head and found himself looking Steve-O in the eye.

With a tip of the Stetson, Steve-O said, "What's up, Lee?"

"Opportunity knocks, that's what, Steve-O." Craning to see past the brim on the man's hat, Riker said to Shorty, "The Dodge is a diesel. Want to see if there's some fuel left in her tanks?"

Shorty surveyed the wreckage, giving the road in both directions extra scrutiny. Nodding, he threw the transmission into Park. Leaving the motor running, he exited the cab, looped around back, and disappeared inside the camper.

Tara lowered her window. "A bit of tension back there at the armory, eh?"

Riker made a face. "I have a favor to ask."

"What is it?"

"Bury the hatchet. Last thing we need is for Shorty to take out his frustrations on the wrong folks." A door slammed. Shifting his gaze to the side mirror, he went on, saying, "It nearly got ugly back there."

"How so?"

"Long story. But trust me, we were literally on a hair-trigger at the gate. I'm talking Def-Con 1. Lucky for us the major has a good head on her shoulders. No kind of power trip going on with that one. Probably comes with the territory, what with her being brought up by someone working in corrections."

Steve-O said, "Her mom is the lady Lee rescued from the jail."

"*We* is the operative word," Riker said, matching Lia's gaze. "It took the two of us to get those people off the roof. It took a group effort to get us all out of the parking lot in one piece." He stuck his arm out the window and bumped fists with Steve-O. "You pulled your weight that day, too."

Steve-O's face was turning red when Shorty reappeared in front of the Roamer. In one hand was the siphon tool. In the other was one end of a length of twine he'd threaded through the handles of half a dozen plastic ten-gallon gas cans. The cans were dragging the ground behind Shorty and collected around his hikers when he stopped outside of Riker's window. "A little help out here? Without a ladder, it's going to be a pain in the ass for me to reach that rig's main fuel door. If I'm going to dip my wick in the external tank, I'm definitely going to need some help getting into the load bed."

"I can make a stirrup with my hands," Steve-O suggested.

Riker said, "You'll figure it out, Shorty. If you're anything, it's resourceful. Have Steve-O and Tara pull security for you. We'll wait right here with the AC running."

Muttering under his breath, Shorty let the Shockwave slip off his shoulder and took hold of it by the bird's head grip. Transferring the twine to the hand holding the siphon tool, he started off across the road, the empty gas cans making way more noise than Riker would have liked.

Tara and Steve-O caught up with Shorty as he was dropping his gear to the blacktop beside the pileup. Calling out to Tara, who had staked out a spot near the first of the crushed imports, Shorty said, "What's up Lee's butt?"

"Probably just wanted to stay in Dolly so he can rest his leg," Steve-O posited. "His wound is still healing, you know."

"That's not it," said Shorty as he fumbled to keep one of the cans level so he could get the hose into its neck. "Lee is *pissed off* about something."

Tara poked her head around front of the elevated pickup. "He's mad because you tend to shoot first and ask questions later."

Shorty didn't respond. He'd kind of figured that was the case, what with the bruised fingers Lee had left him with. Setting the pump aside, he took hold of the Dodge's rear tire. Adopting a wide stance, he pushed and tugged on it. Nothing. The wheel didn't spin, and the pickup didn't budge. It was going nowhere.

Shorty scooped up the pump and long length of rubber hose attached to it. Finding a toehold on what used to be a fender, no telling whether it had been front or rear, he grabbed ahold of the pickup's tire and pulled himself off the road. Body pressed flat to the pickup's rear fender well, cheek in contact with the warm metal, he pried open the fuel door with his knife. Sheathing the knife, he spun off the gas cap, letting it dangle freely on its retaining strap.

The chemical nose of diesel hit him at once. Suddenly the wind changed direction and he was blasted in the face by the sickly-sweet stench of rotting flesh coming from within the wreckage.

Balanced precariously on the crushed import, Shorty released his hold on the pickup long enough to shove the long length of hose attached to the siphon's input port deep into the Dodge's main tank. No sooner had he gotten the end of the hose to what he thought was the bottom of the tank than in his peripheral he saw a pale arm shoot from the wreckage. It was stunted and riddled with puckered oval bite wounds, each crusted with dried blood and oozing a viscous yellow liquid. He felt the sting of fingernails biting the flesh just above his ankle. They'd gone right through the sock. He didn't have eyes on what was happening, but it sure felt as if the punctured skin was tearing slowly, the fingers worming their way into the underlying flesh. The pain was excruciating. Still, he didn't cry out.

He was kicking at the hand gripping his ankle when a second arm snaked out of the dark. Slender fingers clamped around the other ankle, interlacing overtop the sock. Fighting a rising bout of panic, he let go of the hose and grabbed the bed rail. With the fingers on both hands momentarily supporting the brunt of his hundred and fifty-some-odd pounds, he took a second to glance up and down the road.

Tara was out of sight. No doubt she was right where she had said she would be: on the other side of the wreck and keeping an eye out for anything coming from the south and west.

Steve-O was also at his post. Shorty caught a glimpse of the tips of the man's red boots and the brim of the white Stetson peeking past the tailgate. It was clear he was fixated on something in the distance and totally oblivious to what was happening.

Shouting for help was not an option. It went against everything Shorty's father had taught him. *Men of our size*, the equally diminutive elder Twigg had said to Shorty when he was still in middle school and the target of a massive amount of bullying, *are always on our own. Never let another man get something off a high shelf for you. And never, ever consider sitting on a pillow to drive a car.* Finally, the elder fisherman had ordered Shorty to never show or admit weakness. *Do not turn the other cheek. Because if you do,* his father had insisted, *you will never win their respect.* So far for Shorty, at least in the old world before the dead started coming back to life, his father's advice had proven to be more asset than deficit. Right now, given the predicament he had gotten himself into, he was beginning to believe it was time to rethink his position.

Cursing himself for not wearing his Stetson cowboy boots, the same blaze-red items as Steve-O wore, Shorty thought through his options. First off, letting go of the bed rail was not going to happen. With his feet held in check by the cold hands strangling his ankles, his head would be first to smack the road. No way he could break his fall by extending his arms. He'd end up with a pair of broken wrists *and* a closed head wound. With the addition of the second hand applying a vice-like grip to his leg, the likelihood of him being knocked unconscious on impact and then being dragged into the wreckage was too great to chance. He'd become a quick meal to however many dead things were trapped inside there.

The Shockwave was on the road and out of reach. So close yet so far. Lot of good it did him there. Lastly was the Glock. Dragging it from the holster on his hip would require him to hang on with just one hand. A prospect he wouldn't have balked at twenty years ago. Now, a few years north of fifty, given the exertion being put on his muscles by the constant pull of the zombies, he no longer possessed the strength in two hands to suspend his entire weight for much longer, let alone just the one for the time it would take to draw the Glock. Already his fingers were beginning to cramp, the tremors and twinges increasing by the second.

Another wind gust buffeted the pickup. A gauze bandage, black with dried blood, slipped off the second arm and was carried away by the wind. This arm was also peppered from wrist to elbow with pus-filled bite wounds.

Was it a ride share gone wrong? thought Shorty. *Or was it an entire family trying to flee the city and one of them unwittingly brought the Romero virus along for the ride?* He'd seen dozens of vehicles crammed with living dead things. So far, the latter scenario made the most sense.

Didn't matter how they came to be there. All he knew was that the grabby bastards were winning the life-or-death game of tug o' war.

No sooner had Shorty's brain dragged into the equation the specter of being eaten by the unseen monsters inside the wreck than yet another arm emerged from the darkness and grabbed hold of him. He didn't need to look down to know the gnarled fingers had a strong purchase on one pant leg.

With the constant pull of the three arms close to dislodging the North Face hikers from the fender, Shorty's resolve crumbled like a sandcastle to a sneaker wave. *Who cares what they think*. "Steve-O," he bellowed. "Get your Mule over here! And you better *fucking* hustle!"

By the time Steve-O made it to Shorty's side, the forces working against Shorty staying upright won out over his ability to retain his grip on the bed rail.

Head hurtling toward the road like a hair-covered cannonball, Shorty closed his eyes in anticipation of the knockout blow to come. Instead, the fall suddenly arrested, he felt his hat come off and a hand palm his head. The sting of the nails digging into his ankle was accompanied by the same painful sensation occurring near the small of his back. *This is it,* he thought. *After all the scrapes I've been through, I go out siphoning gas.* In the next beat, as he was busy imagining the crushing bites to come, his fall was arrested, and he felt his upper body being lowered slowly to the road. Opening his eyes, he saw Tara's face inches from his. It was twisted and beaded with sweat. The exertion of supporting his weight had her breathing hard. It was a vision from on high.

"Move," said Steve-O as he brushed by a kneeling Tara and thrust the Mule's deadly end deep into the wreckage.

"Never saw such a beautiful sight in my life," admitted Shorty. He pursed his lips. "Since we're already in position … might as well plant one on me."

To the sound of continual bursts of compressed air coming from the Mule, she said, "You almost got yourself *planted.* What were you thinking?"

Shorty made a face. "I wasn't. Most people call it short man's complex. Guess I thought I could get myself out of the jam."

"Well," she said, "you couldn't. That was pretty obvious. And you best clean and bandage those wounds before they get infected." She planted her hands on her hips and bugged her eyes at him. "Next time, holler. Hell, scream like a girl. There's just about nothing you can do in the course of day-to-day operations, Shorty, save for getting bit and hiding it, that will cause me to lose respect for you. I may have harsh words now and again, but dammit, Shorty, you stood on the beach by the campground and took it to the biters. You did that for all of us. Your actions bought us the time we needed to get the pickup going again. You proved you're a team player."

Wearing a sheepish expression, Shorty said, "Message received. There is no I in team. Now about that kiss?"

She slugged him on the shoulder. "You men are always thinking with your little head."

Shorty had heard that particular retort before. So many times that he even had a few choice comebacks ready to go. But to keep on life support any chance he might have of getting with Tara in the future, he wisely bit his tongue.

"Done," said Steve-O. The Mule wand resting over one shoulder, he gestured at the Walgreens with the other. "Better get sucking, Shorty. There's more biters coming from that store."

Shorty regarded Steve-O. "How many were in the car?"

"Three kid zombies. They all had silver tape over their mouths." Steve-O pointed to where the front seats should have been located. "The adults are in there and are as flat as a couple of flapjacks. I don't think they were sick when they wrecked."

Tara said, "Died on impact, I'd imagine."

Shorty shook his head. "The parents couldn't do it. Probably brought the kids to that hospital back there and got turned away." In a funereal voice, he added, "I don't think I could put one of my kids down if I had to. But since they're missing, don't suppose that's a bridge I'll ever have to cross."

"Someday, you might have to put one of us out of our misery," Steve-O said matter-of-factly.

Shorty shook his head. "That's a bridge I hope none of us will ever have to cross."

Tara plucked the siphon tool off the road and started the motor running. Although it was no louder than a fish tank pump, with only the intermittent wind gusts as competition, the mechanical noise it made carried far and wide. Heads snapping in the direction of the wreck, the zombie in the red shirt, as well as two other female zombies loitering nearby, began a slow march across the drug store's trash-strewn parking lot.

Talking over the softly humming motor, Tara said to Shorty, "I got this. I'll fill the tanks for you. And know that my stepping in has nothing to do with size or reach. I'm just trying to conserve ammo." She gestured toward the approaching zombies. "Shocky needs to eat, right? So you may as well put down Red Shirt No Pants and the gang."

"Fair trade-off," Shorty said, racking a round into the chamber. "Be right back." *We all gotta know our strengths and weaknesses* was the mantra bouncing around his head as he trudged off toward the undead welcoming party.

Chapter 12

After leaving the pileup on the outskirts of Rio Rancho in their rearview, sailing had been smooth for a long stretch. It wasn't until Unser cut through several blocks bordered on both sides by densely packed one- and two-level homes that things got hairy for the two-vehicle convoy.

Paradise Hills did not live up to the name. Navigating the subdivision had been a stop-and-go shitshow. Packs of zombies wandered the streets. Dead bodies everywhere Riker looked. Drifts of trash had collected beside abandoned cars. The stoplights in town must have gone out unexpectedly during the mad rush to get out of Dodge. The lack of drivers following even the most basic rules of the road had left nearly every intersection blocked by gruesome scenes of automotive carnage, all of which took a bit of finesse and some driving on sidewalks to circumvent.

Coming out of Paradise Hills, the main drag became a sun-bleached four-lane that seemed to go on forever. It wasn't long before Riker's eyes were drawn to a flock of large birds riding the thermals a mile or so out. A quick glance at the nav screen told him the birds were orbiting over the Double Eagle II Airport's eastern perimeter. There had to be at least a dozen of them. Although they were little more than black dots at this point, it was obvious they were circling something of great interest to them.

Lia had spotted the birds, too. She was pointing in their direction and already bringing the binoculars to bear.

Riker slowed and consulted the rearview mirror. Saw Shorty in the Roamer. He was hunched over the wheel, one arm extended across the dash.

Shorty sees them, too.

"Buzzards?" Riker said.

"Yep. And there's a whole bunch of them," Lia confirmed.

"Can you see what's got their attention?" Riker asked.

She lowered the binoculars and shook her head. "Not from this angle. Line of sight isn't great. You're gonna have to get us closer."

"Not too close," Vern warned. "Until we know what we're looking at, best to keep a good standoff distance. If someone's set up shop at the airport, it's highly likely the entrance is being manned. Worst case scenario, we could be driving straight into an ambush."

Lia lowered the binoculars. "How do you explain the birds in the air?"

"They're taking a break between meals," quipped Vern.

It was one of the first times Riker had heard Vern go out of character. Lifting his foot off the gas, he said, "Understood. We go in slow and deliberate. Take our time and glass the place thoroughly before we commit fully."

***

Five minutes spent slow-rolling forward at less than half the posted limit got them to a distance where Riker thought they would be safe from incoming fire yet still be able to pick out individual details with the naked eye. Only problem with the chosen vantage point was the nearby strip mall. No telling what could be lurking inside the business concerns.

Double Eagle II, a general aviation facility located on the southern end of Albuquerque's west mesa, consisted of two runways surrounded by acres of tarmac. The perimeter fence appeared to be intact all the way around. Razor wire coiled atop the fence gleamed under the sun. Running away from the feeder road at divergent angles were a number of steel airplane hangars. The control tower, situated west of the hangars, rose a good thirty feet above their gently pitched roofs.

The tower was a utilitarian-looking cement structure. Copious amounts of tinted glass fronting the controllers' stations angled up to an octagonal steel roof. It looked as if the stairs were contained within the narrow base supporting the tower's nerve center. Based on the darkened windows and lack of movement anywhere within the perimeter fence, Riker came to the conclusion the place had been abandoned.

A pair of static Black Hawk helicopters sat in the shadow of a ten-wheeled fuel truck. Inside one open hangar, a half dozen fixed-wing aircraft could be seen. Riker guessed they were privately owned, likely Cessna or Beechcraft. Both runways and the vast majority of surrounding tarmac was a sea of empty concrete. No planes. No bowsers. And, most importantly, no zombies inside the fence.

Lia panned the binoculars slowly right to left. Suddenly she froze, her entire body gone rigid. "There's a tan pickup blocking the mouth of the airport feeder road. It has military markings. Words are stenciled on the door, but I can't read them from this angle. That's what the birds are interested in." She drew a deep breath. "Bad news, guys … the truck is surrounded by zombies. In places they're two and three deep. Can't see what's in the bed that they're attracted to."

Riker said, "There's got to be something they want. You can't see anything?"

She shook her head. "The truck's facing us. I can only see inside the cab. Looks empty to me."

Riker said, "The whereabouts of the Humvee is the sixty-four-thousand-dollar question."

"Maybe the pickup ran out of gas," Lia posited. "Then the driver crowded into the Humvee and they continued on."

"Not likely," said Riker. "We're not very far from the armory. Any driver worth his or her salt wouldn't leave the wire without a full tank."

Further ruling out Lia's explanation, Vern said, "Humvees are thirsty gals. Serving in the National Guard is not much different than doing time in the Big Green Machine. They both have protocols that must be followed. That being said, with all that's going on, I can't imagine them leaving the wire without bringing a couple of extra Jerry cans full of diesel."

Lia made a face. "Well, maybe the truck broke down and they abandoned it here."

Riker had a feeling she didn't want to hear the alternative. Didn't want to learn the rig could be where it was due to some level of malfeasance. He said, "Zombie apocalypse or not, you sign a vehicle out of the motor pool, you better damn well bring it back. If that truck is dead, they would have hooked it up to straps and towed it back to the armory."

"Lee's got a point," Vern said. "If you ask me, any way you slice it … *none* of this passes the smell test. Before we proceed, wouldn't it make sense to call and share our thoughts with the others? Get their input on the matter?"

Lia handed over the two-way. "Do you mind?"

"I got it," Vern said, taking the Motorola and thumbing the Talk key.

Wrists already sore from blasting zombies with the Shockwave, steering the Roamer at slow speed to slalom through wrecks and avoid the occasional roaming pack of zombies had started a dull ache radiating from the palm of Shorty's dominant hand. It was the same hand Lee had crushed against the Shockwave back at the armory. It didn't help matters that years of prepping bait, hauling nets, and captaining boats had left Shorty with an intermittent case of arthritis that always seemed to spring up at the most inopportune of times. Back in Florida, he'd always blamed the annoyance on the constantly changing barometric pressure. After spending a couple of weeks in high desert terrain, during which the temperature went through wild swings on a daily basis, he'd begun to think the random nature in which the flare-ups occurred was just old age fucking with him.

He wasn't holding a grudge against Riker. He did have to admit: more often than not, the man's gut instinct had served him well. Not only had he been right about not shooting first at the armory, but he had also been correct in the assumption the high-centered Dodge pickup was a "ranch rig." Finding nearly a hundred gallons of diesel in the tanks had Shorty's mood pendulum momentarily paused on the optimistic side of its swing. Not having to dip into the half dozen cans of backup fuel he'd brought along relieved him of a lot of pressure. The Roamer was a thirsty beast—the closest thing to Miss Abigail he could imagine captaining on land. The last thing he wanted was to have to swap her for a more fuel-efficient rig. He'd only agreed to bring her on this half-assed journey west because Lia needed the HAM setup. That the young woman was damn easy on the eyes helped bolster her case. In a way, she kind of reminded Shorty of a younger version of his late wife, Abigail. Which was both a blessing and a curse.

Reminiscing about how cancer had stolen her from him way too early had the propensity to send him spiraling into a funk that could last hours. So to take his mind off all he'd lost, he followed up with Steve-O on something the man had blurted out earlier, at the armory gate, just prior to the sound of Littlewolf racking a round into the shotgun of hers.

At the time, Shorty had been dying to probe Steve-O for more information about his first-ever boob sighting.

"So, Steve-O, exactly when and where did you see the boobs?" Shorty asked. "I want specifics. Whose, where, and when." He paused, a half-smile forming. He had a hunch whose boobs were exhibits A and B; he just wanted confirmation. "And FYI … zombie boobs *do… not… count.*" He glanced at the rearview and caught Tara staring daggers at him. *Mission accomplished.* If he weren't driving such a big vehicle, he would have taken his hands off the wheel and made a show of rubbing them together. *This is going to be good,* he thought as he awaited Steve-O's response.

Tara placed a hand on Steve-O's shoulder, causing him to start. "Do *not* answer him," she ordered. "He's just trying to stir the pot."

Shorty said nothing. His eyes were locked on the Shelby as it wove through yet another cluster of stalled-out vehicles. It wasn't until the pickup exited a left-hand sweeper and came to a full stop in the middle of the road that Shorty replied to Tara. "I'm the best shit-stirrer this side of the Rockies."

Looking beyond the Shelby, he reacquired the birds he'd spotted a mile or so back. They were circling over a break in the four-lane where a secondary road shot off west toward a two-strip airport. It was basically the same layout as every other general aviation airport he'd seen. The southbound ribbon of gray asphalt running past the eastern perimeter was surrounded on three sides by miles of wide-open desert.

Directly below the buzzards and completely surrounded by zombies was a desert-tan pickup. The bulbous rear fenders and rounded hood led Shorty to believe he was looking at Littlewolf's missing GMC. As the Roamer came to a complete stop a couple of yards shy of the Shelby, Steve-O turned in his seat and addressed the elephant in the cab. Puffing out his chest, he said, "I'm a grown-ass man, Tara. Besides, you shouldn't be embarrassed that I saw your boobs. They are very nice ones." He paused. Tara's jaw was open, no words coming out. "Just be happy it was me and not Vern or Shorty. Me and you have an ongoing relationship. You're still getting to know *them*."

Shorty wanted to laugh. Instead, he looked out his window and performed a drum solo on the wheel. Bad idea. Because it sent bolts of pain up his right arm. He had asked Riker earlier for something for the pain but had forgotten to follow through.

Collecting her jaw off the floorboard, Tara said, "I was wearing a bra. I already told you, Steve-O … that what you saw yesterday was *side boob*. There's a big difference between *full boob* and what you saw."

Shorty took his eyes off the Shelby long enough to gauge Steve-O's reaction to Tara's revelation. The man's face was poker-table ready. No smile. No raised eyebrows. Serious as a heart attack. Steve-O was convinced he saw what he saw. Shorty said, "Side boob can be elevated to full boob on one condition." He looked at Steve-O. "Did you see any nipple?"

Steve-O nodded. "It was pushing up on the material."

Tara shook her head. "It was cold in the shade. Seeing me in my bra is no different than when you saw me in my bathing suit at Villa Jasmine."

Steve-O fixed Shorty with an earnest look. "Tara told me she's not a virgin."

Shorty's foot slipped off the brake pedal, causing the Roamer to lurch and roll toward the trailer. Getting his foot back on the pedal, he said, "And here I thought she was saving herself for Mr. Right." He blew on his nails. Feigned buffing them on his shirt. "Since you're not awaiting your *before anyone else* … I just so happen to be available."

The Motorola suddenly came to life in the center console, its shrill warble mercifully ending the conversation before any more harm could come of it. It was Vern. He said, "We've got buzzards up ahead. There's also a pickup. It's military. Could very well be our lost patrol."

Shorty snatched up the Motorola. "I saw them. Shouldn't we be getting on down there? Might be someone hurt who could benefit from your particular set of skills." It took all of his willpower to not share the lurid details of the previous conversation across the airwaves. Discretion winning out over getting a few laughs, he said, "Anything moving down there?"

"Just biters and buzzards," Vern replied.

Tara leaned over the seatback and plucked Shorty's Bushnell binoculars off the seat.

"Want something done right..." She glassed the distant scene, right to left, then lowered the field glasses. "The pickup is definitely a GMC. The markings suggest it's military. Question is: Where's the Humvee?"

Shorty relayed Tara's findings over the radio. Finished, he said, "Let's charge down there and flush them out," and opened the channel.

Immediately Riker's voice emanated from the Motorola's tiny speaker. "Let's give it a couple of minutes. If anyone is watching, inaction on our part is sure to try their patience."

Tara took the radio from Shorty. Thumbing the Talk button, she said, "I think you're both going about this the wrong way." She looked to Steve-O. "I say we let Steve-O deploy his drone. Have him do an aerial recon of the airport. If anyone's hiding, it might flush them out into the open. At the very least," she added, "we can get a look at whatever's in the pickup bed." She opened the channel.

"Brains *and* beauty," Shorty cooed. "The whole package." He rubbed his hands together.

Riker's voice leapt from the two-way's speaker. "What's Steve-O have to say?"

Shorty regarded Steve-O. "Are we within range of the pickup?"

"Yeppers."

"Can your drone reach the far side of the airport?"

"No problem."

Shorty nodded to Tara.

Radio already poised by her mouth, she said, "He's game. We'll get started setting it up."

In the Shelby, Riker and Lia exchanged glances. She said, "Good a time as any to stretch a leg and use the toilet in Shorty's rig."

Vern chuckled. "Stretch *a* leg. Good one. I'm happy to see you're taking the loss of your leg in *stride*." He grinned at his own joke.

Riker said, "What she's doing is practicing Rule 62."

Now it was Vern and Lia exchanging glances. Neither of them commented.

"Rule 62 is don't take yourself too damn seriously," Riker explained, shoving open his door and pocketing the Shelby's fob. "Practicing that and relying on a good deal of humor has helped me to keep most of my demons at bay. Adhering to the Golden Rule is also pretty damn beneficial."

"Sage advice," Vern put in. "Especially the do unto others component."

Riker said nothing. He was busy checking his surroundings. Although the Shelby was stopped on an elevated stretch of road with nothing but desert on both sides, he still reminded Lia to do the same.

Turning around in her seat, she said, "Were you practicing those the time you screwed the Harlans out of their bought and paid for slot on Shorty's ferry?"

Vern had been listening intently. As he opened his door and was making a mental note to remember that his traveling companion was far from an angel, the man in question said, "Desperate times called for a desperate measure."

Vern knew exactly what the man meant. He'd faced the same dilemma in the jungles of Vietnam. Making triage decisions on the fly was never easy. To this day, he was still haunted by the faces of the men he'd had to ignore in order to save others who weren't actively holding in their guts or screaming for their mother as their lifeblood pulsed from a severed carotid. He'd been put in that unenviable position during that meat grinder of a war more times than he cared to remember.

"You coming, Vern?" It was Riker. He was holding open the door and staring strangely. "Lost you for a moment. You OK?"

"Just the last MRE coming back to haunt me," Vern lied. "Damn indigestion. You have any antacids in that drug baggie of yours?"

Riker waited for the older man to join him on the road, then closed the door. "Sure do," he said. "That reminds me." He grimaced. "Shorty had asked me for Ibuprofen for his arthritis, and I forgot all about it."

"You mean for his crushed fingers?" Vern said. "You had a vice grip on that gun of his."

Riker shook his head and started off for the Roamer. "Sometimes I don't know my own strength."

Chapter 13

Steve-O had the drone out of its case and prepped to fly before everyone had finished taking turns using the Roamer's cramped lavatory.

Riker had found a cactus off the side of the road and relieved himself behind it. Getting stuck in the tiny enclosure in back of the Roamer wasn't something he wanted to chance—especially knowing that Shorty had been the first to conclude his business in there. Riker was zipping his fly when the high-pitched whine of the quadcopter's four engines broke the still.

Pausing on the dashed yellow line, he turned his attention to the half-mile or so of road they'd just traveled. The nearby bend was clear. As was the surrounding desert. But down the straightaway spooling out behind the Roamer, maybe a half-mile back, where a strip mall and row of fast-food joints faced off across the two-lane, he saw movement. He didn't need binoculars to conclude that the small crowd entering the road was made up of zombies. Their stilted gait was the first tell. The tattered clothing, matted hair, and gaunt, talc-white visages confirmed his first impression. So far, none of the two dozen or so living corpses were breaking ranks and charging him. No Bolts was a good thing. No Bolts meant he had a few minutes, maybe even ten if they were especially road-worn specimens, before anything needed to be done about them. That should give Steve-O plenty of time to do his thing. However, should one or more of the rotting flock prove to be fast movers and break from the pack, he and his companions would be caught between the proverbial rock and a hard place.

Riker waved his arms and jumped up and down, the latter action starting a new wave of pain shooting from his healing wound. He watched the shamblers for a few more seconds. Confident there were no Bolts present, he went to rejoin the others. By the time he had returned to the Roamer, whose hood had been used to launch the drone, everyone but Shorty was crowded around the open passenger door and watching Steve-O manipulate the controls.

Lia welcomed Riker back and nodded at Steve-O. Peering over the tops of Tara and Lia's heads, Riker saw that his friend had adopted his usual flight posture: slumped down in the seat, stocking feet on the dash, remote clutched in a two-handed grip and resting against his Wrangler-clad thighs. With the Stetson pulled down low, its brim casting much-needed shade on the wide color screen, Steve-O was in the zone, all of his attention focused on the moving color image being captured by the drone's gimbal-mounted camera.

Riker watched the drone as it zipped away, the noise of its four hard-working electric motors sounding like a swarm of pissed-off hornets. He tracked it all the way to the airport entrance. Three long minutes. Once on station, to the naked eye, the drone was a speck about the size of the vultures orbiting the truck.

A quick glance down the road told Riker the zombies were still coming but had only made it a third of the way to the parked vehicles.

"We've got biters heading our way," he warned.

From the driver's seat in the Roamer, Shorty said, "I got eyes on them." He leaned out the window, the tip of his crooked nose nearly touching the side mirror. His lips moved as he counted the bobbing heads. "Looks like we got the beginnings of a herd coming at us, Steve-O. Better make your recon a quick one."

"Excuse me," Riker said to Lia, placing a hand on her shoulder as he hauled himself onto the Roamer's running board where he'd be out of everyone's way. Ducking his head to clear the camper's overhanging front sleeping loft afforded him a bird's-eye view of the remote control's color screen. He saw the pickup straightaway. It was very small, taking up a tiny fraction of the center of the screen. The tan paint contrasted greatly against the airport feeder road's coal-black surface.

Suddenly a feathered wing swooped by the camera lens. It was nearly as dark as the blacktop the pickup sat upon. For a split second, the screen went completely dark. No sooner had the vulture winged off and the pickup was snapping back into focus than a second bird was invading the drone's airspace. It circled the drone twice before losing interest and rejoining the rest of the flock.

Riker said, "Those birds aren't going to take down my drone, are they?" *That would be a huge loss*, he thought. He'd purchased the thing on a whim over the Internet. Having inherited several million dollars simultaneous to the Romero outbreaks, he'd let his hair down and engaged in an extended late-night spending spree. Amazingly, the goods had been delivered as promised and were awaiting his arrival at Trinity House. But that wasn't all that was waiting for them. A recent prison parolee had wormed his way into Rose's social circle and had shown up uninvited. Riker still occasionally awoke in a cold sweat from nightmares in which Raul was the victor of the brief gun battle that took place in Trinity's courtyard. The same event that had left Benny with a minor gunshot wound that had mostly healed.

"Drop the drone below the birds," Riker urged.

Tara shot a glare over her shoulder. "Leave the man alone, Lee."

Lia also jumped to Steve-O's defense. "How would you feel if someone was hovering over your shoulder and being a backseat pilot?"

Shorty piled on, saying, "He needs to concentrate, Lee."

Taking it all in stride, Steve-O said, "I'm just trying to see where the wind is coming from." He engaged the auto-hover function and released the twin joysticks. "Look, *Dad* … no hands." He glanced up at Riker, who was clearly doing all he could to refrain from snatching up the remote control and taking over.

Lia said, "Looks like you have calm winds aloft, Steve-O." Her vernacular struck Riker as something a pilot's kid might say. She craned and added, "The truck looks like a Hot Wheel from that altitude. Can you zoom in?"

"Not enough to make a difference," responded Steve-O. "This drone isn't a top-of-the-line model. There's no audio, either. Lee was pinching pennies."

"*Jeeeesh* … Steve-O. Cut me some slack," Riker shot back. "I *just* came into money. You come from nothing, doesn't matter how many commas are on your bank statement … it's very easy to remain frugal."

"Won't ever be receiving another bank statement," Vern noted. He had squeezed between the women and found a spot with a clear view of the monitor. "The Wall Street thieves and big-bankster-class bastards biting the dust is probably one of the only good things to come of this calamity."

"Don't forget the politicians," Shorty called. "I'm sure they left as bad a taste in the zombies' mouths as they did mine." He was the only one to laugh at his attempt at humor.

Steve-O regained control of the drone and was starting it on a slow descent toward the pickup. Having lost interest in the noisy mechanical interloper, the vultures continued carving lazy circles over the target.

"What's that in the bed?" Lia asked.

"Bodies," said Vern grimly. "I count four. All of 'em are men."

"They're stripped down to their boxers," Tara said, nose crinkling. "Why would someone take the time to do that?"

"Same reason whoever killed them took the Humvee," Vern replied.

Lia looked a question at him.

Tara beat Vern to the punch. "The fuckers are going to wear the uniforms and pretend to be National Guard soldiers."

Vern nodded. "First thing that came to my mind. With the uniform comes a certain *gravitas*. Put that together with the Humvee and you've got yourself a pretty believable roadblock."

"Bastards," said Riker. "And the people who are still struggling to survive will likely fall for it. Everyone's gotta be grasping for straws by now. Longing for a modicum of order amidst all this chaos. Exactly what we were talking about back at Trinity."

As the truck bed and pale bodies laid out in it grew larger on the screen, Riker saw that three of the men were mid-twenties to early thirties. The fourth was about his age: a couple of years shy of forty. They were all fit and had fresh high-and-tight haircuts. Around each of their necks was a chain and pair of dog tags. Crimson gunshot wounds trailing thin fingers of blood dotted the bodies. One of the younger soldiers had taken a round or two to the face. There was no identifiable exit wound, the brains and blood having instead leaked out of the gaping fleshy chasm where the left eye and temple should have been. The load bed was awash in blood. As Riker looked on, one of the vultures swooped down fast, flaring its wings only when it was a dozen feet above the corpses. Falling slower now, maybe five feet above the dead soldiers and almost within reach of the zombies' kneading fingers, the bird tucked its wings tight to its body and crash-landed on the older soldier's bare chest.

With straining fingers ruffling the dark feathers on one outstretched wing, the bird dipped its beak into a puckered gunshot wound, shook its head violently, then reared back, a jiggling morsel trapped in its bloody beak. Ignoring the threats all around, the bird tipped its head back and swallowed the hunk of flesh whole.

Apparently, that was enough risk-taking for the vulture. For no sooner had the opportunist landed and taken its prize than it was screeching and flapping its wings, clawing its way airborne, twisting its body and snapping away at the many threats. A cloud of drifting feathers was all the zombies got for their efforts as the carrion feeder narrowly escaped the tightening noose of cold dead hands.

As the faint calls of the vulture fighting for its life reached Riker's ears, on the screen he watched the corpse the bird had launched from suddenly come to life. Eyes blue as a mountain lake staring skyward, mouth frozen in a silent O, the soldier's arms scythed the very air the bird had just vacated.

"That one's not dead," Lia blurted. "We have to help him."

"He sure looks dead," replied Steve-O.

"Even with my old eyes I can see that *that* is not a zombie stare," noted Vern. "If we're going to uphold our promise to the major, we better get to him before the biters do."

Shorty said, "Put your drone into a hover. Don't move it until I tell you to."

"Roger, roger," replied Steve-O. He had already stabbed the Auto Hover button and was back to sitting upright in his seat.

"Seatbelt," Shorty ordered.

As Riker watched Steve-O doing as he was told, he said to Shorty, "What are you going to do?"

Shorty matched Riker's gaze through the open window. "It's my turn to shine. *I* have a plan to take care of those things. *You* get to follow my lead this time."

Riker protested, saying, "Your rig isn't the best handling thing on the road."

"You're pulling a trailer loaded with bright blue drums. Some of them are full of *my* diesel. You catch a stray round and you're a rolling Roman candle," Shorty pointed out. "Any way you slice it, I can get there before you." He looked at Vern and hooked a thumb over his shoulder. "Get in, Doc. Your specific set of skills is going to be needed. You'll find a med kit under the seat." Shorty tipped his cap and smiled at Riker. "Trust me, friend … I got this."

Without a word, Vern edged past Riker. Swinging his MP5 around front of him, he boarded the Roamer and settled into the seat behind the driver.

Tara climbed aboard and buckled in behind Steve-O. "Consider the hatchet buried," she said to her brother through the open window. The Roamer's motor revved. Regarding Lia, Tara said, "Looks like you're stuck riding solo with Lee. You two better jump in before the zombies beat you to it." As Tara was finishing her sentence, the Roamer began rolling down the slight decline, quickly picking up speed as Shorty matted the gas pedal.

Lia and Riker were left standing on the road amidst a rising cloud of diesel exhaust.

Tara hadn't been kidding; the clutch of zombies had drawn to within a few yards of the Shelby and, though none were Bolts, seemed to have found second gear.

In the Roamer, fumbling to get ahold of his shoulder belt, Shorty cried, "Grab your *oh shit* handles." Already the overlanding rig was gaining speed. As it neared the posted limit, a strong wind gust hit it broadside, causing it to rock like a ship at sea. Buckling his seatbelt with one hand, the other gripping the wheel white-knuckle tight, Shorty shared his hastily concocted plan with his traveling companions. By the time he had finished talking, the Roamer was coming to the bottom of the runout.

Steve-O nodded that he understood. Taking hold of the remote's twin joysticks, he turned his attention back to the image on the screen. Chewing his lip, he broke the drone from its hover and dove it toward the knot of zombies nearest the National Guard pickup's tailgate.

Riker had boarded the Shelby a couple of seconds behind Lia. He was getting the motor started when the first of the zombies appeared outside his window. Pale palms slapped the glass. The squeaking of clammy dermis dragging the smooth surface was nearly as disconcerting as the keening of the fingernails gouging the Shelby's flanks.

Lia had just buckled in when the first of the shamblers reached her door. Earlier, when Riker had made the unexpected stop here and she had joined him and the others on the road outside the Roamer, she had inadvertently left her window part of the way down. Now, taking full advantage of the six-inch gap, one of the zombies thrust its hands into the cab.

Knocked off her head by the clumsy attack, Lia's ball cap landed on her lap. The zombie's fingers plunged into her blonde hair, the cracked fingernails carving deep furrows into her scalp.

"Get us out of here, Lee," she gasped, blood already trickling from the wounds. Leaning hard over the center console, she felt the thing's forearm brush her cheek. The skin was ice-cold and rubber-like. The zombie's vacant, shark-like eyes locked with hers. Feeling a chill magnitudes colder than the thing's skin race up her spine, she fumbled blindly for the window controls.

Shifting to drive and tromping the pedal, Riker bellowed, "*Do not* run the window up! You'll just trap its arms inside the cab and bring it along for the ride."

As the Shelby hit the decline, the speedometer needle rushing past ten miles per hour, the rest of the zombies fell away. The pickup's forward momentum, combined with gravity's pull, yanked the lone attacker off its feet. As the zombie's arms slithered from the cab, inexplicably the tips of all eight fingers hooked over the pane of tempered glass.

"Shit, shit, shit," Lia cried. With the zombie's sneering face mashed against her window and its shoeless feet being pummeled by the road rushing beneath them, she scooped her aluminum beverage canister from the center cup holder. As she cocked her arm, preparing to bash the fingers with the bottom of the half-full canister, she felt Riker's warm fingers encircling her wrist.

"You trying to break my window?" he asked. Feeling Lia's arm relax, he let go and urged her to pry the fingers away from the glass. Tapping his head with one finger, he said, "Work smarter, not harder."

Lia shook her head hard side to side.

"You want to ride the rest of the way with no glass in your window?"

Again Lia shook her head. Finally, she said, "OK, OK. I'll do it." She grimaced as she worked up the courage to touch the fingers. So far, she'd come into contact with plenty of corpses. Helped remove scores from the turnaround at Trinity. She'd even stabbed a living, breathing person and then watched them bleed out. The metallic stench of the woman's blood as it gushed from her neck would always haunt Lia. The blood had been hot and sticky and had turned black as it soaked into the little sedan's cream-colored front seat.

The zombie that had rent a mouthful of flesh out of Lia's right calf, thus creating the need to amputate the leg before the virus could invade her bloodstream, had wrapped its clammy hands around her bare ankle just prior to getting its teeth into her. Although her leg was gone now, on occasion she could still feel those cold fingers crushing down on her flesh.

The one hurdle Lia had yet to clear since the dead began to walk was her actually being the one to initiate the touching. She had always tried to stay as far away from the things as possible. It just didn't compute how a human body with no respiration or pulse could be mobile. That they consumed human flesh when they didn't really need it to survive really baffled her. If she was to pry the zombie's thick, sausage-like fingers from the glass, she needed to find a way to overcome her squeamishness. And find it fast.

Deciding to make a game of the morbid task, she made a pincer with her thumb and pointer, clamped down on the tip of the zombie's pointer finger, and in her head sang, *This little piggy went to market.*

The skin was frigid, the blood-encrusted fingernail cracked all the way down the center. Yellow pus leaked from the nailbed as the finger went straight and popped free from the glass.

Lia threw a hard shudder and immediately went to work on the middle finger. Absurd as the first verse sounded inside her head, in a high falsetto, she sang the next verse out loud.

"This little piggy stayed home," she crooned, trying hard to not make eye contact with the beast outside her window.

The distraction of trying to remember the words of each new verse as she sang them took the power from the fact she was actually touching one of the monsters that had haunted her since she'd come face to face with that first one in the aisle of the darkened supermarket in Santa Fe.

She didn't get to sing the *Wee wee wee all the way home* verse. Because the second she pried the little piggy deprived of its roast beef from the window, all at once the persistent creature's left hand fell from view, and all four fingers on the other hand let go of the wildly flexing pane of glass.

Looking a lot like a crash test dummy ejected from a rapidly decelerating vehicle, the limp form hit the road at thirty miles an hour and cartwheeled bonelessly next to Lia's window. At first, the zombie was just a blur of flailing arms and legs. After the third full revolution, all inertia spent, it folded in two and ground to a halt, face down and ass up on the centerline, maybe a hundred yards from the bottom of the runout.

No way it's getting back up after that, thought Lia. As she continued to watch the prostrate form grow smaller in her wing mirror, she was proven wrong. To her horror, the zombie raised its head and pushed itself up off the road. The moment the zombie's weight was distributed over both feet, it crumbled back to the asphalt. Undefeated, the zombie resumed its pursuit of the retreating vehicles, clawing hand over hand, its ruined legs leaving bloody trails parallel to the dashed yellow centerline.

Eyes locked on the Roamer, Riker said, "I hope Shorty knows what he's doing. If not, and he knocks his rig out of commission, we're going to have to get that Guard pickup running."

Lia said nothing as she ran her window up. Remaining tightlipped, she peeled off her tee shirt. Sitting there in just a sports bra and jeans, she wet the fabric with water from the canister and went to work cleaning the blood off her face.

Chapter 14

"Get the rotten bastards to the yellow line and keep them there," Shorty instructed.

"I shall do my best," Steve-O promised, the remote for the drone wedged firmly between his upthrust knees.

On the remote's screen, the zombies were filing away from the Guard pickup. In the pickup's bed, once again all four Guardsmen were unmoving. The man who had suddenly come to and taken a swipe at the buzzard was again wedged between the others, eyes closed and looking no different than he had when the carrion feeder had first alit on him. From the sharp viewing angle picked up by the moving drone, there was no telling whether the soldier was playing possum, was unconscious, or had finally expired from the gunshot wounds to his chest. The same was true for the other three Guardsmen. Only way to tell who was alive and who was truly dead was to remove the zombies from the equation and have Vern assess the situation.

Working the twin joysticks, all of his attention focused on the action taking place on the display, Steve-O piloted the drone away from the pickup. Moving in lockstep, the zombies followed the drone onto the main road, where Steve-O hovered the noisy craft a couple of yards above the dozen pair of eyes locked onto it. Only when the entire pack was off the feeder road and gathered near the yellow centerline—arms outstretched, fingers straining to get ahold of the drone—did Steve-O start it moving slowly north, on a collision course with the speeding Roamer.

Propelled by the urge to hunt embedded deep in the reptile part of its brain, the zombie nearest to the drone dropped its arms level to the road and gave chase.

"Fish on," Shorty said. Steve-O had succeeded in drawing the zombies into a ragged line. Although they were close together, they weren't quite *nuts to butts* like Shorty wanted them to be. It would have to do. Flicking his eyes to the speedometer, he saw the needle closing on sixty miles per hour. With maybe a quarter mile separating the Roamer from the zombies, and with the creatures staring straight at the behemoth bearing down on them, Shorty eased up on the pedal and firmed his grip on the wheel.

"You sure you want to do this?" Vern asked.

Sinking low in her seat, Tara said, "One of those things goes over the hood and through this windshield … I'm going to go *Big Momma* on you."

Shorty recognized Tara's statement as a threat, but the movie reference was lost on him. Just seconds from impact, he said, "I got this. They're going *under* my rig." The way he answered, voice oozing with confidence, was hardly convincing. Tara remembered the man lying straight to the elder Harlan's face. Telling the older man to wait with his pickup on the boat ramp in order to allow her brother to load his pickup onto the ferry first. The explanation having to do with proper weight distribution had been as convincing then as Shorty's *I got this* proclamation.

Vern said, "You pop a tire, changing the thing is going to be quite the undertaking."

Shorty shook his head. "Not gonna happen. The tires are run-flats."

A beat later, accompanied by a loud bang, the first of the zombies met the modified F-550's massive grille guard. The halo of pink erupting around the zombie's head rose and spread faster than the eye could track. As the creature was sucked underneath the Roamer, brain matter and teeth and splintered bone hammered the windshield hard, like a sheet of driving rain. The flat affect dominating the zombie's features prior to impact remained unchanged through the entire event. Even as all of the bones in its outstretched arms were being pulverized by several tons of unstoppable Detroit iron, those dead eyes had remained fixed on the meat behind the windshield.

As Shorty lifted his foot from the accelerator and stabbed at the brake pedal, he triggered the wipers and soaked the windshield with a liberal spritz of cleaner. A big mistake, he quickly decided. While the pinkish-gray film being spread across the windshield by the wiper blades spared all of them from seeing the damage the grille guard had wrought on the remaining zombies, for them to continue on, someone was going to have to scrape a porthole in the gore.

After listening to nearly a dozen more gong-like bangs fill the cab and suffering through the wet pops of skulls being flattened underneath the Roamer's nearly impenetrable tires, Shorty belted out a rebel yell.

Bringing the Roamer to a complete stop a few yards beyond the feeder road, Shorty set the emergency brake and shut off the motor. After enduring the prolonged cacophony of the undead caroming off the Roamer's undercarriage, the silence inside the cab was deafening.

Shorty glanced at Steve-O, who was sitting up straight, the remote on the seat between them. "I must have closed my eyes for a split second after the first one's head exploded," Shorty explained. "I saw the drone … then I didn't. Please tell me I didn't run the thing over. Lee will never let me live it down."

Tara said, "I *did* close my damn eyes, you crazy fool. I hope you did run Lee's drone over. Maybe then he'll break your neck. Lord knows I want to."

"If it wasn't for me and my Abigail, you would still be south of the Mason Dixon Line."

Gaze bouncing between the pair, Vern chose to remain silent.

During Tara and Shorty's back and forth, Steve-O had donned and adjusted his Stetson. Delivered with a wink to both parties, he said, "I got Lee's drone to safety." He gestured at the road beside the Roamer.

Looking past the man, Shorty spotted the drone. It was nestled between a pair of cactuses, the high sun glinting off the white fuselage.

First aid kit in one hand, MP5 in the other, Vern opened his door and slithered from the cab.

Steve-O grabbed up the Mule, stuck one arm through the straps, and twisted the valve to the halfway point.

"I'll go with you," said Tara. "Someone needs to watch your back while you work."

Steve-O shook his head. "You should help Vern." Wand in hand, he climbed from the cab.

Grumbling about not wanting to touch another corpse for as long as she lived, Tara followed Steve-O out of the Roamer and closed the door behind them.

Throwing the locks, Shorty drove down his window and stuck his head out. Couldn't miss the trail of destruction. Every couple of yards a crumpled body lay on the road. A few of the zombies were unmoving. The majority, drawn by the prospect of a meal of warm flesh, were struggling to rise and resume their pursuit.

Stretched out on the centerline, maybe ten or fifteen yards beyond the feeder road entrance, the last zombie to be mowed down by the Roamer was emitting a low growl. Carried on the southerly breeze, the guttural rasp stood the hairs on Shorty's neck to attention. It, too, was still hungering for flesh. One hand slapped the concrete continuously as the claw-like fingers scrabbled for a hold. The zombie's torso had ruptured like a ripe fig. The contents of the now hollow body cavity were a glistening slurry of guts and organs painting the road for yards in the crawler's wake. The largest piece, a wedge-shaped hunk of meat dark as obsidian, had come to rest on the shoulder where blacktop met dusty gravel.

Somebody's missing a perfectly good liver, thought Shorty as he turned his attention to the approaching Shelby. As he looked on, Riker drifted the slow-moving vehicle left of the centerline. To avoid the twisted corpses and zombies struggling to stand, Riker had to ride the pickup's left-side tires onto the shoulder. As the trailer followed suit, its wheels kicking up a rooster tail of fine dust, Steve-O was fast approaching the first of the fallen monsters.

By the time the Shelby was sliding in next to the Roamer, Steve-O was hard at work, the *pfft-thwak* of the Mule barely audible over the rumbling V8.

Making eye contact with Lia, Shorty mouthed, "Roll down your window."

A few seconds passed before Lia complied. During the short pause, she had checked her wing mirror and then lifted herself off her seat and craned to inspect the yard-wide sliver of road between the two vehicles.

As the Shelby's window disappeared into the channel, Shorty shot Lia and Riker an *I told you so* look. Brows lifted, he said, "Nary a scratch on the old gal."

Riker leaned forward. Seatbelt biting into his shoulder, he rested his forearms on the steering wheel. "You need to look at your old gal's backside. That vantage tells a different story. I'm just saying … once you get done scouring your windshield clean, you're going to have your hands full with the *out of sight* stuff."

"Plenty of windshield cleaner in the tank." Shorty shrugged. "As for whatever is stuck underneath Marge, I'll let the road work it loose."

Flashing Shorty a wan smile, Lia said, "I would have just driven up beside them and put bullets in each of their heads from the safety of the cab."

Indicating Lia's bloody compress, Shorty said, "Looks like the cab ain't so safe," and shifted his gaze to the guard pickup, where Vern was approaching the tailgate, first aid kit in one hand, MP5 held loosely in the other. Glock drawn and in a low-ready position, Tara was on the man's six and flanking the pickup from the left.

Lia examined the bloody shirt. Looking sheepish, she regarded Shorty. "It was an oversight on my part," she explained. "Just a few minor scratches, that's all."

"Should have seen the other guy," Riker added. "He didn't get back up."

Locking eyes with Lia, Shorty said, "While I'm not entirely discounting your strategy, gunfire does carry for miles and miles out here. If the folks who did this are within earshot, wouldn't be wise to alert them to our presence."

"Man has a point," Riker said. Tilt to his head, he invited her to come along with him.

She inspected the compress. It was totally saturated and heavy in her hand. As a fresh rivulet traced a line down her forehead, she grimaced and shook her head. "I'm one-handed and one-legged. I'd just be in the way."

He fished the first aid kit from the door pocket. Moving a strand of hair from her eyes, he said, "Let's get you cleaned up."

She shook her head. "No us about it. You go on. I'm a big girl." She flipped down the visor and turned on the vanity light. Probing the wound, she said, "It's not as bad as it looks."

"Understood." While his first instinct was to stay and help her clean and properly dress the wound, he had to respect her desire to be self-sufficient. He showed her the Motorola, then placed it in her hand. "Put your two eyes to work. See something, say something. I'll be listening."

Boot heels clicking on sun-warmed blacktop, Steve-O charted a course through puddles of gore, stopping only when he was within arm's reach of what he gauged to be the most mobile of the zombies mowed down by the EarthRoamer. It was a male, maybe forty years old. The jagged ends of shattered bones jutted through bloodless holes in its left forearm. Tread marks were evident against the pale skin of its crushed left hand. The other arm was outstretched, the fingers quivering as they made contact with the tip of Steve-O's boot.

The foot on one leg was facing the opposite direction to normal. Both bones of the other leg were broken in multiple places. When the zombie tried to push itself up with its one good arm, the grossly misshapen leg jiggled like an overcooked noodle.

The zombie looked as if it had been in a fight with Andre the Giant and had lost. In a way, it had. Like the zombies in the crushed import, this one was hard to look at up close.

Pressing the Mule's deadly end hard to the zombie's road-rashed forehead, Steve-O said, "I'm sorry," and caressed the trigger. The resulting *pfft-thwak* was swallowed up by a wind gust. The hollow thunk of the zombie's skull impacting the unforgiving road was not.

Steve-O didn't seem to notice. He was on a mission. One down, many more to go.

"Spent casings everywhere," noted Vern as he bent down and plucked a shiny piece of brass off the road. After turning the item over and inspecting the indented primer, he chucked it away in disgust. "Seven sixty-two by thirty-nine millimeter. I'd bet the house the ambushers were using Kalashnikovs."

Tara lowered her Glock to keep from flagging Vern. Crabbing to her left, she said, "You mean AK-47s, right?"

"One and the same," Vern said. "Designed by Mikhail Kalashnikov in the late forties and adopted by the Soviet army shortly after World War Two. They're pretty much indestructible. They run dirty. Cold weather, jungle moisture, desert heat … doesn't matter. The AK is the Timex of automatic rifles—it takes a licking and keeps on ticking. They're so reliable they were favored by the Viet Cong over captured M-16s. Hell, I've been on the receiving end of one of the chattering lead slingers more times than I care to count." He slowed his gait and stared off into the distance. "Seen too many young G.I.s chewed up by them." His gaze settled on the pickup. "The most widely used battle rifle ever made. Armies and terrorist organizations the world over swear by them." Correcting himself, he said, "Well … they used to. Now it appears they're favored by bandits roaming America's highways." He was back to walking, his pace brisk. He stepped onto the feeder road, eyes downcast, head on a swivel, looking for any other clues as to what had befallen the National Guard patrol.

Tara said, "The war really messed you up, didn't it?" As soon as the question crossed her lips, she regretted asking it. *Who was she to judge a man she'd known for so short a time?* Maybe he wasn't like the prototypical Vietnam vet portrayed on television and in the movies. He was no Rambo, that was for sure. He had said so himself one night after dinner. He was a healer, he had declared, not a killer. He'd even divulged that he had wanted to be a doctor. Was signed up for medical school and preparing to move into student housing when his draft number was drawn.

Loath to use a student deferment to get out of his duty to serve his country, he shelved his dreams and answered the call.

Vern didn't answer Tara's question. Either her words had been drowned out by the wind, or he had purposefully ignored them. *In one ear and out the other* was what Tara's late mother called the tactic. Tara had been guilty of doing the same thing—most recently at the coffee kiosk in the lobby of the university in Middletown. Back then, it was the small talk that irked her. Well-to-do legacy students with no money worries asking her: *Are you here on scholarship? Did you get a Pell Grant? Do they give you a break in tuition for making coffee?* She'd pretended not to hear them. A couple of bursts with the steam wand usually sent them on their way, none the wiser that, though her family had had the means, she was the one paying for her education. It was the last lesson in self-sufficiency her late father had taught her. Though she was proud of the accomplishment, the degree in interior design was not especially useful to her.

She had been scratching by on tips and income from a couple of different jobs when her mother had passed from cancer. As executor of the estate, she knew there was an inheritance of an unknown sum coming her way. Nevertheless, life hadn't improved much by the time Lee had come back into the picture. Together they had learned, through the sale of their late father's many patents, the inheritance had made them instant multimillionaires. Unfortunately, that knowledge had come *after* the zombie apocalypse. It was like winning the Powerball and losing the ticket. Although she'd never admit it to Vern or Shorty, saying she was still bitter about the cards she and Lee had been dealt would be a vast understatement.

Once Vern was within spitting distance of the Guard pickup, he slowed his pace and regarded Tara. "Did you say something?"

"Nope," she lied. "Probably just the wind." While it was true the wind was picking up, she was grateful for the excuse to keep from having to repeat her probing question.

The pair were coming at the pickup from the driver's side, Tara a couple of yards behind Vern, when a much stronger wind gust hit them broadside.

The sudden maelstrom whipped the distant windsock into a frenzy and birthed tiny dust devils that raced across the tarmac. Closer in, it sent the shell casings skittering down the road and started the pickup swaying subtly on its high-clearance suspension. Picked up by the sudden gust, sand pelted the pickup's upwind flank. The air went brown, and the staccato pinging quickly rose in volume. There was no sign of it letting up.

While Vern had let go of the MP5 and covered his face with his hands, he still received a solid pummeling from the airborne grit.

Tara had avoided Vern's fate by crouching down and burying her face in the crook of her arm.

The mini storm lasted a solid ten seconds.

Once the wind died down, Vern lowered his arms and snatched up the slung MP5. Pinching tears from his eyes, he was right back to walking toward the pickup.

Tara rose up from the crouch and swung her gaze around, taking in all there was to see. Above her, the buzzards were nowhere to be seen. She guessed they had scattered prior to the freak wind event. Up the road, Steve-O was back at it. Moving with Terminator-like precision, the steady *pfft-thwak* of the Mule breaking the still, he was close to finishing culling the last of the fallen zombies. Closer in, trucker hat askew and hunched over the steering wheel, Shorty was safely ensconced in the Roamer's cab. On his face was a look of contentment. It was clear he wasn't in favor of stopping here, let alone leaving the safety of the truck in order to inspect the pickup and its load of dead men.

Though she wasn't looking in her brother's direction when the wind kicked up, if she had been, she would have seen him stop in his tracks, clamp a hand atop his Braves hat, and turn his back to the driving sand. Now, the wind having subsided, he walked in her direction as if nothing had happened. She supposed, having been exposed to more than one haboob while deployed in Iraq, this mini dust storm was a mere annoyance to him.

Turning her attention back to the pickup, Tara saw that it was still swaying back and forth. *Strange*, she thought as she shifted her gaze to the airport, where the windsock now hung limply against the pole. As she tried to make sense of the contradictory information, she heard a loud bang, and suddenly the older Guardsman with the ice-blue eyes was standing in the load bed. Only the man's eyes were no longer the color of a glacial pool; they were now black as death and locked onto Vern, who was a few steps from the pickup and just beginning to react.

The thought of warning Vern was still crossing synapses in Tara's brain when the zombie launched itself at the man. The thing had already cleared the bed rail and was tumbling to the ground, arms outstretched and teeth bared, when the impulses became spoken word.

"It's a Bolt!" she called, bringing the Glock to bear. *Too late.* Vern was in the line of fire. All she could do was watch in horror as the fast-mover sprang up from the hard spill and both of its blood-streaked hands went for Vern's face. In the next beat, a whole bunch of things happened in rapid succession. First, mouth forming a silent O, Vern triggered a couple of three-round bursts from his MP5. Then, as the rounds stitched the Bolt diagonally across its bare chest, adding crimson blooms amongst the older puckered bullet wounds, the growling monster fell like a blanket atop the smaller man.

Riker had noticed the pickup moving, too. Spidey Senses jangling, he realized something was off at about the same time the zombie was springing to its feet in the load bed. Before Tara had shouted her warning, he was head down and sprinting toward the pickup.

With hot shell casings still arcing from Vern's MP5, Riker dragged his Sig Legion from the drop-leg holster, threw the safety, and snapped off a trio of rounds.

The first round found its mark. Head reared back, arms on the upswing, the Bolt's left ear was blown clean off. The follow-on rounds missed wide right and punched a pair of closely spaced holes in the pickup's box. Ribbons of bloody flesh that used to be an ear slapped the side of the pickup, just below the twin bullet holes, and started a slow slide to the road.

As Riker lined up to take another shot, he saw that Vern was fighting for his life. The thing's teeth snapped the air inches from the man's upturned face. The only thing keeping it at bay was the MP5 clutched in Vern's hands. Somehow, as the Bolt was coming down on him, he had managed to get the little sub gun wedged underneath its neck.

Vern grunted and groaned and struggled to keep his arms locked. For the moment, he was winning the battle to keep the gaping maw from tasting flesh. But with both hands occupied, there was no defense against the hands clawing at his face and neck.

Riker was just getting to the pickup when he saw the zombie wrap a hand around Vern's neck and plunge four fingers of the opposite hand two knuckles deep into his friend's open mouth. *Better than going for the eyes* was what Riker was thinking as he lowered his Sig. Even at this close a range, he decided the risk of hitting Vern was too great to let another round fly. He was no Wyatt Earp. He definitely knew his limitations. So as he came to within a couple of strides of the struggle taking place on the road, a full head of steam building, he quickly surveyed the ground before him. The blacktop was mostly smooth, with the uneven frost-heaved shoulder a few feet to the left. Not perfect for what he intended to do, but better than nothing.

Vern was silent now, both arms quivering and beginning to show a little bend at the elbow. The much larger Bolt's hand was crushing down on his neck, the snapping teeth a finger's width from his nose.

Vern's silence, Riker sensed, had nothing to do with the fingers rooting around in his mouth. Nor was it a byproduct of his airway being choked off. It was clear the man's tank was close to empty. If the Vietnam veteran were to let his arms go limp, he was going to get bit. While a bite wasn't always a death sentence, in this instance the chances of him living another day were slim to none, with none being the odds-on favorite.

There were exceptions to the rule, Riker remembered. Granted the amputation occurred immediately, a bite on the hand or foot or an appendage was not a death sentence. Lia was living proof. However, should Romero be introduced by a bite to the torso or anywhere above the neck, the only eventual recourse was a bullet to the brain.

The distance to the pickup cut down to a couple of long strides, Riker pushed the grim thoughts from his mind. Focused intently on the Bolt's pistoning maw, he planted one foot on the road and pushed off with all his might. Landing ten feet from where he launched, he stutter-stepped to close the remaining couple of feet, then unleashed a kick Detroit Lion Matt Prater would be proud of.

The tip of the Salomon on the prosthetic caught the Bolt squarely under the chin, snapping its head back with such force that Riker not only felt the impact course up his residual limb but also heard the sharp *crack* of vertebrae breaking. As the Bolt's upper body and arms adopted the same trajectory as its head, a torrent of freshly broken teeth spewed from its mouth.

Arms windmilling wildly, Riker landed on the smooth blacktop several feet beyond Vern and the Bolt. Snaring the pickup's wing mirror with one hand arrested his forward momentum just enough to allow his feet to catch up with the rest of his body. Metal groaned, and the wing mirror broke off the pickup. When he finally came to a complete stop, he was left standing near the pickup's front fender, the wound on his residual limb throbbing in tune with his accelerated heartbeat. As the first hammering of what would no doubt be one hell of a headache began behind his eyes, he realized he was still holding the mirror. Throwing the mirror to the ground, he drew the Sig Legion and spun a quick 180.

The scene that greeted him was far from what he was expecting.

Chapter 15

Vern was still flat on his back, face upturned to the sky, when Riker recovered from the devastating kick he'd unloaded on the Bolt that had been straddling the man. His lips were rimmed with white froth. Puffy red abrasions encircling the man's bruised neck wept blood. The hand on one outstretched arm still grasped the MP5. At first blush, nothing Riker saw convinced him Vern was still alive. And if his assessment rang true, and the life had indeed been choked out of him, a grim task awaited Riker.

Promises made, promises kept. He had made a pact with Vern: No matter the cause of death, whether by blade or bullet, the brain must be destroyed. Dealer's choice. No way he was going to go back on his word.

When Riker was taking his shots at the Bolt, Tara had been frozen in place, the black pistol shaking in her hand. Although she had been gripped by indecision, she was the first to reach the Bolt after the kick had laid it out. Standing beside the pickup, one boot planted on the Bolt's bloody chest, holding it down just in case it made another try for Vern, she said, "I could use a little help here, bro. Shoot the thing. Stab it in the eye. Get Steve-O over here with the Mule of his. I don't care. Anything but standing there and gawking at me would be acceptable."

Before Riker could answer, Lia rounded the pickup's tailgate. At once, he detected the hurt and fear in her eyes. Passing the Motorola off to Tara, Lia immediately dropped to her knees next to Vern's unmoving body. Drawing a deep breath, she pressed two fingers to his neck. After a few seconds, head bowed and shoulders rounded, she exhaled. "It's all my fault," she said. "I saw the soldier turn. It happened real quick. By the time I put the radio to my mouth, the thing was already out of the truck and on top of him."

"Caught us all by surprise," admitted Tara. "I saw Lee coming and didn't know what to do. I didn't do anything because I was afraid I'd shoot one of them."

"It's OK," Riker insisted. "I had to make the same decision."

"Mine wasn't a conscious one, though. I locked up." Taking her foot from its unmoving chest, she said, "Well? Knife, gun, Mule? What's it going to be?"

Riker swallowed hard. His tongue wanted to stick to the roof of his mouth. Suddenly he realized he was thirsty. Crossing the Sahara desert thirsty. Dragging the Randall from its scabbard, he said, "Sorry. I'm not feeling so hot."

Tara said, "Headache coming on?"

Riker nodded. "It's going to be a banger." As he closed the distance with two long strides, he sized up the Bolt. Only stitch of clothing on the thing was the pair of blood-soaked Army-issue boxers. From the neck down, not a muscle was moving. Its pale arms had come to rest at ninety-degree angles to its torso, both palms upturned. On the inside of its right wrist was a barely perceptible ring of indentations. He'd been bitten. The teeth had barely broken the skin. But that's all it took. A little Romero virus in the system and you're toast. Both legs had gone straight as the momentum from the kick had lifted the zombie off of Vern. Returning to earth flat on its back, the impact with the road sent both legs jutting out at odd angles.

The dead eyes, however, were a flurry of movement. Darting around in their sockets, the bloodshot orbs jumped from Tara to Lia and back again. The mostly toothless mouth opened and closed slowly around a lolling hunk of bloody flesh that could hardly pass for a human tongue.

Riker took a knee beside the paralyzed Bolt. "How's Vern?" he gasped as he shoved the Randall's sharp tip into one of the thing's constantly roving eyes. "Is he still with us?"

Lia didn't immediately reply. She was busy inspecting the man for bites. She ran her hands over his neck, back to front. She lifted his head off the road and threaded her fingers through the thinning hair. She looked each arm up and down, giving both hands extra scrutiny.

"Give us something," Tara said to Lia. "Does he have a pulse?"

"He does," Lia replied. "But it's faint. Just a flutter, really."

Riker rose. "You find any bites?"

"None. I thought I was going to. There will be no amputation necessary," she declared. "Only injury I found is the goose egg on the back of his head."

The first aid kit Vern had been carrying was on the road beside him. Unzipping it, Lia rooted around and came out with an ammonia ampule. Crushing it and rolling it around between two fingers, she waved it underneath Vern's nose.

Nothing.

Shorty and Steve-O arrived at the pickup near simultaneously from two different directions. The former had the Mule banging against his back as he walked, the latter was toting the Shockwave and cussing like a sailor.

Addressing Shorty, Tara said, "Relax, pottymouth. Vern's not dead. He just fell and struck his head on the road."

Lia made another pass with the ampule, letting it linger underneath Vern's nose.

All of a sudden, eyes snapping open, Vern gasped and sat upright. At once, his eyes toured his surroundings. It was clear he was more than a little confused.

Lia described to Vern what she had witnessed from her seat in the Shelby, finishing with, "You're lucky to be alive."

Shorty had been nodding as Lia spoke. When she finished, he said, "That's how I saw it. I'm amazed the thing's head is still attached."

Steve-O cracked a wide smile. "Once again, Lee Riker saves the day." Smile morphing to a frown, he said solemnly, "The people who did this to the soldiers need to pay for it."

Vern rubbed the back of his head. "I assumed the soldiers were all dead. Didn't cross my mind that they could have been infected. I'll never make that mistake again," he promised. Locking eyes with Lia, he asked, "Were they *all* carrying the virus? Or just this one?" He lifted his gaze and made eye contact with Riker. "Did anyone check the rest of them for a pulse? Can't risk another of them turning unexpectedly."

Shorty had crawled into the load bed with the corpses. "Working on it," he called. "Steve-O … get over here with that Mule. Be ready to trigger it in case I don't find a pulse."

Riker peered over the bedrail. Watched as Shorty pressed a finger to a young Guardsman's neck.

"Nothing," Shorty said to Steve-O.

Steve-O already had the wand pressed hard to the corpse's temple. Grimacing, he pressed the trigger. The wand went *pfft-thwak* and jerked in his hand. "I'm sorry," he said, moving the wand to the next corpse.

One at a time, Shorty declared the other two Guardsmen dead.

One at a time, Steve-O put the Mule to task.

Shorty rose up from the bed. Standing head and shoulders taller than everyone, he said, "Now that that's out of the way, what do you propose we do with the bodies?"

Riker swung his gaze to Tara. "Check the cab for anything of use. A radio. Military I.D.s."

She nodded. "I'll check the fuel gauge, too."

As Tara opened the driver's side door, Riker picked the twice-dead Guardsman off the road. Lifting the limp corpse over the pickup's bedrail, he deposited the soldier in the load bed with his fallen comrades.

Steve-O fixed Riker with a questioning look. "We're not going to bury them?"

"Ground's too hard," Riker stated. "We'd need a backhoe."

Overhead the vultures were back to flying lazy circles above the pickup. Pointing skyward, Shorty said, "We can't just leave them for those bastards to eat."

Lia was propping Vern up and giving him water from her bottle. Looking up, she said, "These men don't deserve to be left out in the elements."

Riker tore off the Guardsman's boxers and used them to clean his hands of the dead man's blood. Tossing the shorts to the road, he said, "I have a plan. But first, I need to get Littlewolf on your radio and relay the bad news."

Leaping to the road, Shorty said, "Knock yourself out. She's unlocked."

As Riker strode off for the Roamer, Shorty helped Vern to stand.

"Thank you," Vern called to a retreating Riker. "I owe you one."

***

Riker returned from the Roamer a couple of minutes later. In one hand was a five-gallon gas can. His companions were standing in a loose knot near the pickup's tailgate and conversing in hushed tones. After acknowledging Vern's gratitude and telling the man there was no scorekeeping amongst friends, Riker looked at Tara. "Find anything of use in their rig?"

She held up one hand. In it was a roll of toilet paper. Trapped between her fingers were two pairs of dog tags. "Just this stuff. Found the dog tags on the seat. It was as if they'd been left where they'd be found. If you ask me, it seems like a big middle finger to whoever would come looking for the patrol."

Running a handkerchief over his bloody hands, Shorty said, "Gas in the tank?"

Tara made a face. "It's bone dry. And the assholes also put a bullet in the radio."

"Figures," Shorty said. "What's it say on the tags?"

Tara tossed the toilet paper roll to Lia. "For your head." She then palmed the dog tags and read off of them one at a time. "Dehen, Katelyn B. Long string of numbers. Not gonna read them. Her blood type is A positive. And it says here at the bottom that she's Catholic."

Vern was leaning against the pickup. The color had returned to his face. Whereas before the man had looked like a corpse, now, with the rosy cheeks and twinkle in his eyes, he looked fit as a fiddle. Lifting his chin, he said, "What about the other one? I assume it belongs to the other woman soldier Littlewolf spoke of."

Tara said, "Jackson, LaTasha P. Long string of numbers, only different. She's O negative in the blood department. Says here she's also Catholic." She looked at her brother. "We're looking for a white girl and a sister."

"What makes you say that?" asked Lia.

Tara dropped her chin to her chest. Had she been wearing glasses, she would have been peering over them. Slowly, she said, "Katelyn Dehen is definitely a white girl's name. LaTasha Jackson speaks for itself."

"Agreed," Shorty said.

Vern nodded. "Ditto."

Head cocked to one side, a hint of skepticism in his tone, Steve-O said, "I don't get how you can tell a person's skin color by their name alone."

"It's a long story," said Riker. "I'll fill you in later."

That was good enough for Steve-O. He turned back around, all of his attention focused on a new pack of zombies trundling down the highway toward them.

Following Steve-O's gaze, Riker said, "Let us know when they get to the point in the road where Shorty's handiwork begins."

Still staring up the highway, Steve-O said, "Will do, boss."

Shorty regarded Riker. "What now?"

"I spoke with Littlewolf," Riker replied. "Apparently, the patrol consisted of half of the troops under her command."

"Explains the Fort Apache moniker," Vern put in.

Tara planted her palms on her hips. "We're not taking the bodies back to her, are we?"

Riker shook his head. "I offered. She thought it would be too risky."

"No way we're *digging* a hole in this hardpan," Shorty declared. "It'd take us hours. My back would probably go out with the first shovelful."

"Nope," Riker said, "I promised her they would get a proper sendoff, though."

Vern gestured at the gas can by Riker's feet. "Are we giving them a Norse funeral?"

Riker nodded. "The pickup will have to take the place of the boat."

Another wind gust hit them out of the blue. It rocked the pickup and sent a dust cloud drifting over the feeder road.

Riker opened the cap on the gas can and poured most of its contents over the corpses. The small amount he left in the can was enough to wet the pickup's bench seats.

Vern produced a Zippo lighter. "You do the honors. Better say a few words first."

Riker shook his head. "I'm no Eleven Bravo. I was just a driver over there."

"Bullshit," Tara called. "You got a Purple Heart and everything that goes with it. Your time spent over there meant something. If anyone is worthy of saying some kind words about these men, it's you."

Vern took Riker's hand in his and forced the Zippo on him. "My war ended a long time ago. You'll think of something."

"All right," Riker said. "Everyone step back." He looked across the load bed. "How much time do we have, Steve-O?"

Hat in hand, head bowed, Steve-O said, "Probably five minutes."

"Get on with it," Shorty urged. "We're burning daylight."

That's not the only thing, Riker thought as he lit the lighter and touched the flame to the gasoline pooled in the bed.

Chapter 16

Interstate 40 – 100 miles west of Double Eagle II Airport

Two hours after leaving the smoldering National Guard pickup in the rearview, Riker was still smelling smoke and the disconcerting odor of burning flesh. It was in his clothes, in his beard, and had seemingly wormed its way into his very pores. If he had hair on his head, no doubt it would have attached itself to every follicle.

They were back to their initial seating arrangements: Lia and Vern riding with Riker in the Shelby. Tara and Steve-O were back to riding in the Roamer with Shorty. Tara hadn't put up a fight when Shorty asked her to rejoin him and Steve-O. That the ask was prefaced by a promise to cut the crudeness and a less than believable oath to keep the off-color jokes to a minimum made no difference to the woman. It was Steve-O she was worried about. She'd even pulled Shorty aside and had told him so. While she couldn't attribute Steve-O's recent affinity for cursing to him spending a lot of time with Shorty—mainly because she was one of the worst offenders and had acknowledged that fact—she did have a hunch the way Shorty carried himself had, in a small way, helped to feed Steve-O's emerging ego. She liked the old, sweet, and somewhat naïve Steve-O a lot more than the new cocksure version.

Chased by the sun, the two-vehicle convoy wheeled west on Interstate 40, the Shelby in the lead, with Lia in the front passenger seat and scouting ahead with the high-powered binoculars. The handful of stops they'd made to search clusters of stalled vehicles had turned up little in the way of supplies and barely enough fuel to replace what Riker had used to start the makeshift funeral pyre.

Over the last thirty miles or so, as the convoy burned through the bleak New Mexican landscape between Thoreau and Coolidge, barreling toward Gallup and the Arizona state line beyond, all conversation in the Shelby had ceased.

In the backseat, Vern was asleep and snoring softly. Ten minutes after being choked near to death by the undead Guardsman, his color had returned, and he had recovered his full range of voice. The fight for his life had left him spent and aching all over. He'd fallen asleep before the smoke from the pyre was out of sight and had been out like a light ever since.

Before joining a brooding Riker in his cone of silence, Lia had been trying to assure him that he had done the right thing back at the airport. Prior to Riker drawing inward, he had confessed to her that his decision to leave the airport without searching for fuel had had more to do with the plume of greasy smoke roiling off the burning corpses than the "waste of time" he had initially attributed it to. The sight of the burning Guard pickup and immolated soldiers, he had explained to her, had transported him back to that fateful day in Iraq when an improvised explosive device had added him, his passengers, and the up-armored Land Cruiser he'd been driving to the burgeoning numbers of insurgent-caused casualties, death, and destruction so commonplace on Route Irish.

Interstate 40 West cut through a broad valley beneath a large escarpment of Entrada sandstone, marking the southern boundary of the Colorado Plateau to the north.

All along the way, four-by-eight sheets of plywood with NO GAS, NO FOOD, NO FEDS, NATIVES ONLY! spray-painted on them fronted a myriad of vehicles blocking entry to towns small and large. The roadblocks had been manned by Native American men and women brandishing long rifles, shotguns, and AR-15s. Riker did spot a white face here and there, but the sightings were few and far between. What he didn't see was a single person who looked like him.

While the local militia had seemed nice enough from a distance, waving and flashing thumbs-up at the Shelby and Roamer as they rolled past, their stony countenances told a different story.

Riker had seen it all before. Not so much on the Eastern Seaboard. Those folks had been in the grip of normalcy bias and had quickly become zombie chow. Nonetheless, with few exceptions, armed Americans were seen guarding off-ramps and feeder roads from South Beach, Florida all the way to the bridge closure near where he'd made Shorty's acquaintance. For 700 miles, citizens exercising their Second Amendment rights were doing what the already stretched thin law enforcement and military could not: protecting their communities from the infected and criminals alike, the latter well known for taking advantage of *every* emergency—hurricane or zombie outbreak, there was no crisis the criminals would not exploit.

Having had enough of the silent treatment, Lia lowered the Steiners and looked sidelong at Riker. "I thought the Lord's Prayer was appropriate, Lee. You did good back there."

Riker said nothing. Kept his gaze boring into the bluebird sky beyond the Shelby's hood.

"You're not a preacher," Lia pressed. "I don't think anyone expected more of an oration than what you delivered." She made a face. "What does '*Until Valhalla*' mean?"

Suddenly Vern's disembodied voice emanated from the backseat. "Valhalla … the hall of the fallen … is the great hall in Norse Mythology where heroes killed in combat are received. No matter who or what the fallen soldier believes in—Until Valhalla is a sign of great respect. It's assuring the fallen that we will see them again."

Riker glanced at Lia. "I only said it because Littlewolf asked me to."

"How to say '*I'm not worthy*' without saying '*I'm not worthy*' for two hundred, Alex." Lia shook her head. "You need to quit that *bullcrap*. Back there, when the zombie got a jump on Vern, you acted without thinking about your own safety. When you kicked that zombie, it could have just as easily turned its head and taken a bite out of *your* leg."

"It was the leg fitted with my bionic," Riker pointed out. "Romero doesn't transmit through carbon fiber and aerospace-grade titanium."

Lia pounded a fist on her thigh. "What am I going to do with you, Lee? What you did outside the airport was an act of valor. Therefore, you have every right to a seat at the table in Valhalla."

"That's a pretty deep dive," Vern said. He was sitting up now, arms hooked over the seatback and looking at Lia. "I agree with you wholeheartedly, young lady. I wouldn't be on this side of the grass if it wasn't for George Blanda here."

"Who?" Lia asked.

Vern snickered. "Only one of the best kickers of all time."

"Soccer?"

"Football," replied Vern. "NFL football. The only football, in my opinion. Blanda played for the Raiders when I was about your age."

"Don't hate on soccer, Vern." Riker cracked a rare smile. "It's loved by billions of people ... just not you and me."

"I can take it or leave it now," Vern admitted. "All the damn commercials. If it weren't for Romero, sooner or later the players' uniforms would be plastered with product endorsements. Have to start calling it the Nascar Football League."

"Give me golf over football or soccer any day," Lia said. "It's relaxing to watch."

"Hell to play," Vern said. "Damn expensive, too. Some call it a 'good walk spoiled.'"

Riker didn't have an opinion on the matter. He'd always considered golf a rich man's sport. And now that he was a rich man and could afford the green fee of any course he wanted to play, anywhere in the world, the Romero virus and the zombies it had created made the point moot.

Sun glinting off the snaking body of water that had been keeping pace with the Interstate for nearly thirty miles redirected Riker's train of thought. Seeing the Puerco River reappear a half-mile north of the Interstate prompted him to glance at the Shelby's navigation panel to get an idea where they were in relation to the state line. The Puerco presented as a blue squiggle on the screen. It struck off north and then dove back down south before cutting through a town on the map called Gallup. As soon as Riker lifted his gaze from the nav screen, he spotted a roadside sign bearing the message **Now Entering Gallup - Population 21,481**.

"If memory serves," Vern said, "Gallup's population is made up mostly of First Nations Native Americans: Pueblo, Zuni, Navajo, Hopi—"

Riker snatched up the two-way and hailed the Roamer.

Tara came back straightaway. "What's up, Lee?"

"You see that sign? We're coming up on a city of twenty thousand. Bound to come across snarls on the highway. Keep your eyes peeled for zombies, too."

"Goes without saying, bro," Tara replied. "It's good to hear your voice, though."

"Likewise," Riker radioed. "You see me stop, you guys do the same. Remember to keep a safe following distance."

After a brief pause, Shorty came on over the radio. "Roger that," he said. "Don't forget about your flammable cargo."

"Understood," Riker replied. "Everything looking good back there? Barrels still straight? Nothing's shifted?"

Tara radioed the reply. "You're good, bro. Now you better focus on driving."

***

A couple of minutes later, as they approached the first interchange east of Gallup's city center, a series of looping ramps connecting I-40 to a long stretch of Historic Route 66, they saw the first indication that the locals had their city on lockdown. In addition to parked vehicles and sternly worded signs discouraging travelers from even thinking about trying to leave the Interstate, the armed Native Americans guarding the conduits into the city leveled their weapons at the approaching two-vehicle convoy. The locals remained vigilant, keeping their assortment of AR-15s and long rifles trained on the Shelby and Roamer until they were committed to the fenced-in elevated stretch of I-40 that took them over Route 66. Riker didn't shake the feeling they were being watched until they reached the west end of town and the final group of heavily armed locals was growing small in the rearview.

A total of ten minutes had elapsed between Riker seeing the sign announcing Gallup's eastern limits and the one coming up fast on the town's western border. Along the entire eight-mile run of I-40, they hadn't encountered a single abandoned vehicle or wandering zombie. All lanes in both directions had been entirely cleared of debris. It was so spotless Riker wondered if someone had put the city's street sweeper to use.

Coming up on Gallup Municipal Airport, a single strip affair three miles southwest of downtown Gallup, Riker noted the length the locals had gone to in order to keep the outside world at bay. The runway was a parking lot for all manner of emergency and ground support vehicles. It was bookended by a Day-Glo-yellow fire engine and a like-colored low-slung crash tender Riker thought looked a lot like the Oshkosh rigs he'd driven in Iraq. Ambulances, a snowplow, and a pair of fuel bowsers were left parked at staggered intervals between the hard-to-miss rescue equipment.

"Those folks are hell-bent on keeping Gallup sterile," Vern noted.

"Isn't blocking runways illegal?" Lia wondered. "Where in the hell was my dad supposed to land his plane if this bullshit is what he encountered at Portland International?"

Riker said, "Pretty hard to argue with all those guns back there. No doubt there's some of them guarding the airport."

"It's a good thing what they did here," Vern opined. "I think history is going to show that proximity to a large airport is a main contributing factor to how fast a city falls to the dead."

As Riker was nodding in agreement with Vern, another city limit sign whipped by on the right. While the easternmost boundary sign had been mostly informative, the message on this one merely thanked them for visiting and urged them to **COME BACK SOON**.

Riker thought it funny that those in charge of isolating Gallup from the outside world hadn't thought of changing the messaging on the city limit signs. Maybe they wanted to maintain the element of surprise. The lockdown sure as hell came as a surprise to Riker and the gang.

No sooner had the Roamer passed the sign demarking Gallup's western border than Shorty's voice sprang from the Motorola in Lia's lap. "Pucker time is over," he quipped. "Everyone can stop making diamonds."

Vern clucked his tongue. "Nary a serious bone in that man's body."

Riker kind of liked the comment. As soon as he heard it, the visual it produced started the headache that had been stalking him since the airport to wane. As I-40 transitioned from a long straightaway to a shallow left-hand curve, he spotted a trio of bright yellow dump trucks. They were the type used by mining concerns, with wheels as tall as a man and an elevated cab that required a ladder to access. Though they were parked in the desert a hundred yards or so north of the right shoulder, it was easy to see that all three were filled to overflowing with twice-dead zombies. Partially shielded by the dump trucks, a like-colored digger was busy scraping flat the bottom of a massive communal grave. Three identical-sized parcels of land stretched away from the one still in progress. They were far from flat and a couple of shades darker than the surrounding desert. No doubt the finished graves held tens of thousands of zombie corpses.

Lowering the binoculars, Lia said, "There's the answer to why we didn't see a single zombie roaming Gallup."

A half dozen workers milling about graveside turned and stared at the convoy as it passed them by. Weapons emerged and heads panned until both vehicles had moved on.

Once the dump trucks were small dots in the rearview, Riker said, "They mean business." He paused, thinking. "We should ask the Littlewolf ladies if either of them have connections with the Gallup sheriff or native elders. If so, it would be smart to see if they're willing to make introductions. Allies are damn hard to come by these days."

Vern shook his head. "The messages on those signs were pretty clear to me."

"Agreed," said Lia. "We're lucky they allowed us safe passage. I think sticking our noses where they don't belong is a *bad* idea."

Shrugging, Riker said, "Nothing ventured, nothing gained."

Vern stuck his arm between Riker and Lia. Stabbing a finger at something out there, he said, "See that? Way out on the horizon."

Riker squinted. "What is it?"

Brow arched, Lia said, "Smoke."

Nodding, Vern said, "Yep. Smoke."

Instantly the one-syllable word started a throbbing behind Riker's eyes. "Where?" he asked, grimacing. "Is it on the road?"

"Can't tell," Lia said. "It's *real* faint."

Riker tapped his finger on the SYNC monitor. "We're headed south by west right now. Up ahead, the 40 takes a sharp bend west. Judging by our icon on the nav pane, I'd put the source of the smoke near the state line."

"I've driven this route a few times with Shane," Vern said. "I think you're right, Lee. First services are three or four miles ahead. It's a pretty big truck plaza right across the state line."

Lia bit her lip. Lowering the binoculars, she said, "Maybe that's what's burning."

Just what we need, thought Riker. *Where there's smoke, there's fire.* And the type of fire he was seeing in his mind's eye was coming from the barrel of a semi-automatic weapon.

Back to scouting ahead with the binoculars, Lia said, "Up ahead on the right. About a mile or so. There's a bunch of big rigs backed up on the right shoulder. When we get to the first of them, slow down and creep forward. I have an idea." She thumbed the Motorola alive and filled Shorty and the others in on what she had in mind.

Chapter 17

"Get closer?" Shorty called across the divide. "What kind of plan is that?"

The Roamer was pulled up tight to a semi-tractor hooked to a trailer emblazoned with giant-sized nacho-cheese-flavored tortilla chips, the colors so vivid and enticing Steve-O couldn't stop staring at them. The Doritos logo in four-foot-tall red font rose a couple of feet over the Roamer's front sleeping loft. At first sight of the larger-than-life advertisement, Tara had been obsessing about needing to find a bag of that particular brand of chips.

Riker had let the Roamer overtake them shortly after Lia had voiced her "plan." The Shelby was parked on the larger vehicle's left side, a couple of yards separating the cabs.

Lia lowered the Steiners and shot Shorty a sour look. "We know something's happening at the truck plaza. First off, while I'm no expert on military vehicles, I think the tan vehicle next to the fuel pumps is the missing Humvee. Secondly"—she glanced at Riker—"I'm pretty sure panel vans don't spontaneously combust."

Calling out from his seat in the Roamer, Steve-O said, "I can fly the drone over the truck stop. Make it hover behind the smoke and see what's happening."

Regarding Steve-O, Riker said, "Slow your roll, Chuck Yeager. I don't want to risk getting my drone shot out of the sky. Damn buzzards got close enough as it is. We're probably going to need it to save the kids. That's assuming we even get to Vegas before the shit bags move them someplace else." Turning his attention back to Lia, he asked, "What's the distance to the first building?"

She handed him the Steiners. "You go ahead. You know what you're looking for."

Riker raised the binoculars and spent a minute or so glassing the distant plaza. It consisted of two smaller metal-frame buildings fronted by a third, much larger metal-frame building. Signage on the smaller buildings indicated they housed a self-service laundromat, a cardio gym, a technology center offering Wi-Fi and High-Speed Internet, and a spa complete with Jacuzzi tub, steam sauna, and private showers. *Only things missing,* thought Riker, *are a massage parlor and an on-site barber.*

The darkened sign towering over the plaza was a neon item. The bent glass tubing spelled out **HOLL-EE's FULL SERVICE TRUCK PLAZA**. *False advertising,* thought Riker as he watched smoke from the burning panel van drift across the sign. Holl-Ee's was a veritable oasis in the middle of nowhere. Still, the zombie outbreak hadn't missed it. There was no service of any kind happening here. The massive windows of all three cube-like buildings were boarded over with sheets of plywood. That there was no broken glass littering the ground led Riker to believe the boards had gone up early on. Probably shortly after the mayhem at Battery Park in New York City was broadcast on televisions the world over.

Two fueling islands flanked the main building—one to a side. Both islands sprouted a dozen pumps and appeared to be dedicated solely to automobiles. The much larger fuel island was in back of the main building. It stretched away to the west and consisted of twelve drive-thru fueling bays, each long enough to accommodate big rigs towing triple trailers. Half of the fueling bays had a tractor and attached trailer sitting idle in the oil-stained lane. A dozen or so trailers, the contents already looted, sat on the graded dirt lot at the west edge of the plaza. Riker saw a handful of zombies moving amongst the sea of eighteen-wheelers. He also spotted a couple of people closer in, near the automobile fuel islands. The discovery was immediately punctuated by something that started a cold ball to form in his gut.

Lowering the Steiners, a concerned look on his face, he said in a low voice, "Rangefinder says distance to the first building is just shy of eighteen hundred meters. That rig Lia saw *is* a Humvee. A squared-off rear end like that is near impossible to confuse with anything else on the road. Whoever was driving it had parked close to the first row of pumps. The nozzle to one of the pumps is on the ground beside where you'd find the fuel cap on one of those rigs. Leads me to believe someone was probably trying to coax some fuel out of the pumps and got caught with their pants down." He paused and looked the others over. Continuing, he said, "And there's zombies milling about the trucks parked on the far edge of the property." He went quiet for a couple of seconds.

"And?" Shorty pressed. "Why the mime act?"

"Because closer in, beside the pumps to the left of the bigger of the three buildings, I saw two people hunkering down." He shook his head. "Then I saw muzzle flashes coming from the north side. The gunfire was answered immediately by someone hiding behind the Humvee."

Vern stated the obvious. "So someone's engaged in a firefight at the truck plaza."

Brows arched, Lia said, "People are shooting at each other?"

Shorty said, "That's the definition of *firefight*." He regarded Riker. "What's the distance to the place? This time in *English*, please."

Lia answered for him. "It's a little over a mile, smartass."

Vern looked to Shorty. "If we push forward, stop maybe seven or eight rigs back, you'll be at a perfect distance to glass the place. If needs be, we'll also be close enough to engage the enemy."

Now Shorty was wearing the concerned look. "What's going to keep the bad guys from seeing Large Marge coming?"

Vern said, "Every one of those big rigs are taller than your Roamer. Not to mention, if Lee saw what he thinks he saw, they're *all* a bit preoccupied down there. If you stick close to the rigs, you'll have cover *and* concealment the entire way." To Riker, he said, "You keep a close following distance, should they make us, the only vehicle they'll see is the Roamer. That'll leave us as the trump card."

Tara poked her head over the seatback in the Roamer. Fixing her brother with a steely glare, she said, "Whether they think we're one vehicle or two, what good does getting closer do for us? We'll just put ourselves within reach of their weapons." She looked at Shorty. "I think we should keep our noses out of whatever is going on over there. We can backtrack and go around, right?"

"We have no choice," Riker interjected. "There are two *Is* in integrity. *I* will, and *I* did. I made a promise to Littlewolf that I'd help her troops if we came across them. The fact that the Humvee is down there means Jackson and Dehen could be, too. I intend on staying true to my word."

"Lee Riker is right," Steve-O put in. "A man is only as good as his word."

Lia rested her hand on Riker's thigh. Peering at the plaza through the Steiners, she said, "Until Valhalla," and gave a little squeeze.

Shorty said, "Backtracking will burn a lot of fuel. I'm with Lee and Steve-O."

Concern evident in her voice, Lia said, "What do we do if they're at a stalemate? What happens if both sides just keep their heads down and decide to wait for the sun to set? Last I checked, we don't have night-vision goggles."

Tara said, "She has a point. If that happens and we're forced to flip on the headlights and try to speed on by, we'll make for one hell of a target. We could end up with both sides shooting at us."

Riker said, "We cross that bridge when we come to it. Best not get ahead of ourselves."

"We do have the sun at our backs right now," Vern noted. "That's one thing we have going for us."

Though Riker knew the sun always rose in the east and could feel its rays warm on his exposed left arm, he still checked for it in the side mirror. Sure enough, it was up there, in a low azimuth and climbing toward high noon, doing what it had been doing for millennia, totally oblivious to what had befallen planet Earth.

Not only were they burning fuel, thought Riker, they were also burning daylight. Keeping his thoughts to himself, he walked his gaze down the long line of static eighteen-wheelers. Sun glinted from all the chrome. Parked grille to trailer, the colorful parade of Kenworths, Peterbilts, Volvos, and Freightliners stretched all the way to the plaza entrance. Riker imagined the drivers waiting patiently to refuel, all the while the world was going to shit around them. No doubt those drivers' hopes had been dashed when the plaza's tanks went dry, leaving them stranded in the middle of the desert. He didn't need to do the math in his head. With the sheer number of trucks abandoned here, the plaza had to have been the epicenter of a zombie outbreak.

The evidence supported Riker's theory. Here and there, on down the line, pools of dried blood and brass shell casings reflected the sun. A tennis shoe sat alone by a rig with an open door, the white leather and undone laces dappled with crimson spots. The knot of walking corpses shambling in from the west was the smoking gun. They were all male and mostly middle-aged. Some wore coveralls over blood-stippled tee shirts. Others were dressed in jeans and Western-style shirts. Though none of them wore a mesh trucker hat on its bobbing head, Riker figured they all fit the profile of the average long-haul trucker.

Riker walked the Steiners along the queue, counting up from one until his gaze fell on the eighth semi from the front. It was a purple Freightliner wearing a thick coating of dust. A face-shot corpse with multiple bite marks running up one tanned forearm hung from the open driver's door. Only thing keeping it from tumbling to the road was the shoulder belt looped around its bloated neck.

One thing that really stood out was that about half of the trailers had no tractors attached to them. To spare themselves a slow death baking in the sun or to escape the flash outbreak that had likely occurred, he figured the operators had decided to literally *lighten their load* and continue on down the road without their cargo. Every one of the trailers on down the line had been broken into, the cut locks discarded on the road below yawning doors.

Most trailers were empty, the cargo long gone. Here and there, useless items littered the road. Plush toys bound for stores in Flagstaff and Phoenix presented as a colorful mound behind one trailer. Halloween decorations spilled from another—plastic skeletons, fuzzy black cats, and blaze-orange jack-o-lanterns that would never see a porch or a front yard, let alone frighten a host of young trick-or-treaters. Burst bags of potting soil and wood-slat crates full of shattered clay pots littered the road below the open doors of yet another trailer. One flatbed was loaded high with lumber and dozens of rolls of coiled chain-link fence.

Lowering the Steiners, Riker looked from face to face. "What do you all think? Should we cut the distance and get a better feel for what's going on at the plaza?"

Heads nodded all around.

"Looks like the *ayes* have it," Shorty said, letting his foot off the brake. "But if we start taking fire"—he called through the open window—"you all had better be ready to return it."

Riker nodded and watched the Roamer pull away, its idling diesel engine providing just enough torque to propel it forward at walking speed. It was rather quiet, the usual rattle clatter of the motor no louder than a sewing machine. He waited until the Roamer had a two-truck-length lead before easing up on the Shelby's brakes.

The Shelby's idling V8 easily provided enough power to the wheels to keep pace with the Roamer. Although the Shelby's sound signature, with the exhaust exiting through Borla pipes, was far from quiet. *No matter*, Riker thought as he goosed the engine to close the distance to the Roamer. *Combatants in the middle of a firefight with ringing in their ears and a vehicle burning nearby would be hard-pressed to hear themselves think, let alone detect a couple of idling engines a mile out.*

The two trucks slow-rolled the better part of a mile, bumper-to-bumper and hugging so close to the line of semis anyone in the passenger seats could reach out and touch them if they wanted to. Halfway down the line of trucks, the opposite occurred. As the Roamer was passing by a blaze-red Peterbilt decorated with neon-green pinstriping, a pale arm shot out of the tractor's open window. Face twisted into a toothy snarl, the zombie in the driver's seat thrust its other arm into space and made a play for the back of the Roamer's camper shell, missing it entirely. While the Roamer escaped contact with the undead trucker, the Shelby wasn't so lucky.

The loud report of the palm slapping the windshield caused Lia to jump. Fight or flight instincts kicking in, she leaned hard away from the window and drew her legs up onto the seat. Hands raised in a defensive posture, she tracked the hand with her eyes as the fingers raked across her window just inches from her face. Walking her gaze the length of the extended arm culminated in a split-second staring contest with the zombie. It was half out the window, its upper body bobbing as it strained to reach the trailer passing it by.

"Better a hand hitting the glass than a noggin," observed Vern. "Not going to find a Safelite AutoGlass all the way out here."

"Came out of nowhere," Riker said, glancing at Lia. "Would have swerved had I seen it in time. My bad."

Back to sitting upright in her seat, Lia said, "No worries. Probably best that you didn't swerve. Shorty would have shit a brick if the barrels tipped and his diesel ended up on the road."

Vern chuckled. "That would have been a sight to see."

"That's a headache avoided." Truth was, he had been plagued by a subtle throbbing behind his eyes since leaving the airport. Every new surprise caused the pain to spike behind his eyes.

Ruffling her hair, Lia said, "Thanks to you, Lee, this time my window was rolled up."

Meeting Vern's gaze in the mirror, Riker said, "We're all still learning the ins and outs of this madness."

"That we are," Vern said. "That we are."

Seeing Shorty pull the Roamer next to the agreed-upon eighteen-wheeler—the purple Freightliner with the dead body half at the wheel—Riker nosed the Shelby up to the back of the Roamer, set the brake, then killed the engine. Through his open window he could smell the dead driver. It was that sickly sweet pong that, once introduced to, one could never equate with anything but death. The hollow pops of sporadic gunfire also infiltrated the cab.

No sooner had the gunfire subsided than the Motorola on the seat beside Lia belched white noise. "We're closer now," Shorty quipped. "Question is: Who is gonna get on top of my rig and play Peeping Tom?"

"My idea," Lia radioed back. "I'll do it." Radio and Steiners in hand, she stepped to the road and shut her door.

Passing the key fob to Vern, Riker said, "I'll be her extra set of eyes while she's up there," and elbowed open his door. He reached into the Shelby's backseat and grabbed his F4 AR from the floor. Slinging the carbine, he hinged over the load bed and retrieved a black Pelican case and a small black nylon bag.

Lia was already climbing the Roamer's shell-mounted ladder when Riker caught up with her. She was negotiating the steps pretty well for someone new to wearing a prosthesis. Although she did stop once to dig a finger into the sleeve fitted to her stump and attack an itch. When she finally reached the top, Riker got her attention and handed up the Pelican case.

Riker was just beginning his ascent when Vern showed up behind the Roamer. Pausing halfway up the ladder, he said, "What's up?"

Hands on hips, Vern said, "I want to have a look."

Riker made a face. "Then who'll be watching our six?"

Vern said, "Tara's on it," and grabbed hold of a rung.

Seeing Tara taking up station behind the Shelby, Riker returned his attention to Vern. "You up for this?"

"I'm old," said Vern. "Not decrepit."

Vern *had* suffered a pretty solid blow to the head. Still, Riker didn't want to argue with the man. *Will the roof hold all of our weight?* was what Riker was thinking as he bellied onto the camper shell and commando-crawled past the roof-mounted AC unit. His question was answered when Vern slithered up next to Lia and there was no keening of metal and no detectable sag to the roof underneath the three of them.

Benefitting from years of experience as an Olympic caliber shooter, Lia knew her way around bolt-action rifles. By the time Riker was next to her and taking the spare magazines from the nylon sack, she had already removed the Klepto long rifle from the Pelican case, deployed its Atlas bi-pod, and flipped the dust covers away from the lenses of the high-power Leupold scope.

As Riker passed Lia a five-round magazine topped with .308 Winchester, he caught her looking at her watch. Casting a furtive glance at the plaza, she bit her lip and seated the magazine into the magwell. She had just finished chambering a round and was settling in behind the rifle when firecracker-like reports from a sustained burst of automatic rifle fire rolled over their heads.

Raising the Steiners to his face, Riker painted three objects with the built-in laser rangefinder. The readout indicated the main building was 400 meters out. The Humvee parked next to the fuel island south of the main building was ten meters closer. Lasing the Dodge Ram pickup partially hidden behind the main building's northeast corner came up with a distance just shy of 450 meters. While the Ram's load bed was shielding a trio of men from fire directed at them by two camo-clad men kneeling beside the Humvee, their left flank was fully exposed to Riker and company.

Riker said, "I count five shooters."

Vern said, "There's bound to be more."

Klepto snugged tight to her shoulder, staring one-eyed into the scope, Lia said, "Vern's right. There's two more men on the ground behind the far fuel island. They've got the pack of zombies coming at them from their eight o' clock."

Riker said, "I see the biters. I don't see the shooters. Garbage can at the building's far corner is blocking my view. Are they wearing stolen camos?" As soon as he posed the question, one of the men came into view. He was indeed wearing desert camos. M4 cradled across his arms, he was low-crawling across the blacktop, angling toward the burning panel van, trying to get behind it without being seen.

Lia was saying, "He's trying to flank the men behind the Dodge," when a three-round burst fired from somewhere behind the main building cut into the man. From shoulder to buttock, blood splotches bloomed red on the tan fatigues.

Itching to get into the action, Riker chambered a round, shouldered the F4, and peered down the scope. "I'll get the ones on the right, by the pickup. You pick off the dirtbags behind the Hummer."

Lia had already drawn a deep breath and had a few pounds of pressure applied to the Klepto's trigger when she felt a hand on her right shoulder.

Dialed in and busy reciting a prayer of absolution in his head, Riker was just touching his finger to the trigger when a hand gripped his left shoulder.

Simultaneously, Lia and Riker heard Vern implore them to stand down.

"Why?" Riker said, taking his finger off the trigger. "They're sitting ducks."

Lia released the breath trapped in her lungs, engaged the rifle's safety, then shot the older man a questioning look.

Vern was surveying the truck plaza through the discarded Steiners. Without missing a beat, he said, "Because you *never* interfere with your enemy when he is destroying himself."

Riker backed off from the F4's scope. Looking side-eye at Vern, he said, "Sun Tzu?"

"Him or Napoleon. I'm getting old. I can never remember who said what." Vern panned the Steiners up a degree. "Also," he added, "one should never interrupt a herd of biters when they're stalking your enemies. That one's an original Vern Rossi quote."

Exasperated, Lia said, "The zombies are a couple of blocks away and won't pose a problem for some time. Right now I have clean shots on the ambushers by the Humvee."

"They're *all* ambushers," noted Vern. "Just so happens the new ambushers got the jump on the previous ambushers. They *all* need to go."

Another burst of gunfire from the fake Guardsman by the fuel island took out the feet of one of the shooters behind the Ram. Letting go of his short-barreled carbine, the redhead—dressed in blue jeans and wearing body armor over a flannel shirt—went down hard. Issuing a scream only those near to him could hear, he drew his legs up to his chest. A blink later a second burst from the fake Guardsman found the fallen man. The body jerked under the impact of several rounds and then went still, a pool of blood quickly spreading on the white cement.

As another one of the shooters behind the Dodge—an overweight middle-aged man wearing mismatched camos and a plate carrier way too small for him—went to the aid of the redhead, he was caught from behind by a fusillade of automatic rifle fire.

Startled look on his face, the third shooter—a teenager with bad acne and a recently shaved head—clambered into the load bed and laid down flat on his stomach.

"Wait for the fake Guardsman behind the building to come out from cover," Vern urged. "No doubt he thinks they have the upper hand. They sure as hell have the numbers."

Lia looked up from the rifle. "You think it's really three to one? Nobody from the kid's side hiding in the building?"

Riker shook his head. "They're boarded up real good. Pretty hard to engage your enemy if you can't see him."

"Agreed," said Vern. "I wouldn't trust that plywood to stop a BB." He went quiet for a tick and pointed to the main building's north side. "And here comes our flanker."

Sure enough, it was the man in camos who'd been low-crawling behind the burning panel van.

A series of loud pops sounded at the plaza and the panel van settled unevenly on three blown-out tires.

Hearing the out-of-place sounds, the kid in the Ram's load bed poked his head over the bed rail. His action was immediately answered by a volley fired from the flanker's M4.

Vern had been watching through the Steiners. When no new combatants entered the fray, he said, "Go ahead and hit them. Hit them hard. But be sure to leave one of them alive so we can question him."

Knowing how the firefight with the kids on her block in Santa Fe had left Lia rattled for days, Riker said, "On three. I'll get the teen in the truck and the crawler wearing the dead Guardsman's camos."

"OK," Lia said. She took a deep breath, flicked off the safety, and peered down the scope.

The pair of fake Guardsmen were still crouching behind the Hummer and conversing with one another when Lia found them with the Leupold. Feeling a lot like the Grim Reaper, an arbiter of who would live and who was going to die, she settled the crosshairs over the younger of the two men and transitioned her finger to the trigger.

When Riker's count reached three, a pair of reports broke the still. As the crack from Lia's rifle rolled across the open desert and the twenty-something man with half a mouthful of teeth took a round to the temple, the hollow *pop* emanating from Riker's F4 was instantly followed by a handful of closely spaced reports.

The flanker wore a surprised look as Riker's first three rounds pocked the asphalt to his fore. A millisecond later, the expression was erased from his face when two of the follow-on shots caved it in from chin to brow. The man was dead before shots five and six plowed harmlessly into the asphalt between his splayed-out legs.

"Two down, two to go," was crossing Riker's lips when the Klepto roared again. He took his eyes off the kid in the truck bed just long enough to see the last of the fake Guardsmen have his right arm nearly blown from the socket. Arm flailing uselessly, hands no longer gripping the black rifle, the man's mouth formed a silent O and he crashed face-first to the ground.

Obviously in the firm grip of the fog of battle, the kid in the pickup bed went to his knees, leveled a carbine at the Humvee, and proceeded to empty its magazine.

"Three down, one to go." Riker aimed for the swastika tattoo on the kid's neck, then pumped half a dozen rounds down range, easing up on the trigger only when the kid was slumped over the wheel well and unmoving.

As Lia rolled the bolt open and the spent brass tumbled forth, she stole another look at her watch.

In the process of swapping magazines, Riker said, "It's getting close to check-in time with the Cole kid, isn't it?"

Lia nodded. He saw she was still chewing her lip. Something was eating away at her. He had a feeling it had to do with what was happening to the kids in Vegas. Shelving the question on his mind until the time and place was right to ask it, he said, "We better get down there and check on the one you winged before the biters beat us to him."

Chapter 18

Shorty parked the Roamer on the east/west feeder road fronting Holl-Ee's. As agreed upon ahead of time, Riker slid the Shelby in next to the Roamer, on the driver's side, where the volatile cargo in the trailer would be shielded by the larger vehicle. While the trailer was out of the line of fire, the Shelby was still exposed from the front wheels forward. Which was perfect for Lia, because even before Riker had cut the engine, she was out and looping around front of the pickup. Using the Shelby's tall front end for cover, she deployed the Klepto's bi-pod and laid the long gun across the pickup's hood. Her job was to cover their left flank, which encompassed a couple of dozen eighteen-wheelers and half as many abandoned trailers scattered about the dirt overflow lot. The fuel island dedicated to the truckers and the two smaller buildings housing Holl-Ee's many amenities were also hers to watch.

For the time being, the only threat to her was the pack of trucker zombies angling in from her left.

After glassing the truck plaza one last time, Tara set the Bushnells on Steve-O's lap, shouldered open her door, and met her brother and Vern on the road between the two trucks.

MP5 at a low-ready, she said, "Nothing's moving but the zombies coming in on the feeder road. They'll be all over the injured dude in a couple of minutes. What the heck are we waiting for? Christmas?"

Riker had just popped some Advil and was busy massaging his temples with both thumbs. "I don't give a shit about that *dude*," he put in. "If they get him, they get him. I care about us. I'm calling a huddle so we can go over the plan one more time."

Reluctant to join the huddle—solely because she didn't like her brother's tone of voice—Tara stayed put and cocked an ear.

Also within earshot, Lia stayed behind the rifle and listened in.

Shorty remained in the Roamer, window open. As he took in the impromptu SITREP from his elevated position, he kept a close eye on the plaza and surrounding desert.

Riker quickly rehashed their agreed-upon plan, making sure each person knew their role. He would have one radio with him. Shorty would man his radio and remain in his elevated position, acting as their eyes and ears. Once all heads were bobbing in unison, Riker firmed his grip on the F4 and struck off toward the rear of the Roamer.

When Riker emerged from between the vehicles with Vern and Tara close on his heels, he was crouched down low and half-expecting to draw fire from the trucks in the field. Trusting Lia to have his back, to immediately return any incoming fire, he entered no-man's-land. Hustling across the first leg of open ground, some twenty feet sandwiched between the feeder road and run of pristine white sidewalk demarking Holl-Ee's southern border, he spent the entire time scrutinizing the plaza.

On the far side of a wide strip of dead lawn bordering the sidewalk, parked sideways to one of the smaller fuel islands, was the National Guard Humvee. Bullet holes riddled the top and side facing Riker. The windshield was spidered but still intact. Reaching the familiar vehicle, he looked in a side window. *Nothing moving inside.*

On the cement apron beside the stolen vehicle, clumped brains leaking slowly from his destroyed skull, was the first dirtbag Lia had dropped. Nearby, beginning next to an M4 on the ground beside the Humvee's rear wheel, was a trail of blood. The ragged crimson streak curled around back of the squat vehicle and ended a few feet away, where the man who had taken the round to the shoulder lay slumped, his one-armed commando crawl reduced to just the fingers of his left hand scrabbling futilely to find some kind of purchase on the smooth cement.

He's going nowhere, thought Riker as he knelt and scooped up the M4.

"Want me to render aid?" asked Vern.

Riker shook his head. "We stick to the plan. If he dies, he dies."

After relieving the injured man of a Beretta and several loaded magazines, Riker peered over his left shoulder. He picked up the zombie truckers shambling in on the feeder road. The first of the pack had just reached the plaza's western border and were using the curb cut to get onto the property. *Damn things are acting on snippets of retained memory.* Judging the open ground between the zombies and Humvee to be about a city block or so, he estimated they had two, three minutes tops to sweep the plaza for additional bad guys.

Equidistant to the Hummer and long row of oversized-vehicle fueling lanes, maybe twenty yards on the diagonal from Riker's position, was the panel van. It was fully engulfed, licks of flame and smoke pouring from its open front windows. It had been occupied by at least one person. The stink of burning rubber and cooking flesh hung heavy over the plaza. The latter was another of the things one could never forget once exposed to. Riker felt the heat of the fire warm on his face and left arm. Grateful he wasn't the crispy critter draped over the van's steering wheel, he continued on to his objective.

Angling away from the Humvee, Riker entered the shadow of the pump island canopy and stepped between a pair of gas pumps shoulder-high to him. After a quick left to right scan of the ground before him, he sprinted for the plaza's main building. The sound of retreating footsteps told him Tara and Vern had just split from him and were making their way around back of the main building.

As Riker made the southeast corner, roughly thirty yards south of the Dodge pickup, in his left side vision he saw Tara and Vern forming up on the building's southwest corner.

A quick turkey peek around his corner assured Riker there was nobody waiting in ambush near the Ram. Making eye contact with Tara, he held up a fist. Seeing her nod, he started the agreed-upon silent countdown. Arriving at one in unison, they all rolled around their respective corners.

Approaching the Ram, F4 tucked in tight to his shoulder, Riker got his first look at the damage inflicted on the ambushers. Slack face turned toward the blue sky, bloody gunshot-riddled legs akimbo, the redhead was lying in the shadow of the pickup atop a yellow puddle of his own urine.

After the redhead had had his legs shot out from underneath him, he had been struck by several follow-on shots. The one that killed him was to the temple. Clumps of brain matter had leaked from the ragged fissure and formed a broken halo around his head.

The overweight man in mismatched camouflage had come to rest on his stomach, his jowly face in a puddle of his own blood and pressed hard against the Ram's rear tire. Already the off-road tire's sidewall pattern had imprinted on the dead man's pallid forehead. Eyes wide open, mouth agape in a silent scream, the man's arms remained outstretched à la Pete Rose in one of his famous face-first slides into home. All put together, Riker got the impression the man's last attempt at preservation had been a clumsy dive for safety.

The tiny red holes punched through the big man's fatigue blouse told a different story. At best, the tiny plate carrier the man wore over his fatigues covered a third of his back. While some of the sustained burst from the flanker's rifle had likely been stopped by the ballistic plate, the rounds that got by had obviously found vital organs left unprotected.

The skinhead sprawled in the pickup's bed cast an accusing dead-eye stare Riker's way. Propped up, back against the bed rail, one elbow planted on the inner wheel well, the gutshot kid could have been enjoying a feature at the drive-in. In reality, the truth of the matter—which didn't make a blip on Riker's give-a-shit radar—was that the kid had died a horrible death, all alone, in great agony, his life blood pumping red and sticky onto the floor of the scarred metal load bed he had come to rest upon.

You reap what you sow, Riker thought as he unsheathed the Randall. He delivered the "insurance" stab to the brain to the kid first. Kneeling, he thrust the knife into the base of the big man's skull, just above the C1 vertebrae, scrambling what little brains he had behind a quick twist of the wrist.

When Riker was finished making doubly sure none of the ambushers would be coming back sans pulse and respiration, he peeked his head around the next corner. He spotted Vern first. The man was cupping his face with his hands and peering through a crack between a pair of Holl-Ee's boarded-over windows. Drawing back, he flashed Riker a thumbs-up. "All clear," Vern called. "Murderer number five is back here between the buildings. From the number of shell casings scattered about,

I'd bet the ones who did the Guardsmen stumbled upon the panel. This one was first to go. Caught himself a face full of lead."

Tara was stooped over the flanker. Looking up, one hand wrist-deep in a fatigue pocket, she said, "You tore this guy up, Lee. He never knew what hit him."

Do they ever? Riker mused. Out loud, he said, "Do I have time to search the truck?"

Tara craned and looked the length of the building. "If you make it quick." She scooped up the flanker's carbine, dumped the magazine and checked the chamber. "This one left behind a couple of full magazines. Want me to do the zombies?"

Nodding, he said, "Put down all but one of them. Immobilize the one you spare."

"Immobilize?"

"All I need operable on the thing is its mouth."

As if a lightbulb switched on in her head, Tara said slowly, "To make the injured guy sing. You're wicked, bro."

Getting there, Riker thought. Turning back to the Ram, he started rifling through pockets.

The redhead was a collector of identifications. A cursory scan told Riker the man was holding one issued by nearly every state. Men, women, old, young … didn't seem to be a method to the madness. He was also in possession of a short stack of military IDs—six of them belonging to Littlewolf's troops. A chill coursed Riker's spine as he realized he was holding trophies taken from people the group had murdered.

Determining the Ram's tank still held some diesel, he set about searching the cab. He found a daypack stuffed full of dozens of pairs of soiled panties. He emptied the pack of its creepy contents and was busy filling it with canned food and MREs when the gunfire began. A beat later, Shorty's voice sprang from the radio in his pocket, assuring him the gunfire was Tara "redeadening" the zombies. If not for the pounding headache, Riker might have chuckled at Shorty's made-up word. As it was, it was all he could do to not down his entire stockpile of Advil.

Finished policing up all the loose ammo and full magazines he could fit in the pack, Riker radioed Shorty back. "Did the lone survivor make it?"

"Apparently it's touch and go. Vern's tending to him. Your girl Lia is still at her post. Nobody's moving on our six." Shorty finished the SITREP, saying, "Those occupied big rigs we passed on the way in. I was thinking of going back up the road and seeing if there's diesel to be had in their tanks."

"We really can't spare the time," Riker replied. "Besides, the Ram's got a full tank of diesel. Probably twenty or thirty gallons in the main. There's a transfer tank in the bed that needs checking. Looks like one of the thirty-eight-gallon jobs."

"So that's a firm 'no' on Shorty's big adventure?"

Riker exited the Ram and closed the door. "I'm just offering my opinion on the rigs. Time, though … it's a finite commodity." He paused for a tick. "We still have to question the survivor."

"Copy that, boss," Shorty said. "I'll spool up the siphoning operation."

Riker made no further comment. If Shorty was *butt hurt* as Tara was wont to describe his demeanor whenever he was told no, it wasn't evident in his tone. Rolling down the volume and stowing the radio, Riker went about separating the military IDs from the rest. Finished, he put them in the pocket with the dog tags.

Exiting the Ram, Riker tossed the rest of the IDs into the load bed with the dead skinhead. Most of them landed in the pooled blood and stayed there, stuck fast. Some, caught by an errant wind gust, flew back in his face and ended up scattered on the ground near the corpses.

Gaze settling on the dead men, Riker said, "Fuck you, and you, and you … especially *you*, you Aryan Nation piece of shit." He spat on the kid with the swastika tattoo. "I pray you all rot in hell." He was actually wishing far worse for them, envisioning in his head the trio in escape-proof stocks planted in a lake of fire and Satan wearing both a wicked grin and a massive strap-on dildo. Too bad their days of feeling pain were done.

Inside the Roamer, Steve-O gave Shorty a questioning look. Finished relaying his brief SITREP, Shorty said, "You heard the man. No more side journey for us, amigo. What you can do, though, is put on the Mule and grab the siphon. I'll get us some empty cans and meet you at the Ram."

Steve-O didn't jump like he did when Riker spoke up.

"Whatsa matter?" Shorty asked. "You got a turtlehead poking out? Got a poo trying to go prairie dog on you?"

"Nope," replied Steve-O, "But I do have to pee *real* bad. Can I do that first?"

"Of course you can," Shorty replied. "You never have to ask permission from me, Steve-O. Just say 'pull over, motherfucker. I have to piss.'"

One hand clamped on his crotch, Steve-O said, "Pull over motherfucker. I have to piss."

Shorty chuckled as he raised up off his seat and looked out over the hood. Lia was there, only now the rifle was all alone on the hood and she was sitting on the winch mount and watching Tara sell the zombies *insurance*. Each time Tara thrust that black blade of hers through a temple or poked an eye out with its angled tip, he threw a hard shiver. He had to give it to her. She'd gotten good at mentally separating the people the zombies used to be from the mindless flesh-eaters Romero had turned them into.

After a quick glance out both side windows—seeing to his left the deserted freeway a hundred yards distant, and in the opposite direction, Vern working furiously to save the grievously injured ambusher—he checked the dash-mounted monitor. The rear-facing cameras showed that the feeder road behind the Roamer was clear to the extent of their reach: about halfway down the train of abandoned big rigs.

"Go ahead," Shorty instructed. "But make it quick. We still need to siphon the fuel from the Ram."

Steve-O shouldered open his door and climbed from the Roamer.

Catching Steve-O as he was closing the door, Shorty made eye contact. "You know, Steve-O," he said, eyes scanning their surroundings. "It sure would be a shame if you *accidently* pissed on that dead murderer by the Hummer."

Smile curling one corner of his mouth, Steve-O snapped off a pretty good salute and shut his door.

While Steve-O liked Shorty's *suggestion*—a word Steve-O's former caregiver Marcy had told him was just a sneaky way of issuing an order—he was afraid that by following through, his penis would be hanging out for all to see.

Walking with a pronounced limp—a hitch in his gait not brought on because of the siphon in hand or the extra weight of the Mule on his back, but more so because his bladder felt as if it was about to burst—Steve-O crossed no-man's-land and made his way to the dead body sprawled beside the Humvee. As he was unzipping his fly, he saw Riker approaching from the far side of the plaza. To Steve-O's left, beyond the Humvee's canted hood, Tara was luring the last couple of stragglers Shorty had taken to calling "the front row of a Willie Nelson concert" down one of the big rig fueling lanes. She was shooting and moving. No way she could see *Mister Penis* from there. A quick glance over his left shoulder told him Lia couldn't see him, either. All that was visible of her over the Roamer's hood was the very top of her black ball cap.

Shorty hung his head out the open window and hollered, "There's a time and place for a bashful bladder! This ain't it!"

Lia shook her head. "Leave him alone, Shorty."

At the Humvee, Steve-O had been standing so close to its rear door when the dam finally broke that the blowback left his untucked shirt and Wranglers dotted with a constellation of highly visible pee stains.

Taking a step back, Steve-O changed his aim just long enough to wet the head and shoulders of the corpse staring up at him. Unnerved by the dead eyes seemingly fixed on his privates, he turned back toward the window. Instead of focusing on his own reflection, or the two vehicles behind him, he peered inside the Humvee. Unable to see past his own visage transposed over the blue sky in the background, he removed his Stetson and used it to block the glare.

Instantly he learned he was not alone. There, on the floor in front of what passed for a backseat, a pair of disembodied eyes stared back at him.

At first, he was convinced he was staring into his own eyes. That notion was challenged when those eyes blinked, and he had not. The possibility he had been seeing things was proven wrong when he blinked twice and the pair of white orbs remained fixed on him.

Keeping a cool head, he hitched up his Wranglers, tucked in the damp shirt, and buttoned and belted the well-worn blue jeans. With that out of the way, he decided the best course of action was to alert the person nearest to him. Seeing that Vern was digging into the first aid kit and that the man on the ground to his fore was writhing in agony, Steve-O opted for the second closest person.

"Tara. I need help."

She was on one knee near the far fuel island and trussing her brother's zombie with a pair of zip ties taken off one of the ambushers. "I'm no good with buttons, Steve-O. Better have Lee help you."

"I don't need help with my *pants*," Steve-O called back. "I see eyeballs. I think someone … or maybe a monster, is in the Army truck."

Hearing the exchange from a dozen yards away, Riker tucked the F4 to his shoulder and hustled across the oil-stained cement breezeway. Reaching the pumps parallel to the Humvee, his approach bringing him in opposite Steve-O and at an angle he hoped would render any gunfire from the backseat ineffective, he crouched down next to Vern and the injured ambusher.

Waving Steve-O away from the rig, Riker said, "What did you see."

Boot heels scuffing the pavement as he shuffled backward, Steve-O said, "*Eyeballs.* I saw eyeballs."

Edging around back of the Humvee, his large frame filling up the space between the pump and passenger-side rear door, Riker rose up from his crouch and stole a quick peek into the backseat area. Seeing his own face, blurry and reflected back at him, he raised the F4, triggered the tac-light affixed to its Picatinny rail, and trained the cone of brilliant white light at the Humvee's backseat. While there was some glare at first, adjusting the angle of the rifle let him see, in all her naked glory, the woman whose eyeballs had gotten Steve-O all flustered.

Thumbing off the tac-light, Riker called across the plaza. "Sis … get over here. Make it quick." He glanced at the Roamer. "You too, Lia. And bring a blanket or jacket or something."

Chapter 19

Pointing at the Roamer, Tara bellowed, "Avert your eyes, Shorty." Next, she ordered Steve-O to the rear of the Humvee, telling him to stay there with Lee and Vern until she gave them the all-clear.

Standing a dozen feet from the Humvee, on the edge of the cement apron, Steve-O waved the wand of the Mule at Tara. "Won't you need this?"

"Get over here," Riker barked from behind the Humvee. "That's a woman you saw in there, *not* a zombie. And she's totally naked."

Lia arrived from the rear of the Roamer. She'd come with a Patagonia jacket underneath one arm and an unzipped sleeping bag, one end dragging the ground behind her. Placing a hand on Steve-O's shoulder, she gently steered him toward where he needed to be.

Reaching the Humvee, Lia placed her jacket on its roof. Gripping two corners of the sleeping bag, she extended her arms and used the bag as a makeshift blind.

With the bag in the way of prying eyes, Tara opened the Humvee's rear door and leaned inside. "LaTasha?" she asked, her voice low and unthreatening.

The woman blinked once but said nothing.

As Tara shifted in the door, a bar of sunlight illuminated the duct tape covering the woman's mouth. Without warning, she gripped a corner and yanked.

Eyes tearing up, the woman said, "Could have warned me you were gonna do that."

All business, Tara repeated her question. *No time for beating around the bush.*

She nodded subtly. "Sergeant LaTasha Jackson … Army National Guard … Hundred and Eleventh Sustainment Brigade out of Rio Rancho, New Mexico." The African American sergeant's hair was cut short. Suggestive of an undue amount of time spent under the desert sun, her skin was nearly the same dark brown hue as Tara's. The similarities didn't end there: The sergeant was early to mid-thirties and possessed the same wiry physique.

Sergeant Jackson's hands and feet had been zip tied together behind her back. After a cursory examination, during which Tara looked for obvious injuries and any evidence the sergeant had been bitten, she took hold of one of her hands. It was ice cold, the palm dark purple.

As Tara cut through the zip tie binding the sergeant's wrists, she said, "While I don't think you're in danger of losing any fingers, I do think, real soon, they are going to get hit with a shit storm of pins and needles." After cutting the tie around the soldier's ankles, Tara helped her to sit up on the seat.

Rubbing her hands together, the sergeant said, "You're right. Feeling is returning. It ain't the good kind, either."

"Better than the alternative," Tara noted. "How about your feet?"

"Same. Pins and needles."

Tara peered into the front of the Humvee. "Any idea where your clothes ended up?"

"They're probably in the van where the fuckers gang-raped me."

Tara grimaced. *Motherfuckers. What's this world come to?* Craning her head out the Humvee, she ordered anyone within earshot to strip one of the corpses of its fatigues. "Bring me the cleanest pair you can find! The ones with the least amount of brains and blood on them."

Lia handed Jackson the Patagonia.

Jackson took the coat, draped it over her shoulders, then looked up and locked eyes with Lia. "Are they *all* dead? The ones who took us hostage *and* the ones who just ambushed them?"

Eyes roaming the plaza, Lia said, "Except for the one Lee wants alive for questioning, all of them are on their way to hell."

Nodding in agreement, Tara said, "Lia winged the survivor. Nearly blew his damn arm off. Vern patched him up. Still, he's in pretty bad shape. Lost a lot of blood."

"Four of the dead are wearing Guard fatigues," Lia added.

Hooking a thumb over her shoulder, Tara said, "There's a guy cooking in the panel van. He's one of the fuckers who ambushed you and your men at the airport, right?"

"Technically, they weren't my men. Lieutenant Murphy was leading our fuel acquisition mission." She shook her head. "In the Sandbox, LT always had to stop and talk to the villagers. Kids, mostly. He'd hand out candy and such. He was a real good guy. Very religious. Family man. The van was parked off the side of the road by the airport. Flat tire. At least that's what it looked like as we rolled up on them. Guy and a woman trying to change it." She went quiet for a bit.

Tara said, "So you all stopped to help. Then what happened?"

The sergeant bowed her head.

Tara bellowed, "*Clothing please!*" Returning her attention to Jackson, she said, "We found Murphy and three other men back at the airport. All of them were dead and had been stripped of their uniforms. I think my brother removed their dog tags and kept them. I know he has yours and one other that he found on the seat of your pickup." She had purposefully left out the part about the Guardsman turning zombie and attacking Vern. No sense adding to the anguish she was sure the sergeant had to be feeling after learning none of her fellows had survived.

After peering through the Humvee's windows for any movement that might indicate the fatigues were on the way, Tara locked eyes with the seated sergeant. "The other tags belonged to Katelyn Dehen. Do you know where she is?"

"They raped her, too," Jackson said. A tear traced her cheek. "They separated us after they were done taking turns. I got put in here ...." She started to sob.

Tara didn't need to hear the rest to know that Katelyn had been in the van, bound and trussed with no way to escape, and had likely burned alive. *What a fucking terrible way to go.* Stomach clenching, she repeated her request for fatigues.

Heard you the first time, Riker thought. He was on his knees behind the Humvee and struggling mightily to undress the young man Lia had killed. While the fatigue blouse was stippled with blood and gore and came off easily, the pants were a different story. Already a couple of sizes too small for the dead man, they were damp and sticking to his clammy skin. Riker stopped what he was doing long enough to touch one of the dark stains and sniff his fingers.

Urine?

"Steve-O," Riker called. "Get over here."

Still weighted down by the Mule, the siphon pump, and several empty gas cans, Steve-O waddled over, whistling a happy tune.

Riker regarded the man. "Did you piss on this guy?"

Without hesitation, Steve-O said, "Guilty as charged."

Riker extended a fist. "My man."

Steve-O set the cans on the ground. Reciprocating the fist bump, he said, "It was Shorty's idea. I enjoyed it, though."

"Great minds run on the same track," Riker said as he yanked the pant legs over the uncooperative corpse's bare feet. "I was contemplating dropping a deuce on *Nazi Boy* over there. Just wish I had one in the chamber."

Again Tara bellowed, "Clothing? Anyone working on getting Sergeant Jackson here some fatigues. Damn it … seems like all the men I'm riding with have turned mute on me."

Riker balled up the fatigues. Gripping the uniform and boots in one mitt-sized hand, he made his way around the Humvee and passed the items over top of the sleeping bag. "Cleanest pair out here," he said. "I'd tell you the wet spots are water, but I'd be lying."

Arms beginning to tremble from holding the bag aloft, Lia peered around one side. Meeting Riker's gaze, she whispered, "What is it?"

"You don't want to know," Riker whispered back. "Just forget about it."

The response further piqued Lia's interest. She made a face and mouthed her question again.

Riker made no reply.

Tara poked her head around the sleeping bag. "You can put it down now, Lia. Sergeant Jackson's decent."

As Lia folded the bag and threw it over her shoulder, Tara backed away from the open door. When Jackson finally emerged, fully clothed in the ill-fitting fatigues and oversized boots, Tara made formal introductions.

Riker nodded. "Sergeant. Wish we were meeting under better circumstances. Sorry about what happened to your unit."

Lia grabbed her Patagonia off the seat. "If you're not needing this, I'll take it all back to the Roamer."

"I'm good," Jackson said. She regarded the dead man. "Phenomenal shooting, ma'am. Thanks for your help. Thanks for everything you guys did here."

As Lia set course for the Roamer, Riker said to Jackson, "We're heading to Vegas. You're welcome to come along." He gave her the Cliff's Notes version of what had led to the quest he had come to think of as *Lia's Jihad.* While he hadn't gone so far as to call it that out loud, until he heard from Cole again, he put their odds of doing any good at fifty/fifty.

Jackson shook her head. "I'd be AWOL if I did. Besides, I signed this vehicle out, I intend on bringing her back." She went quiet for a beat. "Major Littlewolf was expecting us back."

"Our friend Shorty has a long-range comms suite in his Roamer. You're welcome to use it to hail the major." He gestured toward the Ram. "I took some food and a couple hundred rounds of 5.56 out of the pickup. You can take what you need."

Jackson shook her head. "We just stood up the armory on one September of this year. We're flush with food, weapons, ammunition. What we lack is manpower. Troops were trickling in when the Romero bug popped. Since then, only a handful have reported for duty."

Riker nodded knowingly. "Explains why Littlewolf called the armory 'Fort Apache.'"

"We've had to fight off our fair share of opportunists," Jackson admitted. "Didn't end well for most of them."

Vern emerged from behind the Humvee. He tipped his cap to the sergeant and introduced himself. Finished with introductions, he faced Riker. "This guy's fading fast, Lee. If you're going to interrogate him, better do it real soon."

"We don't need him anymore," Riker said. "Sergeant Jackson here already filled in the blanks. Steve-O, on your way to the pickup, go ahead and finish him with the Mule. And while you're at it, might as well do Tara's zombie, too. Won't be needing it."

Jackson arched a brow. "What's the Mule?"

Tara pointed to Vern's invention, giving it high praise when she was finished describing how it worked. To Steve-O, she called, "Why don't you show the sergeant how quiet it is in action."

Eyes going wide, Jackson said, "No, no, no. Can't let the murdering piece of shit get off that easily." She shook her head vigorously. "No way. Me and Mr. Rapist have unfinished business to attend to."

Riker tugged from his waistband the Beretta he'd taken off the dead man. "Military issue. Likely one of yours."

"I'm not using that either," Jackson scoffed. She pointed to the Randall riding on Riker's hip. "I'll be needing *that*." She looked over the group. "I'll also require someone to hold him down while I work."

Hearing that the Mule wouldn't be needed, Steve-O headed off to siphon the fuel from the pickup.

Lia and Tara didn't jump. In fact, having a good idea what the sergeant had in store for the injured captive, they both clammed up and averted their gazes.

Riker's hesitation lasted just long enough to allow Vern to volunteer for the job. When the older man finally spoke up, Riker released the breath trapped in his lungs. While he couldn't blame the sergeant for wanting to do what he feared she was about to, he didn't need any more nightmare fuel. Since the dead began to rise, uninterrupted sleep had been hard to come by.

Telling himself the act of loaning the Randall to the sergeant wasn't the same as being an accessory to an especially gory murder, he yanked it from its sheath and, reluctantly, handed it to her hilt first.

A wicked expression ghosted across the sergeant's face. Smiling, she said, "Thank you, kind sir," and disappeared around back of the Humvee, Vern in tow.

If the older man had any sense of what kind of punishment was about to be meted out to the rapist/murderer, it wasn't betrayed by his expression. Wearing the mother of all poker faces, he passed by the others without saying a word.

The moment Tara's admonishment issued from the radio on the seat beside Shorty, he had averted his eyes from the Humvee. After a few seconds of staring straight ahead, he took a quick peek out the Roamer's passenger window. Lia was back to standing beside the Humvee, only now she was blocking his view of the desert-tan vehicle with his sleeping bag.

Next, he watched in amusement as Riker struggled to strip the corpse of its fatigues. Tiring of the one-sided battle taking place behind the Humvee, he switched to watching Vern trying to save the man whose right arm Lia had nearly amputated with a single .308 round. It had been one hell of a shot. Seeing as how the Olympic-caliber athlete had had the benefit of shooting without having just finished a prolonged sprint on cross-country skis (a feat that would have anyone's heartrate and respiration elevated and caused all kinds of aiming problems), her accuracy, even taking into account the added distance, was to be expected. Shooting down the draw behind Trinity House, the woman had drilled a moving zombie behind the ear from twice the distance.

For the first couple of minutes, Vern had been in full-on medic mode. Seemingly in a trance, gloved hands a blur and dipping in and out of his first aid kit, he poured some kind of powder into the gaping gunshot wound, lifted the detached arm off the ground and reintroduced its ball joint to the rotator cuff, then deftly bandaged the man up. Shorty saw all of the lifesaving actions as a lost cause, nevertheless he understood why Vern was going through the trouble.

When the sleeping bag blind finally came down, Shorty liked what he saw. While he wasn't into the Grace Jones look, the African American woman wearing the baggy uniform was very easy on the eyes. Shorty's eyes remained glued to her as she conversed with the others. They never left her as she took the Randall in hand. And though he had a hunch what was to come, he remained mesmerized as she grabbed the prisoner's flaccid member in one hand and introduced the blade to the base just below the swollen scrotum. Watching her remove his manhood in one fell swoop was like witnessing a slow-moving train wreck; nothing short of a mushroom cloud blooming on the horizon could have broken the trance.

Only when the deed was done, the castrated man being held down by Vern screaming bloody murder, did Shorty scoop up the radio. Thumbing the Talk button, he said, "You there, Lee?"

Shorty saw his friend's gaze swing up and lock on the Roamer. Slowly, the radio in the man's hand closed the distance to his mouth. Amplified screams coming from the radio filled the cab. A tick later, speaking loudly to be heard over the wails of the dying man, Riker said, "What's up?"

"You were onboard with that?"

"Least I could do, considering what they did to the sergeant and her comrades."

"For the record," said Shorty, "it didn't break my heart to see that piece of work lose his twig and berries. Seeing 'em go flying across the plaza was the cherry on the sundae." He chuckled into the radio. "Sergeant Lorena Bobbit there has an arm like Randy Johnson. Damn near hit Steve-O with the guy's junk."

"Thanks for the play-by-play," said Riker. "Now I have a visual to go along with the soundtrack." There was a short pause. "Anything else on your mind?"

"Is she coming with us? If so, she can ride in Large Marge with me and the gang."

"No, she isn't," Riker radioed back. "After Steve-O's done transferring fuel from the Ram to the Humvee, Sergeant Jackson is heading back to the armory. In the meantime, I told her she could use your long-range radio to contact Major Littlewolf."

Smile curling the corners of Shorty's mouth, he said, "Red Rover, Red Rover, send the Nubian beauty over."

Chapter 20

Trinity House

Rose was dressed all in black leather and sitting on a folding chair in the bunker beneath Trinity's great room. On the table beside the HAM radio, collapsed in on itself and looking like a misshapen human face, was the leather half-mask that had been paired with the costume she had on. A cat o' nine tails—not necessarily a thing Catwoman might employ against Batman—sat next to the mask.

The shiny black costume had come with the trove of oddities Shorty had taken from a suburban home he'd plundered earlier in the week. The smooth leather touching her skin made her think of Benny. He had gone off to the Lazarus facility dressed as Batman. That his arms, chest, and legs didn't quite fill out the matte-black latex suit was of no concern to her. She liked him just the way he was—all sinew and muscle. Running her hands over the suit's vacuum-formed six-pack abs was just a reminder of what lay inside the *package*. Who knew introducing her new man to cosplay in a mansion they had all to themselves would be so much fun? Unwilling to change into the clothes that reminded her of her usual mousy self, the persona that had let her glide unnoticed amongst the denizens of the old world, she convinced Benny to do the same. In her mind's eye, she pictured him moving about the Lazarus facility, in costume—the master of his lair. If anything could come close to being a real Batcave, the subterranean bunker up the hill from Trinity was it.

Though ten minutes remained until Cole's usual check-in time, Rose had been at her post with the radio powered up for double that. Having worked restaurants for years in her old life, she still adhered to the adage that "showing up five minutes early to shift was akin to being late." It was her manager's favorite way of telling her and the rest of the front-of-the-house staff at the well-known chain Italian restaurant that they were to be suited up and clocked in before the first guest was seated. The burned-out lifer was also subtly warning them that if he had to venture from the office and greet tables for anyone coming in late to shift, there would be hell to pay, which usually meant the offending party would be saddled with extra after-shift cleaning duties.

If there was one thing Rose would never miss from her old *existence*—and this sentiment was shared wholeheartedly by Tara—it was the ungrateful slice of humanity that couldn't bring themselves to treat restaurant staff as equals.

On the table beside the radio was a monitor displaying images fed to it by the many closed-circuit cameras around Trinity's perimeter. In the pane in the monitor's upper right corner, the pair of zombies drawn in by the noise of the convoy leaving earlier in the morning still paced the cul-de-sac. They'd arrived two hours ago, approached the gate fronting the parking pad, loitered there for a spell, then began to wander the length of the wall.

Rose had started a mantra in hopes they would turn around and leave the way they had come. When repeating *go away zombies* over and over in her head hadn't worked, she became resigned to the fact she would be the one putting down the bloated pair of walking corpses she'd named Stay Puft and Mama Cass.

Time and the elements had not been kind to the male zombie. Morbidly obese to begin with, the pasty-white corpse had bloated to the point where its butt cheeks were seemingly eating its skid-marked underpants. Each step it took sent an equally pasty pair of man boobs moving in concentric circles. Below the Cro-Magnon brow, the thing's eyes were black dots crowded by leaden lids and chipmunk-like cheeks. Cheeks to clavicle, the thing was all neck. Now and again, when Stay Puft opened its slit of a mouth to emit a hollow-sounding moan, what passed for a chin would briefly emerge from the sea of fat.

The name Rose had bestowed on the latter had nothing to do with physical appearance. It had all to do with the message on the undead woman's soiled tee shirt. Bracketed by neon green palm trees, the words *California Dreamin'* had instantly started the song of the same name playing in Rose's head. Mama Cass was the only member of the Mamas and Papas whose name she could recall. Something about the woman's untimely death, choking on a ham sandwich, had caused her name to stand out.

"Go away, damn it." She tapped the monitor. "Santa Fe is that way. Go find someone else to redead you." Rose still had a hard time with the K word. Psychopaths killed things. Serial killers didn't blink when snuffing out a human life. She was still convinced there was a little spark of life somewhere inside the undead. Every one she'd put down so far, in her mind, put her one step closer to being just like John Wayne Gacy or Gary Leon Ridgway—killers she had no doubt now were hanging in Hell with Mao Zedong, Adolf Hitler, and Joseph Stalin. As a believer in her savior, Jesus Christ, ending up in the hot place was a fate she wanted to avoid at all costs.

Just as the pair of zombies was joined by an especially road-worn shambler, a kid of about ten whose left arm was a bloody stump ending just below the elbow, the radio's external speaker came alive.

Rose immediately forgot about weighing the hell on earth she was currently living against the one she had been taught awaited her should she stray from the tenets of her religion. Looking at the bank of clocks high up on the wall, she saw Cole had hit his mark.

On the heels of the hiss of white noise coming from the speaker, a voice, faint and tinged with notes of the South, said, "Lia? Are you there, Lia?"

Donning the headphones, Rose adjusted the volume to a comfortable level. After drawing a deep breath to calm her nerves, she thumbed the button on the handheld microphone and introduced herself to Cole Parker.

After a prolonged silence, the boy asked, "Where is Lia?"

Peering down at the handwritten instructions left behind by Lia, the first line on which was written **DO NOT TELL COLE ABOUT THE PLAN**, Rose opened the channel. Telling herself it was just a little white lie, she said, "Lia's not here, Cole. She's gone out on a foraging run."

Voice cracking, Cole said, "I told her this was the only time I might be able to get back on the radio."

"Lia didn't want to leave," Rose responded. "She wanted to be here. She cares about you, Cole. She really does. That's why I'm here in her place."

The channel opened on Cole's end. Rose could hear ragged breathing and an occasional whimper. Finally, he said, "When are you guys coming to rescue us?"

Lia put the Sharpie between her teeth and bit down on it. She longed to give him the shred of hope he so badly needed. Her eyes dropped to the pad. **DO NOT TELL COLE ABOUT THE PLAN**. Then her gaze wandered down the page, lingering on each of Lia's questions as she posed them.

"Where are Janice and Kurt right now?"

Cole said, "They're both passed out drunk. Unless we're moving on, they do this just about every day."

"Has the man returned from the recon?" Reading Lia's question verbatim sounded strange to Rose.

"Not that I know of. I think he's their son, though."

Deviating from the line of questioning, Rose asked, "What's your best guess? Have you heard any vehicles coming and going?"

"Nobody is going in or out," replied Cole. "Too many biters hanging around the parking lot." She knew he was telling the truth. Could hear the fear in his voice. She wrote down **Nobody in and out. ZOMBIES in the parking lot** and circled it twice.

"How is Cole … er, how are you, Cole?" Angry at herself for reading the question as it was written, Rose lowered her head and pressed her forehead to the desk blotter.

"I'm OK," he answered. "I can take care of myself. It's the others I'm worried about. Charlie and Missy keep crying. Last night Kurt tied them up and taped their mouths shut. He only does that when he takes one of them to the back room. He didn't this time. He kept drinking." Rose didn't like the sound of that. It all but confirmed Lia's assumption that the couple was actively abusing the kids—likely sexually. The kids' ages were listed beside the names jotted down on the pad. *Six and two. Damn those monsters.* Swallowing hard, she again went off-script. "The tape was left on them all night long?" She released the Talk button and pinched away newly forming tears.

When Cole came back on, he said, "Charlie is fine." He paused for a long three-count. "Missy … she's had a breathing problem the whole time I've known her. This morning, when we all woke up, she was still tied and had the tape over her mouth. But she was blue in the face and wasn't moving." There was a long pause. "Kurt took her into the back room." Another long pause was punctuated by Cole crying. "He came back out alone. When I asked if she was dead, he slapped me across the face and told me to keep quiet about it."

Rose's gaze drifted up the yellow pad, to the top. **DO NOT TELL COLE ABOUT THE PLAN.**

Screw that, she thought. *One's already gone and sounds like Cole's barely hanging on.* She thumbed the Talk button, lifted the microphone to her lips, and let it linger there as she wrestled with what she saw as a life and death decision that needed to be made. Finally, mind made up, she said, "Hang tight, Cole. Good people are coming to help you. Just be smart and don't make Kurt or Janice angry. Pray for Missy but be strong for the others."

When the channel opened up, Rose could hear Cole sniffling. The sound of dry lips parting preceded Cole asking her if Lia was going to abandon him and the others.

Sensing the strong bond that had formed between Lia and the boy and not wanting Cole to give up, Rose said, "No, she's not. She's coming with a whole bunch of friends who hate bad people just about as much as she does."

After a short silence, Cole whispered, "I'm going to make it so the back door stays unlocked." He went on, telling her in great detail all he had learned about where he was being held since he'd last talked to Lia.

Rose listened, all the while jotting everything down in Lia's spiral notebook.

"That's real helpful," she said. "I'll pass it on."

After a long silence, Cole said, "I think I just heard some noise coming from next door. I gotta go now."

"Bye for now, Cole," Rose whispered. "You hang in there." Heavy of heart, she peeled off the headphones and hung them on the closed-circuit monitor.

As she set the microphone on the desk and rolled the volume down, the enormity of what she'd just done hit her like a ton of bricks. Leaving out the betrayal part, she scooped up the Iridium satellite phone and typed out an SMS message. She let her finger hover over the button for a full minute before sending the message on its way.

Suddenly disgusted with herself, in more ways than one, she headed upstairs so she could get out of the ridiculous costume.

Indian Route 12

Southeast Arizona

"The reds and oranges are *sooo* vivid," Lia gushed. She was leaning forward in her seat, seatbelt taut against her shoulder, chin nearly resting on the Shelby's dusty dash. "It's like God finished with Sedona and went to work here with the same palette and brush."

Heeding Sergeant Jackson's warning to avoid Flagstaff because it was a hotbed of infection, with the majority of its eighty thousand residents minus a pulse and roaming the streets in search of the living, Lia had pored over the map and found them an alternate route to Las Vegas, one that would, to her chagrin, set them back a few hours and add roughly two hundred extra miles to their trip.

According to Jackson, three days into the outbreak, jetliner after fully loaded jetliner started arriving at Flagstaff's Pulliam Airport. Commercial and private planes, some belonging to carriers that had never before touched down there, had come from all points of the compass—domestic *and* international. A scant few had arrived with a full manifest of healthy passengers and crew. Many more had brought with them passengers already infected with Romero, which quickly introduced death and destruction on a massive scale to the nearby city.

As the two-vehicle convoy entered a stretch of highway crowded on both sides by stands of ponderosa pines, Vern said, "This is Navajo country we're cutting through. I'd expect us to have some kind of contact with local law enforcement before we reach the western boundary." He paused for a second, thinking. "Me and Shane came this way last time we road tripped to Vegas. If I remember correctly, before we shoot off west on SR-264, we'll get a good look at Window Rock. It's a sight to behold. In my opinion, it puts Snoopy Rock in Sedona to shame."

Back to scanning the road ahead through the Steiners, Lia said, "We'll soon find out."

After a few long seconds of silence, Riker caught Vern's gaze in the rearview mirror. "What's it got on castrating a man?" There was an icy tone to his voice. "Is that a *sight* to behold, too?"

Vern said nothing at first. Then, after a minute had ticked into the past, he said calmly, "That line of questioning is a bit passive-aggressive, don't you think?"

Death grip on the steering wheel, eyes locked on a point in space only he could see, Riker remained tightlipped. If the headache coming on was any indicator, he was afraid anything he had to say on the matter would come from a place of anger. Conversely, if he were to use comedy to diffuse the situation—a tool taught to him by more than one therapist—his traveling companions would assume he had lost it completely.

"She didn't just castrate that mutt," Vern put in. "She took it *all* off. The whole kit and caboodle. And if Steve-O hadn't already put down your *solution* to the problem, she would have fed the rapist's shriveled member to the undead bastard."

Pounding a palm on the steering wheel, Riker said, "So now we're resorting to frontier justice?"

"I'd rather call it *biblical reckoning.* An eye for an eye, so to speak." Vern shook his head. "The longer I listened to that young sergeant unload on that man, telling him how she felt with those four sweaty bodies taking turns defiling her and the other woman in the stifling heat inside of that van, the more I wanted to take a pound of flesh from the son of a bitch. Enact a little *frontier justice* for those four dead soldiers at the airport."

Lia had purposefully kept quiet, content to keep scanning the road ahead. Now, though, with Lee under attack, she felt the urge to posit her take on what had gone down at Holl-Ee's. Lowering the Steiners, she said to Vern, "I think what Lee is getting at is that the man was already dying. He had *one arm* blown completely off. I own that. But, Vern, for crying out loud, he was defenseless."

The tension inside the cab was palpable. It only added to the incessant throbbing behind Riker's eyes. "I don't need anyone speaking for me," he shot. "I'm just addressing the elephant in the room."

"It's true the man was defenseless," Vern conceded. "In every sense of the word. But what he did is unconscionable. I'm at peace with my part in it. Reap what you sow, and all that. Let's face it, Lee … we are the law now. Those natives in Thoreau and Coolidge have had to become the law for their people. Pretty soon, though, once society falls further into anarchy, the one who's carrying the biggest stick will be the law. Ask yourself this, Lee. You're standing in front of Peter and arguing your fate … would you want to be the one who has sinned but with good intention, or the rapist/murderer seeking absolution?"

Grudgingly, Riker matched Vern's gaze in the mirror. "The former, of course."

Vern slumped back into his seat.

Incredulous, Riker said, "So you're telling me you feel zero remorse for what you did?"

"I'd say so with a megaphone if I had one," Vern replied. *It was you who provided the knife*, was what he wanted to add. Discretion being the better part of valor, he kept it to himself.

Riker said, "Elephant addressed," and clammed up.

Lia went back to scanning the road through the Steiners.

Since exiting I-40 west of Holl-Ee's, they had traveled north along Defiance Plateau for sixteen miles, cut through Oak Springs (population sixty-three), and then passed by a small cluster of farms north of town, all without seeing a single soul. Along the way, on the left and right, standing out starkly against the blue sky, were remarkable rock formations: monoliths, mesas, high rock spikes and spires. It was almost as if they were on a road trip, the zombie apocalypse a mere figment of their collective imaginations.

Fifteen minutes after the heated conversation, the sat-phone in Lia's door pocket made a strange noise. As soon as she got the phone into the light of day, she saw there was a new SMS message from Rose waiting to be read.

Vern's prediction of *some kind of contact with local law enforcement* came true when, emerging from a sharp right-to-left bend in the road, a blind curve with lanes so narrow that, for once, Riker actually observed the thirty-miles-per-hour posted limit, they came up against a formidable roadblock.

Riker braked and flicked his eyes to the rearview. Saw that the Roamer was just creeping into view around the bend.

What to do? he thought as he brought the Shelby to a complete stop with, maybe, a dozen yards to spare.

As the Roamer closed with the trailer hitched to the Shelby, Riker took a second to scan their surroundings. He quickly came to the conclusion that reversing out of the jam he'd gotten them into was not an option. The left side of the road fell away into a brush-choked arroyo. Horror gripped him when he spotted the mangled husks of a number of vehicles that had come to rest where the arroyo widened, some fifty feet or so downhill. Some of the vehicles, presumably with their occupants still in them, had been consumed by fire. Most showed signs of having tangled with the spike strips that had caused Riker to brake.

An import SUV, tires flattened, hood and doors full of bullet holes, sat atop a pile of zombie corpses. A younger woman was draped limply over a deflated airbag. The corpse looked fresh and was sans the usual slack-faced expression of the twice-dead. Frozen on the narrow face was a look of complete surprise. If anyone had died along with her in the SUV, it wasn't evident from the road.

On the Shelby's right flank, a byproduct of the heavy machinery that had cut the road through one side of a sandstone formation loosely resembling Australia's Ayer's Rock, a head-high berm of red soil dashed any hope of getting turned around here.

Dead ahead, parked behind the spike strips, was a pair of white vehicles. On the left, nosed away from the arroyo, was a Dodge Charger police cruiser. On the right, its tubular grille guard aimed directly at the Shelby, was a Chevy Tahoe police cruiser. Parked on the narrow shoulder, roughly a hundred yards back from the Tahoe, was a yellow Caterpillar bulldozer.

Caught between the proverbial rock and a hard place, Riker killed the engine, pulsed his window down, and put his hands where the unseen occupants of the cruisers could see them.

Chapter 21

The two vehicles blocking Indian Route 12 sported low-profile light bars, roof-mounted needle antenna, spotlights on the A-pillars, and wide high-performance tires. NAVAJO NATION POLICE was splashed across their hoods and doors.

As soon as Riker had parked his hands atop the Shelby's steering wheel, both driver's doors on the cruisers hinged open. A squat fireplug of a man wearing a khaki NNP uniform and brandishing a pump shotgun emerged from the Charger. Donning a tan, wide-brimmed hat, the officer turned his head and spit a stream of tobacco juice onto the gray asphalt. The Native American's eyes were hidden behind mirrored sunglasses. His pockmarked face showed no emotion as, using his door for cover, he crouched down and leveled his weapon at the Shelby.

Out of the Tahoe came an imposing figure wearing the same uniform. If the middle-aged Native American wasn't taller than Riker, he was very close. Six foot three, at least. And just as muscular. A long, thick braid of jet-black hair snaked from under the black ball cap pulled down low over tinted aviators. The man's utility belt was a finely tooled leather item sporting a saucer-sized silver buckle inlaid with pale green and red stone. In the man's hands was a short-barreled rifle, its muzzle currently aimed groundward. The weapon was fitted with some kind of compact optic and a short sling, nothing more. Compared to Riker's F4, and most of the AR-15s he had handled since the apocalypse popped off, the lawman's rifle was fairly pedestrian.

Instead of remaining with his Tahoe, the tall officer slung the SBR over one shoulder and strode confidently down the centerline. Right hand never leaving the general vicinity of the chrome revolver holstered on his right hip, he continued to advance until he was a dozen feet from the Shelby's left front fender.

Raising his left hand, palm facing the Shelby, the man said, "I'm Lieutenant David Nez." He hooked a thumb at the Charger. "Officer Percy Begay." Nez flashed a toothy smile. "Percy is a hell of a shot with that Mossberg of his. It's loaded with slugs that'll punch right through metal." He looked over one shoulder. "Percy's nephew's a Marine Scout Sniper. Kid's a crack shot with that M40 of his. Thirty-two confirmed kills over thirteen days in Fallujah back in oh-four. Seventeen more confirmed in the mountains of Afghanistan in oh-six. He's also sitting with a .50 caliber Barrett that'll leave a nice sized hole in an engine block." He swung his gaze over to the Roamer. "Noah came out of boot with his Expert Marksmanship Badge and returned from the war with a Silver Star, a Purple Heart, and a bunch of unconfirmed scalps. He's out there somewhere … watching and waiting. He's real good at both." That smile again as he parked his gaze on Riker. "So what's your business on Navajo land?"

A look passed between Riker and Lia, his worried, her defiant.

"Sergeant Jackson said Flagstaff is a shitshow," interjected Steve-O. One arm, sunburned beyond belief, hung out the open window.

Riker kept both hands where they'd been since the cruiser doors hinged open: clasped atop the steering wheel, unmoving. "What my friend means," he said, "is that we were warned to steer clear of Flagstaff. Apparently, the city is more dead than alive. We have no intention of stopping in Window Rock or anywhere else. Just passing through, is all."

Lieutenant Nez hitched up his gun belt. "What's your final destination?" he asked. "You all heading home, or are you outbound from somewhere? We're real careful who we let come onto our land." He gestured to the arroyo. "That's where our would-be looters and marauders end up. Infected, too. Any of you carrying the Romero?" He shook his head. "Damn strange name for a little bug."

Leaning toward Riker's window, Lia said, "None of us are infected. As for why we're coming this way … we're outbound from Santa Fe. Hoping to get to Vegas to help some kids who are being kept captive by people who aren't their parents or guardians."

The lieutenant made no reply.

Riker asked, "Do you have any lines of communication open with Las Vegas PD?"

"Vegas is radio silent," said Nez. "As is most of the United States." He cocked his head to one side, a cold stare fixed on Riker. "You have any proof to back up your claim about the kids in need? Names and ages? Maybe an address where they're being held?" All were questions even a seasoned liar would have a hard time answering on the fly. Without hesitation, Riker lifted one hand off the wheel and made the universal *gimme* motion at Lia.

Vern said to Lia, "Sure you want to show them all your cards? What if they keep the phone?"

Then we end this fool's errand, thought Riker. Speaking to Vern, he said, "Do you have a better idea?"

No sooner had Riker stopped speaking than Shorty called across the divide. "Just show the man the text message from Rose. Hell, have them call and talk to her if they need confirmation."

Regarding the Roamer, Nez said, "Text message?"

"The SMS on this sat-phone," replied Riker as he passed the Iridium out the window.

Nez closed the distance and took the phone from Riker. He replaced his Aviators with a pair of readers with thick, clear lenses. He squinted and his eyes ticked left and right as he read the entire message. Finished, he handed the sat-phone up to Riker. "It's a good thing you're doing for complete strangers. While it's against our new charter to allow any outsiders on our land, and I *should* have you all turn around and go through Flagstaff, you getting to where those kids are far outweighs ink on paper."

Smiling wide, Steve-O said, "Thank you, sir."

"We're good people," Riker said. *At least when we're not castrating folks.* He couldn't shake the man's shrill cries and the sound his *package* had made when it fell back to earth. The wet squelch was right up there with the sound of a zombie skull popping under weight of the Shelby.

"I'm going to allow you through. But that's not all," Nez said. "Window Rock is under quarantine. Closed to outsiders."

He gestured at the trailer. "I see you're carrying extra fuel for these thirsty beasts. So what I'm going to have you do is drive straight through to our western roadblock. No stopping. I'll let my men know you're coming. Don't dawdle. You take too long, I'll send Noah after you on his dirt bike. He's one hell of a tracker." He swapped out his glasses. Staring at Riker through the Aviators, he went on, saying, "If you need potable water, you're welcome to fill up at the water truck. Can't miss it. It's where you'll connect with 264 West. You'll find a portable john there, too." He backed away from the vehicles. Gesturing with his left hand, he said, "While I'm inclined to believe none of you are infected, I'm going to have to ask you all to unass the vehicles and assemble before me. Then I'm going to have you all strip down to your underwear. Ladies can keep their bras on."

"Fuck I will," Tara shot from the Roamer's backseat.

"Only way I can allow you on our lands," Nez pointed out. "Me and Percy aren't pervs. Noah … while he's a watcher, he ain't a voyeur. He's got a wife and three kids in Window Rock." He looked at Percy and shrugged.

The shrug struck Riker as the action of a person who didn't have a dog in the fight. "It's a reasonable request," he said, elbowing open his door. He figured leading by example would expedite things.

The others followed suit, with Tara the last one out and staring daggers at the officers.

Once everyone had complied—Riker, Vern, and Steve-O stripped down to just their boxers, the women wearing only bras and panties, and Shorty, clad in neon green bikini briefs—Nez walked the line, having each person perform a slow pirouette as he looked for bite marks.

The whole time, seeing Tara nearly naked, vulnerable in front of Nez and Percy, took Riker back to the time he'd learned she had been drugged and raped. If he could have found the guy responsible—if he was being honest with himself—castrating the guy would have seemed totally acceptable. Hell, it would have been the jumping-off point of a long night of misery and suffering he had planned for the guy. However, with Tara unable to remember enough of the night's events to finger the rapist, the crime had gone unpunished. It had been a bitter pill to swallow. A pill that, during uncomfortable times like this, was still seemingly stuck in his craw.

Finished inspecting Shorty, the lieutenant said, "Good to go. You all can get dressed." Singling out Lia and Riker, he asked when and where their respective amputations had occurred. It was clear, because his gaze never left Lia as he spoke, that he was more interested in learning how she had lost the lower third of her right leg.

"What are we … chopped liver?" quipped Shorty as he pulled on his jeans.

Nez didn't answer. Nor did he waver. "I'm guessing Big Man left part of his leg overseas. You've got that look in your eyes, Lee Riker. I see it in Noah's eyes, too. The look that says: I've seen my fill of death and destruction."

Riker nodded. "IED on Route Irish took it. Took some good men, too."

Nez removed his Aviators and met Lia's gaze. He maintained eye contact with her as she dressed. Never once did his gaze drop below her neck. After she had pulled on her shirt, he said, "When did you get the bite that necessitated the amputation?"

"A few days ago."

"Who saved your life?"

She gestured to Vern. "He did."

Vern said, "I didn't do the chopping." He shook his head, slowly, side to side. "I just cleaned up the messy ends and sewed it all up."

Nez asked, "How'd you know what to do?"

"I was a combat medic."

"Nam?"

Vern nodded.

"Don't like to talk about it, eh? Can't blame you," Nez said. "My pops never talked about his tours of duty in the jungle. Didn't say a peep until he was on his deathbed. The shit he went through." Nez shook his head.

"I'd just as soon forget it altogether," Vern admitted. "The person who did that to Lia's leg is an Army aviator. She just acted. Strode right over to where Lia had fallen, machete in hand, and hacked the leg off a couple of inches above the bite."

"Doesn't always work out," Nez said. "I've seen plenty of failures. Key is you gotta get it done inside the two-minute window."

"Thankfully, Rhoads knew what she was doing," said Riker. After cinching his belt, he dug in a pocket and came out with the Crown Royal bag.

"I don't drink," said Nez, displaying a hand as if warding off a hot flame.

Riker shook the bag. The items inside made a dull clinking sound. He reached a hand in and plucked out two of the items. The sun glinted off the items as he held them out to the lieutenant. "There's a half-ounce of gold here. I have no idea what it's trading for right now. That's if the markets are open anywhere in the world. Consider it my way of showing appreciation for you allowing us safe passage."

Again with the raised hand. "That's not necessary. Just respect my people and our lands." Looking to the Charger, he said, "Percy … these are the first ones today. Is the color green?"

Percy flashed Nez a thumbs-up.

Nez reached into a pocket and came out with a stack of sticky notes. Each was a different color. Peeling a page off the green pad, he signed his name on it. "Don't let this blow out the window. You lose it and you might find yourself getting naked again." He stuck the sticky note on the inside of the Shelby's windshield.

He signed his name to another and handed it up to Steve-O. Then, as if the Shelby were a metal Appaloosa, he slapped a hand on her flank. "Hottest part of the day is still to come. Y'all better get a move on."

Didn't need to tell Riker twice. He pocketed the bag of gold and clambered aboard the Shelby. As soon as Percy had reversed the Dodge cruiser out of the way, Riker swung his rig past the Roamer and continued on.

Around the next bend, a hundred yards or so from the roadblock, was a cluster of colorful tents, several dusty pickups lined up on the outside shoulder, and a popup canopy with a slew of dirt bikes parked underneath it. Nearby, all eyes tracking the two-vehicle convoy, was a dozen armed Navajo. They were men and women, old and young, all taking refuge from the sun under a second popup canopy.

"Quick reaction force," said Riker. "I figured Noah wasn't their only backup."

Vern leaned over the seatback. "Appear weak when you are strong, and strong when you are weak."

Riker met Vern's gaze in the mirror. "More Sun Tzu?"

"Yep. He's got one for every battlefield situation."

As the Roamer passed the tent city, Shorty tooted the air horn. Smiling wide, Steve-O waved a sunburned arm at the camo-clad Navajo. There was no reciprocity on their part. Their expressions remained stony. Weapons didn't waver. They were all business.

Which made sense to Riker, considering the new normal. He only hoped that what awaited them at the western boundary was expecting them. Last thing he wanted was to have to negotiate their exit from the Navajo Nation with a similar group.

The mound of red stone slowly eroded over millennia by winds sweeping the Colorado Plateau was only visible for a short duration from Route 12. Rising over its namesake town, even from half a mile out and viewed from a vehicle on the move, Window Rock was an impressive sight.

"In the park at the base of the rock is a monument to the Navajo Code Talkers," Vern explained. "It's a statue of a U.S. Marine kneeling by his radio. Thing's close to twenty feet tall. Pretty damn impressive, even if it's a jarhead on the pedestal."

"Can't put a price on the Navajo's contribution to World War II," said Riker as he slowed to make the left turn onto State-Route 264, the main artery in and out of the town of Window Rock. "Their code was never broken by the Axis. Without them, the Marines would not have taken Iwo Jima."

Vern said, "You know that ubiquitous picture? The one of the six Marines raising the flag over Mount Suribachi? It would never have been snapped had it not been for the Talkers. Shameful their contribution wasn't recognized formally until 2001." He shook his head. "Should have happened right after the bombs went *kaboom* over Japan." He threw a crisp salute in the general direction of the rock.

Shortly after the Shelby was tracking west on 264, the water trucks and portable toilets came into view. They were on a vast field of gravel and watched over by a force about half the size of the one they'd left behind them on Route 12.

"We're here," said Lia. "Can we switch off the History Channel?"

"If you don't remember your past," said Vern, "you're doomed to repeat it."

Flashing a wan smile, Lia said, "That's if the biters don't eat all the historians."

Vern said, "Touché, young lady," and clicked out of his seatbelt. He'd been holding in a piss since they turned off of I-40. He admitted to Lia and Riker that if he didn't get inside that ugly gray porta john in the next thirty seconds or so, he was afraid he'd be disrobing for the second time today. If so, burying a soiled pair of Fruit of the Looms would be the next order of business.

Inside the Roamer, Shorty, too, was rushing to click out of his seatbelt. Next to him, Steve-O had already unbuckled, elbowed his door open, and was climbing down from the cab.

Tara sipped from a water. "What's the rush, fellas?"

Steve-O said nothing. Head down, arms pumping, he was on a mission.

Shorty threw open his door. "Captain Flatulence destroyed the Roamer's john back at the truck plaza. Toilet's totally clogged with toilet paper and Steve-O poo." As he climbed to the road, he said, "Last thing I want to be is stuck in the porta john with one of his noxious farts."

"Better hustle," Tara chided. "Vern just ducked inside, and Steve-O's already got a big head start on you." As she watched Shorty looping around front of the Roamer, she made herself a mental note to keep her eyes peeled for a plunger.

Riker and Lia had remained inside the Shelby, wrapped in a cocoon of uncomfortable silence, both staring at the Navajo officers seated underneath the sun canopy. While Vern was on his way out the door, Riker had jokingly implored him to "warm the toilet seat for him" and had put his hand atop Lia's hand to keep her from unbuckling her seatbelt. His real intention for doing so was known only to him.

Taken aback, Lia said, "What? You don't want to stretch your *leg*?" She remained straight-faced for a second or two, then started laughing. "Get it? *Leg*. Singular."

"Hardy har har," Riker brayed. "Never heard that one before."

"Just trying to break the ice," said Lia. "You've been so serious since the Viking funeral. You *totally* ignored me giving your leg a squeeze."

He smiled and bowed his head.

"I thought that maybe you were too preoccupied with all that was going on," she explained. "That maybe you didn't or couldn't feel it."

"Oh, I felt it alright." He turned toward her, the smile dissolving. "I didn't acknowledge it because I have … *questions*."

She shifted in her seat. After a beat or two spent looking him in the eyes, she said, "What do you want to know?"

"Why the fixation with Cole and the others? I get it … they're kids. Innocents in harm's way." Eyes misting over, he shook his head. "Only a monster would be capable of thinking up the things Cole says his captors are subjecting him and the others to."

"My first gymnastics trainer was one of those *monsters*," she divulged, on the brink of tears. "The abuse was mental at first. Grooming me to trust him instead of my parents. I didn't know. I was ten, for fuck's sake. The nuance of our relationship was lost on me." A tear traced her cheek. Riker reached over and wiped it away for her. Her lips quivered as she said, "It became sexual real quick. Digital penetration. When I told him I was going to tell my dad, he threatened to kill him and my mom." She went quiet for a beat, then looked up at the headliner. "He even said he was going to kill my dog, Pappy. And he was very graphic in detailing how he was going to do it."

"That's awful," said Riker. "No kid should ever be put in that position." *Nor should an adult woman*, he thought, Tara's ordeal still in the backseat of his mind.

"It wasn't a one-off," said Lia. "The abuse escalated from there and continued from the time I was ten until I was thirteen. That was when I convinced my parents I was done with the balance beam … all gymnastics, really."

"What happened to the trainer? Did he finally get his?"

She shook her head. "He threw a clot. Brain aneurysm. Dropped dead at a meet. Fucker got off easy. Later on, it came to light that I was one of six girls he was molesting."

"So you took up shooting and skiing as a diversion?"

"I had an ulterior motive for learning to shoot. But that's a story for another day." She reached out and clamped thumb and pointer finger on his bearded chin. Pulling his face to hers, she kissed him hard on the lips. Breaking away, eyes boring into his, she said, "You're a good man, Lee. Don't ever tell yourself you're not. And the leg squeeze, there's more where that came from."

Smile parting his lips, Riker said, "And the kiss? More of them, too?"

"We'll see," she said, a twinkle in her eyes. "Let's both savor the first one for a while."

They exited the Shelby in tandem, both of them embarking on an unspoken mission to beat the other to the porta john.

Outside the Shelby, Tara, Vern, and Steve-O were crouched beside the portable toilet. On the ground between them, its four corners held down by fist-sized rocks, was the map of the western United States Vern had brought up from the bunker underneath the great room at Trinity. He was pointing at something on the map when the door to the toilet hinged open. All heads turned as Shorty stumbled through the yawning door, one hand holding up his pants, the other clamped firmly over his nose. Settling his watery gaze on Steve-O, he said, "What crawled up inside of you and died?"

Steve-O looked a question at Tara. She shrugged. Head cocked to one side, dog-like, Steve-O regarded Vern, who said, "It's an expression. Don't worry, you're not carrying a chestburster."

This further confused Steve-O.

"It's that thing from Alien. The little bullet-headed creature that burst from John Hurt's chest. Hence the name: chestburster."

"I saw Aliens," said Steve-O. "The Colonial Marines were kickass. Hicks is my favorite. He survived, you know."

"Yeah," said Vern, "because he threw everyone else to the proverbial wolves. He survived all of ten minutes into the third installment."

Shorty's color was returning. Cinching his belt tight, he looked to Vern. "Big sci-fi fan, are you?"

"Huge," replied Vern. "I took Shane to see Alien in the theater when it first came out. He was a teenager by then, I think. That movie scared the shit out of both of us."

Having just been aced out of entering the porta john by Lia, Riker joined the huddle. Looking down on the map, he said, "What are we doing?"

Vern said, "We're trying to decide where we're going to spend the night."

Riker studied the map. "What's the consensus?"

Tara said, "Somewhere outside of Vegas. That way, we can get up before first light and move into position under cover of darkness."

Shorty pointed to the map. "I want to stay somewhere near this Sierra facility. We can go up the road and check it out before we set up camp."

"I already told you," Vern said, "it's out of our way." He tapped a finger on the map. "I still think this cache is the one we check out first. It's on our way. It's not far off the highway. If it's a dry hole … by that I mean if it's already plundered, we can move on to the next one on the map."

Lia emerged from the porta john three minutes after she had entered. Only when she was a dozen feet away did she release the breath trapped in her lungs.

"Wow!" said Shorty. "You held your breath the entire time you were in there?"

A little red in the face, Lia nodded. "That was nothing," she bragged. "With my heartrate at ninety percent max rate, I used to be able to suspend my breathing *and* hit a four-inch target from a hundred and sixty feet."

Shorty said, "Well shit, Lia. Had I known that I would have barred the door so you'd have to suffer along with the rest of us."

"My farts do not stink," Steve-O insisted.

Ignoring the potty talk, Tara said, "That second cache is pretty damn close to town. No way I'm closing my eyes anywhere near there. Not even to take a little catnap. Going to sleep for a few hours? No effin' way. That is *not* going to happen."

"Let's compromise, then." Shorty pointed to the same spot on the map as he had before. "Why don't we try this one."

"That's the one you already pointed to," Steve-O shot. "Quit trying to pull a fast one, wise guy."

Shaking his head, Shorty strode away, muttering under his breath something about never getting his way.

Under scrutiny by the Navajo officers, Vern put his map away and helped Steve-O fill their water bottles. Meanwhile, Shorty and Riker popped the hoods on their vehicles and went about checking fluid levels.

When the two vehicles were loaded up and slow-rolling back onto 264, fifteen minutes had slipped into the past, all without a single word having been said between the watchers and the watched.

Chapter 22

The Navajo Nation was locked down tight from Window Rock to Navajo Bridge, a nine-hundred-foot-long steel spandrel arch bridge spanning Marble Canyon at the western edge of their current exclusionary zone. All of the little towns and small cities in between had been under strict quarantine. Security usually consisted of a number of armed citizens, their vehicles parked across off-ramps or access roads. Tuba City was the exception. Situated one hundred and fifty miles west of Window Rock and sixty miles south of the Navajo Bridge, Tuba City was encircled by a wall of concrete freeway noise abatement panels and, seemingly, home to more MRAPs and Humvees than civilian vehicles. There was even a makeshift airbase complete with circular landing pads carved into the desert soil. On the pads sat a number of civilian and military helicopters. A pair of orange fuel bowsers with TUBA T03 stenciled on the tanks in big white font were parked close by. From a distance, the whole thing had the look of a Forward Operating Base straight out of the Sandbox. Up close, it had the feel of a fledgling Fort Kit Carson. Clearly, the Navajo were serious about maintaining their autonomy from the crumbling United States.

When Riker and company finally reached the crossing, roughly four hours after their surprise encounter with Nez and Percy at their roadblock south of Window Rock, they had gone the entire time without seeing a single zombie—ambulatory or otherwise. The Navajo Bridge they were approaching consisted of two separate spans. One had been built in the late twenties and was now dedicated to only pedestrians and crossers on horseback. The second span was erected in the nineties. It was wider by half and open for business. Judging by the security on both sides of Marble Canyon, Riker had a sinking feeling they'd be seeing plenty of zombies once they got to the other side.

While the easternmost roadblock had been a bit porous, its counterpart here—fortified by a twelve-foot-tall concertina-wire-topped cement wall and dozens of Jersey barriers, patrolled by a small army of armed officers, and backstopped by several desert-tan MRAP armored vehicles—was nearly impenetrable. A pair of guard towers rose up on either end of the bridge. Constructed with two-by-fours and sheet plywood and fitted with stretched canvas roofs, the crude fifteen-foot-tall structures looked sturdy enough to easily accommodate the Browning Ma Deuce heavy machineguns and uniformed personnel manning them.

A trio of single-wide mobile homes sat end to end opposite the bridge access. They appeared to be new additions to the operation. There was no landscaping. The drapes appeared to be just sheets put up over the windows. Also a new addition, erected along the canyon edge, shiny chain-link fence stretched north and south for as far as the eye could see. Running off to the east, perpendicular to the canyon rim, was the beginning of a wall of cement freeway barriers. It was a new endeavor. Maybe one-third completed. A long line of flatbed trailers, each piled high with cement panels, stretched off to the east. Riker supposed they demarked the path the wall was supposed to follow. With surveyors likely few and far between, it was as good a strategy as any to keep everything tracking straight. From the looks of it, there was at least a half-mile of wall to be completed before its eventual merger with the base of Echo Cliffs.

Access to Navajo Bridge from the west was blocked by a lone MRAP. At the moment, the armored vehicle was being moved from the road to allow a trio of eastbound eighteen-wheelers to cross.

The longer Riker took it all in, the more the whole operation reminded him of the 14th of July Bridge entrance to the Green Zone in Baghdad, Iraq. But instead of the survivable thirty-foot drop from the 14th of July Bridge to the Tigris flowing under it, here the Navajo Bridge and Colorado River were separated by a deadly five-hundred-foot plunge.

It was clear to Riker the Navajo Nation had themselves one hell of a defensible position. *No doubt*, he thought as he slowed the Shelby to walking speed, *the twin spans are also wired with explosives and could be dropped into the Colorado at a moment's notice.*

As the two vehicles came to a halt before a break in the cement Jersey barriers, Shelby in the lead, Roamer a couple of truck lengths behind, they were approached by a twentysomething officer dressed in a khaki uniform similar to those worn by Nez and Percy.

There was no fanfare. Nobody was asked to exit their vehicle and undress. Just a cursory look inside each vehicle. As the officer conducted his inspection, Riker caught him performing a covert headcount. The eyes roving behind the smoked lenses of wraparound Oakley sunglasses didn't give it away; it was the subtle movement of the officer's lips as he did the counting.

From his perch in the Shelby, Riker sized the officer up as the man went about his job. Green sergeant's chevrons trimmed with gold thread adorned the uniform's right shoulder. On the sergeant's left hip was a holstered Glock pistol. Nestled in a tooled-leather sheath on the opposite hip was a war tomahawk. The man carried an M4 carbine in a low ready position. He looked comfortable with it. The imprint of the plate carrier underneath his uniform blouse was distinct. A nametag pinned to his breast pocket read YAZZIE.

Sergeant Yazzie was close to six feet tall, lean and wiry, and looked as if he would be at home in a boxing ring. He stalked around the vehicles like a big cat on the hunt.

He struck Riker as a man who was versed in the arts of killing.

Finished inspecting the Roamer, Sergeant Yazzie returned to the Shelby and took up station outside of Riker's open window.

After introducing himself to the officer, Riker peeled the square of paper off the windshield and handed it over. "Signed by Lieutenant Nez at the Window Rock entry."

"Not necessary. We've been expecting you." Yazzie didn't even bother to look for Nez's signature. Just glanced at his watch. It was a bulky armored item similar to the one on Riker's wrist. "You're a little late, Riker. But we'll let it slide, seeing as how you've got the trailer in tow."

"For what it's worth," Riker offered, "we didn't deviate. We stopped once to top off our tanks and scarf down some

MREs. That's it. We didn't do any exploring or sticking our noses where they don't belong."

"We know." A pained smile ghosted across the sergeant's face. "We've been keeping tabs on you."

Though Riker knew the Navajo Nation had somehow obtained dozens of military vehicles, he doubted they had procured Predator or Reaper drones. And there was no way on earth they had gotten their hands on anything more advanced—Global Hawks and the like took more than a trailer full of advanced electronics and communications gear to operate. Furthermore, he didn't recall seeing any private planes or helicopters dogging them. Then it hit him: the drivers of the eastbound eighteen-wheelers they had encountered intermittently along the way had been calling in their location. Though the plates on the rigs he had been able to make out in passing were from states west and north of Arizona, mostly California with some Idaho and Oregon sprinkled in, he had a hunch the drivers behind the tinted glass were Navajo bringing home the spoils of successful foraging missions. Some of the trailers were emblazoned with Amazon's ubiquitous Smile. Others bore Target's impossible to miss red and white logo. He even remembered seeing quite a few tractors pulling UPS and FedEx tandem trailers.

Sergeant Yazzie took a long second look at the trailer hooked to the Shelby. "I highly recommend you put those barrels in back of your rig and jettison that trailer. It'll just slow you down. You can leave it here. We'll hold it for you until you return." He grimaced. "You come across a horde out there, you'll be hamstrung. Unable to turn around, you'll be trapped inside your vehicle, surrounded by eaters." He tsked. "Those things are worse than the Taliban. We may have the watches, but the dead have the time. All the time in the world. They *will* wait you out. Doesn't matter how long. Rain or shine … they don't care. You'll either go crazy or starve to death. Don't know which is worse."

No way was Riker leaving behind the trailer. He was still holding out hope they'd find one of Vern's caches stocked full of fuel and food. Instead of acknowledging the sergeant's advice, he said, "Are we good to go, sir?"

Yazzie nodded at the bridge. The first of the three semis was just rolling off the east end. "We're keeping to strict weight limits," he said. "Once they're all on this side, you can proceed."

From the backseat, Vern urged Riker to ask the officer what to expect on the other side.

As soon as the noisy Peterbilt rumbled past the Shelby, likely on its way to Tuba City, Riker picked the officer's brain, inquiring about the road conditions, zombie sightings, and whether the United States still maintained a military presence west of the crossing.

Shorty had exited the Roamer, made his way to the Shelby, and staked out a spot on the road close to Riker's door.

Acknowledging Shorty with a curt nod, the sergeant slung his M4 over one shoulder. After downing some water from a bottle and dabbing at his forehead with a red handkerchief, he said, "*Daaztsánée yigáłígíí* are everywhere beyond the crossing." He pointed out the red rock cliffs due west of them. They were imposing, the uneven tops seemingly touching the sky. In places they rose nearly a thousand feet from the desert floor. "There will be many. On the roads and on the range. Until you can no longer see Echo Cliffs, do not stop for anything. Steer well clear of the campgrounds. Nothing but death there. If you do stop and get stuck and surrounded by *daaztsánée yigáłígíí*, we will not be able to save you."

"I was wondering what those cliffs were called," Shorty interjected. "They've been keeping pace with us for damn near sixty miles." He made a face. "But what's the other thing you said? I'm not even going to try to repeat it."

"*Daaztsánée yigáłígíí* is what we Navajo call the living dead. There are other names. This is the one I prefer." The sergeant backed away from the road, waving a hand at dust kicked up off the far shoulder by a passing eighteen-wheeler.

Once the dust had settled, Riker said, "So it's Navajo for *zombie*?"

"Roughly translated."

Shorty adjusted his trucker hat. On the front, in big red letters, was the saying: No Grass, No Ass, No Cash. He said, "I thought you'd call them *skin walkers* or *spiritless corpses* or something cool like that."

"Maybe in a campy B movie," Yazzie replied. "There's nothing 'campy' about what you all are going to find once you reach Nevada. Especially in and around Las Vegas and Henderson. Both are overrun by zombies. Crawling with them." He looked at Riker. "The military's been trying to clear them out." He turned his face away from the road as the last of the eighteen-wheelers—a lime green Freightliner pulling a refrigerated trailer wrapped with larger-than-life graphics depicting all types of dairy products—rumbled by them. Like the first two big rigs, this one showed obvious signs of contact with the dead. The front bull bar was coated with bloody chunks of detritus and unidentifiable bodily fluids. Crimson handprints painted the trailer all down its sides. Snagged on the trailer's undercarriage, colorful scraps of fabric fluttered in the tractor's slipstream.

Picking up where he'd left off, Yazzie said, "The military is fractured. Word is they suffered catastrophic losses trying to put down the rising in the east. The West Coast didn't fare much better. At least not in the heavily populated areas. Los Angeles is a no-go zone. Frisco and Oakland, too. A lot of survivors have scattered inland. We take in only our own, for now. We make exceptions for law enforcement personnel and active-duty military. Over the last few days, we've granted many military patrols sanctuary on Navajo land."

Lia was out of the Shelby and had quietly sidled up next to Riker. "What about the zombies we'll likely come across?" she asked. "Are there slow *and* fast movers? If both, what's the ratio?"

"There will be walkers and sprinters. The fast ones are few and far between, though." He drew in a deep breath, then exhaled sharply. "The *daaztsánée yigáłígíí* are forming up and hunting in packs. Hordes, actually. Thousands. Sometimes tens of thousands." He stared off into the distance. It was hard to tell if he was recollecting something or just trying to read what was going on across the bridge. "They follow our foraging teams out of the suburbs around Vegas and Henderson. Once they catch sight of the tractor-trailers, they follow. And once they get on the highway, they keep going. Two hundred miles in lockstep. They just keep coming, picking up more from cities and little towns they pass along the way. Some of the larger herds that have made it all the way here remind me of the old film reel footage of bison they showed us in school when I was young. Before this, the only herds we saw out this way were metal and chrome and heading to Sturgis. Now, it's wave after wave of soulless monsters wanting only to feed on those of us left behind."

Always thinking of himself, Shorty said, "Know where a guy might find a plunger around here?"

Incredulous, Yazzie stared over his glasses at Shorty. "A plunger?"

Shorty put his fists together and made plunging motions. "In the immortal words of Cousin Eddie, the shitter's full."

Yazzie made a face. "Sure," he said dryly. "Just swing by the True Value in Fredonia. I'm sure the staff is *dying* for your business."

Shouting to be heard from the Shelby's backseat, Vern said, "Use the canister on the Mule. Take off the wand and blow out the blockage."

"And risk the blowback?" Shorty shook his head. "Hard pass. Last thing I need is a face full of Steve-O poo."

If Yazzie was amused by Shorty's problem, it wasn't evident on his face. Once the *all clear* call came through the radio clipped to his belt, he bowed his head momentarily. "May the Creator look after you." He made eye contact with Riker. "The culling crews have the right of way. As do our men and women coming back from foraging runs." With a nod, he added, "You're good to go now," and struck off for the nearest trailer.

Viewed from the middle of the Navajo Bridge, the Colorado River, some five hundred feet below the Shelby, was wide and dark green and moving much slower than Riker was expecting. While he and Vern weren't spooked by the plunge, Lia was terrified. She had gripped the grab-bar by her head white-knuckle tight, releasing her hold on it only when the Shelby was on the opposite side, all four of its wheels and the trailer safely on terra firma.

In the Roamer, Steve-O was the one affected most by the depth of the gorge. Shielding his eyes with one arm, he said, "Tell me when we're done."

"If you can't handle heights, how in the heck can you stand to pilot the drone?" Shorty asked. "All that dipping and diving at altitude, eyes glued to that little screen. What's the difference?"

Incredulous, Tara said, "You're a moron, Shorty. He's not *inside* the drone while it's five hundred or a thousand feet above ground. Here and now, we are five hundred feet in the air." She paused for a long three-count. While she was not talking, the thrum of the Roamer's off-road tires on the span resounded in the cab. "A plunger? Really?" she went on. "You have a potential wellspring of information standing in front of you, and you ask where you can find a *plunger*." She shook her head and slumped into the backseat, arms crossed, accusatory glare directed at the rearview mirror.

The Shelby had just rolled through the western gate and was being ushered on by uniformed officers of the Navajo Nation. As the Roamer neared the opening in the cement wall, looking sheepish, Shorty said, "You heard that?"

"My window was open, and my hearing is exceptional."

Shorty went quiet and punched the button to start the Roamer's mirrors retracting. Once they were flush to the cab, he slow-rolled them through the gate. Though the modified Ford pickup was no taller than the trailers hitched to the tractors that had passed them by on the eastern end, and the opening in the western end appeared to be the same dimension, Shorty was taking no chances. Only when they were through the gate and on their way did he respond. "It was on the front of my mind," he said. "Besides, Vern and your brother had already asked all the pertinent questions."

Tara said nothing. Just continued to stare at the mirror as the Roamer hit the incline leading to the canyon rim.

Always the icebreaker, Steve-O said, "Shorty is not a moron, Tara. He's way older than twelve."

"OK," she said, raising her voice to be heard over the low growl of the Roamer's diesel engine. "Shorty's an *imbecile* for inquiring about bathroom accouterments instead of asking the sergeant what we should expect to find when we get away from whatever's awaiting us beyond the canyon rim."

Steve-O's hat brim cut the air as he shook his head. "Wrong again, Tara. Shorty can't be an imbecile. He's still too old."

"OK … enlighten me, Steve-O. What's the age cutoff to be classified an *imbecile*?"

Steve-O crossed his arms, the sunburned right arm contrasting sharply with the other ghostly-white appendage.

"Seven," he said with all the authority of a scientist declaring the properties of an element on the periodic table.

Tara parked her elbows on the seatbacks. "As in *second grade* seven?"

"I didn't mean seven *months*, guys. *Everyone* knows babies can't be imbeciles."

"So I'm an idiot," Shorty declared as the Roamer crested the hill behind the Shelby. "I should have asked Yazzie about road conditions and probed him for the weather forecast. I'll give you that."

"Wrongo," Steve-O corrected. "A baby can be an idiot. So can a two-year-old. Technically, Shorty, a fifty-five-year-old man cannot be an idiot."

Exasperated, Tara said, "I take it all back." She looked at Shorty. "I'm sorry for name-calling." To Steve-O, she went on, saying, "Where did you learn all those medical terms?"

"From my mother," Steve-O said matter of fact. "Whenever kids called me names at school, she would explain to me how they were wrong. My dad, on the other hand, told me to box them on the ears if they kept it up."

Taking his eyes off the scene unfolding before the Roamer, Shorty said, "Did you box anyone's ears?"

"I never had to," said Steve-O as he balled a fist and shook it at Shorty. "Doing this always made them stop it."

Stifling the urge to laugh, Shorty said, "Walk softly and carry a big stick. I like your style, Steve-O."

Chapter 23

The Marble Canyon crossing, with its sheer stone walls and dizzying views of the river below, had nothing on the scene Riker and the others had thrust upon them once the two vehicles crested the canyon's western rim. It was as if they were staring out across a vast battlefield. Zombie bodies were heaped everywhere. A particularly large pile near the canyon rim had just been set afire by a Navajo officer. Although the man was wearing a full set of what appeared to be the type of body armor worn by correctional officers sent in to cells to subdue uncooperative inmates, he had no problem working his way around the head-high mound, stooping and bending here and there as he touched flame to a head of frazzled hair, a torn and bloodied shirt, a ratty dried tumbleweed trapped between the legs of a twice-dead kid. As the wind-whipped tongues of red and orange licked from body to body, fingers of black smoke coiled skyward, twisting and turning before finally twining into one continuous, fast-rising plume. And though the smoke was being pulled away from the canyon, Riker couldn't help imagining the stench coming off the burning bodies.

"It's like the culmination of the Battle of the Bastards," said Vern. "Minus the dead horses and siege engines, of course."

"I don't remember there being Native Americans in Game of Thrones," Lia pointed out.

Vern said, "You watched? My wife wouldn't. Said it was 'too violent.'"

"Had the DVR set to record every episode," Lia confessed. "The violence is what made it believable. That and the grittiness of it all. Life wasn't easy back then." *It's not easy now*, she quickly reminded herself.

Riker had been listening but made no comment. He didn't obsess over television shows. If he found something he liked while channel surfing, he watched it. Simple as that. Save for his beloved Atlanta Braves, there was no hierarchy to his viewing preference. If pressed to declare a favorite channel, it would be a toss-up between Discovery or the History channel. Watching squads of armored Navajo officers converging on a knot of zombies amassed near a distant cluster of buildings was akin to some of the programming on those channels. *Vikings* came to mind at once.

The electronic sign above the Marble Canyon Trading Post was dark as a slab of polished obsidian. The charred remains of the once rambling structure gleamed almost as bright as the sign that had escaped the all-consuming conflagration. Beyond the chained drive to the trading post was an empty parking lot fronting a budget motel with whole banks of its windows broken out. Sharing the lot was a brick post office, Old Glory forever at half-staff.

Next door to the post office was a chain gas station and attached convenience store. Smaller by half, the layout was similar to Holl-Ee's, with two opposing canopied fuel islands and a handful of smaller, detached buildings flanking it on two sides. Still, the place was inundated with just as many (if not more) dust-covered big rigs as Holl-Ee's had been. Dozens and dozens of them sat idle on the parking lot and desert bordering it to the north and west. Boarded-over windows with NO FUEL and CLOSED INDEFINITELY sprayed across them were clearly visible from half a mile out.

Yazzie's "culling crews" were employing lifted 4x4 pickups to lure small groups of zombies from larger packs shambling eastbound on the highway. Once the proverbial fish was on the hook and had been drawn a safe distance from the main body of walking dead, the pickups would stop suddenly and disgorge their cargo of armored Navajo officers—a combined squad of twelve or so. The front echelon of each squad employed clear riot shields. The second echelon wielded long wooden tridents. As the zombies came up against the shields, the second echelon would thrust their tridents over the bowed heads of the shield bearers. The zombies that caught a barbed tine to the eye fell at the feet of the shield bearers. The zombies that survived the initial thrusts became fodder for the shield bearers' tomahawks.

Working with lethal efficiency, the ranks of Navajo deputies quickly divided and conquered the zombies on the road by half. Even as the first squads were breaking ranks and clambering back aboard their respective rides, new teams of armored tomahawk-wielding officers were being dropped off on the remaining zombies' left and right flank. Immediately the dismounts went about cleaving skulls. Unlike Riker's Randall or Vern's machete, the tomahawks never seemed to get stuck. Not once did Riker see any of the dismounts struggling to free their weapon from a zombie's split skull.

Swing, yank … swing, yank … swing, yank. Over and over, the cullers' blades flashed in the early afternoon sun.

The whole scene was backstopped by a wide-angle shot, the dominant feature the Vermillion Cliffs—a massive blaze-red wall of sandstone soaring thousands of feet skyward. To the left, softened by distance, a vast swath of mesas rambled away to the south. Closer in, the tan wind-swept basin was shot through here and there with shadow-filled arroyos and deep canyons. The cloudless blue sky crushing down on it all seemed close enough to touch. The road taking them west shot off diagonally through the middle.

As the Shelby and Roamer coasted slowly down the curving section of 89A, bypassing the entrance to the Navajo Bridge Interpretive Center cum culling crew staging area, all aboard witnessed zombies falling to ancestral weaponry like wheat to a combine. Riker was mesmerized. He wanted so badly to stop at the interpretive center and watch through the Steiners, if only to glean something from seeing the Navajo culling crews in action.

Until you can no longer see Echo Cliffs, do not stop for anything.

With Yazzie's admonition playing in his head like an Emergency Broadcast Signal, Riker swept his gaze forward and fed the motor fuel.

The first mile or so was touch and go, with the zombies on the highway forcing Riker to be creative to get by them. Feinting one way or the other, Riker would get the small packs lurching toward whichever shoulder was closest to them. When a wide enough slice of daylight appeared between the periphery of a pack and the inside breakdown lane or the outside shoulder, he would stab the pedal and make a mad dash for wherever the newly created opening presented itself. The tactic worked more often than not. The times it failed saw the Shelby forced off the road, into the unforgiving desert, where even the Baja model's long-travel suspension was put to the test.

The tactic was not without its consequences. The short stints of forced off-roading threw everyone around inside the Shelby. Although Lia had a firm grip on the grab-handle near her head and was belted in tight, the vibration transiting her prosthetic caused the constant throbbing in her residual limb to escalate to wave after wave of shooting pains the likes of which she hadn't known since the first time Vern had changed the dressing.

Another victim to the prolonged shaking and shimmying: a good portion of Shorty's diesel was lost when one of the rain barrels in the trailer split its seams.

Riker had been so preoccupied with getting past the major pockets of walking dead that he hadn't paid much attention to how Shorty was faring. He did keep one ear cocked in case a call for help came over the radio.

On one occasion, after an off-road sprint around a slow-moving herd a good hundred zombies strong, he had stolen a quick glance at the rearview, only to see the Roamer parting the shamblers like an icebreaker cleaving pack ice. Another time, after swerving around a herd half the size as the first big one, he'd witnessed Shorty speed up and take the Roamer right over top of them. As the broken bodies built up underneath the top-heavy rig, it slowed considerably and started to sway to and fro like a skyscraper riding out a major temblor. Riker had caught himself holding his breath as he watched the rig, its slab front end red with blood, buck and shimmy and gyrate as all forward momentum ceased. Just as Riker thought the high-centered Roamer was going to flip over and mounting a rescue was imminent, the two-way channel had opened up and he got to listen to what was happening in the cab. In the background, between incoming barbs from Steve-O and Tara, Shorty could be heard apologizing profusely. A beat later, as Tara came on the radio asking for a tow, the Roamer's tonnage won out over the organic matter trapped underneath it.

Riker imagined the awful sounds of skulls popping and gasses escaping crushed bodies as he watched the Roamer go nose down. He didn't have to imagine what came next. In fact, he couldn't tear his eyes from the carnage as the spinning front wheels grabbed the road and the Roamer came down off the drift of mangled corpses. A pale arm, severed by the knobby tires, went airborne, spinning end over end as the accelerating Roamer left twin rooster tails of flesh and blood in its wake.

Lia had been watching, too. She'd been so engrossed, radio hovering near her mouth, that she hadn't replied to Tara.

Swiping the radio, Riker thumbed the Talk key. "What was that all about, Shorty?"

"He's got Little Man Syndrome," Tara responded snippily.

Once Riker saw the Roamer closing the distance to the trailer, he accelerated to the posted limit.

"Not good enough of an excuse, Tara." Riker paused for a beat, the radio in front of his mouth. Finally, after wrestling with how he was going to respond to the bullshit he knew Shorty was about to spew, he said, "Put him on. I want to hear it from the horse's mouth."

Shorty responded at once, saying, "I miscalculated. Nothing more, nothing less. I'm sorry for putting all of our lives at risk."

Riker was so blindsided by the humble response he didn't know what to say. The ass-chewing he had locked and loaded was appropriate for anything but Shorty's wholly unexpected mea culpa. Collecting his thoughts, he said, "We're all human, Shorty. Just be careful, man … you're carrying precious cargo."

Apparently, Tara had snatched the radio from Shorty. She came back on immediately. "Might as well get a 'baby sister on board' sign for this land yacht. While you're at it, pick up a pair of matching rings for you and your new crush."

All Riker could come up with was to offer Tara a seat in the Shelby. When that was rebuffed, her reason being that she liked the legroom in the Roamer, he signed off with a curt, "Suit yourself." On a scale of one to ten, with ten being near fisticuffs, this sibling tiff was a two or three.

Riker drove on in silence, perturbed at his inability to juggle all the different personalities. Mediation was never his strong suit. Nor was turning the other cheek. That's why he had been living alone in Atlanta before Romero went and changed everything. He blended in there. The proverbial gray man. Nobody struck up conversations with him. He glided through life without having to make life-altering decisions. All of that had changed with his mother's death. Now he was thrust back into the big brother role. And he was damn rusty at it.

As Route 89A cut south by west through the vast basin, off to their right, Vermilion Cliffs—the second step in the five-step Grand Staircase of the Colorado Plateau—was their constant companion. It wasn't until Riker spotted a sign announcing Kaibab National Forest and the climbing serpentine stretch of blacktop was being crowded on both sides by scattered stands of juniper and pinion pine that he realized he could no longer see Echo Cliffs. While the road here remained clear, he did see patches of snow among the trees. It was also here, thirty miles west of the Navajo Bridge, that the encounters with packs of roving dead suddenly became fewer and farther between. The sign also marked the beginning of a three-thousand-foot elevation gain that culminated near the unincorporated community of Jacob Lake, where the map on the Shelby's navigation screen showed 89A crossing paths with State Route 67—the only paved road leading to the North Rim of the Grand Canyon, forty-four miles to the south.

Riker took the initial snow sighting as a portent of things to come. He highly doubted, even if anyone from ADOT was still alive, that they were showing up for work, let alone actively plowing the road leading to the pass. If that were the case, the Shelby's four-wheel drive capabilities would soon be tested.

A couple of miles into the ascent, where spotty accumulations of packed snow began to appear on the road, Riker engaged the Shelby's four-wheel drive. A minute later, his lane was totally obscured by a two-inch layer of snow. Across the centerline, the downhill lane was not pristine. It showed signs of heavy travel. No doubt the parallel tracks in the snow had been scoured by the tires on fully loaded big rigs heading to Marble Canyon.

Riker checked the Roamer's progress in the rearview. Saw that it was keeping pace and immediately tossed out the idea of moving over to the left lane to take advantage of the clear patches. With his luck as of late, the second he moved over he'd find himself in the path of an eastbound eighteen-wheeler.

Though the going was slower than Riker had hoped, save for having to bull through a couple of packs of dead making their way downhill, and being forced into the left lane a few times to pass the occasional abandoned trailer, all of which had already given up their cargo to previous passersby, the long uphill climb was uneventful.

As the sign announcing **Jacob Lake Pop. 1,321** slid by on the right, Tara's voice sprang from the two-way in Lia's lap. "Shorty requests that we pull over." Her tone was less than enthusiastic.

"Is everything OK?" Lia radioed back, each word sending a fresh wave of pain coursing the length of her residual limb. The vibration from all the driving had awakened the nerves. There was no amount of Ibuprofen that would put them back to sleep. Twice Vern had offered her something stronger from the National Guard first aid kit. Both times she had turned him down.

"He wants to stop and look at the map," Tara replied. "Says he thinks there's a point of interest near here we should consider looking into."

As Riker scanned the road ahead for the first signs of civilization, he kicked up the heat and turned on the A/C to help fight the condensation and start the window defogging. Looking to Lia briefly, then meeting Vern's gaze in the rearview, he said, "Did either of you get a good look at the biters we passed on the way up?"

Lia nodded. "I glanced at them. Why do you ask?"

"Because I noticed they weren't adversely affected by the drop in temperature."

"I doubt it's freezing out there," Vern put in. "Probably just keeping cold enough so the snow hangs around."

Riker consulted the Shelby's SYNC Home screen and noted the outside temperature displayed there. "It's thirty-three here. And we're almost at the pass. Last group we passed was a couple miles back. I'd guess that was around the six-thousand-foot level."

"I'd bet the temp was nudging up on forty back there," Vern posited. "I'm curious to know how subfreezing temps affect the things. Does it stop them completely? Do they just slow down?" He walked his gaze from Lia to Riker. "Or do they *die*? I mean really *die*. If so, that would be a game changer."

Riker smiled. "First real snow event we get at Trinity we could venture out with no worries. We'll be able to forage day and night. *That* would really be a game changer."

"The dead aren't our only worry," Lia reminded. "We have to be wary of other humans." *The type of human trash I hope I get to kill when we get to Vegas*, she thought to herself, a smile curling the corners of her lips.

"Sadly, she's right." Vern sighed. "Think you could still ski if we find a proper prosthetic and ski boot to fit it?"

Lia pointed across the hood. "See that?" She pressed the Steiners to her face. As she glassed the road ahead, the trees quickly thinning out, she said to Vern, "Baby steps. I need to learn to walk on it as good as Lee does on his. Then run. Then I'll contemplate strapping on some planks." She winced. "None of that is going to happen if these damn nerve endings don't stop effing with me."

"It'll happen," Riker answered. "In due time." He was speaking from experience. Everyone's path to healing was different, inevitably their physical wounds would heal. The mental ones, though, were a different story.

"I'm ready for the nerves to fuck off and die." She stopped panning the binoculars and grunted.

Slowing the Shelby, Riker said, "What is it? What do you see?"

"A lodge or something. Store, maybe. Gas pumps. Sign that says *no gas*. Whole lot of cars and trucks sitting idle in front of the place. There's a few parked around back, too. I see some cabins behind it all, in the shadow of the trees."

"Any zombies?" Vern asked.

"Not that I can see."

Riker slowed further and signaled a left turn. "Any fresh tracks in the snow?"

"Can't tell," she replied. "Gotta get us closer."

Closer was a fifteen-foot-wide strip of dirty snow bordering a short, looping feeder road splitting from 89A's eastbound lane. It was large enough to allow both vehicles to park side by side while still leaving room for the doors to open.

Riker kept the engine running. "We wait here for a bit. See if anything takes interest in us." No sooner had he said it than a pair of mule deer ambled from the rear of the main building, sniffed the air, then hightailed it toward a nearby road.

The sign posted at the road's entrance was a trove of information: Grand Canyon's North Rim was 44 miles south on State Route 67. Closer in was the unincorporated community of Jacob Lake as well as the lake itself. And in bold black font atop the sign was the proclamation that Jacob Lake was the **Gateway to the Grand Canyon**.

Chapter 24

Jacob Lake's namesake inn was nestled on a couple of acres cleared out of a dense forest of fir, spruce, and aspen. The *inn* was more rustic lodge than the ubiquitous cube-shaped motel Riker was expecting to see. It was clad in hewn wood siding and featured a recessed entry paneled with pale pine. The wide pine door was flanked by columns of stacked river rock. Though there was an attached restaurant that looked more like a Denny's than a joint where one might find pioneer fare, there was nothing Best Western or Howard Johnson about the inn. If the windows hadn't been boarded over with blood-streaked sheets of plywood, Riker would have made a motion to ration a few minutes to do some exploring.

In the Shelby's cab, a loud rumbling could be heard coming from the west.

Instantly placing the sound, Riker said, "That's a big rig compression braking." Three heartbeats later, with Lia firing a questioning look his way, he was proven correct. Not one big rig, but three came at them from the west. The rigs had just reached the turnoff to the inn and were using their engine compression to slow down prior to beginning the long trip downhill. As the lead semi, a Volvo tractor pulling a refrigerated trailer, hit the stretch of 89A bordering a copse of trees growing in front of the feeder loop, Riker saw the driver's head turn his way and recognition flash across the man's deeply tanned face. The rig's air horn unexpectedly emitted a long, drawn-out *blaaappp.* A Freightliner tractor pulling linked chrome fuel tanks—SHELL emblazoned on one, CHEVRON the other—slid past next. Following close behind was a second Freightliner tractor. It was pulling a flatbed heaped high with cargo, all of it concealed from view by a number of wildly flapping tarps.

As the trailing rigs passed by the inn, their horns belched a greeting, too.

"If that doesn't bring out the dead, nothing will," Lia intoned.

Riker heard a hand slap the Shelby's flank. Shifting his gaze to the wing mirror, he saw Tara. She was out of the Roamer ahead of Shorty and Steve-O and leading them by a few yards. MP5 in hand, head on a swivel, she made her way around to his door.

Tilt to her head, she said, "What's up?"

"I should be asking you that," grumbled Riker. "I was waiting to see if we're alone here before venturing out."

"Should have radioed your intention," Tara replied. "I would have stayed in the truck."

Lia said, "Since we're stopped, and so far it looks like we're alone, makes sense to top off our tanks. We're less than two hundred miles out from Vegas. The map shows us dipping in and out of southern Utah before we reach the Arizona/Vegas border. Better than doing so near population centers." She looked all around. Focusing on something beyond the inn, a man-sized shape moving about in the deep shadows between a pair of tall pines, she said, "Famous last words." She scowled. "Why'd those truckers have to go and blow their horns?"

"Maybe it was a warning," Steve-O said. He was strapped with the Mule and peeling the wrapper off a cereal bar. "The Indians are the good guys."

"Native Americans," Tara reminded. "It's not cool to call them *Indians*."

Shorty leaned on the Shelby, Shockwave in a two-handed grip, and grinned at Riker. "When you were little Lee Riker … not that your little was really *little* … did you play cowboys and *Indians* or was it cowboys and *Native Americans*?"

"The former." He shook his head. "I don't care what word Steve-O used. We all know he wasn't using it as a pejorative."

"It's still problematic," said Tara.

"I think you worked too long at the college," Riker intoned. "Growing up, you were never into splitting hairs."

Tara said nothing. She was watching the thing in the shadows. As it neared the forest edge, it was clear it was not another deer. And it had companions. Three to be exact.

"I got this," she said, hefting the MP5.

"Your shots will carry," Riker said. He realized how stupid that sounded as soon as it had slipped his tongue. "Go ahead." As Tara strode off, Steve-O in tow, Riker looked to Shorty. "So what's this point of interest?"

Shorty spread out his arms, indicating the gas station and inn. "The Gateway to the Grand Canyon. It popped up on my navigation pane." He pretended to pray. "It's only fifty miles south of here."

"That'll be a hundred-mile round trip," Riker said.

"Then there's the possibility there may be snow on the road," Vern put in.

Squashing all thought of a side trip, Lia said, "We don't have time to spare. We need to be close to Vegas before nightfall."

"I expected that," Shorty conceded. "Vern gets his way when he asks to explore the cache outside of Vegas." He regarded Riker. "What do I have to do to be a shot caller?"

Riker shrugged. "This is a group effort. Had you gotten truly high centered on the herd back there… if you went and flipped your rig on its side, I was ready to come to your rescue. We're a team, Shorty."

"There is no *I* in team," Shorty mumbled. "I get it. I'm just used to being a lone wolf. Not answering to nobody. Now that my kids are gone, I got nothing to look forward to. Nothing driving me."

"Even though they're little, just pretend Cole and the others are your kids." Lia shrugged. "You're adding positive karma to your karma bank. Who knows," she said, staring him in the eyes, "maybe your kids are still out there. Maybe they're looking for you at this very moment."

Riker said, "I already told him that. Shorty's glass is half empty."

Looking past Riker, Vern said to Shorty, "Not too late for you to turn over a new leaf. I've lost people near and dear to me. If I can rebound, so can you."

Riker hollered at Tara and Steve-O, urging them to hurry back. Speaking to Shorty and Vern, he said, "Lucy's advice stand is closed, fellas. Put your nickels away … because Lia is right, we need to get a move on." He consulted his fuel gauge.

Three-quarters full. "I can easily reach the cache on what I have in the tank."

"I'm good for now," Shorty added. "But if we don't find diesel to replace the stuff that got spilled, I may be singing a different tune on the return trip."

"Cross that bridge when we get—" Riker's words were cut off by a flurry of gunshots. The seconds-long fusillade was followed by Steve-O bellowing, "Monsters!" and then another pair of closely spaced gunshots.

As Riker urged Shorty to go see what was happening, he was already scooping up the radio and depressing the Talk key. His shouted requests for a SITREP went unanswered. He was drawing his Sig Legion and elbowing open his door when he heard the distinct sound of Steve-O's Mule firing.

As Tara entered the tree line, MP5 shouldered and lining up the iron sights on a trio of zombies, she heard branches snapping deep in the forest on her right. As her finger tensed on the trigger, a chorus of low timbre moans drifted from the open door of a cabin to her left. Engaging the lurching zombies a dozen feet to her fore, her first shot landed precisely where she'd been aiming: dead center on the leader's wide forehead. As a dime-sized hole appeared and the thing's frontal lobe was reduced to mush, all hell broke loose.

From the right, a Bolt burst from the forest. It was a younger dark-skinned man with a full head of oily black hair. A ragged blood-crusted gash ran from ear to Adam's apple, the second mouth opening and closing with each step. As the thing was illuminated by bars of rainbow-colored light lancing diagonally through the canopy, she saw that its black Adidas tracksuit had picked up wisps of spider web and long strands of feathery green lichen. It was fifteen away, head down and arms pumping, and quickly closing the distance.

Keeping her cool, Tara face-shot the pair of zombies coming up behind her first kill. Even as they were falling to the forest floor, she was swinging her weapon right, finger continuously slapping the trigger. Six of the dozen rounds fired blindly at Track Suit sailed harmlessly into the forest. The remaining rounds stitched him from groin to shoulder and opened up his belly, sending several feet of steaming intestine on a one-way trip to the forest floor. Stood up by the kinetic energy behind the screaming hunks of lead, the Bolt lost all forward momentum and collapsed in a heap on the ground a couple of yards distant.

Tara was lining up her kill shot, the iron sights bracketing the rear of the fallen Bolt's wagging head, when Steve-O shouted his one-word warning. Coming to realize the *monsters* Steve-O was seeing were the ones whose moaning she'd heard coming from the direction of the cabins, she finished Track Suit with two rounds to the head, then turned to face the new threats. As she did, several things happened all at once. The *pfft-thwak* report produced by Steve-O's Mule reached her ears. Simultaneous to that, she watched his kill, a geriatric male zombie, fall and get hung up on the waist-high tree stump Steve-O was backing away from.

Swinging her gaze left, she spotted a pair of zombies advancing on Steve-O's blind side. They were having a hard time navigating the trees. Which was a good thing, because in the background, maybe twenty feet from the first pair of zombies, more were surging from the cabin's gloomy interior.

Hearing footsteps coming up fast from behind, and the accompanying sound of someone's labored breathing, Tara emptied the magazine into the zombies threatening her friend. As her rounds staggered the zombies, one of them collapsing a dozen feet from Steve-O, a loud *boom* and the reassuring follow-on reports of a smaller caliber weapon told her the cavalry had arrived. She was lining up on the zombies in front of the cabin steps when she heard the *pfft-thwak* of the Mule. A half beat later, Steve-O was calling for help.

Shorty swept by her, a gossamer wisp of gun smoke trailing the Shockwave's barrel. "Steve-O's OK," he called in passing. "The Mule is caught up on a branch."

Relieved her worst fear hadn't been realized, Tara crabbed left, swapping mags as she went. Content to let Shorty finish the zombie left standing after her last volley, she made her way to Steve-O's side. He had already freed the Mule from some grabby branches and was sitting on a stump. Her brother was there, too. Somehow, he'd swept around from the left and had remained outside of her peripheral vision as he took down three zombies lurking beside a second cabin.

So much for situational awareness was what she was thinking as another half dozen zombies emerged from behind the cabin, where someone had tried to conceal a pair of full-size RVs under camouflage netting. If it wasn't for the dusting of snow, she wouldn't have realized what she was looking at. "Lee," she called out, "you have six coming at you from your twelve o'clock."

No sooner had Riker acknowledged the shouted warning than Shorty's shotgun boomed three times in quick succession. "Cabin's clear," the man bellowed from somewhere out of sight. "I'm gonna loop around and check out the RVs."

Riker let Shorty's report go unanswered. Picking up through the trees the flitting movement of the zombies Tara had just warned him about, he worked his way forward, engaging them individually with his Legion whenever he was presented a clean shot. By the time silence had returned to the forest, he had expended half a magazine, and all six zombies were down for good, their brains leaking from shattered skulls.

Riker doubled back and found Tara and Steve-O where he'd seen them last. He was sitting on a stump, the wand to the Mule balanced on one shoulder. She was standing nearby, on high alert, her MP5 aimed at the ground.

Gun smoke drifting between the branches on the forest edge parted as Shorty emerged from between a pair of tall pines. The Shockwave was dangling on its sling. Clutched in one hand was the black Glock. In the other, he was carrying a wooden-handled plunger. Gesturing at Riker with the plunger, he said, "That's all she wrote. The RVs are clear. Nothing moving south of here, either."

Steve-O rose from the stump. "Anything need to be tapped with the Mule?"

Shorty shook his head. "No need. There's really nothing left of them to tap." Beaming and hooking a thumb at the RVs, he said, "All the ammo we just expended. It was definitely worth its weight in gold."

"All that just to unclog your shitter?" Tara quipped.

"*All that just to unclog your shitter?*" Shorty mimicked in a singsong voice.

"What else did you find?" Tara pressed. "That can't be it. You're smiling way too hard."

"In addition to this lifesaving tool," Shorty said, "the rigs are treasure troves of stuff we need."

Surveying the forest to their fore, Riker swapped magazines. Eyeing Shorty, he said, "Is the treasure in the form of fuel, ammo, or food?"

Shorty nodded. "Yes."

Tara said, "Which is it, smartass?"

"All three and then some."

Riker's two-way came to life. "You all OK back there?" Lia asked. Her words were clipped. She sounded stressed. "We heard lots of gunfire."

"It's all under control," he radioed. "Are you two OK?"

"Coast is clear," she responded. "Can we get going?"

"After we transfer some fuel. Think you're up to driving?"

"It's not a stick shift," she joked.

Remembering the story of how she had to leave behind a perfectly good getaway car because she couldn't drive a stick caused him to smile. Considering all the dead bodies littering the forest, he welcomed the momentary distraction. "Get on the highway. Loop back around and take the first right. You'll see some cabins and a couple of RVs. That's where we'll be waiting."

"Where do you want me to park?"

"Just get Dolly close." He winked at Steve-O, drawing a tight smile out of the man.

"Should I back it in?" asked Lia.

Riker saw Shorty and Tara both shaking their heads. Agreeing with them, Riker said, "No need. Just park with the trailer broadside to the RVs."

She said, "We'll be there in a sec," and ended the transmission.

Pocketing the radio, Riker smiled at Shorty. "Show us what you got."

Chapter 25

From the amount of trash heaped alongside the RVs, Riker gleaned that the group of survivors had been idle at Jacob Lake for several days. From going through the pockets of the dead, they concluded the group had been made up of two married couples in their late twenties whose IDs suggested they had fled together from Seattle, a family of three from Vancouver, British Columbia, a geriatric couple hailing from sunny Pasadena, California, and a lone thirty-three-year-old man carrying only a .38 special and the receipt for it issued by a gun store in Las Vegas.

As luck would have it, the thirty-seven-foot Newmar Ventana belonging to the elderly couple was powered by a Cummins diesel. Shorty was able to siphon enough fuel from its tank to fill one of the fifty-five-gallon rainwater collection barrels in the U-Haul trailer. The RV also yielded a couple of bags of potato chips and a good deal of canned food. The couple was fond of red wine. Lia had found three cases stacked vertically inside a closet, most of it Pinot Noir bearing labels from Oregon vineyards. Save for some board games, a few of which Steve-O pilfered, nothing else in the Ventana was worth taking.

The fuel tank in the rental Winnebago Brave gave up seventy gallons of gasoline. It would be more than enough to get the Shelby back to Santa Fe. While poking around inside the retro-styled RV, Tara found the fridge in the modest kitchen filled with two dozen bottled micro beers and half as many cans of Diet Coke. In the cupboards above the sink, several boxes of 9mm had been stashed behind bags of dried pasta and stacked-up cans of chili and beef stew. All total, there were four hundred rounds and enough food to fill up three grocery bags. Only thing missing food-wise were the staples: eggs, meat, milk. That stuff,

Vern had said at the time, was probably a relic of the past unless individuals got back to farming.

After leaving Jacob Lake, the convoy followed 89A as it descended 3,000 feet through the northwestern edge of the vast Kaibab National Forest. The small groups of zombies trudging uphill in the snow toward the sleepy lake town usually had a bell cow out ahead of the main body and a number of stragglers bringing up the rear. The lone zombies found on the road were mostly crawlers or ambulatory specimens injured so severely that, instead of miles per hour, their forward progress was measured in yards per hour.

Once 89A came out of the trees, the highway all the way to Fredonia, Arizona, some thirty miles north by west of Jacob Lake, was mostly free of wrecks and stalls. The majority of the zombies they came upon were combined into large packs, all of them migrating east.

Formerly a logging town, Fredonia, Arizona, population 1,300, was now a ghost town. The Chevron station on the edge of town was clogged with vehicles, many of them still occupied by their undead drivers and passengers. A block from the gas station, where 89A curved gently north, the country store on the right demanded their attention. It had been thoroughly looted. A pair of dust-covered SUVs were nosed in close to the store's boarded-over front doors. Both vehicles were pocked with bullet holes. All of the windows in the nearest rig, a dark green Isuzu Rodeo, were spidered and punched through with fist-sized holes. A number of corpses, their limbs frozen at curious angles, facial features twisted in grotesque final expressions, were scattered about the ground behind the SUVs. Whether they had been alive or undead before suffering their separate fates, Riker had no way of telling. The passage of time and exposure to the elements made it impossible to determine age, sex, or cause of death. The bullet holes in the Isuzu led him to believe that whatever had gone down here likely had something to do with the current state of the little convenience store. Two sides had clashed. That much was clear. He supposed the bodies represented the side that had wanted something that was not theirs to take. And for ignoring societal mores, they had all paid the ultimate price.

Further down the road, a ranger station on their left caught Riker's eye. Suggestive of a hasty retreat, it was dark inside and surrounded by a fenced-in parking lot devoid of vehicles. The nearby dollar store was an empty shell of its former self.

"I can think of a thousand stores I'd loot before I took a thing from their shelves," Lia sneered. "Seems like everything they sell is made in *China*. I went in one once thinking I would buy some toys for a local toy drive." She shook her head, nose crinkling. "Everything. And I do mean *everything* on the toy aisle smelled like toxic chemicals."

Riker said nothing. He was busy watching the road and side streets, making doubly sure nothing untoward happened that would cause them to have to spend one second longer in Fredonia. The deserted town was giving him the creeps.

Vern said, "They use slave labor over there. What'd you expect? Wooden masterpieces carved by the Amish?"

"Just caught me by surprise, that's all." She looked earnestly at Riker. "I wasn't being classist. Swear to God and hope to die."

"I know that last part you said is *just* a saying," Riker replied. "But given the state of the world, it's probably something you shouldn't be thinking, let alone saying out loud." Gesturing at the nav screen, he asked her for an update.

Consulting the screen on the dash, she said, "If we follow the route the computer wants us to, we'll be going through a lot of little towns. The alternate route has us staying on this road until we get to State Route 389. It's coming up quick." She motioned with one hand. "Take a left there and head west. Colorado City is the next town we'll come to. Looks like it's thirty miles from here to there."

"How about points of interest along the way that Shorty might bust my balls to stop and see?"

"Nope," she said as she snaked a couple of fingers into her prosthetic and jabbed furiously at a hard-to-scratch itch. "Looks like smooth sailing all the way."

Riker made a face. *Shouldn't say that either* he thought as he made the turn-off of 89A. Tempting the Grim Reaper and Murphy of Murphy's Law fame all in the span of a few minutes wasn't good practice. In fact, it was inviting trouble.

For three blocks, SR-389 passed through a small residential area. Save for a lone windblown tumbleweed and trash littering the streets, the only thing Riker saw moving when he cast his gaze about was already long dead.

The two-vehicle convoy didn't slow or stop on the way out of town. There was no reason to. Fredonia belonged to the dead.

Transiting the northern Arizona desert between Fredonia and Colorado City, the Shelby and Roamer had the road all to themselves. The drivers in the big rigs that had honked at them in Jacob Lake, triggering the event that had led to them tangling with the zombies and, ultimately finding the fuel and supplies, were the last living beings they saw until they rolled into Colorado City and *trouble* found them.

Women and kids, the latter outnumbering the former by a huge margin, were staged at most of the entry points into the city of 4,500. There were very few men in the mix. Riker got the impression their purpose was to keep an eye on the women, who vastly outnumbered them.

The adults were all visibly displaying rifles and shotguns. Many of the older kids were armed, too. A select few who appeared to be grade school age also brought rifles to bear on the convoy as it approached the first exit. To a person, they wore what appeared to be handmade clothes. The women had on long-sleeved blouses over flowing ankle-length dresses. The men and boys were clad in white button-up shirts, the tails spilling over gray or black pants. Leather shoes and boots seemed to be the norm. The women and girls had their hair pulled tight and secured in buns atop their heads. The boys and men all wore wide-brimmed hats pulled down low so their eyes were cloaked in shadow.

The exits not guarded by locals were blocked with Jersey barriers and static automobiles.

Signs at each exit, manned or not, forbid entrance by outsiders. It was also made clear gas and food were not available in Colorado City.

Whoever these people were, Riker thought, they had their little slice of Arizona locked down every bit as tight as the Navajo did theirs.

"What did I just see?" Riker asked as he was waved past the first road feeding into the city.

"Looks like a casting call for the Handmaid's Tale," quipped Lia.

"I think these people are hardcore members of the FLDS," said Vern. "They're an offshoot of the LDS."

Riker wore a fake smile and waved at the knot of grim-faced people as they slipped by on the right. "LDS is Latter-day Saints," said Riker. "So these are Mormons, right?"

"Basically," said Vern.

"What's the F stand for in FLDS?" asked Lia.

"Definitely not *fly*," joked Riker as he slowed the Shelby so as not to appear threatening to the next group of locals crowding the Jersey barriers at an upcoming offshoot. "Because nothing those folks were wearing would cut it at the nightclub. A honkytonk, maybe." He chuckled at his own attempt at humor.

Vern said, "The F stands for fundamental. They practice polygamy."

"Oh yeah," said Lia. "That Jeff guy from a couple of years back. I remember he was kicking men and boys out so he'd have the ladies all to himself."

"I think you're correct," said Vern. "Not sure if his first name was Jeff, or if it was his last name. Rings a bell, either way." To get a better look at the next group coming up on the right, he scooted to the edge of his seat and pulsed down the window. Catching the eye of a forty-something woman holding a lever-action rifle, he mouthed, "We're just passing through." She nodded as if she understood the message. But the portly man wearing a straw hat and wielding a stubby AR-15 who stepped into Riker's lane a dozen yards past the main group was not on the same page. He raised one hand, universal semaphore for halt, then gestured with his stubby rifle for them to move to the outside shoulder.

Riker didn't like being put in this situation, but, short of shooting first and risking the dire consequences such an act would precipitate, he saw no way out of it. Plus, they still had to pass through Utah's southwest corner to get to the crossing into Nevada. So, lifting a hand off the steering wheel, he waved at the man and nodded. As he started to slow and steer for the shoulder, the radio issued a burst of squelch. "Oh, hell no," Tara protested. "We cannot stop here. It's like The Hills Have Eyes and shit. Do you see a single face that looks like ours, bro?"

Riker rolled down the volume. Then he pulsed down his window and greeted the man with a smile and introduced himself.

The man skipped the formalities and delivered a message Riker was sure he had uttered hundreds of times since the world went to shit. It might as well have been Lieutenant Nez standing there and running down the rules required for passage. The little man's rules differed in only one respect: a tithe to the FLDS Church was required.

"Fuel, food, or …" the man said as he looked Lia squarely in the face.

Producing the Crown Royal bag, Riker shook it so the man could hear the precious metals jangling inside. "One-quarter ounce of gold for us to pass. Gold was blowing through the roof before the financial system collapsed. I figure that's a couple of grand to the church."

The man bit his lip, thinking.

Barely audible coming through the two-way, Riker heard Tara asking if she could shoot the teenage boys leering at her.

Lifting the radio to his lips, Riker whispered, "Only if you're fearing for your life."

She said, "Whatever. They're staring the clothes off my body." In the background, Steve-O was going on about seeing a mass grave in a graded plat of dirt bordering the opposite lanes.

"Two ounces," said the man with no name.

So you want to play the game. "One-half ounce," Riker said firmly.

"One and three-quarters ounces." The man crossed his arms and tilted his head. *The ball is in your court.*

Sighing, Riker said, "Let's cut the back and forth and meet in the middle." He paused for effect. "Three-quarter ounce pieces for passage. That's a high price to pay, if you ask me."

"You can backtrack and go around," said the man, a knowing smile lifting his mustache.

"OK," said Riker, "you win. One ounce for passage."

"Deal," said the man. He sounded like a satisfied customer. Like he'd talked the auto sales closer up on the value of his trade-in. Eyes narrowing as he accepted the gold Krugerrand from Riker, the man reiterated the rules, finishing with, "No stopping, whatsoever. And no leering at the women folk." Then, like Nez had earlier in the day, as if the Shelby were a metal steed, the man with no name slapped its sheet metal flank and instructed Riker to carry on.

They burned ninety minutes on an eighty-mile sprint through the southwest corner of Utah. The route Lia inputted had them jump onto Utah 59. They stayed on 59 and skirted Zion National Park to the south before the state route shot off due west, passing through Hurricane and curling around Quail Creek Reservoir's southern shore.

After 59 merged with I-15 South and cut through Washington, Saint George, and dipped back into Arizona, it became clear every effort had been taken to keep all lanes of travel open. While there was a considerable zombie presence in and around the cities, the interstate was, to regurgitate Lia's taboo expression, "smooth sailing" all the way to Mesquite, Nevada, a stone's throw west of the state line with Arizona.

The Nevada Department of Transportation sign emblazoned with the words WELCOME TO MESQUITE was the size of a ping pong table and plastered with all kinds of information. For one, the elevation here was listed as 1,630 feet above sea level. Which would explain why, even with sunset rapidly approaching, it was still a balmy seventy-five degrees outside. A number of badges on the sign indicated when and where one could find a weekly meeting of the local Rotary Club, the Lions International, and the Benevolent and Protective Order of the Elks. Something Riker had never seen displayed on a city limits sign was the type and location of churches that could be found in a city. There were three different denominations on offer. Granted, Mesquite was purported to have a population of just north of 18,000, but he still found it strange to lump that in with everything else.

Commissioned and installed by the Chamber of Commerce was a separate sign fashioned out of red rock. Chiseled on its face was a repeat of the welcome on the NDOT sign. Below the foot-tall words embossed in rock was what Riker guessed had to be the city slogan: YOUR FUTURE IS HERE.

Yeah, right, thought Riker. Judging by the dust-streaked vehicles and small packs of undead patrolling the nearby Casablanca Casino and Hotel's palm-tree-lined parking lots, most of the city's population had either fallen to Romero or had gone elsewhere in search of the future promised on the sign. A future more conducive to remaining in the still-possessing-a-heartbeat-and-respiration column.

"Eighteen thousand people," said Vern. "Where are they all?"

"Don't jinx us," shot Lia. "Apparently that's my job."

Though Riker knew the subtle barb had been directed at him, he addressed Vern's question. "I'm guessing many of them left early on. I would have. Las Vegas is what, eighty miles from here? That's a lot of desperate people real close. And as Rage Against the Machine so succinctly put it: Hungry people don't stay hungry for long."

"Neither do zombies," Lia put in.

"Desperation will cause a man to do things he never fathomed he is capable of," Vern said. "Case in point: The rugby team whose plane crashed in the Andes. Out of fifty-some-odd people aboard, less than twenty survived. They had to resort to eating the frozen bodies of their coaches and teammates."

"They were Uruguayan," Lia pointed out. "And they didn't eat the guts and stuff. Just strips of flesh, if my memory serves. "Still"—she threw a hard shiver—"the mere thought of cannibalism turns my stomach."

"That's how I feel about MREs," quipped Riker. He pointed to a distant fast-food sign, the unlit arches a depressing shade of yellow. "What I wouldn't give for a Big Mac right about now."

"And some fries," Lia added. "They have the best fries."

"Had," said Vern shaking his head. "Hard to believe it's all gone the way of the dodo."

It looked like war had been waged in the middle of Mesquite. Perhaps one had. If so, it was evident the wrong side had won. If a window remained in any of the business concerns, Riker would be hard pressed to point it out. An Audi dealership's entire fleet of new vehicles had been torched. Rows and rows of charred metal husks sat on warped rims.

The fast-food joints that hadn't been shored up with plywood had also been set upon by the firebugs. It was here, near the middle I-15's short run through the center of Mesquite, where Lia pointed out that there were just as many zombies heading westbound with them as there were moving in the opposite direction.

"Damn things are fire and forget," Riker grumbled. "My guess is they're following the big rigs coming out of Henderson and Vegas."

Lia looked at Riker. "How do you explain the ones heading toward Henderson and Vegas?"

"Light," said Vern. "Even if Cole is right and Vegas is dead, solar power was big before the fall. I wouldn't be surprised if Sin City lights up like a torch once the sun sets." Vern nodded as if he could see it in his mind's eye. "It'll be a bubble of light at first. As you get closer, drawn like bugs to the zapper"—he chuckled—"it takes on a glow filled with all the colors in the rainbow. The beacon in the valley shining like the riches it promises, yet rarely delivers."

"We'll find out if you're right"—Riker consulted his watch—"in about an hour or so."

The Motorola crackled then Steve-O's voice filled the cab. "Tara sees something up ahead."

"Shit," Lia said, lifting the Steiners to her face, "I'm falling asleep on the job." Through the binoculars, about half a mile distant, she saw the outskirts of Mesquite giving way to desert. She also had eyes on what Tara was reporting. The short hairs on her neck snapped to attention when she realized the freeway was funneling them toward the threat.

"What do we do?" she asked.

Slowing to thirty miles per hour, Riker said, "Gun up and stay alert."

"I concur," Vern said. "Something tells me the third time is a charm thing is not going to apply here and now."

Chapter 26

Less than a mile outside of Mesquite was where smooth sailing ended and the proverbial waters got choppy. The roadblock was haphazard, at best. On the left was a hot-rodded late-sixties Chevrolet Camaro. It was canary yellow, the hood and fenders decorated with photorealistic flames. The nose-down stance was aggressive and complemented the big chrome Cragar rims and wide fifty-series tires wrapping them. Blocking the right lane was a black Cadillac hearse. It was late model, frilly curtains drawn over the rear windows, the westering sun reflecting off paint and chrome.

The way the vehicles had been left on the freeway, grille to grille, with a couple of yards of open space between bumpers, told Riker he was looking at the work of someone who knew nothing about physics. Even though the Chevy was old-school Detroit metal, and the hearse was heavy and low to the ground, no way were they going to stop a determined driver at the wheel of anything larger than a Prius.

Another clue to the lack of thought put into the roadblock was the total absence of zombie corpses. Surely with the number of dead transiting I-15, if the roadblock had been here for any amount of time, at the very least the parties responsible would have already had to deal with a straggler or two.

The more Riker thought about it, the more convinced he became that he was looking at someone's spur of the moment decision. And the people responsible weren't guarding ancestral lands or their many wives and children. *Hell*, he thought, *they didn't even park their vehicles with a modicum of conviction.* As the realization that he was dealing with garden variety highway robbers turned to resignation that conflict was looming, he vowed he wasn't going to disrobe for anyone, nor was he willing to give up anything to travel the highways and byways of what he still believed to be a free country. His free country.

"Come out, come out, wherever you are," Riker said under his breath. As he continued with the chant, he was drifting the Shelby to the outside shoulder and drawing his Sig Legion. The words "come out" had just crossed his lips for the third time when the perpetrators popped up from behind the hearse and made their way to the gap between the vehicles. There were three of them. A woman toting a bullhorn and two younger men. All were armed with black AR-15 carbines. The woman, with her graying hair, sunken cheeks, and dark, unblinking eyes, looked old enough to be mother to the men.

Strangely, the trio wore matching black leather jackets, the epaulets bristling with inch-long chrome spikes. Thick leather belts studded with more spikes held up their stiff denim jeans, the legs of which were rolled into inch-wide cuffs that left their identical Doc Martens boots on full display.

Still peering through the Steiners, Lia said, "Isn't that cute. Looks like Mom and the boys are living their best post-apocalyptic lives."

As if she had been privy to Lia's dis, the woman slipped between the vehicles and squared up to the approaching Shelby. Holding the AR-15 in one hand, she raised the bullhorn to her lips. "Halt. We know you have fuel. Give it to us or you do not pass."

Shaking his head, Riker said, "Not today, lady," and pressed down on the accelerator. As the truck lurched and the turbocharger whine filled the cab, he was telling Vern to fire warning shots if the men brought their rifles up even an inch. Indicating the woman, he said, "And if that one sets the bullhorn down and shoulders her rifle, light them all up. No mercy."

"For issuing an ultimatum?" Lia asked.

"I'm done with all the talking," Riker said. Still a couple of hundred feet from the woman, he laid on the horn. It wasn't a short *How goes it?* kind of toot. It was a full-blown, drawn-out *Get the hell out of our way!* warning that could be construed as nothing but.

In the Roamer, Shorty saw twin puffs of exhaust belch from the Shelby's rear pipes. While the ultimatum hadn't reached his ears, he did hear the blaring horn. Incredulous, he said, "I think Lee is going to ram them," and applied the brakes. If metal was about to be reshaped, he didn't want his Roamer to be involved.

"He's just testing them," Tara said. "He knows he's got the fuel in the trailer. You just watch, he'll slow down. But what he does after depends on their response."

Their response was far from ideal. The woman dropped the bullhorn, moved her hand to the rifle's forestock, and started dragging the muzzle up. Simultaneously, she was tilting her head to the right and dropping her cheek to the rising buttstock. Behind her, the men were following suit. Behind them, maybe thirty feet distant, a pair of zombies crossing the median had just set foot on I-15. If the men were aware they were being stalked, they didn't seem concerned.

As Tara's prophecy came true, the Shelby's brake lights flaring red all the proof Shorty needed, he witnessed a black muzzle protrude from the pickup's left-side passenger window. Instantly licks of flame erupted from the weapon and shell casings cascaded to the road.

A look of surprise flitted across the woman's face as bullets stitched her body from navel to neck. Bloody intestines poked through the initial wound. The leather jacket obscured whatever damage the middle rounds had wrought on her chest. The hit to the neck was a grazing one. Still, her carotid artery must have been nicked, because a spray of blood, fanning out on a flat plane, wet the Camaro's hood. Forgetting all about the rifle, the woman let go of it and clamped both hands over the pulsating wound.

The Shelby had been moving at walking speed when the first shots were fired. It was at a complete stop when the horn went quiet and Riker's arm, Sig prominent in his hand, emerged from the open window. A series of loud reports reached Shorty's ears and he saw the pistol and hand jerk multiple times. The firing lasted longer than the horn blast. By the time the Sig's slide had locked open, the two men were each hit multiple times and had fallen out of sight behind the Camaro's front end. Some of the rounds found the Camaro's passenger window. It was spidered and slowly disintegrating, the tiny pieces of safety glass bouncing as they hit the road.

Next to Shorty, Steve-O was on the edge of his seat, Stetson on his lap, both hands wringing its brim. After having sat through the two previous encounters with folks manning roadblocks, he wasn't expecting the violence that followed the woman's action. When it was all said and done, the woman lying on the road and ashen-faced from loss of blood, the pair of zombies dropping down to their knees behind the Camaro and the shrill screams that followed, there was nothing he could do to stop the rise of bile.

"They were about to fire on Lee," Tara pointed out. No stranger to the look on her friend's face, she scrounged a plastic bag from the backseat floor and held it open underneath his chin. Hooking the handles behind his ears, she instructed him to hold it there until the nausea passed. While the sight reminded her of a horse on the feedbag, the shock from what she had just witnessed overrode any chance of her finding the situation even the least bit amusing.

With the wails of the dying rising over the Shelby's idling motor, Riker quickly swapped mags, thumbed the Sig's slide-lock, and elbowed open his door. Legion in hand, two-way radio clutched in the other, he stepped to the road and stepped clear of the Shelby. Eyes never leaving his would-be attackers, he thumbed the Talk key. "Anyone copy?"

"Tara here. We're just now rolling up on the trailer."

Riker could hear the Roamer's tires hissing on the blacktop but kept all his attention directed at the roadblock, where the screaming had just ceased. "Tell Steve-O to bring the Mule. We're going to need it."

"Will do," Tara responded. "Don't mind his pallor. Those three getting shot up just about made him lose his cookies."

Riker couldn't blame the man. The scene was upsetting to him, too. Pocketing the radio, he cut the distance to the dead woman, about thirty yards, his pace slow and deliberate, the Sig never wavering. Hit in the face by the metallic odor of the pooling blood, he stepped over the dead woman, crabbed between the vehicles, and got eyes on the zombies. They were on all fours and stuffing ropy intestine into their gnashing maws. He whistled to get their attention.

Hair slicked with blood, jaws pistoning nonstop, the zombies fixed Riker with a pair of dead-eyed stares. As if a switch was flicked, the creatures forgot all about the bullet-riddled corpses. Riker matched their stares as their jaws stopped moving. It was at that moment he detected a subtle shifting of gears he'd seen before. Though they didn't show emotion or communicate in any way, it was clear his presence had them slipping back into hunt mode.

"I got your back, Lee," said Steve-O as he hovered the wand over the dead woman's left eye and hit the trigger. The Mule produced the usual *pfft-thwak* and the spike did its thing.

Riker said, "One down, four to go," and stepped aside to let the man work.

Steve-O tiptoed through the growing crimson puddle. Steadying himself with one hand on the Camaro's hood, he leaned forward, arm holding the wand at full extension, and touched the flange at the end to the nearest zombie's forehead. Reacting to the intrusion, the zombie took hold of the wand and moved it toward its open mouth. In response, Steve-O gave the wand a firm forward thrust and hit the trigger. As the spike punctured the creature's cranium through the soft palate, scrambling the brain from below, so did the compressed air propelling the deadly projectile. Instantly the zombie's eyes bugged from their sockets and a geyser of blood shot from one ear. One moment the zombie was eyeing the meat from Steve-O's bones, the next it was seemingly boneless and collapsing atop the dead man it had just been making a meal of.

Extending one arm, Riker detained Steve-O long enough to pump a pair of 9mm rounds into the brain of the second zombie. "OK," he said, letting his arm fall to his side, "time to sell the Leather Jacket twins some insurance."

"I still don't get why that seems funny to you and Tara," said Steve-O as he shuffled between the vehicles.

"It just is," Riker said. "It's called *gallows humor*. Keeps the specter of our own death from weighing too heavily on us."

Steve-O pursed his lips and shrugged. All business, he pressed the wand to the ear of the man nearest to him and triggered the kill shot. The *pfft-thwak* precipitated an immediate blowback of brain tissue. Getting hit in the face by a spritz of gray matter finished what the gunplay had started. After emptying his stomach on the ground beside the Camaro, Steve-

O dragged a sleeve across his mouth and picked up where he had left off.

Rounding the front of the Camaro, Steve-O saw that the second man had already turned and was rising from the road. Hands leaving bloody prints on the Camaro's left front fender, the fresh turn pushed off the car and spun to face him. Guttural growl issuing over bared teeth, both claw-like hands sweeping up, the zombie charged.

Riker was a dozen feet away when the flash of movement dragged his attention from the hearse. Unlike the other zombies, the one facing off with Steve-O was not exhibiting the usual stiffness and compromised range of motion. Riker's stomach clenched as he realized one-half of the Leather Jacket twins had come back as a *Bolt*.

As Steve-O raised both hands, a defensive posture born out of his close proximity to the rushing Bolt, the wand clattered to the road, useless.

Riker was shouting a warning and swinging the Sig around when, simultaneously, he heard the *snap-crackle* of live rounds passing close by and witnessed a geyser of brain tissue erupt from the zombie's head. The report that followed was familiar. It was made by his F4. And though he knew Lia was a deadly shot from just about any distance, with just about any rifle on earth, the fact that the rounds had passed *between* him and Steve-O before hitting the intended target was not lost on him.

Legs suddenly gone rubbery, Riker steadied himself on the hearse and stole a quick look up the road. Lia was out of the Shelby, the AR resting on the hood, and peering at him through the scope. She waved but remained vigilant, rifle tucked tight to her shoulder.

The Roamer was on the right shoulder, Shorty at the wheel. Tara was on the road and scanning all points of the compass with Shorty's Bushnells.

Steve-O was still throwing up. When he finally hinged up from between the cars, wiping a thin rope of yellow bile on his sleeve, he gestured with the wand at the face-shot zombie. "That was a Bolt." He traced a trio of red welts running horizontally across his neck. "And it almost had me."

Riker nodded. "That's three Bolts in one day. Common denominator is they were all young men who had just recently turned. I should have just put them all down myself." He hung his head and massaged his temples. Mr. Headache had come a-calling. He fished out the baggie of Advil and swallowed a handful. Regarding Steve-O, he said, "Lia saved your butt. She also spared me a lifetime of regret."

Steve-O placed a hand on Riker's back. "I'm a grown-ass man, Lee. You aren't responsible for me. Neither is Tara. You can tell her I can handle Shorty all by myself. If she wants to ride with you, she should."

"Agreed," Riker said. "She's hardheaded, though. She won't do anything you tell her to do. Best let nature run its course." He tapped Steve-O on the shoulder. "I think if we ever find a live tattoo artist, you should get Lia's face added to your country music Mount Rushmore. At least put her name somewhere on your body."

Steve-O grinned. "I think you should do that, Lee Riker. You're sweet on her. Even Ray Charles could see that."

"Very astute observation, friend." Riker clapped him on the back. "I'm going to check these vehicles for anything of value. Then I'm going to write my name with piss in the desert. After that, we ride. The day isn't getting any younger."

Steve-O harumphed and adjusted the Mule's tank on his back. "I have to pee, too, Lee. But not here. No siree. There could be a lady hiding in the long car."

Have to admit, Riker thought, *the man has a way of making mountains into molehills.* The big life-altering events most people feared didn't weigh out the same on Steve-O's give a shit scale. "I'll inspect them both for you, Steve-O."

Riker peeked inside the hearse. *Nobody home.* Where a casket would ride, camping gear, amplifiers, and various musical instruments were stacked to the roof. He didn't see any food or propane canisters or anything that looked likely to be holding fuel. On the seat up front was a Mossberg pump shotgun. He opened the door and racked the slide. *Empty.* A quick glance at the fuel gauge confirmed the reason for all the desperation: the needle was pegged on E.

Walking over to the Camaro, he looked inside. Nothing but food wrappers and miscellaneous articles of clothing and a couple of winter coats. The dash revealed that the gas tank held less fuel than the hearse. Why the gas-guzzling muscle car? At least his gas-guzzling Shelby was not all show. It was utilitarian and could go just about anywhere. A combination that had already paid off in spades since the dead began to walk.

Riker caught Steve-O's attention. "Coast is clear. No women folk lurking in the vehicles. You may now release the Kraken and write your name in the desert." He gestured toward the left shoulder with the empty Mossberg. "You do your thing over there." He turned and started peeing on the road. "I'm doing mine right here."

Finished, Riker flashed a thumbs down at the others. "No food or fuel. Nothing of value." Beckoning Shorty to pull forward, he said, "Release the winch. We pull the Camaro straight and we'll be on our way."

Lowering the Bushnells, Tara said, "Make it quick. We've got biters coming in from both directions."

Snatching up the F4, Lia said, "Bolts?"

"Not yet," replied Tara. "Better stay frosty, though."

Lia and Tara stood on either end of the stretch of I-15 and pulled security while Vern and Riker hooked the cable around the Camaro's front suspension.

Moving the Camaro was nothing for the Roamer. A stab of the pedal and puff of diesel exhaust and it was parallel to the left-side shoulder, the only evidence it had been blocking the road the pair of skid marks and tiny pebbles of window glass.

Five minutes after the first shots were fired in the sad one-sided skirmish, the shooters burdened with many unanswered questions, the small group of survivors were back in the saddle and had resumed their pursuit of the westering sun.

Raven Rock Mountain Complex

Sitting in a black leather chair emblazoned with the Presidential seal, President Henry Tillman leaned forward, planted his elbows on the table whose identical counterpart sat in the White House situation room seventy miles away, and steepled his fingers. On the wall-mounted monitor before him was a sight he found hard to comprehend. While the dead were known to form packs and follow the highways and byways of the United States, not in his wildest dreams did he think one would ever grow to the size of what sixty-one-year-old Chairman of the Joint Chiefs of Staff, Marine Corps General Gerald F. Dunlap had taken to calling a mega-horde.

The monsters shuffling northbound on a four-lane freeway deep in the western desert were comprised of three smaller hordes called LA-1, SF-1, and SAC-1. They got their names from the regions they'd migrated from. Having combined near Modesto, California where the Reaper drone had first picked them up, the mega, estimated to number more than half a million, had been leaving death and destruction in its wake ever since.

After enduring a full ten minutes of deep, brooding silence, General Dunlap cleared his throat and said, "Hank. Have you given any thought about what you want to do?"

"There's no stopping them, is there, Jerry?"

On the screen, the front echelon of the mega was surging past a small town. A car lot near the freeway was swept up in the peripheral flow of marching dead things. Cars and trucks were pushed aside like toys, and the single structure wavered once, then folded in on itself.

Bowing his head, the general said, "Hank. The bombing campaign barely slowed LA-1 down. That was prior to the three coalescing." He paused, shaking his head. "I hate to admit this, but I think all we're going to accomplish by throwing more conventional munitions at them is minor attrition amid major destruction of infrastructure."

Tillman said, "Collateral damage?"

"We stopped seeing the living coming out in great numbers since week one."

The President exhaled sharply. "So how long until we have to think about evacuating assets and personnel?"

The general scowled at the row of clocks above the monitor. "Eight to ten hours, they'll be on the doorstep."

"What's your recommendation?"

"Fuel up every available bird. Load munitions, then personnel."

"How about French? Utilize it?"

The general nodded. "Just for the last to leave. Best to have them close in case you want to stand the base back up."

"We can do that? Even after—"

"Not right away," replied the general. "But they'll be secure, nonetheless."

The President scowled at the monitor. "Bastards just keep coming. Like the march of time, unstoppable." He looked up at Dunlap. "Get General Conklin on the horn and begin the process."

"Already done, sir."

"Something to be said about initiative." The President poured bourbon from a decanter into the crystal highball in front of him. Sitting back in his chair, he added, "Until I have to make the final decision, I want Conk to keep the pressure on. Keep pounding them. If we can't turn them into hamburger, maybe we can get them to fracture and head out into the open desert." He lifted the glass and sipped at the room temperature Knob Creek. "I really don't want to escalate unless there is no other way."

"Understood. I know you'll make the right call, sir." The general held the President's gaze. Couldn't help but note the dark bags under his eyes. "Hank," he said, "you really should get some sleep. I'll wake you if anything changes."

The President grunted.

Taking this to mean his longtime friend was not receptive to the suggestion, Dunlap saluted and left the room without another word.

Chapter 27

The two-vehicle convoy had made good time after the unanticipated stop outside of Mesquite. Nevertheless, their pursuit of the rapidly setting sun had been a futile endeavor. By the time they exited I-15, their sole aim to find the unnamed road Vern had pointed to on the map back at Trinity House, the orb was partly obscured by the distant mountains and a faint bubble of man-made light was beginning to emerge just over the horizon.

Riker was pointing it out to Lia and Vern when Shorty's voice came out of the two-way radio. "That's a sailor's sky if I've ever seen one."

Red skies at night, sailor's delight. Red skies in morning, sailors take warning, thought Riker. With a burned-out truck plaza slipping by off to the left of US-93 North, he scooped up the Motorola and radioed back. "It sure is a beautiful sunset brewing. But we're not at sea, Shorty." He paused for a few seconds, the channel still open. "I'm more interested in the colorful lights on the lower horizon. Think that's Henderson?"

Vern didn't wait for Shorty to answer. "Henderson is farther off to the left. That's Las Vegas," he put in. "No doubt a lot of their electricity is derived from those." He was pointing to a vast solar panel farm in the desert on their right. There must have been several acres of the shiny black panels, all angled slightly and facing due south, the reflection of the setting sun making them look like a thousand unblinking eyes.

"Last ones out forgot to turn out the lights," Lia quipped. "Either that or life is mimicking art, and Randall Flagg has finally set up shop in Sin City. If so, that would explain the pedophiles putting their stakes down in North Vegas. Birds of a feather and all that."

"I get most of what you're saying," Riker said as he slalomed the Shelby around a pair of mangled cars that had burned completely and now sat fused together on the northbound lane. "But who the hell is this Flagg guy?"

"The Stand, man," Vern shot. "You don't read King?"

Riker shook his head. "Not so much. Sports autobiographies were my jam. Chipper Jones … Ballplayer. Bo knows Bo. *Anything* about Larry Bird." Switching the subject, he said to Vern, "Where's this secret road of yours?"

"Should be coming up on the right." His window was down, and he was scanning the desert for any sign of a break in the fence bordering the two-lane. They were sixty-five miles southwest of Mesquite, where they'd left the bodies of the three would-be robbers on the road for the crows to eat.

Lia tapped the SYNC screen. "It's still not showing on this thing."

"Wouldn't expect a road the government really didn't want found would appear on widely circulated maps," said Vern.

"The map with the caches, bunkers, and Lazarus on it *was* marked *top secret*," Lia said. "Maybe the road is top secret, too."

They were three miles north of the freeway into Las Vegas when Vern spotted something out of place on his side of the road. It was a fifteen-foot-long break in the drainage ditch that had been a constant companion to the road since it branched off I-15. The entire run of ditch was filled in, the top graded smooth. There was also a ten-inch galvanized steel culvert running through the filled-in section of ditch.

"Stop, stop, stop," Vern urged. He was pointing behind them, now.

Riker tapped his brakes, then began to slow. Flicking his gaze to the rearview, he saw Shorty also begin to slow the Roamer and move over to the southbound lane.

Before the Roamer had come to a complete stop, Vern was out of the Shelby, gunned up with the MP5, and heading back toward the anomaly in the ditch.

By the time the others formed up on the road behind Vern, he was taking a knee and inspecting the drainage ditch.

"It's a culvert," said Shorty. "Lots of runoff from the mountains around here. Flash flooding too, I'd imagine. So what's the big deal?"

"It's the only one I saw along the entire stretch of road." He let the MP5 hang on its sling. Hands on his hips, he said, "The fence here is strange, too."

Steve-O was the first to venture across the yard-deep section of tamped-down earth. The reddish-brown soil was brittle on the surface. When he crouched before the fence, he pointed to a mosaic of diamonds and squares imprinted in the dirt. He grabbed a strand of barbed wire and shook it back and forth, causing the nearby post to vibrate. "The fence is loose. I also can see tire tracks. They start here and continue on the other side." He rose and turned to face the group. Hands on hips, a serious look on his face, he said, "Looks like people on motorcycles came through here."

"Recently, too," Vern added as he approached the fence. He ran his hands along the back side of the post. "It's not just a loose run of fence: This is a gate. And there's a padlock back here. It's close to the ground. Almost like it's not supposed to be found."

"I'm sure lots of people ride all kinds of off-road vehicles up here," Tara said. "Maybe this used to be a secret drug smuggling route or something."

Riker was shaking his head. "Vern's Occam's razor theory begs to differ."

"I agree," said Shorty. "Can't think of a reason for either of these features other than to allow access to something out there." He pointed across the desert. All that lay between the tip of his finger and the distant mountain range was scrub and cactus.

Steve-O said, "I'll fetch the bolt cutters," and set off for the Shelby. When he returned, he held the tool out, waiting to see who wanted to do the honors.

"You took the initiative to get the tool," said Riker. "Honor is all yours."

The group remained patient while the man struggled to cut the lock. After some serious contorting and having to ultimately resort to sticking his upper body through the lower two runs of barbed wire, he found the angle he needed. Grunting from exertion, he muscled the rubberized handles together. Only sound to indicate success was the dull thud of the defeated lock striking dirt.

"It's off," Steve-O declared proudly.

"Good job, buddy." Riker traded the Stetson for the bolt cutters.

Vern and Shorty pulled the post out of the ground. It had been inserted into a tight-fitting cement sleeve. They both agreed the craftsmanship was head and shoulders above anything one would expect from a county work crew. Working together, they rolled the length of fence around the post and left it propped next to the opposing post.

Vern stooped to examine the tire tracks. Hinging up, he said, "Knobby items. Looks like there were two riders. They entered here." He shook his head. "But they didn't come back this way."

Lia said, "Any idea how long ago?"

"More importantly," Tara added, "Do you think we're going to run into them?"

Vern said, "Wish I knew when it rained last. If I did, we'd at least have a window of time to speculate from."

"These are pretty degraded," Riker posited. "My gut tells me they're days old."

Tara sized up the Roamer. "Think both rigs will fit through here?"

"Oh yeah," Shorty said nonchalantly. "No problemo."

Steve-O had collected the cut lock. He presented it to Riker. "Want to save this?"

"Not necessary," Riker said. "Tara, still got some of those zip ties in your pocket?"

She nodded. "I'll close and secure the fence behind us."

The Shelby fit through the gap in the fence with a few inches to spare. The Roamer, on the other hand, initially got caught up on the gnarled wooden posts. To prevent important components from being torn off the sides of the camper shell, Shorty flicked a switch on the dash. After a short wait, enough compressed air was added to the Roamer's suspension to let it squeak through without anything important coming into contact with the posts. His *"Oh yeah. No problem"* comment earned him a lot of ribbing as the two vehicles tooled the vast desert in search of the GPS location taken off the map.

Tara was hanging over the seatback, eyes scanning the desert. "You know, Shorty," she joked, "they say beauty is in the eye of the beholder. Maybe it's the same with size." When Shorty made no reply, she added, "To be fair, I thought it would fit."

In his best Andrew Dice Clay, Shorty said, "That's what she said. Ohhh … give the man a rimshot." Shooting Tara some side-eye, he made like he was striking an imaginary drum with an imaginary drumstick.

Tara was about to pretend to be offended when Lia's voice came out of the two-way radio. "My Garmin says we're getting close. Everyone keep an eye out for anything out of place."

From her seat in the taller Roamer, Tara had a commanding view of their surroundings. On her next visual sweep of the desert, focusing mainly on everything in middle distance, what she had initially thought to be a large cactus blending in with the background seemed to morph before her eyes. She knew it was just a trick of distance and lighting. Still, it had been strange seeing what she thought to be a tall, somewhat round form sharpen at the edges and come across as what it actually was: a structure roughly the size of a large garden shed. On the roof, facing south and angled upward a few degrees, was a single solar panel. A platform high up on a pole protruding from the back of the roof bristled with needle antenna, a utilitarian-looking directional weathervane, and what appeared to be a device for measuring wind speed.

Chain-link fence surrounded the structure. To discourage would-be trespassers, the fence was topped with multiple strands of barbed wire, all strung on sturdy brackets jutting out at a forty-five-degree angle.

"Right there, Shorty," Tara said. "There's a building at your nine o'clock."

"Good eye, Tara." He radioed her finding as he steered toward the tiny structure.

"I don't have eyes on," Riker came back. "Too many cactuses."

Steve-O gestured for Shorty to hand over the radio. Thumbing the Talk button, he said, "Cactuses is not a word, Lee Riker. It's cactus … or cacti."

"You're wrong," Riker responded. "I've seen cactuses used in print more than once."

Steve-O said, "Want to bet on it?"

"I don't bet anymore," Riker came back. "See if someone else wants to prove you wrong."

Steve-O shot Shorty a questioning look.

Shorty shook his head. "Nope. I want none of that action."

Steve-O extended a hand toward Tara, "Wanna bet? My MRE pound cake is yours if I'm wrong."

"Lee is right," she said. "And I hate that shit. Tastes like foam torn out of a car seat. Texture's about the same, too." Her eyes narrowed. "I'm curious, Steve-O. What's spurring on this new vice of yours?"

"It's called a gentleman's bet, right, Shorty?"

She glared at Shorty. "So it's your doing? All the wanting to bet on mundane shit?"

Shorty threw his arms up in mock surrender. Taking the wheel back, he said, "Lots of time to kill in the zombie apocalypse."

Tara looked to Steve-O. "What's next, friend? You going to pick up smoking and drinking?"

Steve-O shook his head. "Never, Tara. Both of those will kill you."

"I hate to interrupt your PSA, Steve-O … but we're here. Better Mule up, just in case." Shorty slowed and parked the Roamer beside the building. In the failing light, the rectangular, windowless structure stood out significantly against the darkening jagged silhouette of a distant mountain range.

Shorty had an epiphany. He took the radio back from Steve-O. "Lee," he radioed, "we're here. You want me to back up to the fence and hit the building with the camper's external flood lights?"

"Negative," replied Riker. "Kill your engine and go dark."

Shorty was muttering about once again being *kneecapped* when the Shelby, running dark, slid up on the right and came to a complete stop. Though the larger vehicle had been eating the Shelby's dust since leaving the paved road, the column of dust that descended on the static vehicles when Riker pulled up left both coated with even more of the reddish-orange dirt.

After letting the dust swirl and settle, Riker cut the motor and stepped from the Shelby. First thing he noticed was the all-encompassing silence. Soon the sky would turn from its current shade of burnt orange to deep purple. Before long, the entire desert would be under a shroud of impenetrable darkness.

Elbowing open his door, Shorty said, "You heard the man. Going with headlamps only." He had a suspicion thwarting the lone door on the building under the meager cones of light thrown by their headlamps was going to be a pain in the ass. If they stayed the night here, setting up camp with the same limited light sources was also going to be a challenge. Hell, it was Shorty's experience erecting one of those newfangled dome tents in full light and with instructions was harder than solving a Rubik's Cube in welder's gloves.

The Shelby emptied out and doors sucked shut. Beams from headlamps cut the air as Lia and Vern looped around the truck.

Riker dipped an arm into the bed and came out with the bolt cutters. He approached the fence and immediately noticed tire tracks. They were the same depth and bore the same tread pattern as the ones by the road. The tracks stopped beside the fence where a pair of inch-square impressions in the soil led him to believe the dirt bikes were left here, resting on their kickstands, while the riders were doing whatever they'd come here to do.

A two-foot square metal sign was affixed to the gate head-high to him. NO TRESPASSING — PROPERTY OF THE NATIONAL WEATHER SERVICE was emblazoned on it, the letters red and bold and backed up by a felony penal code and the promise that if the warning was ignored, prosecution by both the federal government and Clark County was the penalty.

Riker wasn't buying it. Why put a weather monitoring station on the desert floor? Especially with the solar farm a few miles distant. No doubt that facility was equipped with top-of-the-line weather monitoring equipment.

Once the group was assembled around Riker, he said, "Volunteers?"

Staring at the sign, Steve-O said, "This is a *cache*?"

Hand resting on her holstered Glock, Tara said, "Looks more like a garden shed to me."

Vern said, "If it isn't the cache, shame on me." He gestured with his MP5 to the desert behind the Shelby. "I need to write my name in the dirt. Afterward, I'll pull security. Holler if I steered us wrong."

Riker nodded and watched the man thread between the vehicles and disappear into the enveloping darkness. Lia and Tara both raised a hand. "Spokes of a wheel?" he said. "Lia, you want to take nine o'clock?"

She nodded and ranged off to the left, borrowed F4 at a low-ready, headlight beam sweeping the ground.

"I'll take three o'clock," Tara said, and she strode off for the open desert beyond the Shelby.

Shorty and Steve-O stayed put.

Riker said, "That leaves us three amigos to crack this nut." He lifted the padlock. It was a heavy brass item. Looked like something a government agency would overpay grossly to buy in bulk. He let go of the lock and gestured at Steve-O with the bolt cutters. "Want to refine your technique?"

Without a word, the man took the heavy tool and moved to the front. He had the lock snipped in half the time as it had taken him to defeat the one on the gate by the road. Beaming, he handed the tool back to Riker.

"Smooth like butter." Riker hauled the gate open. Nothing about the way it moved was smooth. It groaned and squealed in protest. Leaving the gate standing half-open, he stepped into the fenced-in area. The desert underfoot here felt firmer than it had outside the fence. Scraping a toe along the ground revealed smooth poured concrete beneath a thin layer of sandy dirt. *Strange. Why pour a cement pad this large for a structure half the size?*

A wind gust coming off the distant range ripped through the ground-hugging bushes behind the building and rattled the chain-link fence. Riker tilted his head back and scrutinized the gear atop the pole. While the vane had changed direction, pivoting on the pole and stopping with the arrow pointing south, the wind speed indicator was not spinning. A second gust came a moment later. The vane shimmied left and right; the indicator remained fixed.

"Wind gauge is a prop," Shorty noted. "All of this is for show." He hung his head. "Chalk this win up for Vern."

"Maybe it's just stuck and needs some oil," Steve-O posited.

Shorty planted his hands on his hips, thinking. "Then why didn't the scientists taking the readings fix it when they were here? You'd think they'd do something about those hinges on the gate, too."

"That troubled me as well," answered Riker. Approaching the door, he said, "Only one way we're going to find out."

Expecting to find a locked door with just enough of a weather seal to keep out windblown dirt and sand, instead he found one very similar to the smaller door to the Lazarus bunker. While the door here wasn't cut from any kind of exotic alloy, it was a thick single plate of steel that completely concealed the hinges and locking mechanism. There was no lock to cut, and no seams to speak of around the jamb.

Riker put his hands on his hips and gave Shorty a look.

"No palm reader. No keypad. No padlock." Shorty shook his head. "I don't like it."

"I do," Riker said. "It leads me to believe we're where we want to be."

Swinging the headlamp beam from the door and parking it on Riker's face, Shorty said, "So what do you want to do? We going crowbar, power saw, or acetylene torch?"

Riker raised a hand to shield his eyes. "Let's start with the crowbar." He sent Steve-O off to get it from the Shelby's bed.

Watching Steve-O go, Shorty said, "Shouldn't we just go with him and bring all of the breaching tools back here? The welder is on wheels, isn't it?"

"It is, but first I want to see where brute force gets us."

Chapter 28

Nevada Desert Northeast of Las Vegas

Steve-O returned from the Shelby carrying the crowbar and trailing the remnants of a noxious fart.

"Damn," said Shorty, waving a hand in front of his face, "we better not fire up the torch around you."

Taking the crowbar, Riker said, "Holy shit, Steve-O. What the hell did you eat that turned you into a human skunk?"

"Doritos and Twinkies."

Riker moved the tool around the door's right-hand side, probing for a seam. "Strange combo. Are you pregnant?"

"Impossible," said Steve-O. "I'm a man."

"Lee's joking. Pregnant women crave weird food," Shorty explained. "Stuff like peanut butter and pickle sandwiches. Or fish on pizza."

Steve-O pressed two fingers against his lips. "Pineapple is bad enough. Fish? Really? People like that?" He groaned. "I think I'm going to throw up again."

Finally achieving a good bite under the metal lip with the crowbar, Riker had Shorty and Steve-O stand back. Wiping his palms on his pants, he went to work, putting all his weight into trying to pry an opening wide enough to get the tool deeper under the door's edge. He grunted and groaned, and his muscles rippled underneath his light fleece top. The more he leaned into it, the more his Salomons slipped on the loose dirt underfoot. Beads of sweat were rolling down his forehead when he finally gave up, the seam barely wider than when he'd started.

A hint of satisfaction in his voice, Shorty said, "Saw time?"

Riker set the crowbar on the ground by the bolt cutters. "Too noisy. Sound travels way too far out here."

Steve-O said, "Torch it is," and again struck off for the Shelby.

Shorty said, "Need a hand getting it to the ground?"

Waving him off, Steve-O said, "I'm a grown-ass man. I got it."

Shorty said to Riker, "How do you think this door opens?"

"Signal from space."

Brow arched, Shorty said, "Like from a satellite?"

Riker nodded. "Kind of like the Cadillac thing. OnStar, I think it's called. The signal is bounced into space from whatever device sends it. Also," he added, "it's likely it can be opened remotely from a central ground-based location."

"What about a fob? You know, like a car alarm?"

"I suppose so. An RF signal transmitted by one could actuate solenoids that pop the locks."

Shorty stepped aside to allow Steve-O to wheel in the trolley with the welder and tanks strapped to it. "Your theory sounds like black ops voodoo," Shorty said to Riker.

"Maybe we're both wrong." Riker fired the torch and twisted knobs until the torch nozzle was putting out a pinpoint of flame. "At the very least, if it's truly a weather station, we'll know when it rained last."

Smartass tone to his voice, Shorty said, "Lot of good that will do us. Rigs don't run on rain."

Starting at a point on the right side of the door, where a knob or pull would usually reside, Riker introduced the flame to metal and walked it up a foot or so. Sparks flew and the metal glowed cherry red. Finished with the first cut, he returned the flame to where he had started, then, feeding the flame more oxygen, walked it slowly downward, along the door's edge, until he had a yard-long fissure cut between door and jamb. Wisps of smoke curled off the rapidly cooling metal.

Extinguishing the flame, Riker said, "My leg's killing me. Who's going to try to kick this in?"

Shorty rose to the occasion. When he hauled off and kicked the door near where Riker had started the cutting, there was zero give. Only thing that moved was Shorty. Windmilling his arms forward as he was repulsed backward was the only thing that kept him from butt planting in the dirt.

"I had a feeling that would be the case." Reigniting the torch, Riker held the concentrated flame near where he imagined a deadbolt to be. Sparks flew as he worked the flame up and down and left to right, creating a fist-sized hole whose edges glowed red and orange for a few seconds. He extinguished the flame and traded the torch for the crowbar.

"Fingers crossed," said Steve-O, both hands twisted into pretzels.

Riker didn't need to expend one-tenth the effort as he had before. A little forward press on the crowbar and the door was free and swinging out at him. He quickly dropped the crowbar and drew his Sig. Stepping aside, he saw the building's shadowy interior revealed in tiny increments. A little voice in his head told him to feel around the jamb for a light switch. Ignoring the voice, just in case someone was inside, he stepped over the threshold. Sig following his gaze, the headlamp beam illuminating the walls and ceiling, he turned a slow 360 and took it all in.

Nobody home. While the wall to Riker's left was home to weather monitoring equipment, none of it seemed operational. The needle on the wind speed indicator was pegged on zero miles per hour. A trio of zeros beside an LED gauge labeled PEAK WIND GUST glowed red in the dark. A conduit snaked down the wall from the ceiling, ran alongside the rectangular metal box, then shot down to the floor, where it disappeared through a hole bored into the cement pad.

The remaining walls were bare metal painted battleship gray. The light switch was indeed next to the door. It had been singed by the torch, the plastic and metal housing partially melted on the side facing the jamb. Also revealed in the light of his beam was a pair of recessed deadbolts. The torch had done a number on them, too, the extreme heat leaving a rainbow-like discoloration near the cut edges. It was definitely something other than metal. *Titanium?*

Regarding Shorty and Steve-O, he said, "This is all for show." He jumped up and down. Just an inch or two, though. He didn't want to hit his head on the low ceiling.

Shorty said, "Sounds hollow underfoot. Trap door?"

"That's a weird noise," Steve-O put in. "There's cement out here. Look." He jumped up and down on the pad outside the door to demonstrate the difference. It was night and day.

Riker backed out of the glorified shed and kneeled by the threshold. Extending a hand toward Steve-O, he said, "Crowbar."

Feeling the cool metal hit his palm, Riker spun the tool around and probed the floor with the chisel edge. He got the edge worked underneath the floor. There was substantial give and the steel plate flexed when he put all of his weight on the crowbar. Spinning the tool back around, he pushed the bent-claw end in the opening, sat on his butt, and planted both Salomons on the opposing door jambs. Gripping the tool two-handed, he leaned back and straightened his legs. There was a groan and the metal plate rent free from the floor.

The trapdoor was five feet deep by three wide and hinged on the end opposite the door to outside. As Riker slowly lifted the trapdoor, his headlamp beam revealed the beginnings of a run of steel stairs that descended into a black hole of darkness. The treads he could see were textured with raised metal nubs.

Riker passed the crowbar to Shorty. Scooping up the Sig, he whispered, "Going in," and started down the stairs. He was four steps down when he detected a hissing sound coming from the ceiling behind him. His first thought was that a snake was about to strike. Before he could swing the headlamp beam toward the sound, he was blinded by a sudden flare of blue-white light. Resisting the urge to fire blindly into the void, he blinked furiously and felt around for a handrail. Just as his vision was returning and his left hand fell on cold steel, he heard Steve-O's voice drift down from above. "I found the light switch for you, Lee."

Riker grimaced. He was mad at himself for not first pointing it out to Shorty and Steve-O and instructing them to leave it be.

Crouching on the sixth stair from the bottom, he was afforded a good view of both the ceiling and the entire room below the fake weather station. He was at one end of a steel intermodal shipping container. It was standard size: eight feet wide by forty deep. Suspended from the low ceiling and now humming softly were two rows of single-bulb fluorescent light fixtures, four in all. The air was cool and dry, likely somewhere in the high fifties. The sweet smell of gun oil mingled with an odor he instantly associated with new tires.

What appeared to be communications gear—most hardwired, some portable, the major components powered off—sat on a deep shelf affixed to one wall. Below the shelf were a half dozen sealed boxes of United States military MREs. One box had been emptied and folded flat and was tucked away behind the others. Another shelf on the same wall was stacked high with eight hard-side Pelican cases. The cases were the size of a small carry-on bag. "Night Observation Device" was stenciled in white on the side of each case. Rifles and sidearms were visible behind steel mesh screens fronting cabinets on the opposite wall. Two pairs of spoked motorcycle rims wrapped with knobby off-road tires leaned against the far wall. A number of plastic five-gallon cans labeled FUEL sat on the floor next to plastic bottles containing all of the lubricants necessary to keep a motorcycle running smoothly.

A wheeled toolbox was pushed into the far corner. Stacked to the roof beside it was row after row of olive-green ammunition canisters. Most of the calibers Riker knew of were represented. A few canisters contained calibers he'd never heard of.

Preceded by the ringing echoes of their boot heels striking the stairs, Shorty and Steve-O formed up next to Riker.

"Eureka," said Shorty upon surveying the spoils. "Vern was right. This is a cache, all right. We definitely *will not* be wanting for anything more on this little trip west." He looked at Riker. "The Roamer's previous owners hoarded Ikea bags like they were going out of style. I'll get some and we can start hauling this stuff topside."

Poking his head around Shorty, Stetson in hand and wearing a look of surprise, Steve-O said, "Did we just strike gold?"

"Just another of Uncle Shorty's favorite utterings is all," Shorty explained, rubbing his hands together. "We struck booty." He looked to Steve-O. "Not as in the 'buttocks' kind of booty. But in the 'pirate's treasure' kind of booty." He edged around Riker, going for the gun cabinets.

"Not so fast, Blackbeard." Riker reached out and planted a palm on the cabinet door.

Stopping in his tracks, Shorty said, "I thought we came here looking for a cache to plunder."

Steve-O said, "Who's going to miss what we take?"

"If this were a Cold-War-era cache, I'd have no qualms about cleaning it out." Riker surveyed the room. "But it's clear to me this is still in use. Whoever was riding those motorcycles will be needing this stuff. Judging by the quality and quantity of this gear, I'd be willing to bet the house a Delta team or another Tier One group is operating nearby. It's pretty evident they came here very recently to replenish."

Shorty planted his hands on his hips. "Doesn't mean we can't *replenish*, too."

"We don't *know* the true origin of Romero," Riker said. "Sure, there's speculation it was that big-pharma biotech group headquartered in the building that burned and partially collapsed in Manhattan." He paused, thinking. "Zen Pharmaceuticals, I believe. But that's not settled. Neither is the thing that happened at Logan Airport. It was supposedly some of the Zen owners or corporate guys involved in that shootout with the Johnnys … or F.B.I. or whatever three-letter agency interdicted them there. With all the money at stake, the Zen guys could very well be working with our enemies. Lots of other countries would love to see us knocked down a few pegs."

"We do a lot of good around the world," Steve-O pointed out. "World War Two is one example."

"Yeah … agreed," Riker said. "But for every country we help after an earthquake, major flood, Ebola outbreak … etcetera, the perception is that we harm many more through military intervention and nation-building. That's the vibe some foreign leaders were putting out before all this went down."

"Can we at least take some MREs?" asked Steve-O.

"So you can mine them for pound cake?" Shorty said.

Steve-O smiled. "Busted by Blackbeard."

"We're going to *borrow* some things," Riker said to Shorty. "Bring back a couple of bags. And while you're at it, tell Tara and the others we're staying the night here."

Shorty took a step toward the stairs, then turned around. "Borrow would imply we are coming back this way to replace said items. Which tells me you're leaning toward us *not* going out of our way to check out the Sierra facility."

"No matter what the consensus is, eventually we have to come back this way. I'm leaving the trailer here." He paused to let that sink in. Regarding Shorty, he added, "And I think we should leave the Roamer here, too. We can make better time if we do."

Immediately, Shorty's head began to swing side-to-side. "No way," he said. "I'm not letting Marge out of my sight."

Steve-O said, "Fitting six people in Dolly will *not* be easy."

"That's what she said," Shorty quipped. "In all seriousness, we need the communications gear in the Roamer."

Riker pointed to the shelves full of gear. "There's a MIL-SPEC portable HAM handset right there. Probably newer than the one in your rig."

Shorty crossed his arms. "There's another reason we should take Marge."

Riker looked a question at the shorter man.

"What are you thinking?" asked Steve-O. "Use it for surveillance? It's got a lot of windows."

"There is that added benefit," acknowledged Shorty.

Riker said, "Maybe Shorty's just afraid of getting trapped in the Shelby with one of your farts."

Shorty chuckled, then proceeded to lay out the entirety of his plan.

Finished listening, Riker nodded. Shorty's reason was legit. "We take two rigs," he said. "We need to leave at zero dark thirty, though."

"Driving through North Vegas with our lights on will be suicide," Shorty said. "It'll draw the biters to our rigs like moths to a flame."

Gesturing toward the Pelican cases on the shelf, Riker said, "We borrow some night vision goggles. Driving in the dark with our lights off will give us a huge advantage over the dead."

"What about the engine noise?" Shorty cocked his head and stared at Riker. "Said it yourself that sound travels really far out here."

Nodding agreeably, Steve-O said, "They will hear us coming for miles around." He started to wring his hands on the Stetson's shaped brim.

"Out here it does," Riker acknowledged. "Not so much in the city. It bounces off the buildings and will stir up the biters.

Get them moaning, and it'll be hard for anyone listening to pinpoint our exact location."

"Lee's right," said Shorty. "Desert is like open water … sound has nothing stopping it from traveling far and wide." With no warning, he slapped Steve-O's hands. "Knock that off. You're ruining a perfectly shaped hat."

Steve-O donned the hat, but not without muttering a profanity or two.

Riker ignored the exchange. The two bickered like siblings at times. He said, "We'll be splitting up once we get close. I figure we'll be far enough out that we won't be made when we set up overwatch. Especially not by a couple of passed-out drunks."

Shorty said nothing. He was back to eyeing the guns.

"Sound like a plan?" Riker asked. "Yours and mine combined?"

"Sure," Shorty said. "On one condition."

"Shoot," Riker said. "What is it?"

"I want to *borrow* one of those suppressed weapons."

"Saying no would be hypocritical," Riker conceded. "Just make sure there's more than one of whatever you decide on."

"I'll think on it," Shorty said, a sly smile emerging. "In the meantime, I'll get the others up to speed."

Steve-O said, "Bring back the Ikea bags."

"Got it," Shorty said as he started up the stairs. Pausing on the second step, he turned and asked, "You really know how to use those goggles? More importantly, can you show me the ins and outs? Wouldn't want to accidentally run Marge into a herd of bitey meat sacks or crash into a pileup."

"You already got her stuck on a pile of them once today," Steve-O pointed out. "What're the odds it would happen twice?"

Riker said nothing. He was already done fretting over the dumb move that could very well have led to one of them getting bit or dying.

Playfully flipping Steve-O the bird, Shorty resumed climbing the stairs.

After loading the borrowed items into the bags and lugging them topside, Riker and Shorty fueled the vehicles.

Removing the trailer from the Shelby, they stowed it behind the building. They parked the two vehicles in a wedge angling out from the door to the building. The way they were positioned left the inside corner of each rig's rear bumper touching a corner of the chain-link enclosure. With the front fenders close to touching, there was just enough room remaining on the ground between the vehicles to erect camp chairs and spread out a couple of sleeping bags. It was akin to circling the wagons.

After seeing how crowded it had become once the chairs were set up, Shorty decided against erecting his tent.

Their dinner was MRE washed down with the beers they had taken from the RV back at Jacob Lake. Riker and Steve-O both declined the beers offered to them by Shorty, opting instead to go with Diet Cokes.

The group conversed under the stars for an hour or so, listening to the distant intermittent howls of coyotes on the hunt. Now and again Riker would climb atop the Roamer and sweep the desert wearing a pair of the NVGs, each time seeing only cacti and scrub glowing green against the desert floor. The coyotes didn't make an appearance. Likely they wanted nothing to do with humans—living or dead. Steve-O was asleep first, curled up in his bag by the Shelby's rear tire and snoring softly, the chain-link pressing in on him from one side.

Vern retired to the Shelby, sleeping in his bag stretched out across the backseat.

Shorty offered the Roamer to Tara and Lia. The overture was quickly accepted.

That left Riker and Shorty to pull watch while the others slept.

Riker plucked a Pelican case off the ground. "I left a note down there explaining why we took what we did."

"No IOUs, Lloyd Christmas?"

Riker shot him a questioning look. "Who?"

"The gap-tooth guy with the bowl cut Jim Carrey played in Dumb and Dumber. He wrote IOUs for everything he bought with money he and his dumbass buddy stole from some very bad guys." He chuckled softly. "Even had one written out to cover a red Lamborghini they picked up to impress some girls."

"When did it come out?"

After a short pause, Shorty said, "About twenty years ago."

Crossing his arms, Riker said, "If I watched it, I was probably drunk."

"You a quitter? That why you didn't partake in the beers tonight?"

"Sore subject." Riker popped open the Pelican case and powered on the NVGs. "These are much newer than the ones I trained with."

"Did you wear them when you were driving over there?"

"Sometimes," Riker said. He pointed out the features and handed the goggles to Shorty.

Shorty adjusted the band and slipped the device over his head. When he pressed his eyes to the cups, he nearly fell out of his chair. "Holy mother of …"

"Surroundings rush up on you?"

Shorty nodded. "Sure did." He panned his head all around and then shook it back and forth. The goggles remained firm to his face the entire time, the stubby dual lenses staying in perfect sync with the motion of his head. "Wow! I never thought these things would offer this kind of depth perception."

"You can adjust them for clarity and brightness. Range is about five hundred feet or so. Think you can drive with a pair on?"

"I'll know if I can well before we get to the main road."

"Good to go then." Riker handed him the case. "Go ahead and get acquainted with them. Spare batteries are tucked inside the foam."

"Will we need the spares?"

"Supposed to get thirty to forty hours use out of this generation of NVGs. To be safe, we should change out the batteries before we get on the road."

"Who's gonna be wearing the other two pairs?"

"Whoever rides shotgun for us. I figure we can get them up to speed along the way."

"Let's just hope they haven't moved the kids."

Riker nodded. "Lia will be crushed."

Shorty didn't know what to say to that. So he addressed the obvious. "One of us turns in now, we'll both get a solid three hours apiece."

They slept in shifts, with Riker getting his three hours out of the way first.

Chapter 29

Riker was awakened by the hollow thuds of boots treading the ground near his head. He was on his back in his bag and shivering so hard his teeth were chattering. When the light put out by a headlamp passed close by, he saw his breath rising toward the star-filled sky.

"Sorry for waking you," said Shorty. "I gotta pee. Couldn't go the other way. Thought I heard something moving out there. Probably just a coyote or rabbit or something. Doubt any biters followed us way out here."

Shielding his eyes, Riker said, "You'd be surprised. We're not far from Vegas. I bet a lot of folks headed for the hills to avoid the dead."

Shorty turned away from Riker, unzipped his fly, and farted loudly. "And then they themselves became the dead," he said over the patter of a hard, steady stream of urine striking dirt.

"You got it," Riker said. "Did you scan the desert through the NVGs."

Aiming the translucent yellow flow through the chain-link, he said, "Honestly, I did not. I was afraid it might be the guys whose stuff we pilfered."

"Borrowed," Riker reminded. "If it were them coming back, we'd both already be staring down the barrels of suppressed weapons."

Steam rose from the dark stain in the dirt, curling and twining in the headlamp beam. "Go back to sleep," Shorty urged as he zipped his pants. "You've still got thirty minutes."

"You go ahead," Riker said. "I'm up now." He slid from the bag fully clothed, prosthetic on, Salomons laced tight. After saying some words for his fallen friends, he rolled over and knocked out his customary twenty-five pushups.

Shorty said, "You don't have to tell me twice. But first, let's do a quick recon of the surrounding desert. Maybe we find out what's breaking brush out there."

Riker donned the NVGs and strapped on the Sig. Everything around him was instantly rendered in varying shades of green.

Shorty was struggling to power on his NVGs by feel, so Riker helped him out. While Riker was not fully aware of all the limitations that came with wearing the newer gen devices, it was good to know he could accomplish a task that required fine motor skills. Finished, he passed Shorty the Heckler & Koch MP7A1 the man had taken from the cache's mini armory. Designated as a personal defense weapon, even when fitted with a suppressor and EOTech holographic sight, it was substantially more compact than its predecessor, the MP5.

"What about you?" Shorty asked as he dumped the mag and racked the bolt back.

Dragging the Sig from its holster, Riker spun a suppressor on the pre-threaded barrel.

"Where'd you get the can?"

Smiling, Riker said, "Borrowed it."

Viewed through the NVGs, Riker's toothy smile was a bit unnerving to Shorty. Aiming the little personal defense weapon at the ground, he slapped the full mag home and chambered a round.

Riker said, "Good to go?"

Shorty nodded. "Looking at the world through these things is a bit disconcerting, but I'll manage."

"Whatever you do," Riker implored, "do not flag me with that thing."

"It's not my first rodeo," Shorty said. "I checked. It's on safe."

Riker said nothing and made his way to the front of the Shelby. Seeing that the gap separating the two vehicles was much too narrow to allow Shorty to squeeze through, let alone a guy the size of the average NFL tight end, Riker reached out and planted a hand on each of the rigs' hoods. Issuing a pained grunt, he leaped off the ground and quickly tucked both knees to his chest. As his feet went level with his hands, he pushed off hard with both arms. The combined actions propelled him cleanly to the other side, where he landed rather clumsily, flailing away to keep from ending up sprawled on the cold desert floor.

Shorty reached up and palmed the hoods where Riker had placed his hands. The angle was drastically different. Shaking his head, he said, "Ain't gonna happen. At least not without a trampoline or jetpack."

"Come on," Riker chided, peering between the rigs. "It's no different than jumping a turnstile."

Shorty said, "Since there's no subway anywhere near the Florida Panhandle, I'm a bit out of practice." To join Riker, he resorted to commando crawling underneath the Roamer's front bumper.

Riker helped Shorty to his feet, then turned and struck off across the desert. He had only taken a few long strides when he caught sight of the pair of zombies responsible for the night sounds Shorty had described. They were about twenty yards out and jostling with each other in the dark. Somehow, they had become trapped together within a tight cluster of mature cacti.

Shorty was still dusting himself off and fighting with the MP7's twisted sling when Riker whistled to get his attention. Once the two locked gazes, Riker waved the smaller man forward. When Shorty was within earshot, Riker pointed out the zombies and instructed him to fall in behind him and stay close.

It didn't take Riker long to get used to moving while wearing the NVGs. Behind him, Shorty was stumbling around and muttering obscenities under his breath.

Edging around the larger of the three cacti hemming in the zombies, Riker drew close enough to see they were both African American and bristling with cactus needles. Judging by the male's sagging paunch, Riker put him in his mid-forties. The woman was in her early to mid-twenties and had been smoking hot before Romero claimed her. *Was she his daughter? Trophy wife?* Whichever, she was wearing only G-string panties and the remnants of a tank top bearing the word SEDONA. The tank and one exposed breast bore dark stains from the multiple bite wounds peppering her neck and left arm.

The male had died wearing cargo shorts and a light-colored polo-style shirt. Blood was spattered all across the front of both. The hand the male was batting at the cactus with was missing three fingers. From wrist to elbow on the same arm, bone glistened where dermis and flesh had been stripped away.

Viewed through the NVGs, the zombies' unblinking eyes glowed eerily from within deep-set sockets several shades darker than the surrounding features.

"That's some nightmare fuel, right there," whispered Shorty.

"They got nothing on my nightmares," Riker whispered back.

In response to the approaching footfalls and whispered words, both zombies pressed hard against the cactus nearest to Riker. He could see their eyes flitting back and forth as they tried hard to get a lock on what they were hearing.

Riker clucked his tongue to get them looking in his direction. Gesturing for Shorty to halt, he leveled the Sig at the male zombie, edged a few steps closer, then pressed the suppressor hard against its high forehead. Pressing the trigger produced a report much quieter than Riker had been expecting. The fact the projectile and escaping gasses entered the zombie's skull through the same nickel-sized hole may have contributed to the phenomenon. Whatever the case, the metallic sound made by the weapon's slide seemed louder to Riker than the report.

The zombie dropped to its knees, chest against the cactus, unmoving.

Holstering the still-smoking pistol, Riker took a step back to escape the reach of the female zombie's claw-like hands. Directing his gaze at Shorty, the toothy smile returning, he said, "Your turn, *Blackbeard*."

"Whatever you say, *Lloyd*," Shorty said as he ranged around to the zombie's blind side. Leaving the MP7's shoulder stock collapsed, he extended the weapon until the suppressor was within an inch of the zombie's temple, then threw off the safety. Anticipating the weapon's recoil, he firmed up his grip and pressed the trigger.

The *pop* was no louder than that produced by those New Year's Eve party favors that belched confetti at the pull of a string. The damage was subtle as well. There was only a puff of aerated flesh as the speeding seventy-seven-grain hunk of lead entered the zombie's skull. Other than the thing's glowing eyes bugging out, that was it. No blood from the ears or nose. No eruption of splintered bone and brains from an opposing exit point. It was a clean single tap that dropped the zombie where it stood, leaving the mess of scrambled gray matter contained safely within its skull.

"Like a mouse farting," Shorty said, patting the weapon.

The subsonic ammunition taken from the cache, when fired through the suppressor, made Shorty's MP7 the quietest weapon Riker had ever known. "You win," he said. "Damn, that's quiet. Wonder if the others heard anything. Mine, maybe. Yours, doubtful."

"Nothing coming from the radio," Shorty said. "You know … there's three more of these in the bunker. Plenty of magazines. Lots of ammo, too. I can hook one up for you before I turn in."

"No need," Riker said. "I can help myself to one. And I think I will do just that."

They left the zombies where they had fallen. Moving them was out of the question. It would only lead to getting stuck by the cactus needles protruding from nearly every square inch of the creatures' exposed skin.

The camp was quiet when Riker and Shorty returned. Riker powered down his NVGs and flipped them away from his eyes. The contrast was striking. He fumbled around in the dark and finally came up with a camp chair to sit on. Normal night vision returning, he surveyed the two vehicles. *All quiet.* If anyone had heard the suppressed gunshots, there was no evidence of it.

On the ground by his feet, Steve-O was still as a corpse in his sleeping bag and snoring softly. Both vehicles were dark as tombs inside. When Shorty opened the Roamer's driver-side door to stow the MP7, the dome light flared. Not only did it illuminate a good deal of desert and flood the entire cab with its pale-yellow glow, it also lit a bulb in Riker's head.

"Shorty," he whispered. "That overhead light is going to be a problem in the city. Before we head out, we better pull interior bulbs and tape over our brake lights, side markers, and running lights."

Shorty was still wearing his NVGs. "Didn't notice," he replied, peeling them off. "These things must have a built-in feature to keep sudden exposure to light from blinding the user."

"They do," Riker said. "These newer models are so responsive, you lose very little in reaction time."

"I'll take your word for it," Shorty said, cracking the seal on a bottled water. He took a long swig. "You have duct tape?"

Riker nodded.

Shorty said, "Fuck sleep. I'll get plenty when I'm dead and gone. Get the tape and let's get it done before we wake the others."

***

It was 2 a.m. when Riker and Shorty roused their companions. They broke camp in the dark and set off for the paved road, all lights extinguished and NVGs deployed. Forty-five minutes later, as Shorty was turning the Roamer onto the ramp to I-15 West, he had gotten so used to driving with the NVGs that he was no longer flinching each time he passed by a road sign or static vehicle. Still, he was a bit apprehensive when it came to the walking dead. The second a zombie was aware of the approaching convoy, it would actively start to search in the dark for the source of the sound. Searching was not limited to roving eyes and panning heads. Whether alone or members of a group, zombies were prone to lurching this way and that, arms outstretched, every movement completely reactionary in nature, as they vectored in on the sounds they instinctively related to a meal of fresh meat.

Two times prior to making it to the leveled truck plaza near the ramp to I-15 West, a zombie had initiated a collision with the Roamer. The first had been a young female Bolt. One second, Shorty had been following the Shelby at a safe distance; the next, the runner was entering from the left, both arms swiping at the spot in the road the Shelby had just vacated. Though the unavoidable collision had been sudden and very violent, the heavy grille guard and high clearance had spared the Roamer from any real damage.

The other encounter occurred seconds later, the Roamer's wing mirror nearly decapitating the Slog. Prior to the sudden lurch into the southbound lane, the undead woman wearing a nightgown and curlers had been ambling slowly along the right-side shoulder. The minor damage had been to Shorty's ego. He'd thought his quick reflexes would make up for any deficiencies in peripheral vision that came with driving while wearing the goggles. The real damage had been to his right shoulder, where Tara had dug her nails in so deeply that she had drawn blood.

In the seat next to Shorty, NVGs in front of her face, Tara shook her head. "I don't like these," she said. "It's like I'm looking at the world through Kermit the Frog's puckered butthole. No peripheral vision. It's clear yours is hampered, otherwise you would have avoided Grandma Zombie back there. Hell, a tree sloth moves faster than those old Slogs."

Shorty had been taking it all in. In the backseat, Steve-O was on his back, snoring and gasping intermittently. During a quiet moment between snuffling noises that reminded Shorty of a bulldog he once owned, he said, "Tara … I think, based on your experience, you can answer for me an age-old question."

Arms crossed, Tara glared at Shorty through the NVGs. "What question might that be?" she snapped.

Shorty didn't answer right away. He was busy steering the bigger rig through a corridor of broken-down vehicles the Shelby barely made it through. After a couple of keens of metal on metal and clipping off a mirror or two with the camper shell, they emerged onto a stretch of highway bracketed on both sides by hundreds of homes. Viewed through the NVGs, nothing struck Shorty as out of the ordinary. If he had been seeing it all with the naked eye, he would have had an entirely different impression. Nothing moved. There wasn't a single light burning. At least nothing was picked up by the NVGs. Soon they were out of the residential area and the signs beside I-15 were announcing upcoming exits and which business concerns lay beyond certain ramps.

"You going to leave me hanging?" Tara needled. "Or is this age-old question going to remain unanswered for another … *age* … or whatever?"

Shorty chuckled. "Since you've apparently spent some time in Kermit's butt." He paused, and she shot him a death glare sans the NVGs.

"Go on," she ordered.

"Is a frog's ass really watertight?" Shorty choked out. Then he laughed so loud that he woke up Steve-O, who immediately sat bolt upright and hooked his arms over the seatback.

"What happened?" asked Steve-O. "Was I farting in my sleep?"

"No," said Tara. "Our driver thinks he's Sam Kinnison. About as loud as the mofo, too." She grinned at Shorty, anger melting away, and started to laugh with him.

"I knew there was a reason I liked you," Shorty said. "You can take a joke. Plus, you're the first woman who's raked my back with her nails in decades."

Tara was formulating an appropriate response—one that would discourage the man from further advances, yet still not crush his fragile ego—when Lia's voice issued from the two-way radio.

Chapter 30

Riker was steering the Shelby around a small herd of zombies partially obstructing his lane when Lia let out a whoop that caused him to visibly start. Eyes never leaving the gently curving stretch of vehicle- and zombie-choked highway rendered in a dozen shades of green, Riker said, "What the hell, Lia? You almost made me crap my pants."

"We just received some good news," she said as she put down the satellite phone and grabbed up the Motorola. "Listen in while I tell the others."

Through clenched teeth, Riker said, "Just tell me, already."

"Work smarter, not harder," Lia replied, a coquettish smile curling her lip. "Isn't that what you're fond of saying?"

Touché, thought Riker. As he waited to learn the nature of the lengthy SMS message Lia had been reading on the phone's illuminated screen prior to her sudden exclamation, he met Vern's gaze in the rearview. The man was also wearing NVGs. While Vern had no experience with any type of night observation devices, he seemed to have adapted to using them faster than the others. Prior to moving out from the cache site, he'd taken target practice on a cactus with the MP5, seeing three out of four rounds find their mark from fifteen yards out. Closer in, he was nearly as accurate with the little sub gun as he was when not wearing the prohibitive devices.

Lia raised the two-way to her mouth and radioed Tara in the Roamer. "I just heard from Rose," she said. "Wade and Sarah landed at Trinity a few minutes ago."

"Better late than never," interjected Vern as Tara came on over the radio.

"What'd they have to say?" Tara asked. "Any word on how the rest of the country is doing?"

"Only information I got out of the text," Lia radioed back, "is they had to land in the turnaround outside the gate. Rose says the helicopter they came in is bigger than the last one."

"Any other details?" Riker probed. "Are they keeping the biters at the gate thinned out?"

"They must have been," Vern offered. "If they weren't keeping up, landing a helicopter outside the gate would be a dangerous proposition. One zombie walking into the tail rotor could likely ground the bird for good."

Regarding Riker, Lia thumbed the Talk button. "Nothing more than what I just told you." Finally, with the glow of Vegas on the horizon growing larger by the second and the tops of the largest buildings taking on some definition, Lia asked Tara if she was getting used to the NVGs.

Tara answered the question exactly as she had when Shorty posed it. Verbatim. Down to the inflection of her voice and timing of the delivery. When she was finished, Shorty's voice replaced hers, and he inserted his age-old-question comeback.

"Thanks for the visual," radioed Lia. "Now I'm glad I'm not wearing a pair of those things."

When Shorty delivered his punchline, Riker and Vern began to laugh hysterically.

Riker was still wiping tears from his eyes a minute later when it came to him that he should start thinking about finding a place to pull over. Given that Lia had only recently found the strip mall using the nav unit, and that they didn't yet know if it would be in a blacked-out part of Vegas, he wanted to rehash the bare-bones plan they'd all agreed on before breaking camp. If any adjustments needed to be made, hammering them out before the two vehicles parted ways would be more efficient in person than trying to do so on the fly and over the radio. Plus, with their target just a few miles west of their current location, for their plan to work the way they'd gamed it out, Lia and Tara were going to have to switch places. There was also the matter of calibrating watches.

"We're still five miles out," said Riker. "Once the SYNC has us closing in on the ramp we need to take to get to the target, I'm going to pick a spot on the road free of rotters and pull over."

Lia radioed the information to the others.

Tara came back right away, saying, "Make sure it's a real dark stretch of road."

Riker knew what she was thinking. Though the glare they had seen miles out was the byproduct of a scant few casinos and hotels lit up like Christmas trees on the strip, there were a few small pockets of the sprawling city where streetlights and signals appeared to be operating normally. Whether the infrastructure was run on solar power or was on a grid somehow still receiving electricity from whatever supplied Vegas with its power, nobody had an answer. Tara's thinking was sound no matter the case: Night was their friend. And they had to use any advantage at their disposal if they were going to slip in undetected. Riker hoped and prayed the part of North Vegas the navigation computer was taking them to was in one of the many huge swaths of Vegas that remained cloaked in impenetrable darkness.

Off to the left of I-15, maybe a half-mile distant, was a large tract of flat land. Several low buildings rose up near an oval racetrack. Closer to the freeway was a smaller racetrack featuring long looping turns, tight chicanes, and several straightaways.

An enormous billboard rose up beside the road on the right. It was advertising the Las Vegas Supercar Experience. Their hook was: Treat Yourself to the Ride of a Lifetime. A trio of exotic cars, arranged to show off their sleek lines, dominated the billboard. Standing beside what appeared to be a Ferrari or Lamborghini was a man wearing a huge smile and holding aloft a full-face racing helmet.

In the middle distance, beyond the racetrack, was Nellis Air Force Base. In places, zombies three and four deep were crowding the run of fence facing the racetrack. Corpses littered the ground outside the fence. They were left where they had been put down. In places, accumulations of twice-dead zombies corpses rose head-high to the ambulatory specimens.

At the moment, it appeared air operations had ceased at the humongous multi-strip facility. The smattering of vehicles he could see—fuel bowsers, ambulances, and fire suppression vehicles—sat inert near the sprawl of hangars. If there were guards present on the perimeter, or snipers strategically positioned to thin out the accumulating zombies, Riker detected neither.

Lia said, "Want to hit the *supercar experience* on the way back?"

"I've always wanted to drive one," Riker admitted. "And just when I come into supercar money, the zombie apocalypse yanks the rug out from under my Lambo dreams."

Vern said, "If you even entertain that idea around Shorty, at least without first fulfilling his wish to check out the Sierra facility, we'll *never* hear the end of it."

"I was half joking," Lia said. "No reason you can't get a Lambo, Lee. There's got to be one sitting in a garage close to Santa Fe. There may even be a dealer in town."

Changing the subject to one not apt to bring on a new headache, Riker said, "Nellis is lit up pretty good. I find it strange that the only things moving out there are biters."

"I expected it to be dark," Vern replied. "Not seemingly deserted. Me and the boy went to a show there way back when. Place was a beehive of activity all day. We got to see an SR-71 perform a high-speed low-pass. Damn impressive aircraft. Louder than anything I'd heard before or since."

Riker said, "They tested that one at Area 51, right? It's somewhere in the desert north of Vegas, I believe."

Vern nodded. "Groom Lake and Area 51 are basically one and the same. They're about seventy … eighty miles north/northwest. Groom is supposed to have one hell of a long runway."

"Take Exit 52," Lia commanded. "It's coming up soon on the right. It'll feed the Vegas Beltway. Also known as County Road 215 West, looks like. Then the best place I can see on here for us to pull over and do what we need to do is one of these." She tapped the SYNC screen. "They're both overpasses that feed into North Vegas. Looks like a mile or so between them. The second one is the exit we're *supposed* to take to get to where we're going."

"First overpass makes the most sense," Vern put in. "You won't need to backtrack to access the exit we want."

The ramp feeding the Vegas Beltway was partially blocked by a static eighteen-wheeler. Open rear doors revealed an empty trailer.

Both vehicles passed the stall without trading paint with the tractor or trailer.

Three minutes after entering the beltway, Riker was parking the Shelby on the outside shoulder underneath the first of the pair of overpasses Lia had pointed to on the navigation pane.

He reviewed the SYNC screen. The graphic displayed there showed wide-open range north of their current position. To the south, the entire screen was dominated by the North Las Vegas VA Medical Center. Running away to the west and south from the sprawl of multi-story buildings surrounded by acres of parking was a residential neighborhood that looked like it had been expanded over time by the completion of one subdivision after another. The straight yellow line extending south from the crudely rendered overpass dead center on the screen was labeled North Pecos Road. Its terminus wasn't evident on the small slice of Vegas currently displayed on the screen.

What Riker did see was that the entire neighborhood beyond the cement noise-abatement panels bordering the beltway to the south and west looked no different than the desert to the north. Both areas were the same dark green when viewed through the NVGs. Very little variation. From left to right, as far as he could see, not a single pinprick of light was picked up by his goggles. To be sure his eyes weren't playing tricks on him, he flipped up the NVGs and scanned the southern horizon without them. Only thing visible to the naked eye was the soft neon glow floating over the downtown area several miles distant. The rest of North Vegas and West Vegas was completely blacked out. No streetlights. No traffic signals unnecessarily cycling from green to yellow to red. No signs of life whatsoever. Nothing to differentiate the built-up areas from the vast desert bordering the beltway to their right.

"Radio the others," Riker said to Lia. "I'm calling an audible."

"No need," she said. "They're pulling up now. You can tell them yourself."

The Roamer parked next to the Shelby and quickly emptied out.

Satisfied he didn't see the interior lights flare on when the doors hinged open, Riker grabbed the map of Vegas, a headlamp, and elbowed open his door.

Map of Vegas spread out on the Shelby's warm hood, headlamp in place of the NVGs, Riker shared his thoughts with the people assembled around him underneath the overpass. He pointed out the block the strip mall sat on, then dragged his finger to two points on the map where he suggested they would eventually park the vehicles. The Roamer would be a little more than a block east of the target, the Shelby several blocks to the west. If the satellite images provided by the navigation computer were to be believed, an undeveloped lot stood between the Roamer's final destination and the target building. It encompassed a couple of city blocks and was abutted to the east by what looked like a medium-sized apartment complex. From there, Riker reasoned, the view of the parking lot fronting the strip mall would be unimpeded.

With their intended approach out of the way, Riker assigned duties and jumping-off points. Finally, when there were no objections to everyone getting into position before first light and striking the target under cover of darkness, he opened the floor for debate.

Vern spoke up first. "What about collateral damage?"

Riker gestured to Lia.

"If we wait until first light," she replied, "the possibility would be minimal. If we wait to hear from Cole, we'd have a clearer idea of what we'll be up against."

It was clear to Riker that Lia couldn't let go of the idea of waiting for the call to come over the Roamer's HAM radio. It wasn't a given. Which was why they were going in before first light. "It's up to those of us with night vision to relay exactly what we're seeing as we approach. We'll all have a radio," he said. "Just be sure to maintain noise discipline. And be sure to reopen the channel as soon as you finish saying your piece. I'm not pointing fingers. Lord knows I'm guilty of keeping my fat thumb pressed down on the Talk button."

"I'm worried about them hearing us coming in," Shorty admitted. "The Roamer isn't the quietest rig on the planet."

"The walls fronting the complex should help with that," Riker said. "If Tara's idea works, it won't matter if they hear us while we're parking the Roamer."

"It's a feint," Tara put in. "I saw it on an A-Team episode. Might have been Magnum P.I. now that I think about it."

"The transfer is key," Vern said. "Gotta accomplish it as planned so the pause isn't detectable." He looked the others over. "So that we're all less detectable, I'd suggest we wear our darkest clothes. Nothing that'll make noise, though. No windbreakers."

"Agreed," Riker said. Now he was the one looking the others over. "Any questions?"

When nobody spoke up, Steve-O adjusted his Stetson and launched into a pretty fine rendition of Folsom Prison Blues. *The train's a comin' all right*, thought Riker as he folded the map and tucked it away. *Let's just hope nobody is awake at the station.* By the second verse, Steve-O was really getting into it. It was as if he were channeling Johnny Cash. So much so that a chill traced Riker's spine. His friend was singing the lyric in which Cash is confessing he shot a man in Reno just to watch him die when the thought struck Riker that one of them getting shot in Vegas was a distinct possibility. He just hoped the Reaper would be collecting souls from the pedophiles, *not* the white hats.

Raven Rock Mountain Complex

By the time the call needed to be made, President Tillman hadn't slept in close to forty-eight hours. He was operating on coffee, bourbon, and some kind of stimulant given to him by his personal physician.

General Dunlap had just entered the situation room and caught him fingering a photo of his late wife. Clearing his throat, Dunlap said, "They're approaching the point of no return, sir."

The President gave his chairman a rheumy-eyed stare. After a short pause, he said, "We have no other alternative. Begin the process."

"Alpha or Omega Protocol, sir?"

The President took a long time to answer. When he did, it was one word: "Omega."

This time eschewing the salute, Dunlap snatched up the handset to the red phone and rattled off an authentication code known to only him and three other humans on earth, one of the three sitting near his elbow.

Replacing the handset, Dunlap said, "Done, sir. Paladin is airborne and en route."

Pouring himself another three fingers of bourbon, the President said, "God help all of those in harm's way."

Chapter 31

Steve-O had moved on to singing an old Montgomery and Gentry song softly under his breath and was just getting to the final verse when the group broke huddle and returned to their vehicles.

Riker wasted no time getting the Shelby moving west on the beltway. Tara was now riding shotgun opposite him. Vern was where he'd been for most of their trip west: in the backseat, both elbows planted on the seatbacks, and taking it all in. All three of them were wearing NVGs.

Keeping the speedometer needle below the twenty miles per hour hash, Riker drove another mile or so west. He took the Losee Road exit, swung a left at the T, then proceeded south, keeping the Shelby moving along at half the posted limit.

For the first half a mile or so, the four-lane cut through a parcel of flat, undeveloped land. Realtor signs suggested it had been slated for development prior to Romero forever changing those plans.

When the first of many subdivisions slid by on the left, Riker was relieved to see that it was indeed fronted by a formidable cement wall. The satellite imagery had been accurate. He hoped the trend continued.

Wide strips of dead grass occupied the area between the wall and run of sidewalk stretching endlessly to the south. A palm tree rose up from the grass strip every dozen feet or so. The drooping fronds seemed to be embracing the top of the wall in places.

Where business concerns bumped up to Losee, the walls were either nonexistent or were just waist-high versions of those surrounding the subdivisions.

A wide cement divider running down the center of Losee went on for as far as Riker could see, breaking briefly only when intersected by crossing streets.

While zombie sightings had initially been few and far between, the further they dipped into North Vegas, the more prevalent they became. Riker guessed the dead things were leaking from the subdivisions. One of the first things he'd noticed after the dead began to walk was not only were they prone to going through motions once routine to them, but they also seemed to gravitate toward places once familiar to them.

Coming to E. Rome Boulevard, an east/west arterial a block north of the strip mall, the vehicles both slow-rolled left, onto Rome, and continued eastbound.

Though the dozen or so zombies trundling north on Losee couldn't see the vehicles closing with them in the dark, they were greatly confused by the engines' noise. Steering left, Riker saw heads start to swivel and tilt. Some in the group halted in place. He could see eyes probing the dark wildly as the creatures caromed off one another. If the Slogs weren't so deadly, the scene might have been humorous to Riker.

Straightening out on Rome, Riker checked his wing mirror. Seeing the Roamer complete the turn and close ranks, he slowed and swung wide left. Tires nearly brushing the curb in front of a gas station with NO GAS signs and strung chains blocking every entrance, he watched the Roamer pass on the right. Once it was ahead by a truck length, Riker accelerated quickly and tucked in close behind the larger vehicle.

A block east of Losee, the Roamer cut right off of Rome and eased onto the tenant lot fronting the apartment complex they had spotted on the SYNC screen. Shorty continued onward another fifty yards before bringing the Roamer to a complete stop beside the cement wall across the lot from the building's west-facing elevation. The only thing standing between the Roamer and the wall was a pair of mature palms and a narrow cement walk. The palms' fronds hung nearly to the Roamer's roof, coming together in the center like a pair of crossed scimitars.

Though Riker intuitively knew the Roamer's brake lights had flared beneath the two layers of silver duct tape he and Shorty had applied before leaving the cache site, any light that had escaped the tape job wasn't enough to be picked up and enhanced by his NVGs. It was exactly what they had been striving for.

The second the Roamer's diesel engine went silent, three doors opened together. Shorty spilled from one, MP7 in hand, backpack slung on one shoulder. From the other left-side door came Steve-O. He set the Mule on the ground and started hauling items off the backseat and placing them on the ground by his feet. When Riker saw Lia emerge from between the two-foot gap Shorty had left between the wall and Roamer, he released the breath he'd been holding. He watched her loop around back, grab a rung on the ladder attached to the camper shell, and start climbing.

When Riker swung his gaze left, Shorty had already closed his door and was actively scanning the dark for threats. On the ground beside the Roamer was the long, narrow Pelican case containing Riker's long rifle. Next to it was the cube-shaped case with the drone packed inside. Steve-O was just closing his door when Riker picked up movement to the left of him. Across the lot, near the entrance to the apartment building's central courtyard, two zombies were coming down the furthest of two walkways. They were both kids, one half the size of the other.

Riker glanced at his watch. A little over ten seconds had passed since Shorty cut his engine. If this was going to work, they had better pick up the pace.

Shorty had spotted the zombies, too. His body language said it all. After tensing up and swinging the MP7 toward the moaning interlopers, he quickly lowered the weapon, then let go of it altogether. Weapon now dangling on its single-point sling, he snatched the cases off the ground, one to a hand, and hustled to the rear of the Roamer, where Lia was already on the roof and helping Steve-O to navigate the final two rungs.

Again Riker glanced at his watch. *Twenty-three seconds.* "Come on," he said under his breath. "Hurry it up." Twilight was fast approaching, and he wanted enough time beforehand to get everyone in place.

Standing on the passenger seat, upper torso protruding from the Shelby's open moonroof, Tara was focusing all of her attention on the strip mall's east-facing elevation. The sign on the roof was dark. Above the cement walk fronting the building was a series of awnings, each one bearing the name of the establishment it belonged to. The Suburban was still there, nosed in against Eazy Pawn's plate glass window. On the SUV's right side, backed in close to the building's northeast corner, was a U-Haul sprinter van.

The Suburban was nosed in close to the pawnshop's front door—a steel item from the looks of it. Head-high on the door was a rectangular window. Both the store's picture window and the one on the door were fitted with burglar bars and backed by closed horizontal mini blinds. The barred-window theme was continued on down to a bail bond operation and the liquor store next door to it, with the latter's bars no kind of deterrent to the looters who had thoroughly cleaned it out. Not a single bottle remained on the shelves. Like a big middle finger to the liquor store's owner, the mangled set of burglar bars rested atop the sea of broken glass littering the walk below a long run of empty window frames.

Tara could see slivers of weak light leeching between the slats of the blinds in the pawnshop's picture window. Whispering down through the moonroof, she said, "There's about a dozen or so biters in the lot. Blinds on the target are drawn. I see some light coming from inside. It's real faint, though. Might be a lantern or flashlight. Definitely not overhead lights."

"Any movement inside?" Riker asked.

"Not that I can see."

"The Suburban still there?" Vern asked.

Tara said, "It is. And there's a small moving van next to it."

"Might belong to the son," Riker said. "If so, there's the monkey wrench in our plan I was worried about."

Tara said nothing. Just kept watching the place through the NVGs.

Shifting his gaze from the undead kids to Shorty, Riker watched the man place the drone case on the ground by his feet. Spinning the rifle case to vertical, Shorty palmed it on one end, balanced it with the other, then guided it up lengthwise to a waiting Lia. Getting the smaller drone case up to Lia wasn't so easy. Due to the delicate nature of the drone's electronics, tossing it up to her was not an option. So Shorty resorted to scaling the ladder halfway and swinging the case by the handle, pendulum-like, until Lia was able to get a hold on it.

Seeing Shorty spin around and set off walking toward the Shelby's left-side passenger door, Riker tugged on Tara's pants and instructed her to sit and buckle up.

The undead kids were a good twenty feet off the Shelby's left front fender when Shorty hauled open the door behind Riker. Hearing the door suck open, Riker started the Shelby wheeling around the Roamer at a walking speed. He didn't wait for Shorty to close the door before feeding the motor gas. As soon as he saw the man hit the seat via the reflection in the rearview mirror, he tromped the pedal. Instantly there was a throaty *whoosh* of air and peal of belts on pulleys as the Whipple supercharger spooled up. The equal and opposite component of Newton's Law of Motion kicked in a half-beat later. Simultaneously Shorty's door was thrown closed—its lower edge coming very close to clipping the toe on one of his prized Stetson boots—and the pickup began to fishtail.

As Riker braked and whipped his pickup around the wall's southern end, passing diagonally across the empty lot of a standalone building housing a fifties-themed diner, he caught a fleeting glimpse of the strip mall. Though the angle wasn't great, and everything was rendered in green, in passing he did get a pretty good idea of where the doors to each business were located, the locations of the vehicles on the lot, and where the majority of the lingering zombies were concentrated. He also got eyes on the chain-link enclosure at the building's north end that Cole had described. Although it was partially obscured behind the U-Haul, Riker could still make out the boxy outline of the industrial-sized garbage can on wheels the boy had mentioned.

Details already rooted in Riker's pre-constructed mental image of the strip mall were instantly dispelled after seeing the place in person. He'd been expecting a rambling building little more than a series of single-wide trailers arranged end to end. Neon signage and faded placards offering a myriad of services decorated the windows.

Instead of a bunch of low, run-down buildings, he saw a series of interconnected brick structures of varying heights. Starting at the squat, single-level pawnshop, the buildings stepped up in height, finally ending at the liquor store, which stood nearly twice as tall as the business concern in which Cole and the others were being held. If anyone had been alerted to the engine noise, he hadn't picked up anything to suggest so.

"You could have waited until I got my door closed," complained Shorty as he got settled into his seat. "And I missed the part of the plan about us *not* leaving as quietly as we arrived."

"That's one component of a feint," Riker explained. "If they heard us coming in, I wanted to convince them we were just passing through. Make them think we came and went."

Vern nodded. "No different than when a helicopter pilot performs a few fake insertions before and after he really commits to infil the troops he's carrying. Really confuses the enemy."

"We were there for more than thirty seconds," Tara added. "If they heard us on the way in, the thirty seconds should have been enough time for someone to get to a window and look out." She shook her head. "I didn't see anything at all. Blinds didn't move. No green shadows flitting behind them, either."

"I trust Tara's judgment," Shorty declared. "Doesn't mean Rusty Wallace here didn't go and change all that. If they heard us driving away and caught a glimpse of this rig ducking behind the diner, chances are they're now all on high alert."

"I'm banking on the fact the only ones sleeping light enough to have heard that from a block and a half out are the kids." Riker slalomed the Shelby through the divider on Losee. "Cole's a smart kid," he went on. "He figured out how to work the radio. If he picked up on that, he'll put two and two together." He looked around the cab. "I want him to be up and ready. We need all the help we can get. Especially if it's coming from someone on the inside."

"From someone on the inside," Shorty said. "Makes me think of Escape from Alcatraz or The Rock. You packing a spoon in your prison pocket, Lee?"

Tara said, "You're nasty, Shorty."

Vern simply shook his head in disbelief. Not a topic that little man wouldn't broach. Nor was there a time or place Shorty deemed inappropriate to do so. He simply did not possess a filter. Which explained the lightning bolt of a nose. When asked how many times it had been broken, the answer was always that he had lost count over the years. Without fail, the vague answer was always punctuated by: You should have seen the other guys.

While Riker had never put his to use, he knew exactly what a prison pocket was, no thanks to Shorty. The spoon reference was lost on him. He didn't dwell on it, though, because two blocks west of the strip mall, he slowed the Shelby to a walking speed and hung a right turn.

On the Shelby's right was the scrub-covered lot Cole had mistaken for open desert. On the left stood the entrance to one of the walled-in subdivisions depicted digitally on the SYNC screen. The pixelated image didn't do Javelina Estates justice. Most of the homes visible from the road were two-story affairs with tile roofs. Viewed through the NVGs, the darkened windows on the homes' upper stories stood out starkly against their much lighter exterior walls. Palm trees rose above a few of the multi-pitched roofs. Compared to the run-down strip mall, this place was Beverly Hills. No doubt when the graded parcels of land nearby got their own version of Javelina Estates, it would be out with the old and in with the new. If the world hadn't been brought to a screeching halt by the zombie apocalypse, the remnants of a seedier era would have been replaced by Starbucks, Panda Express, and, maybe, an In-N-Out Burger or Shake Shack. Best case scenario would see the pawnshop replaced by one of the chain operations ubiquitous to the distant Vegas Strip. The liquor store would have probably been usurped by a Whole Foods or some other upscale grocery store complete with their large selection of alcoholic beverages.

Partway down the block, with the strip mall and Losee Road a couple of long city blocks to the east, Riker pulled hard to the curb and killed the engine. "We go across the lot on foot and split up at the next corner. Keep a few feet of separation and your eyes on the target. You see anything at all. A light. Person poking their head over the wall behind the target. Anything. Alert your neighbor and go to ground." He held up his two-way radio and thumbed the Talk button a few times. "Set your volume low. Maintain noise discipline. Speak only when necessary. Three clicks from us means we're in place and ready to go. One of you respond in kind if you're good to go. I'll hit you back with three more. After that, it's on. No turning back. You all know your roles." He scanned their faces, moving from Vern, to Tara, then finally settling on Shorty, who he trusted in tactical situations as much as, if not more than the others. "And remember," he added, singling out Tara and Vern, "respond to everything else with one click for yes, two for no."

Once everyone had their radios dialed in and had gunned up, they struck out across the graded dirt lot, four abreast, heads on a swivel, trigger fingers more than a bit itchy.

Chapter 32

Viewed from a distance through NVGs, the wide-open parcel of land slated for future development had appeared to Riker to be as flat as a billiard table. Up close, he could see clearly the many divots and trenches and ruts created by the heavy machinery used to clear the lot.

"Watch your step," Riker whispered to the others. *Especially the clown in the red cowboy boots.* He had tried to talk Shorty out of wearing them. Having had his ankles shredded by the kid zombies the day before, there was no changing his mind. "Sprain an ankle and there goes our plan." Motioning Tara over, Riker wrapped her up in a bear hug and ordered her to be careful. As he let go of her, he told her he was relieved she had taken his advice. Though she had on a thick black hoodie, he had felt the rigid edges of the plate carrier taken off the big guy at Holl-Ee's. It certainly was a better fit on her than the dead man.

Shorty adjusted his backpack. In addition to the Shockwave protruding from its partially zipped main compartment, it contained all the tools he and Riker would be needing to accomplish their roles. "Can't we just take the sidewalk?" he groused. "This is like walking on the moon."

Riker didn't respond to the complaint. He was too busy allocating his attention between the ground ahead of him and the back side of the strip mall. From this vantage, the HAM antenna stood out like a sore thumb. It was a sturdy-looking item and towered a good thirty feet over the tallest palm tree. Nothing he saw across the distant boulevard suggested the pedophiles knew what was about to hit them. Despite the dull throb emanating from deep within his stump, and a couple of close calls navigating the uneven terrain, he maintained a fairly steady pace crossing the lot.

Off to Riker's right, Vern and Tara were also picking their way methodically across the pocked ground. With their NVGs deployed and suppressed MP5s in hand, the pair looked more special ops than the regular folks he knew them to be. He only hoped they could rise to half the height of the pedestal his imagination had just put them on.

Riker stayed behind as the others crossed Losee, one at a time, with Tara going first and Vern bringing up the rear. Once Riker saw Vern formed up with Tara and Shorty, who were already crouching beside the wall rising up behind the strip mall, he spent a few seconds watching a number of zombies loitering in the intersection a block south of him. Confident the biters were unaware they had company, he sprinted across the street, MP7 at the ready, eyes never leaving the wall beyond the far sidewalk.

"All quiet on the Western Front," whispered Shorty as Riker took a knee at the base of a large palm. "I already radioed your girl a quick SITREP. She's set up and ready to rock."

"The drone's ready if we need it?"

Shorty nodded.

Riker fished a handful of Ibuprofen from a pocket and swallowed them dry. "I missed it all," he said. "Must have been on the move. She pick up on anything new over there?"

Shorty shook his head. "Status quo at Eazy's. And you ripping through the diner's parking lot like you did got the biters moving away from the mall. Win, win." Respecting Lia's wishes, he withheld from Riker that the Roamer had already attracted its own crowd of biters. It wasn't a cardinal sin. He figured they were safe up there and capable enough of culling the things should it be warranted.

Riker viewed his watch. *Eight minutes until astronomical twilight, another hour and twenty until sunrise.* Astronomical twilight is the first phase of dawn when the sun's disk is still well below the eastern horizon. While the sun itself wouldn't be cresting the distant mountains until nautical and civil twilight had passed, the upper atmosphere would immediately begin to show signs of the transition. With Las Vegas emitting nearly zero ambient light, once the sequence started, the changes would be notable. He wanted to be in place and ready to go before the shroud of darkness began to lift.

The spot on the block where Riker and the others had convened was nearly equidistant to the north and south ends of the wall. From there, he and Shorty struck off north, keeping close to the wall until they reached the far end, where a chain-link enclosure barred access to the rear of the strip mall. Maybe twenty feet deep, the foot of the L-shaped enclosure ran along the building's entire north side, where it narrowed down considerably before shooting off around back of the brick structure.

Cole had been spot on with his intel. The top of the fence was nearly four feet above Riker's head and topped by coiled razor wire. "Twice as tall as me" was how Cole had described the fence. That would put the kid at close to five feet tall. While Riker didn't know the average height of a kid Cole's age, the estimation sounded plausible to him. The gate to the pawnshop's allocated section of the enclosure faced north and was secured with a large padlock. To keep people from parking and blocking the gate, the asphalt abutting the enclosure was painted over with diagonal yellow stripes.

To Riker's left, pushed against the enclosure's northeast corner, was the dumpster he had spotted from the diner's back lot. The five-gallon buckets Cole and the others were being forced to relieve themselves in were lined up in front of the dumpster. Cole's description of the enclosure was spot on. Pretty impressive for anyone under duress, let alone a kid. Riker only hoped the rest of what Cole had relayed to Lia and Rose was as accurate as what he had seen so far.

"Here you go, boss." Shorty handed over the bolt cutters he'd been lugging around in his pack. "Gonna do the lock or the fence?"

"Lock," Riker whispered. "Close the gate behind us with a zip tie."

Riker attacked the lock with the bolt cutters. The tool cut through the tempered steel with ease. Tossing aside the lock remnants, he traded the bolt cutters for the can of WD 40. After giving the hinges a couple of liberal blasts of the sweet-smelling lubricant, he passed the can back to Shorty.

While they waited a few seconds for the lubricant to penetrate, Shorty crept forward and poked his head around the enclosure. Apparently, what he saw was to his liking because the second he started back, he was all smiles and flashing a thumbs-up.

Riker said, "Spill. What'd you see?"

"Vern and Tara are both in place."

"The biters?"

"Still down by the diner. There are quite a few corpses stacked on the strip across from the liquor store. Looks like Tara and Vern escaped detection on the way in."

Riker clicked his radio's Talk button three times in rapid succession. *Ready?*

The response was three clicks. *Yes.*

Riker responded with three more clicks. *Going in.*

Pocketing the radio, Riker pulled on the gate. It swung out smooth and steady. No metal-on-metal squeal. Releasing the breath trapped in his lungs, he went right and made his way to the rear of the building. A quick turkey peek told him the rest of the narrow enclosure was cluttered with junk and a few antique motorcycles. He saw nothing moving, living or dead.

The pawnshop's rear door was a few paces south of the building's northwest corner. It was a windowless steel item fitted with a utilitarian pull. There was no external locking mechanism. After waiting for Shorty to finish securing the gate, Riker crept to the door and grasped the pull. Taking a deep breath and holding it, he pulled ever so gently. The door moved silent and easy. Cole had come through again. While Riker had only cracked the door, he did spot the wadded-up paper the kid promised Rose he would stuff into the strike plate opening to keep the latch from engaging.

Riker let Shorty by. Shutting the door behind them, he checked his watch. Four minutes until the agreed-upon go time. So far, Mr. Murphy was minding his own business.

Without a word passing between them, both men inspected their new weapons. Satisfied all was as it should be—full mags, rounds chambered—they threw selectors to fire and pressed their backs against the brick wall.

The hollow rasps and keen of nails raking the Roamer's camper shell had the hairs on Lia's neck standing to attention. She was on her belly, legs splayed out a few degrees, elbows planted firmly on the metal roof. Though she couldn't see Tara or Vern, going by what she had just heard coming from the radio by her elbow, she knew they were in place. And when things started to happen, the combination of nautical twilight and the high-powered scope atop the long rifle would render moot the fact that she wasn't wearing NVGs.

Steve-O was on his belly on the roof beside her. The Mule and Stetson were by his side. Casting his gaze groundward, he said, "Amelia."

Eye never leaving the scope, she said, "Yes, Steve-O. What is it?"

"Are you sure biters can't climb a ladder?"

She had already reassured him twice since the dead had begun to arrive in ones and twos from the apartment complex's courtyard. "I promise," she reiterated a third time. "I have never seen one climb a ladder."

"Shorty always says there's a first time for everything."

"Not this." She checked her Garmin. *One minute to go.* As soon as she put her eye back to the scope, she detected with two of her senses one thing she was expecting and another she was not. Between the Suburban and sprinter van, she saw movement. Just a flit of something transiting the black chasm between vehicles. Intuitively her imagination filled in the blanks. In her mind's eye she was seeing Vern preparing his diversion. Somewhere out there, in the dark and on high alert, Tara was watching his back while he went about finishing his task.

The thing initially out of place to Lia was a distant low rumble. It was at the very bottom of the sound frequency spectrum. In addition to hearing it, it manifested as a slight vibration in her chest and stomach. Being the daughter of an airline captain, it quickly dawned on her it was jet engines spooling up. A tick later, the focused roar of a jet engine going from military power to full afterburner reached her position. *Jets launching from Nellis. Plural.* She'd been to enough air shows with her dad to know she was hearing multiple F-15 Eagles launching from the distant base. Soon the familiar roar was accompanied by the rumble of distinctly different sounding jet engines—ones she could not place. *Fifth-generation fighters? Bombers?* She'd rarely seen the former in person. An F-22 once or twice. And though she couldn't identify one bomber from the other by ear, she could identify all of the models her father had flown over his lengthy career as an Air Force bomber driver.

Fearful the pedos would peer out one of the windows and spot Vern or Tara before the countdown on her watch hit zero, she placed the crosshairs over the window where she guessed the dirtbag would show his or her face first. Used to shooting minuscule targets while under cardiopulmonary duress, putting a round through the barred window in the door from a few hundred yards out was child's play.

No sooner had she steadied her breathing, slipped her finger onto the trigger, and drew up a few pounds of trigger pull, than the blinds moved and a face appeared in the window. She was looking at a clean-shaven man in his late twenties or early thirties. Long dark bangs hung down over intense, deep-set eyes. A light source inside the pawnshop bathed the left side of his face with its soft orange glow.

Now or never was what Lia was thinking when Vern's Zippo flared. It was a yellow pinpoint of light between the vehicles that instantly birthed a conflagration that quickly engulfed the Suburban's windshield and hood. Releasing the trapped breath, she finished the trigger pull. At the same instant she started the irreversible process of sending the round downrange, Phantom Limb Syndrome had her thinking her nonexistent right foot was under direct attack by the mother of all cramps. Sometimes PLS manifested as a hot or cold sensation. Other times it was a raging attack of pin and needles. The worst was the itch she could never scratch. This phantom cramp was a first for her. And it just leapfrogged the phantom itch in the discomfort column.

Poised by the backdoor, Riker had also detected the distant rumble of jet engines. He, too, pegged them as coming from Nellis and had instantly deduced it was *not* civilian in nature.

"What the hell is that," whispered Shorty.

"Jet aircraft launching from Nellis," replied Riker. By the time the noise from the second sortie launching was hitting their ears, it was go time and Riker had the door swinging open and was striding across the threshold.

MP7 tucked tight to his shoulder, NVGs deployed, Riker entered the narrow hallway. It was pitch black inside and ran the length of Eazy's. A quick peep left showed a dead-end stacked high with Rubbermaid bins brimming with canned goods. Atop stacked bags of rice and beans was a Coleman camp stove. It was surrounded by dirty dishes and disposable propane tanks. To the right, the hall shot off straight for a good seventy-five feet. As Cole had previously relayed to Lia, the one locked door accessing the rest of the place was in the center of the longest section of hallway. Pushed into the corner beyond the lone interior door was a rolling bucket and mop. Against the wall next to the bucket was a shelf system stocked with cleaning supplies and rolls of toilet paper and paper towels. The hall smelled of spoiled food and disinfectant.

The locked door on Riker's left was windowless and constructed with a light wood that glowed a pale green in the NVGs. First glance at the sturdy metal frame told him that, even from a guy his size, this was the type of door that could easily survive a solid kick.

With five seconds to go until the introduction of the well-timed distraction, Riker placed his back to the interior wall and waved Shorty forward.

Understanding his role, Shorty let the MP7 dangle from its sling and retrieved the Shockwave from his pack. No need to check the weapon. He already had a slug chambered. Throwing off the safety, he nodded to Riker. *Ready.*

When the sweeping hand on Riker's watch was one second from the mark, he nodded to Shorty, then turned his head and cupped a hand over his left ear.

The Shockwave discharging in the enclosed space was extremely loud. But it was the only way in. No doubt it got the people inside stirring and wondering what the hell was happening. *Part of the plan.* Because in a couple of seconds, the main distraction would also be fighting for their attention.

Chapter 33

With one ear ringing from the concussion, Riker wheeled around and kicked the spot on the door ravaged by the lead slug. There was a loud crack and the door swung freely inward. Head on a swivel, he went into a combat crouch and pushed into the main room. On his six, Shorty covered the closed door to their right with his MP7.

Gun smoke swirling the air was quickly overpowered by the acrid stench of sweat and fear. The snapshot in time processed by Riker's mind as he entered the dimly lit room was rendered in many shades of green. His hunch that the place would be crowded with glass display cases full of treasures acquired from desperate people for pennies on the dollar was accurate. The kids were not to his left and asleep on the floor in the corner of the "cage" as Cole had led Lia to believe. They were nowhere to be seen. In the corner to Riker's right was a massive safe. It was four feet tall and nearly as deep. The safe's circular door was closed.

A waist-high counter cluttered with papers and desktop computers ran the length of the room, right to left, in front of Riker. A single pane of ballistic glass rose up from the front edge of the counter. Secured at the ceiling, the glass sealed off the back third of the room from the front of the store. The glass featured a couple of bank-style pass-through windows and was fitted with a single door—also ballistic glass. The door was one long stride to Riker's fore and was half open.

Kurt and Janice were both in the customer area. She was off to the left. He was nearly dead center to Riker. They appeared to be in their late fifties or early sixties and were incredibly thin. The deep-set eyes, sunken cheeks, and crooked teeth on display were no doubt derived from decades of hard living. They were exactly where Cole had said they would be. Kurt in his plush recliner, kicked all the way back, the headrest close to touching the yard-wide section of wall between the window and front door. On the floor beside the recliner was a half-empty bottle of Jack Daniels and a dozen crumpled beer cans. The shotgun resting on his lap had an open porno mag draped across its stubby barrel. The man's hands were in his lap, the fingers on the right curled loosely around the shotgun's pistol grip. *No string or finger on the trigger. Both good things.* Riker only hoped the pump gun's safety was engaged. At this point, outnumbered three to one, he would take every advantage he could get, even if it only amounted to an extra second or two of response time.

Janice was atop a sleeping bag that had been unzipped and spread out on the floor in front of a glass case containing coins and jewelry. Surrounding her feet was a menagerie of dolls. Apparently other people's kids weren't the only thing she collected. On the woman's rail-thin chest was an open romance novel. She wore reading glasses and a headlamp and had fallen asleep with the latter switched on. The weak beam jerked and tracked across the dolls' leering faces when she gasped and sat up.

As if the couple was expecting to bolt on a moment's notice, they were both fully dressed and shod in matching hikers.

The wild card, person number three, was the wiry man dressed all in black. He was stumbling backward, away from the front door, a spritz of blood erupting from one side of his face. Though Cole had mentioned Kurt and Janice having an adult son, and that the son was supposedly en route to the pawnshop, as of the last check-in the son had yet to arrive. It was crystal clear now to Riker all of that had changed.

As the glare from the burning SUV infiltrated the blinds fronting the big picture window, Riker heard a sharp crack and a cloudy, oblong divot suddenly appeared in the bulletproof door head-high to him. As he was struck by the realization the sound and divot were related and caused by an incoming bullet—likely the same projectile that had struck the man in black—his brain kicked into overdrive, dumping enough adrenaline into his body to suddenly snap everything into sharp focus and, seemingly, bring time to a screeching halt. He'd heard the Tier One guys accompanying the VIPs he chauffeured around Baghdad in armored SUVs call the phenomenon "*combat high*." He could count the times it had happened to him on one hand and still leave a finger or two out of the tally.

Breathe, breathe, breathe, he told himself. It was the only advice he remembered Grayson offering up when he'd tried to pick the Delta shooter's brain on what to do if he ever found himself under its spell.

Breathe he did. Sucking in a huge lungful of precious air, he edged around the door, peered through the MP7's holographic sight, and superimposed the red dot over the lean man's back.

"Don't move," he bellowed. "I *will* kill you."

The man didn't heed the advice. Instead, he twisted around from the door and dove for the floor, the muzzle of what looked like an AK-47 sweeping toward Riker. At the same time Janice had started to scream and kick and flail her arms, clawing futilely at the air in front of her. The dolls at her feet were sent careening across the floor and the headlamp slipped down her face, coming to rest around her neck.

Meanwhile, as all of that was happening, Kurt was snapping out of the fog of sleep and groping for the shotgun in the dark.

Riker pressed the trigger two times, sending a pair of 4.6x30mm subsonic rounds across the room at the immediate threat. Behind him, Shorty was pushing through the ballistic door, screaming orders of his own at the woman. "Hands where I can see them. Keep them up, lady." Apparently, the apple hadn't fallen far from the tree, because Janice's bony right hand darted under a plush teddy bear and came out clutching a snub-nosed .38 special.

The suppressed reports and muzzle flashes from the pair of MP7s seemed to have occurred all at once. In reality, they happened back-to-back in quick succession, all four erupting from the suppressors in the span of two short seconds. Thankfully the strobe effect from the four muzzle flashes had been mitigated by the NVG's built-in dimming feature.

A half-beat after Shorty and Riker's MP7s went silent, multiple concussive booms rattled the window and started the merchandise in the cabinets shaking.

Due to the angle of the man's body in relation to the floor when Riker had triggered his two rounds—arms outstretched and nearly prone—the speeding hunks of lead missed erasing the scowl from the man's face by a whisker. Instead, the first round entered between the C3 and C4 vertebra, caromed downward, and punched a hole in one lung. Round number two struck the base of the man's spine at about the same time he was crashing to the carpeted floor. While Riker had no way of knowing, partly because the man's AK-47 was stuttering and sending rounds in his general direction, the first round he had fired had instantly rendered the man paralyzed from the neck down.

Nerve impulses ceased transiting the man's spinal cord the second it was severed. As a result, hands going numb, the Soviet Bloc weapon stopped belching lead. Dead cat bounce in full effect, the man's body rebounded from the floor and his feet went in two different directions. The left foot skidded across the floor and went still. The right, however, impacted the carpet and kicked off toward the recliner. The low heel of the man's combat boot hit the wooden handle on the recliner's left side. The impact released sprung weight and sent the plush chair snapping back to the upright position. Still fumbling with the shotgun, Kurt went along for the ride.

Riker didn't see Shorty's rounds strike Janice. He was swinging his weapon around to Kurt and ordering him to show his hands. He did hear the woman cry out. In his peripheral vision he saw a black pistol skitter across the floor and stop a foot or two from Kurt's recliner.

Second time was the charm for Kurt. He'd apparently seen enough of his predicament illuminated by muzzle flashes to know he was outgunned. Pushing the shotgun off his lap, he raised his arms in surrender.

"I don't know who you are," he growled, voice raspy from decades of smoking and drinking. "But I do know you two have bitten off way more than you can chew." Eyes going wide in the dark, he added, "You're going to come to regret this day."

"Oh, I doubt that," Riker growled back. He looked to Shorty, then flicked his eyes to Janice. Her hand had absorbed at least one of the rounds. Blood was streaming from the mangled knuckles. Gaze returning to Shorty, he said, "Good shooting, Wyatt. Were you aiming for her gun hand?"

He shook his head. "Lucky shot."

Turning his attention back to Kurt, Riker said, "Where are the kids?"

Kurt remained tightlipped.

Riker pressed the suppressor to the man's left knee and pressed the trigger. No hesitation. No warning.

There was a flash and a soft report and the man's eyes went wide. The high-pitched warble that came out of his mouth was about the worst thing Riker had ever heard. It was trumped only by the awful peals and screams made by men burning alive in the Land Cruiser he'd been driving when the insurgents' IED changed his life forever. This was a close second. Riker shifted his gaze to Janice and touched the suppressor to the man's other knee.

Janice spilled at once, saying between sobs, "They're in Junior's van." She nodded toward the front of the pawnshop.

Riker tossed Shorty a pair of zip ties. "You do the honors. I'll radio the others." Watching Janice shaking and clutching her destroyed hand to her bosom, the blood darkening the front of a sweater emblazoned with *World's Best Nana*, he dug out the two-way radio. Pressing the Talk button, he said, "Lee here. Everything's under control. Me and Shorty are both OK."

"Speak for yourself," Shorty said. "That bullet that came through the window ricocheted and grazed my left shoulder. Minor flesh wound, though."

As soon as Riker opened the channel, Lia was on the radio. "What about Cole?" she asked, sounding short of breath. "Is he OK? How about the others?"

Riker grimaced. Seeing only adults had him fearing the worst. "I'm not sure," he conceded. "They're not in here. Nana … I mean Janice … says they're in the van outside." Addressing Vern and Tara, he said, "I need you two to check it out. We're still mopping up in here."

After his request was acknowledged, Riker kneeled beside the man he'd inadvertently shot in the back. First thing he noted was the deep chasm plowed in one cheek by what had to have been Lia's shot. After probing the other two wounds, he checked for a pulse. It was faint. The man's mouth was opening and closing, and a froth of blood rimed his lips. He looked like a fish out of water. It was clear he was dying. Riker was pretty sure one of his rounds had paralyzed the man. He guessed the other had ripped through important internal organs.

Lia came back on the Motorola. "Did I hit one of them? Looked like a younger white guy."

"You hit him, all right." Riker intentionally left out the part about the bullet continuing on and him being saved by the ballistic glass. If Shorty wanted to broach the subject later, bring up the ricochet, it was up to him. "I got him, too," Riker divulged. He lifted one of the man's arms off the floor. It was limp. No movement whatsoever. "He's paralyzed. In my book, there's nothing worse than that."

More hollow concussions from somewhere south and west of the strip mall. They were followed at once by someone rapping sharply on the door.

Seeing that Shorty had finished making sure the unlucky couple would be going nowhere, cuffing their wrists and ankles with thick nylon zip ties, Riker rose and dragged the fallen man away from the door. Throwing the lock, he said, "Come in. Watch your step. There's trash on the floor."

Vern came through the door, smiling. "Good call on the diversion." He looked at the Suburban. "Fire's almost burned itself out. Only wasted half a gallon of gas." He exhaled. "Huge relief I didn't choose the van."

"Cole and the others are in there?"

Vern nodded. "Tara's seeing to them."

"What's their condition?"

Shaking his head, Vern said, "All I saw is that they were all trussed and lying on the floor. Looked like five kids in all." He made a motion like he was eating an apple. "And they had these orange balls strapped to their faces."

Shorty stepped forward, the MP7 hanging by its strap. He was busy undressing one of the dolls. Wadding up the frilly white dress, he used it as a compress to staunch the blood wetting his sleeve. "Ball gags." He shook his head. "Fucking perverts." It was all he could do not to kick the moaning man in his horribly mangled knee. Instead, he spit in the man's face. "You're a piece of work, man. You're way past due for a comeuppance."

Reaching for the makeshift bandage, Vern said, "Let me see. How bad is it?"

Shorty moved his hand. The dress was nearly soaked through. Between clenched teeth, Shorty said, "Hurts like a bitch. Nothing to worry your pretty little head about."

"Whatever, Rambo." Vern gently probed the wound with one finger. "It's going to eventually need to be stitched up. You gonna do it … or will you allow me the honor?"

Shorty raised his eyebrows at Riker. "You call in Lia and Steve-O yet?"

"I'm about to." As he raised the radio to his mouth, Tara appeared at the door. A boy and two little girls stood behind her. The girls, blonde and blue-eyed, looked like they could be sisters. They were five, maybe six years old at best and barely came up to Tara's navel. Their matching knee-length nightgowns were filthy, the thin fabric spotted with blood.

The boy came up to Tara's chin. With long black hair and bangs hanging in his eyes, he looked like a miniature version of the guy on the floor.

Tara said, "We need to get out of here. The biters by the diner are on to us." More concussions rattled the window. "Then there's *that*."

Riker reached out a fist. "Cole?"

The kid nodded.

"Great job disabling the door catch."

Ignoring the offered fist bump, Cole slipped into the store. With no warning, the kid hauled off and kicked the prone man between the legs. It was a solid kick. All toe. He said, "That's for Diana." A second kick followed the first. "And that's for Dena. I hate you, Junior. You're a monster. You need to die for what you did to them."

The man didn't flinch once. Or cry out. Just continued to move his lips and bleed on the carpet throughout the entire ordeal.

"Chill, Pelè," Shorty said, extending his good arm. "Junior's paralyzed. Unfortunately, he didn't feel any of that."

Cole shrugged off Shorty's attempt at detaining him and slammed the sole of his shoe to Junior's face. The man's lips pulled back from his teeth and a broken molar appeared on his bloody tongue. Cole delivered another swift kick. In addition to the pooling blood and molar, a few of Junior's front teeth now decorated the grimy carpet. The kid's tennis shoe was bloody, too.

Riker said, "Leave something for the biters, Cole." He radioed Lia. "Get the Roamer over here. We need to be going."

"No shit," she replied at once. "I'm standing on the roof and watching one hell of a bombing campaign."

"We hear it," Riker radioed back. As he put the radio away, the explosions were accompanied by a faint tearing sound he knew all too well. Regarding Vern, he said, "A-10s doing gun runs. They're pretty close. Five, maybe ten miles out."

"Agreed." Vern patted the fresh dressing. "All done, Shorty." He stuffed the first aid kit back into the man's pack. "What do we do with Ma and Pa Kiddie-diddler?"

Riker said, "We leave them for the dead." He bent down, grabbed Junior by the legs, and dragged him into the doorway. Leaving him on his left side so he wouldn't choke on his own blood, Riker turned the man's head so that he could see the approaching zombies. "I figure you have five minutes or so to live. Better get to praying."

When Riker went back into the pawnshop, Janice was whimpering and rocking back and forth on the sleeping bag. Kurt was still in the recliner. With his hands and feet bound, there was almost zero chance of him surviving what was to come. To be certain the dead would find a captive audience to Junior's eventual demise, Riker closed the ballistic door. To be doubly sure Kurt wasn't going to somehow figure a way to pull his son inside the shop and bar the door, he touched the MP7's suppressor to the man's good knee and pressed the trigger.

The howls of pain weren't quite as bad the second time around. To the hungry dead, thought Riker, it was a siren song. He thought it ironic that Kurt had become the dinner bell to a feast in which he was the main course.

"Leave me my gun," Janice begged. "I don't want to become one of them."

"I didn't want you touching me with your dolls, either," hissed Cole. "But you did anyway. We said stop and you didn't. You all deserve what you got."

The twins were clutching Tara's legs and nodding in agreement.

"Better tell Lia to hurry up," urged Vern. "There's more biters coming from the north."

"Custer's last stand is not what I signed up for," Shorty said. "Come all this way to save the kids only to end up zombie chow alongside them."

The gas on the Suburban's hood had burned off, leaving the paint bubbled and peeling. Overhead, the sky was going from deep purple to lavender. Riker flipped up his NVGs and looked toward the distant apartment complex. Between the palm trees, he could just make out the boxy outline of the top third of the Roamer's camper shell. That was it, though. Whatever was happening behind the palm fronds was known only to Lia and Steve-O.

Atop the Roamer, Lia had ahold of Steve-O's boots, anchoring him to the roof as he put the Mule to work. She had already tossed the rifle and drone, sans cases, onto the Roamer's hood. It was the way they were going to get down once the zombies were dealt with.

Three minutes after the first *pffft-thwak* had the zombies crowding the Roamer beneath Steve-O, he had put down close to twenty of the moaning things.

Dragging the cases after her, Lia climbed down onto the hood. Stacking the cases on the hood allowed Steve-O to climb down from the roof.

Double checking that the coast was clear, they got down from the hood and loaded the gear into the cab.

Slamming their doors near concurrently, the pair fist-bumped.

"Close call," said Steve-O.

"Sure was," Lia replied. She fired the engine and got the Roamer rolling south. Cutting through the diner parking lot, she swerved around the small pack of zombies lurching across the strip mall lot. The scene when she nosed the Roamer in beside the Suburban was about what she was expecting to see. The only exception was the man and woman who had both been trussed and sat tied to individual folding chairs. They were positioned just inside the pawnshop entry. Both had been gagged. Nevertheless, they were wild-eyed and obviously trying to plead their case through the fabric jammed into their mouths.

On the ground, halfway across the threshold and keeping the door from closing, was the man she had had in her crosshairs. He was face up, head turned toward the approaching dead, his bloody mouth moving a mile a minute. It was satisfying to know they all were going to pay for what they did. Even if they came back without a pulse, unless the rope rotted away over time, they were going nowhere. Their days of hurting people were over.

The kids looked like Lia had imagined. Though she wanted to get out and hug them all, beginning with Cole, she was already crawling over the seatback to make room for Shorty.

While Tara and Vern helped Cole and the other kids into the Roamer through the rear door, Riker piled in back with Lia. They exchanged knowing looks. The message conveyed: We did it.

Shorty pulled away from the pawnshop as dawn was breaking. At the end of the sweeping J-turn, Lia implored him to stop.

"What's up?" he asked. "The biters are getting close."

"I want to watch."

"Hell," said Shorty, "can't be worse than seeing a man lose his junk."

Riker said nothing. With the kids in back and unable to see their captors being eaten, Steve-O was the only other person to be worried about. Knowing the comeback would be the stock one if he brought it up, he sat back and watched the biters swarm the pawnshop.

It was over in less than a minute. All the while, the bombing seemed to be intensifying.

Shorty met Riker's eyes in the rearview. "Home, James?"

"To my rig," he said. "Then we go back to the cache and settle business."

"After that, we go find the Sierra complex?" Shorty asked, brows arched. "Just for shits and giggles."

Opposition to the request collapsing faster than the folding chairs had under the combined weight of Kurt and Janice and the zombies feeding on them, Riker closed his eyes and nodded.

Epilogue

They left the feeding frenzy behind. Picking up the Shelby, they went back to their former traveling arrangements, the only difference being the kids in back of the Roamer.

Backtracking to the beltway, they found it crowded with zombies. Packs numbering in the hundreds, all moving east, clogged every available lane.

On the seat next to Riker, Shorty's voice issued from the Motorola. "Anybody home?"

Riker thumbed the Talk button. "What do you want?"

"Looks like I may be getting my way after all."

"Meaning?"

"The Sierra site. Tara has it up on the map. At least its general location." He paused for a beat, the channel still open. "I can get us there. It's not far."

There was a series of loud booms. The prolonged rumble came next. It was felt by everyone.

Lia plucked the radio from Riker's hand. "What about all that? It's clear it has something to do with all the zombies on the march. Didn't you see the dogs and cats scurrying east when we exited the strip mall?"

"I did," Shorty acknowledged. "A few rats, too. But all that's happening south of Vegas. Looking at the map, I'd guess it's going down on the I-15 near Henderson. If we sprint, we should be at the junction to the feeder road in less than thirty minutes. We'll be ahead of whatever is happening. Win, win."

Riker reclaimed the radio. "How far is Sierra from here?"

Shorty said, "A little over twenty miles. Most of it is highway. Some is dirt road."

Riker got Lia's attention, then pointed at the SYNC screen. "Where is it again?"

"Backside of Sunrise Mountain. On the map, the mountain is diagonal and looks like it's about to ram Nellis from the south."

"Great description," Lia replied. "I see a job as a cartographer in your future."

"Well?" Shorty asked.

Riker was staring at his wing mirror, thinking, when he saw the Roamer reverse and begin the first of three turns necessary to get the rig facing south. Knowing there was no changing the man's mind, he threw the transmission into Reverse and followed suit.

Two miles southeast of the beltway, southbound Losee intersected with US-95 North. Riker was listening to Lia warn they were closing with the turnoff to the road that would shoot them east, toward Sunrise Mountain, when Vern launched from his seat. "Lookie there," he blurted. He was out of his seatbelt, one arm hooked over the seatback, and pointing straight ahead.

Filling up the middle of the Shelby's bug-spattered windshield, the red sky of morning bracketing it on two sides, was a wide dirt plume. It was rising and roiling and being blown steadily west by a building wind.

Lia said, "It's too wide to be a dirt devil. Maybe it's the beginnings of one of those dust storms that hit these parts now and again."

Seeing the Roamer begin the turn onto the highway, Riker tapped his brakes and began to steer left. "You're not far off," he said. "But I think this thing isn't the work of Mother Nature." He remembered hearing about a similar occurrence hitting some populated areas in Arizona. While it had made the national news, he couldn't recall the names of the towns affected by it. He had seen a couple of haboobs during his deployment in Iraq. While they were a rare occurrence, the suddenly appearing sandstorms were known to reach hundreds of feet into the sky and blot out the sun, turning day to night. Driving during a haboob was especially dangerous.

He had also watched the Baja 500 one time on television. The sand-rails and souped-up pickups—the latter being the inspiration for his Shelby Baja model pickup—tearing ass across the California and Mexico desert kicked up dirt contrails very similar to what they were all seeing.

This, he quickly concluded, was *not* a haboob. Nor was it created by dozens of vehicles running single-file through the distant desert.

Riker said, "That's the byproduct of bombs being dropped on a bunch of zombies on the move."

Punctuating the statement, a fighter jet screamed overhead. It was gray, the wings loaded with ordnance. A beat later, a fireball bloomed on the southern horizon. It rose and spread quickly, sucking up ochre dust and sending it roiling angrily away.

Vern had plucked the Steiners off the front seat and was glassing the plume and stretch of I-15. "You're right, Lee. The freeway is wall-to-wall zombies." Lowering the binoculars, he said, "Get us far away from here."

***

Ten minutes later, Riker was still seeing the dust plume in the right-wing mirror. Swinging his gaze ahead, he watched the Roamer slow and slew left. With the taillights taped over, the maneuver had come as a surprise. *Can't be zombies*, he thought. They'd all been drawn south by the fireworks. Even the strip and east Vegas had been a ghost town. Save for the trash in the streets and the Bellagio fountains doing their thing, nothing was stirring.

Realizing what Shorty was up to—going against what all of them had decided upon seeing the horde of dead things—Riker snatched up the radio. "We voted," he radioed. "We are not fulfilling your Sierra fantasy."

No reply.

"The turn is coming," Lia reminded.

Riker said nothing.

"The kids are in the Roamer. I can see your sister taking care of them." She looked at him. "But Shorty and Steve-O? Tara's going to need help."

Through gritted teeth, Riker said, "Fine. We get stuck camping in the hills to keep from getting eaten by that horde, it's on Mister Radio Silent." He steered left, slowing considerably because the road was unimproved and already the Roamer was kicking up quite the dust cloud.

The entrance to Shorty's Sierra facility was at the end of a gravel road. The fence went on north and south for as far as the eye could see. The gate was tall and topped with coiled razor wire. There was a squat guard booth. It was fitted with ballistic glass and had a host of antennas jutting from the roof. Strangely, it was unmanned. What they all failed to notice was the small black dome affixed to the side of the cinder-block structure.

There were signs on the fence with statements on them warning of the legal ramifications of trespass. None of the signs bore any clues as to who the land beyond the booth and fence belonged to.

The radio in Lia's hand hissed static. It was Shorty. "Tell Lee we'll need the saw."

"You tell him," Lia radioed back, then handed over the Motorola.

Thumbing open the channel, so as not to give Shorty the satisfaction of getting the first word in, Riker said, "Seems like your radio isn't broken after all."

"Just low batteries," Shorty replied. "We're here now, though. Better not waste this moment."

"Put Tara on," Riker demanded.

"She's in back with the kids. Want me to disturb them?"

Riker threw the Motorola down on the seat, disgusted. He elbowed open his door, looped around to the Shelby's bed, and reached inside.

Passing the Roamer with no acknowledgement to the man at the wheel, Riker strode up to the gate, fired up the saw, and got to cutting.

***

The road widened and was paved from the gate to the point high up on the mountainside where it ended. Five minutes of sharp switchbacks and steep elevation gain and Riker was watching the Roamer cutting across a vast plateau of white cement. The cement pad disappeared a dozen feet into the mountain face. There was another fence stretched across a flat surface a hundred feet wide by fifty high. Behind the fence were what looked like blast doors. They were smooth and shiny and took up half of the opening.

There was no guard stationed here, either.

Riker parked the Shelby beside the Roamer and jumped out. Only this time, after grabbing the saw from the bed, he stopped at Shorty's door and beckoned for the man to join him.

The gate looked no more formidable than the one at the base of the mountain. The blast doors were another story. Up close, though they had spotted a smaller Judas door on the right of the main blast door, neither Riker nor Shorty had any confidence any of the tools they had with them could breach it.

"Only one way to find out," Shorty said.

"Waste of time," Riker shot as he put the saw on one shoulder and turned to head back to the Shelby.

"What's up, guys?" Steve-O had snuck up on them in stocking feet.

Shorty said, "Where's your boots?"

Steve-O was opening his mouth to answer when a trio of soldiers in full MOPP protective suits emerged from the Judas door.

"Do not move," the first to arrive ordered. His voice was muffled by the respirator he wore.

"What in the hell are you doing here?" asked another, the muffled voice definitely belonging to a woman.

As the third soldier fanned left of the lady soldier and aimed an M4 toward the fence, Riker looked to Shorty. "Well, Mister Won't Take No For An Answer. Tell the lady."

"No time for that. You have five minutes to be off the mountain and heading east. I suggest you turn all your mirrors down and refrain from looking to the southwest. Turn around and go."

Incredulous, Riker said, "You're using nukes on the horde?"

The lady soldier maintained eye contact but said nothing.

Riker grabbed Steve-O's shirt and was tugging him along when Shorty said, "We have kids in Marge. They need a doctor."

"Wait," said the lady soldier. "Kids? Are they bit?"

Steve-O shook his head. Removing the Stetson, he said, "We saved them from some evil people."

"We're down to four minutes now," Riker said. He stared daggers at Shorty. "Let's go. It'll take you two of those minutes to get your battleship turned around."

"Wait," said the lady soldier. She ordered the first soldier to open the gate. After sending the other soldier with the M4 off on a mission, she stepped aside. "Get in your vehicles and follow me."

Riker and Shorty exchanged questioning looks.

"You heard the lady," said Steve-O. "Get moving." As he turned to follow the soldier, the low howl of muffled jet engines broke the still air.

At once, Riker, Shorty, and Steve-O stopped in their tracks and looked skyward. The source of the noise was black and triangular. As it passed directly overhead, following a southwesterly course, any notion that the soldier was blowing smoke up their asses just to get them to move was instantly dispelled.

***

When the thunderclap of the low-yield nuke detonating over Henderson rose over the klaxon sounding in the airplane-hangar-sized enclosure, less than a foot of daylight remained between the closing blast doors.

In the Shelby, shocked look on her face, Lia said, "Did I just hear what I think I just heard."

Riker nodded. "Lady soldier saved us from getting fried. Or at the very least, if we escaped the blast and the winds were not in our favor, a lethal dose of radiation."

She looked all around. The place was cavernous. The orange glow cast by the halide lights gave it an eerie vibe. "So we're safe in here?"

Again, he nodded.

"How long do we have to stay in here?"

He smiled. "Long enough for us to get to know each other better."

She was about to grant him kiss number two when Shorty butted in. "My decision back there saved our asses." He looked them both in the eye. "Agreed?"

Too tired to argue, Riker said, "Agreed."

Threading her fingers in his, Lia turned Riker around. Planting a solid kiss on his lips, she said, "Let's go meet the kids."

Look for Book 5 of Riker's Apocalypse Early 2023

###

Thanks for reading! Reviews help. Please consider leaving yours at the place of purchase. Please feel free to Friend Shawn Chesser on Facebook. To receive the latest information on upcoming releases first, please join my mailing list at ShawnChesser.com. Find all of my books on my Amazon Author Page.

Also by Shawn Chesser

SURVIVING THE ZOMBIE APOCALYPSE

TRUDGE

SOLDIER ON

IN HARM'S WAY

A POUND OF FLESH

ALLEGIANCE

MORTAL

WARPATH

GHOSTS

FRAYED

DRAWL: DUNCAN'S STORY

DISTRICT

ABYSS

GONE

HOME

FURY

RIKER'S APOCALYPSE

THE PROMISE

THE PLAN

THE PRECIPICE

CUSTOMERS ALSO PURCHASED:

JOHN O'BRIEN
NEW WORLD
SERIES

JAMES N. COOK
SURVIVING THE DEAD
SERIES

MARK TUFO
ZOMBIE FALLOUT
SERIES

ARMAND
ROSAMILLIA
DYING DAYS
SERIES

HEATH STALLCUP
THE MONSTER
SQUAD

Printed in Great Britain
by Amazon

77991927R00180